BLOOD SISTER

T STEDMAN

BLOOD SISTER

T Stedman

THE ROYAL FAMILIES

OF ATLANTIS

Dubonnetti
Bonaci
Santalini
Florianna

Of Murrtaine
Borge

PROLOGUE

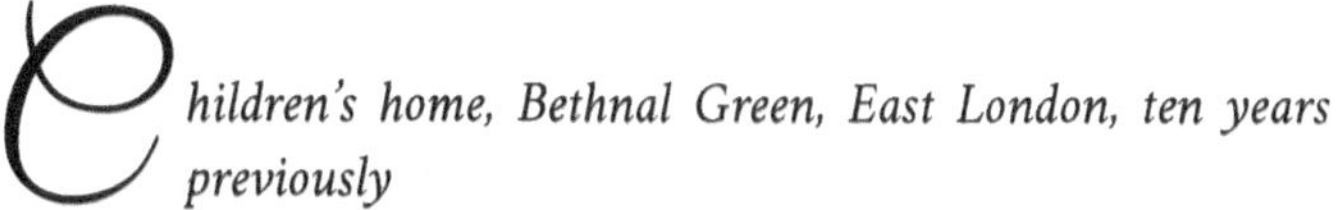

Children's home, Bethnal Green, East London, ten years previously

ALFONZO NESTLED the crying baby girl carefully in the soft bed. "Pass me the boy."

The guard passed the wriggling toddler with a mess of raven hair from his doting nurse's arms to the head of the Bonaci family.

"You have his ring?"

The guard took the ancient white opaque ring from his breast pocket and handed it to Alfonzo.

He lifted the boy's fidgeting hand and pushed the over-sized ring onto the middle finger. The spike penetrated the poor little mite's skin between the knuckles.

He squealed in pain and all the more when he saw the rich red blood run down his fingers.

Everyone around the little bed watched as the ring began to swirl with a white smoke, changed to blood red and then gradually cleared to turquoise.

"She is not…" The guard went to protest.

"Wait! Give it time." Alfonzo reassured him.

Gradually, the ring swirled red again and settled to the deepest purple.

Murmurs of satisfaction came from the big Santalini guardsmen gathered in the room.

Ignoring them, Alfonzo put a drop of the boy's blood on his finger and dabbed it on the little female baby's rooting mouth until she sucked it and removed all trace of the Santalini blood. He then took a pin from a velvet cushion in his pocket and pricked the baby girl's finger and asked the little boy to poke out his tongue, which he did. Alfonzo dabbed the blood onto the boy's tongue. "There. It is done. They are bound till such a time when they can do it for themselves."

The nurse came forward to take the boy. Alfonzo removed the ring from the boy's finger, put it in a velvet pouch and put it back in his breast pocket. "Watch them like your own," he said with a hint of warning. "We will return when the boy reaches puberty, when he will be blooded in truth. Ensure they are never adopted and are known as brother and sister to keep them together. They must never be separated. Is that clear?"

The nurse curtsied. "Yes, sir."

"All is in accordance with the binding contract between the Bonaci and Santalini Houses. That this special dispensation be allowed to safeguard the locations and lives of the Soul Breathers for the king, who is to come. And all accept that this is a sacred gift to the Santalini family. All who agree say aye?"

All present said a resounding "aye".

"You may now say your farewells," Alfonzo said, already making his way to the door.

The guards all said an emotional goodbye to baby

Keenan, the beloved boy whom the cousins and brothers wouldn't see for another ten years.

Alfonzo paused in the doorway, impatient to move on, "Come, we have another three to place. Time is of the essence."

CHAPTER 1

 *en years later*

"I don't wanna go nowhere. It's me birfday," Keenan said, his voice already growing deep with approaching manhood.

"I don't care if you are thirteen now, Keenan, you are still under my care and must go for your check-up. Are you ready to go, Lacy?"

Lacy ignored the nurse and skipped and twirled around in a world of her own. The only person she ever truly took any notice of was Keenan.

The nurse tutted, tidied them up as best she could, then ushered them outside to a waiting taxi.

Eventually, when they arrived at the plush Harley Street clinic, Keenan became immediately nervous. Kids like them didn't get to go to places like this. Not unless someone wanted something. He grasped Lacy's hand while the nurse spoke to Reception. Then they were shown to an examination room towards the back of the clinic.

Keenan's unease grew as they entered the room and he looked around at the faces of several old-looking men. All of them were tall and most of them were built with it. The size he wanted to be— "What's this then?" he said, turning to the nurse, instantly suspicious of the welcoming committee.

He had already built a hot-head reputation at the Home. Everyone knew he wouldn't take any shit from anyone, and that included grown-ups. As well as that, he took his responsibility for his sister seriously, bordering on the insane. In fact, other kids were frightened to go near her.

He leaned down to whisper in her ear, "Get ready to run."

The oldest man then spoke softly in his funny accent, "Welcome, Keenan."

"Whatta you want?" Keenan said aggressively, with a face like thunder.

"I am Alfonzo, Lacy's uncle. And these are two of your brothers, Marius and Drago."

"Yeah right … you never answered my question."

The two men Alfonzo had pointed at smiled at each other with a look like they were proud. Didn't add up.

"You have reached an important crossroads in your life, Keenan. It is time for you to become a man in the culture you come from."

Keenan pulled a face. He'd learned very early on that adults said absolutely anything to get you to do what they wanted. "I dunno what you're going on about. But you make a move on us and you'll be sorry." His whole body was coiling, ready to fight.

"Please calm yourself, Keenan. After today, you won't see us again until Lacy is in her eighteenth year."

"You leave her outta this," Keenan said, pushing Lacy behind the shelter of his larger body.

"Then you will be reunited with your family," Alfonzo persisted.

"I won't go nowhere without my sister … what do you want from us?" Keenan said, narrowing his eyes, trying to back up subtly as he spoke.

Heavy hands landed on his shoulders.

Not willing to give up without a fight, Keenan kicked back with his foot, catching the guard behind him in the shin, making him grunt. One kick was enough and he quickly grabbed Keenan by the scruff of the neck before he could run. The other guard grabbed Lacy. They weren't as stupid as the adults Keenan normally dealt with.

It took two of the brothers to struggle with him to the bed and threaten to strap him down if he didn't quit. Lacy was led to the bed calmly, not willing to go anywhere without Keenan.

"Get on the bed please, Lacy," Alfonzo asked quietly.

Keenan still struggled but his arms and feet were held fast.

"I'm just going to give your finger a little prick okay, Lacy?" Alfonzo said.

"Leave her alone!" Keenan began to struggle wildly as he watched Alfonzo produce a small needle and prick Lacy's finger and squeeze it so a bead of blood welled on the tip. He stopped struggling as soon as he saw it. His eyes never left the droplet of blood. It was as though he was hypnotized.

Lacy was calm throughout the whole thing, but was looking from her finger to Keenan's face. "It's okay, Keenan. It doesn't hurt."

He looked at her face briefly to check she wasn't scared, and then he licked his lips. He frowned with pain as his fangs slowly protruded into his mouth, making it difficult to close. Anxiously, he looked around him, knowing they could all see him changing.

"Easy there," Marius said, trying to steady him.

Keenan started to struggle in fear.

"It's okay, Keenan. You come from a family for whom needing blood at certain times is natural," Marius explained. "Today is just your blooding. All you have to do is bite her and then it's over."

Keenan stilled and looked at the one who spoke, who was meant to be his brother. Then at the one holding his feet, who nodded and smiled, showing teeth similar to his own.

How did they know so much about him being different? "Where?" Keenan asked, which came out in a husky whisper.

Lacy was sitting up, still holding out her finger.

"There is not enough blood on your finger, Lacy, but you can choose where. It can be your wrist or your neck," Alfonzo said kindly to her.

"It's okay, Keenan. You can bite my arm like you always do, I don't mind."

The men looked at each other, a little alarmed, but they said nothing. They didn't want to embarrass them or interrupt the necessary ceremony.

Keenan, unable to resist, crawled closer to Lacy and picked up the hand she was holding out to him. He ran his tongue along the finger with the small bloody stream, never taking his eyes from hers, and then struck her wrist lightning fast, making her jump.

She showed no pain or fear and stroked his thick, wavy hair with her free hand, while his head moved in rhythm with his sucks.

"Has he done that before, Lacy?" Alfonzo asked.

"Yes, but not for a long time. When his teeth hurt, it makes him feel better if he can bite something."

Alfonzo lifted her other arm and saw several bite mark scars. "It appears they have bound themselves."

CHAPTER 2

ix years later

"Take me with you, Keenan. I look old enough." Lacy whined.

"No, Lace. I'm working," Keenan answered flatly.

Keenan walked her up to the children's home front door with difficulty while she dragged her feet. Her curfew was nine-thirty as she was still only sixteen.

Keenan no longer lived at the home because he was now nineteen and was out in the big bad world of trying to scratch a living. He shared a run-down flat with three others of his crew. All Ne'er-do-wells like himself but as tight as brothers. "Go on, go in. I'll see you tomorrow."

"Can't I stay at yours and see you when you finish work?"

He shook his head, smiling. "Nice try. I don't know how late I'm going to be. And you only want to stop me pulling anyone." He pinched her cheek.

Lacy stood on the doorstep for extra height and reached

up and put her arms around his neck. He had to be a foot taller than her now, well over six feet. "I don't know why you bother with the skanks around here," she whispered, looking up into his eyes.

He tried to peel her arms away, but she clung on like a limpet. "Stop, Lace. You're my sister, for god's sake," and he looked around nervously for any witnesses.

"I don't care, Keenan." Her eyes narrowed to that look that was way beyond her years. It heated him in a flash, and he put her forcefully away from him.

"We could go somewhere, Keenan," she whispered. "Just you and me. Then we could be together."

He smiled at her and touched her cheek gently and gave her his most patronising look. "You're just a kid. You haven't lived at all yet. I can't take you for mine until you're old enough to know what you're doing."

Her face fell and she sulked like she would cry. "I am sure, Keenan. There will never be anyone for me except you."

He leaned forward and kissed her chastely on the cheek, then turned and walked back up the path with his hands in his jeans pockets. She couldn't see him close his eyes and take a deep breath to get a grip. "Go in!" he shouted back over his shoulder, but he felt her eyes on him from the shadows.

THE UNLICENSED CLUB WAS SMALL, seedy and smoky and everything went on there. Keenan and his crew mingled with the crowd, supplying weed, speed and various pills.

He wasn't proud of his line of work, but coming from where he did, you made your money where you could. And a couple of pulls by the Old Bill for assault made it hard to get a job in Tesco. So they dealt in anything – mobile phones, credit cards, dope—whatever fell into their light fingers.

When they were younger, they'd shift the dealers' drugs

around on their pushbikes. It was clever. The police never searched little kids. Besides, he was the only white boy in his crew and looked squeaky clean back then.

Nowadays, he sported a slit in his eyebrow, his hair was overlong and his ears were full of shrapnel. He'd also started a love affair with tattoos, which served to further express his severe problem with aggression. So he and his boys fit right in here in the illegal drinking club in East London.

Everything was selling well this particular night. The music was sweet and he'd just decided to take five and spark up a fat one he'd pugged behind his ear, when Vince came up and touched his arm. Vince was his closest friend – well, after Lacy. He'd come from the same children's home. Black as Newgate's Knocker, as the old boys said, Vince was a cockney chancer cut from the same cloth as Keenan, and he always had his back.

Keenan leaned down to hear what Vince wanted to say over the pumping reggae bass.

"Lacy's here," Vince said.

"What the—" Keenan said, with his brows knitted together, annoyed. Then he caught sight of her being pulled up onto a podium and cavorting around with a scantily clad female dancer. She was gyrating and emulating dances much older than her years. "Fucking hell," Keenan spat. He pinched the end of his spliff and put it back behind his ear.

He weaved through the crowd with Vince following behind and stopped in front of the podium. "Get down, Lace," Keenan ordered.

"No, it's okay, they let me in," she said, continuing to dance and looking really cute in a white outfit of a fluffy top showing her toned brown midriff, way too short skirt and black gladiator sandals. Her hair was a mass of brown curls. Every red-blooded male in the place was ogling her, which Keenan was all too aware of.

"Get down, Lace," he repeated. "I'm taking you home."

"I'll only get down if you take me home with you," she said, wiggling cheekily.

Rumours already abounded about their odd relationship. The word incest was never far from people's lips, as their devotion was so obvious and viewed as unnatural. Even though they weren't really brother and sister, they still had to keep their cover, although now they were getting older, they questioned why more and more.

Keenan couldn't help a grin creep onto his features as he watched her trying to look sexy and grown up. Just as well she didn't realize she didn't need to try. She would wipe the floor with him one day. "Now, Lace!" he said, starting to lose patience.

"Nope," she said, as she executed a slut drop so she was low down looking at him provocatively in the eyes.

He seized his chance, grabbed her and threw her over his shoulder. Then he pulled her skirt down to barely cover her behind. He turned to Vince. "Give me the keys to the van. I'll take her home and come back for you all."

"Okay, mate," Vince said, handing them over.

He marched out of the room, up the steep flight of stairs to the peeled-paint front doors leading to the street.

"Reg," Keenan nodded to one of the bouncers, as if carrying his sister over his shoulder was the most natural thing in the world. "She's not allowed in in future, right? … No matter what she says."

The bouncer chuckled. "All right, Keen, no worries."

Lacy heard and screamed. She punched Keenan's back as hard as she could, demanding to be let down.

"Pack it in, Lace, otherwise I'll smack your arse."

She continued to struggle all the way into the next street, where their small white van was parked.

Keenan looked around, opened the rear doors and threw her in.

"Fuck off, Keenan. Let me out!" she screamed. "I'm old enough … you went when you were younger than me."

Keenan got in the back when he was confident no one was about and shut them inside the van. "Shh!" he hissed.

"No I won't! You're just trying to get rid of me so you can go and get off with a girl."

"No I'm not … Shh!" he repeated.

She was about to shout something else when he pushed her down flat, squashing her with his body and put a hand over her highly glossed lips. He stared into her eyes and his breathing was suddenly laboured.

Shocked into silence, she stared up at him, her own chest rising and falling quickly.

Confident that she wasn't going to shout any more, he released his hand from her mouth. His face was mere inches from hers. His blood began to pump fast as it always did when he was in close proximity to her—when he needed to drink.

He hadn't done it in ages, always keeping his distance to lessen the urge. He knew he was weird, but Lacy kept his guilty secret, which bound them together even tighter.

She voiced the words he was thinking: "Do you want to drink?" she said, in barely a whisper.

He closed his eyes. His heart hammered. He could feel her pulse. *Fuck*, he could hear it. *He could fucking smell it*. What was he to do? Feeling helpless, his fangs ached and descended. And always along with it came the damning arousal. His face burned and when he opened his eyes, her cheeks were aflame as well.

She was wild and beautiful, and as he looked down, he could lose himself in her.

Sensing his weakness, she lifted up her arm to expose her

wrist to him. Already scarred with past bites, she wore them like trophies.

Keenan's eyes went from her lips, red and plump, to the tick of her pulse. Then back to her lips again.

Slowly, he bent his head and put his mouth on hers. He'd never allowed himself more than the briefest of kisses before. Terrified of giving himself over to his nature and harming her with his fangs or forcing himself on her young body, not yet ready for him.

He slanted his mouth slowly over hers. Her eyes went wide with surprise and then slowly closed when his tongue pushed into her and probed and gently explored her beautiful, small mouth.

Her tongue tentatively met his and circled and gently stroked his tender fangs, which were now at their full razor-sharp length. The tang of her jasmine-scented blood quickly swamped his mouth and he groaned in approval.

"Stop! Fuck!" he growled, pulling out of the kiss before he lost control and took her here and now in the back of a dingy van.

"Please, Keenan." Her eyes were pleading with him. His tracked back to her wrist. She noticed straight away and put it across her face, kissing distance from his lips, luring, tempting him. He shut his eyes tightly and cursed himself for his weakness, then struck fast and precisely, making her jump and sharply take a breath.

He drew long, hungry, ecstatic sucks. She let out a slow breath and relaxed and put her free hand into his beautiful, black, tousled hair. His head moved in a rhythm that spread down his body to his slim hips, pinning her to the floor. Dangerously aroused, he had to stop his mind from clouding completely with the aphrodisiac quality of Lacy's blood. Slowly using every ounce of his willpower, he withdrew his fangs and licked over the puncture wounds.

A loud bang on the side of the van made both of them jump. Keenan put his finger to his lips to keep Lacy quiet and as sylphlike as he could for such a big bloke, he climbed over and eased himself down into the driver's seat. Just in time for Vince to peer into the side window.

"Fuck, Vince!" Keenan closed his eyes and let out a breath, clutching his heart. He got out of the van and wiped his mouth of any sign of blood or lip gloss. Vince noticed, he was sure of it, but he kept his gaze steady in the way blokes do to say 'your secret's safe with me'.

"Lacy all right?" Vince asked.

"Yeah … she was upset. But she's all right now."

Vince nodded, keeping up the charade. "Okay, mate … later!" And he turned back in the direction of the club.

Keenan got back in the van and started the engine in relief.

CAMBRIDGE

Malleven Mancini walked into the old pub nestled amongst the period buildings near the campus. He stood on the threshold and took no more than two seconds to home in on the easy aura of his cousin, Cesarè Florianna.

He picked his way towards him, through the throng of students who always frequented the place as their local before they went on to parties and clubs. Cesarè was lounging on a sofa, wasted, with a girl on either side of him. Sensing Malleven's approach, they immediately felt the need to go to the ladies. Malleven sank heavily into the vacated space and held up a baggie between his index and middle fingers and shook it.

"Fuck, Malleven!" Cesarè said, snatching it from his hand before anyone could see, and pushing it into his skinny jeans pocket.

"I'm sure you could've washed your own damned coke in seventh grade, Cesarè," Malleven said, throwing him a shrewd sideways glance.

Cesarè smirked, slow-eyed, already stoned from several joints he'd smoked throughout the day. Studying philosophy at the university, he maintained that it helped him reach a higher plane of understanding. "Yeah, but you do it so good, Cousin …" Cesarè's voice trailed off as he spied two girls across the room preening and posing, whilst trying to act natural, to get their attention.

Malleven followed his line of vision. Both of them were very successful with the girls, but there the similarities ended. Cesarè was a lazy student. His hair was wavy, light brown to just past his shoulders and tinted blond by the sun. He had blue eyes, was unshaven and lived in jeans and a tatty shirt. Malleven, on the other hand, was a brilliant student of chemistry, groomed to perfection. His dark coffee skin was always closely shaved, and silk shirt and crisp slacks kissed across his muscled frame.

All the Florianna princes were sent from Italy to Cambridge, paid for by their family's considerable fortune, and Cesarè took that for granted. Malleven had been plucked from an obscure branch of the family and favoured by an uncle with high expectations. That leg up was all he needed. Malleven's determination to succeed and outdo all who looked down on him was strong and overriding. He was so successful at inventing himself that people forgot his humble beginnings. "Go over, Cesarè. Bring them with us if you wish?" Malleven said, bored already. He knew the drill with Cesarè, but he had only a mild interest himself and could take girls or leave them.

"Could be a hassle if I see someone I prefer there," Cesarè sighed.

Malleven went to rise from the sofa; someone infinitely

more interesting had caught his eye. "I will fuddle their fucking mind for you … hell, Ches, call yourself Florianna."

Cesarè laughed easily and got up, clapped Malleven on the back and walked lazily over to the girls.

Malleven gracefully weaved his way to the bar and quickly caught the attention of the striking black boy behind the bar with green eyes. "Scotch and soda and a beer," he rumbled in his beautiful Italian accent.

The boy made the drinks and said the price and looked at Malleven in the eyes. Malleven held his gaze for several seconds while he studied him. He had long perfected his mental persuasion skills, seeing it as an art form and a special hobby of his.

As he gave over the cash, he allowed a finger to stroke the boy's palm and adeptly scanned his consciousness. He quickly discerned that the boy was lower-class Atlantean, which wasn't a surprise given his height and unusual eye colour. Maths was his subject and he was working his way through college – *admirable*.

Malleven prided himself on his telepathic skills, a firm believer in it being like a muscle that grew with exercise. Eventually, he wanted to be good enough to use the skill remotely as the Murrs were rumoured to do and so relieving him of the need to touch skin. "Are you in halls?" Malleven asked, already knowing the answer.

The boy nodded slowly, still held in Malleven's thrall.

"I will come to you later," Malleven said, looking deep into the boy's eyes.

The boy made no remark on the fact that he hadn't told Malleven his floor or door number.

"Later then," Malleven said, smiling. "Steven."

The boy hadn't opened his mouth once, but Malleven felt him stare after him as he turned away and walked back towards his cousin and the two giggling girls.

"Ah, Malleven … meet Genna and Sophie."

Malleven glanced from one to the other, "Incantate …" and bent and kissed each of their hands.

They both looked at one another and giggled.

"Cab for Flor … anna," a cockney voice shouted from the doorway.

Malleven knocked back his drink and Cesarè smacked his beer bottle down on the bar. "Come, girls … your carriage awaits." Cesarè put out his arm to show the girls the way.

Malleven rolled his eyes, already knowing he would give them the cash for a taxi home and they would have no memory of how they came to be in London. Even so, he climbed into the back of the black cab and grabbed the brunette to sit on his lap. "Come, Poppy, keep me warm."

She squealed, "How did you? …" She looked at her friend, shocked. "Only my mum calls me that."

Malleven laughed and shrugged it off. He faced her on his lap so she was forced to put a hand on each of his shoulders to steady herself. "Your mother must have seen what a perfect flower you are." And he kissed her deeply.

Cesarè laughed from his spot on the seat next to him, marvelling as always at his cousin's audacity. "To the West End!" he shouted to the cabbie and grabbed the other girl.

CHAPTER 3

Two years later and Lacy was old enough to leave care. However, as much as he wanted her with him, it was going to cause problems of its own. There was a certain amount of safety in the Home. One thing he was doubly sure of was he didn't want her living with three other blokes, even if they were like brothers to him. And so he was resigned to look for a place of their own.

He knew that it was a turning point. One he wasn't totally happy with, as she was so young. His resolve where she was concerned was tenuous at best and it wouldn't take much for him to sink his teeth into her soft neck and her beautiful body at last. The two things were so connected. The clock was ticking.

The only way he'd kept off her this long was due to a constant string of faceless women. And convincing her that he saw her as a sister. Always telling her she needed more experience before he'd bother with her. He knew he hurt her but he was seriously running out of options.

Keenan despaired at her constant cock blocking with the women he got with. Even finding her in the wardrobe spying on him more than once. Then she'd fall about laughing when the poor naked girl he was with freaked out at the weirdness and stomped out of the place, vowing never to return to such a bunch of raving perverts.

No, time was definitely running out. He would sit her down tonight and tell her his plans.

First, he and Vince had to go to Number Eleven, a little club in Mile End, to collect a couple of ounces from someone and shift it. Then he'd come back and have it out with her, finally.

LACY HAD BEEN in love with Keenan as long as she could remember. He was her knight in the silver hoodie. He fought every battle for her, making people give her a wide berth for fear of angering him, because everyone was scared of him. And when he looked at her, it was as though she were the only person in the world. Her heart flipped at the mere thought of him.

In fact, she could think of no other better-looking or fanciable man than Keenan. She loved the way his deep voice rasped, and the way he smelled clean of soap and maleness. She even loved his temper that he barely kept a rein on. It made his beautiful duck-egg-blue eyes flood with blood, making him look dark and evil, and he would stalk her like his prey. She would pretend to run but let him catch her and allow him to drink her blood till his temper ebbed away and he was contrite and loving.

Although he would always stop himself from making love to her. She knew he became aroused, but he'd always use the brother-sister crap like a contraceptive.

They weren't blood relatives, but when she threw that at him, he'd then switch to excuse number two: that she wasn't experienced enough in life. Not as much as the slappers he fucked, obviously. She threw the soap across the bathroom from her suds-filled bath.

Keenan had given strict orders not to flounce around the flat semi-naked in front of his boys, so he made sure they went out beforehand. She used to think it was because he got jealous, but now she had started to think that it had more to do with her black stripes, which emerged all over her body when she was in water for any length of time.

What a freak. No wonder he didn't want her. He'd tried to make her feel better about them when she was little by showing his arms were the same and that meant they were really related, but it did little to make her feel better when she competed with other girls.

No, he didn't want her. She'd all but begged to go with him tonight, but he'd said he was going south of the river and he didn't want her with him in case of trouble.

Well, she was branching out on her own tonight and getting some of that valuable experience he was always going on about. Razz was collecting her at ten. He was a white, tattooed wide boy who drove a souped-up car and ran with a few boys Keenan knew. Except Keenan and his boys hated Razz and his. Only because they were rivals, Lacy reasoned.

She couldn't win. Keenan didn't like anyone. It was only a week ago that she had been in a club dancing with a really nice black boy from Tottenham, called Desmond, when Keenan had bounded over to them in about three strides and knocked out three of the poor boy's teeth. Then he'd shouted at her, 'You got that boy hurt, Lacy, playing your silly games.'

She'd then screamed at him. 'How was she supposed to get any experience if he never fucking let her?' Then she became acutely aware of the looks on people's faces around them, only then the words were already out, and it was too late.

Well, tonight, Keenan was south of the river and she was

going to Number Eleven, with the dishy Razz. She'd show Keenan how grown up she was.

Determined to see her plan through, she got out of her bath before her markings became too prominent. She'd decided on a black jumpsuit, hair up with curls cascading down, and big hoop earrings. She would wear high heels and hope she didn't have to do too much walking in them.

She was nearly nineteen now and it was about time she was allowed to grow up. Tonight, she was going to make some headway.

KEENAN WAITED in the office at Number Eleven to collect the package that he and Vince were to deliver to Big Frank in Bermondsey.

They'd been kept waiting due to some sort of delay, so they'd been drinking in the bar for the last couple of hours. He was itchy tonight, and it had nothing to do with shifting drugs. He wanted to get it over with so he could go home and check on Lacy and tell her what he'd decided. He just had a funny feeling he couldn't shake off, but he put it down to nerves.

He was called into the office at last, where he received the packet, instructions and walked out into the main club to collect Vince.

LACY STOOD STIFFLY with Razz at the bar, trying to look like she was enjoying herself. She couldn't help but notice the space that had cleared around them. It was like the circle you get when you drop a pebble in a pool.

Maybe Razz had the same effect Keenan did on people. She smiled up at him. He looked at her with shrewd, stone-grey eyes. He wasn't bad-looking, she supposed. Not a candle to Keenan, though. He was tall and stocky, but Keenan had about another six inches in height on him, although probably leaner.

Shit. She had to stop comparing him with every single man she came into contact with.

"Lace!" The stern voice said from behind her.

She froze.

Razz squinted.

She turned and they both looked at Vince.

Her heart stopped. *Fuck!* Anxiously, she looked around.

"Can I have a quick word, Lace?"

She was about to say okay when Razz touched her arm to stop her. "Vince?" Razz said, in a way of greeting.

Vince nodded. "Razz." Then he directed his gaze to Lacy again. "Lace?"

"She's having a drink with me tonight," Razz cut in.

"What are you doing here, Vince?" Lacy asked, worried. "Keenan said you were south of the river tonight?"

Vince nodded, "We're just going. Keenan's in the office." He widened his eyes to communicate a silent warning and a sense of urgency, which was not lost on Lacy.

"Don't worry, mate. I'll look after her," Razz said, grinning, showing a gold tooth.

Her heart hammered.

"Lace, come on!" Vince said, more forcefully.

She went to walk away with Vince to stop a bad situation escalating, when Razz pulled her back to him roughly. "No you don't."

Vince had witnessed enough and stepped between them and went nose to nose with Razz.

Lacy backed away slowly, ready for it to kick off between them. She'd witnessed trouble a thousand times and this was no different.

Then everything happened really fast. There was some

posturing and pushing. Vince swung at Razz. Razz ducked, then he ran at Vince, pushing him into a table. Lacy just got out of the way in time. They rolled around on the floor and then Razz scrambled to his feet and ran through the crowd and up the stairs to the street. Vince rolled onto his side and curled into a ball.

Lacy ran to him and knelt on the floor. Vince was groaning and holding his side. She tried to see what was wrong and went to move his hands that were clutching his side when she noticed the blood. "Bloody hell. Vince!" The blood was on her hands and his were drenched in it.

Heavy hands pulled her up by the shoulders and out of the way. She looked up at the bald bouncer in a daze. Then the world went silent when she saw Keenan push through the crowd.

Everyone moved out of the way.

THE MINUTE KEENAN walked into the club, tension hung in the air like an electric storm. He could smell it. When he saw the crowd surge like scurrying vermin, he homed in and made his way to its focus, his temper ramping up already. *Lacy.* He knew she was there; he could feel her.

When he walked up to her as she was standing with the bouncer, he scented blood instantly. He knew it wasn't hers, but he had to touch her to make sure.

Keenan looked into her face, white with shock, and didn't have a chance to chastise her for being there before she pointed down at Vince's huddled body.

He crouched down and saw the area he was clutching. A stab wound. "Who?" he rasped. His voice was descending with his anger to a bad place and he knew his eyes were flooding as he could only see red like some heat-seeking camera.

"Razz," Vince grit out.

Keenan went to pull away on a roar, but Vince grabbed him with surprising strength, "Wait, Keenan." He breathed heavily to try to steady himself and deal with the pain. "I know what you are going to do ... use your head. Don't lose it, okay?"

Keenan closed his eyes and nodded.

"Go home," Vince continued, "go in my room."

"Shh!" Keenan cut in. "Save your strength."

"No listen, Keen. It's important ... taped under the dressing table is an envelope. Take it, it's yours."

Keenan frowned in confusion.

"It's got a passport for you and Lace, and a credit card. Go to a hotel at the airport; ring the number on the piece of paper. They will get you a flight." Vince grimaced in pain.

"I don't understand," Keenan said in desperation.

"Just do it, mate. The blokes that came before ... they sent it ... now she's past eighteen." Vince lost consciousness for a minute.

When Vince came too again, Keenan felt Ricky at his shoulder, then Dan. He stood up. Facing Dan, he said, "I have to go."

"I'll come with you," Dan replied.

"No!" Keenan said, "I want you two to mind Lacy and Vince. Go with them to the hospital and I'll meet you there."

When Keenan could finally bring himself to face Lacy, he looked daggers while he jabbed his finger at her, "You fucking stay with Ricky and Dan, d'you hear? You don't go anywhere else," he rasped, his voice going completely.

"Where are you going?" she asked.

Keenan ignored the question. "Give me your phone," he demanded.

She handed it over to him immediately. He was glad to see her subdued. Her big mouth shut. "I'll meet you at the hospital." His blood was on a rolling boil and he could not trust himself with her in his present mood. So he left her standing there, exited the club and went into the drizzling night.

HIS FIRST PORT of call was his flat. His mind was troubled by the information Vince had given him. As soon as he let himself in, he grabbed a holdall and stuffed in as many clothes for him and Lacy that would fit. Then he went to Vince's room and found the packet exactly where Vince said it would be.

He couldn't help but take a peek at the contents. Two brand-new passports. He wondered how they'd managed to get two passport-sized photos of them. He didn't dwell on the implications of that. Then there was a credit card with Keenan Santalini on it and not Santos, the name by which he'd always been known. *Fuck! Who were these people? And what did they want – more to the point?*

Well, his options were limited at the moment, so he'd take what help he could get and worry about sorting it out later.

Then, at the bottom of the pile, was a piece of paper with an old-fashioned coat of arms or something on it. It reminded him of a posh school's crest. It had the name Alfonzo Bonaci on it, and an address in Ireland with a phone number. He slipped it in his pocket, stood up and did a quick scan around.

Deciding that he had everything they needed, he closed the door on his flat and his old life.

KEENAN AND RAZZ had crossed paths a few times, being from the same manor. He knew him well enough not to like him and he was sure the feeling was mutual.

The other thing he was sure of, without any shadow of doubt, was that the only reason he had picked Lacy to take out to that particular club was to piss him off and show the watching world he was some sort of big man who would dare go out with Keenan Santos' sister.

So knowing him of old, it didn't take him long to track him down to his part of town. He also knew he'd be mob-handed, tooled-up and waiting for him to come for him. *Oh yeah*, but he didn't know who he was dealing with, especially as he didn't have time to mess about. He dropped off the package he was meant to deliver and collected the money.

He opened the envelope and whistled. There was at least ten K in cash. He ran a thumb through the bundle so it fanned out. Yep, this would be their start. *Fuck Big Frank*, he wouldn't hang around long enough for the fallout.

Wasting no more time, he hit the call-back button on Lacy's phone. Razz picked up in two seconds.

"Keenan … you took your time?" Razz said, with a sneer in his voice, obviously for the entertainment of an audience he had with him.

Keenan tried to calm his anger so his voice was audible, "The garages … Union House … now!" He sounded like gravel.

"I'll be there in ten," Razz said, and laughed.

CHAPTER 4

$\mathcal{K}$eenan stood waiting in the shadows. He needed to stay calm as he could barely see; his eyes were so swamped in blood. He took even breaths – in one two, out one two. He tried anything to keep his head. Vince's words echoed; his old friend knew him so well. Vince knew that when he lost it, there would be no rational thought and he could leave himself vulnerable.

Headlights swung into the large Tarmacked area in front of the garages and brought him to attention. All he could see were yellow blobs with his red vision, but he knew who it was by the pumping bass throbbing from the car.

The car stopped a few feet away from him, but the engine kept running. He heard two doors open and slam, then he stepped out from the shadows.

"You alone," he demanded, pointing to the orange glow of the driver he instinctively knew was Razz.

Then he heard Razz's voice, "This won't take long, Steve." The grin was evident in his voice while he wrapped something jangling around his knuckles.

The passenger door opened and closed again and the

second orange form disappeared, leaving him and Razz alone.

It didn't take much to light his fuse. A simple "How's your mate?" from Razz, and Keenan flew at him.

His fangs descended in a flash so they were clearly visible, and judging by the look of horror that crossed Razz's face, he'd seen his eyes burn red like stop lights.

The rest was a blur.

All Razz could do was bring his fists up to try to protect his face, but Keenan was like a demon possessed. He struck at his neck, ripping his throat out in his first lunge.

Such was Keenan's ferociousness that he shook Razz's body like a Pit Bull until the eerie gurgling stopped from Razz's mouth and he hung limp and boneless like a dog with a rag doll.

Keenan released what was left of Razz so it flopped with a thud on the floor and turned his attention to the stationary car. He bent his knees and cocked his head slightly at an unnatural angle to get a look into the windows. He made out the three glows occupying the car, watching the bloody scene.

Not moving, he watched the frantic actions of the passengers as one jumped into the driver's seat, released the handbrake and tried to make a hasty getaway. If he'd been capable of sane thought, he would have laughed at the car hopping along while the driver panicked until he eventually steadied his foot enough to drive out of the garages and away, shitting himself.

KEENAN WALKED for about an hour after he'd killed Razz. He needed to calm down in order to think straight.

After a while, he got his colour vision and his depth perception back. He looked down at his hands and his shirt and realised he had to clean himself up before anyone saw him.

He headed back to his van that he'd hidden and raked around inside for a change of clothes. Then he threw his soiled ones in a dumpster outside the youth centre nearby. He soon broke in and found the toilets, washed the blood off his face, neck and forearms, as best he could.

LACY HAD BEEN SITTING in the hospital waiting room with Dan and Ricky for what seemed like all night. Vince had been rushed into surgery to stop the internal bleeding, but luckily, he had sustained no major damage, so he was going to be okay.

She'd breathed a sigh of relief when they'd been told. Tonight had been her fault and she was scared stiff of facing Keenan when he eventually rocked up.

Speak of the devil, there he was. Walking down the corridor toward them shrouded in a sports jacket and baseball cap. Everything about him shouted predator. She would know him anywhere. Her heart flipped, then sank. *Shit.*

Dan and Ricky stood up immediately when they saw him approach. They both embraced him and brought him up to speed with what was happening to Vince.

Keenan nodded and spoke to them quietly, but hadn't brought himself to look at her once. Just as she thought she would cry, he looked at her and tilted his head to the side to motion for her to go with him. *Fuck.* She stood warily and slowly walked over to him.

He picked up her hand and held it tightly like you would a small child. She looked down at his hands and saw the blood rubbed into the creases of his fingers. He had clearly tried to wash it off, but had to do it hurriedly. She swallowed hard.

"Later," Keenan said, and hugged each of his boys. "Don't

go back to the flat," he ordered. "As soon as we are settled, I'll send for you."

They both nodded. It was obvious there would be repercussions from Razz's friends, as it looked as though they had to disappear ASAP.

"As soon as Vince is out of surgery, get him out of here," Keenan said.

Both boys looked at each other, then nodded in agreement.

The situation was beginning to dawn on her, but she didn't have time to question anything as Keenan turned away and pulled her along with him.

"Keenan … Keenan," she said over and over, having to run along next to him to keep up. "Where are we going?"

"The airport," he said coldly.

Fuck, this was serious. He must have killed him. She'd never seen him so angry with her. And, for the first time in her life, she didn't feel totally safe with him. It was as though she'd poked the tiger with the stick one too many times.

As soon as they entered the uniform, run-of-the-mill hotel room, Keenan threw down their bag and said he needed a shower. Without further words, he went straight to the adjoining bathroom and switched the shower on to cold. He shed his clothes, stepped under the spray and closed his eyes.

He'd had better fucking days. His blood was still thrumming. Although his anger had given way to a more fundamental need, an overwhelming instinct to claim Lacy as his own, both her blood and her body. He was in turmoil. He was scared of letting go of his emotions, but there was no putting it off any longer. The inevitable was here.

He looked down at his emerging stripes and asked himself for the millionth time who he was kidding. He was a freak. Tonight was proof of that. When he'd ripped Razz apart like a wild animal, it confirmed Lacy deserved better than that.

"Keenan."

Her voice came quietly from the other side of the bathroom door. He sighed and rolled his head back and looked at the ceiling for strength.

"Please, Keenan … I'm sorry." She was crying. He could hear it in her voice.

He swallowed hard and reached a decision quickly. "Come in." He never allowed himself to be naked in front of her … usually. He was always careful in case he lost his cool. However, tonight was a new start. No more games. No going back. She came in.

Keenan watched her eyes, red and puffy, rake over his entire body like a touch, as he stood in the shower. He made no attempt to cover himself.

His gums began to ache and his vision became tinged with red. His mouth opened slightly and he tilted his hair back in the spray. Without words, he was telling her this was him, take him or leave him.

Her beautiful green eyes bored into his. She wasn't going to be frightened off and began to unzip her jumpsuit and step out of it – nervously, he noticed. Then she unclipped her bra and stepped out of her knickers.

His vision went straight to crimson, his temperature shot through the roof and his fangs strained, as they couldn't extend any more. The only thing that could cool him down now was blood. *Back down,* he willed. He wanted her to be scared of him. Instead, she took a step forward.

"I'm hanging by a thread, Lace." His voice went croaky with emotion.

"I want you to let go. That's what I've always wanted." Her

eyes were wide with a mixture of fear and lust. He could smell it.

His eyes closed in one last vain attempt to get a grip on himself, but her body inched so close to him that his large erection touched her and twitched.

A foot taller, he looked down at her menacingly. He touched the tops of her arms as gently as he could manage with shaky fingers and moved her around him to the corner of the shower. There, she was hemmed in by the walls and dominated by his body towering above her.

She still looked up at him unblinking, defiant in challenge. "I'm sorry, Keenan," she said again.

"It wasn't your fault," he growled. "It was mine."

Her chest rose and fell in fear and anticipation. Her pulse raced at her neck. "This is your last chance to back out." His voice was totally unrecognizable now.

"Are you still trying to push me away?" She frowned, pain washing over her eyes.

His resolve snapped and he lunged at her like a cobra.

LACY GAZED up at Keenan in all his terrifying, transformed glory and he was spectacular to her. His messy black hair, piercings, tats and tall muscled frame were all gorgeous enough, but add his beautiful blue eyes flooded with blood, and his sharp canines showing her his physical need, then she was his slave as she had always been.

Amazed, she watched as his dark-grey stripes emerged similar to her own. All over his arms, legs and torso - they were the same. Hers were just more vivid than his. Now she knew without doubt they were meant for each other. So when he uttered the words 'her last chance to back out', she couldn't take any more rejection.

Just when she would snap and pummel her fists into his

chest, he moved fast and slammed her into the corner with his weight and struck with his teeth into the soft part of her shoulder. She let out an involuntary yelp. However, it was merely a grip to hold her, like an animal and not to drink.

Now he had her, he stilled for a few moments. He just breathed. It probably felt longer than it actually was, but he stayed there to allow her to adjust, calm her own breathing and relax into his grip, which she slowly allowed herself to do.

When he seemed convinced that she wouldn't struggle, she felt his teeth retract and begin to kiss her softly up the column of her neck and suck the skin over her pulse and groan. The process was so primal she almost combusted.

Her pulse quadrupled. He answered by pushing himself up against her so she could feel his hardness. Everything, she realized, was to warn her what she was letting herself in for. *Well, to hell with that.* Instead of pushing him back, she pulled him tighter to her by reaching around his muscled back and digging in her nails. Then she turned her face into his shoulder and bit him back hard. She wanted this and she would give as good as she got, so he'd better get used to it.

When she bit him he froze. She released her grip with her teeth and rooted for his mouth, laying light kisses as she went and reaching up with her hands to guide his face down to hers. He quickly found her mouth, but he waited. She ran her tongue along his slightly parted lips and played with the sensitive tips of his fangs. Then she pushed into his mouth. As if he were wary, he tentatively stroked her tongue with his. So gentle, all the while he still had her pinned forcefully in the corner.

Coaxing and goading him, the kiss quickly escalated into something demanding and urgent. She gasped his name when he responded and deepened the kiss. He groaned and ground his hips into her while the loud spray pelted them.

Keenan released her mouth and pushed her head back roughly to expose her throat, but surprised her by kissing gently down her neck. He loosened his hold while he crouched down to kiss her breasts. She moaned in blissful satisfaction. He rolled one beautiful peak between a canine and his tongue and then the other.

Her chest began to ache so badly she thought she would explode. She couldn't explain it. It felt like something inside her that needed to escape. It was her heart, she concluded. No one could love anyone more than she loved Keenan.

Her eyes rolled back into her head in ecstasy when his mouth moved slowly lower down her body. "Oh yes, Keenan."

His teeth grazed and nipped until his fingers touched her searing heat.

KEENAN HOVERED his mouth over the beautiful, soft pulse at her groin. He longed to sink his teeth into her there and taste her jasmine blood, but resisted. Instead, he gently parted her legs and ran his fingers delicately between her folds.

Fuck. She wanted him, and she was so ready but danger-ously hot. She was burning up. He refused to take her here in the shower and risk hurting her more than he needed to. She was a virgin, a fact that weighed heavily on his conscience.

He looked up into her eyes that were full of longing.

"Don't stop," she whimpered.

"I won't," he rasped softly. "It's too late for that."

Slowly, he stood back up to his full height and came to a decision. "You are so hot, Lace. I'm going to bring down your temperature, okay?" It was the only thing he could think of that would work.

She nodded, bleary-eyed. She would have said yes to anything.

"Then I'll take you to bed." He bent down his head and kissed her reverently. But his fangs began to take on a life of their own and began to grow and invade their kiss. He leaned back and checked her eyes again. Then moved slowly forward and kissed down her cheek like feathers until he reached her carotid at her neck. He breathed gently next to her skin while his arms moved softly around her to hold her still, and give her time for her brain to catch up to what he was going to do. He didn't want to rip her delicate skin.

When he was sure she was relaxed, he placed his teeth on her skin and paused for a second. He wanted to savour this. He'd waited his whole life to do it. Then he plunged his teeth deeply into her neck.

Her breath hitched in shock and she froze. He remained still, neither sucking nor removing them. Eventually, she relaxed into his arms and he began to draw long, heavenly mouthfuls of her blood. He groaned as the honey washed over his tongue and overwhelmed his senses.

Keenan felt her body temperature fall along with her blood pressure, and so did his, as it always did when he took her blood. He lifted her up into his arms without breaking the seal of his bite. As always, her blood was the purest aphrodisiac. It spread into his nervous system and ramped his lust higher than it had ever been. Taking more and more of her with each deep pull at her neck, he stalked out of the shower with her and to the bed.

CHAPTER 5

Everything felt like a wonderful dream while Lacy floated in Keenan's strong arms as he carried her from the shower to the bed. She'd imagined them making love a thousand times and what it would be like, and now it was really happening. It exceeded all expectations.

Instead of hurting her, his confidence grew, and he took great care to make sure she had the most wonderful experience. He draped a fluffy white towel around her, then sank slowly with her on top of the bed.

He nestled his weight carefully on top of her and she looked up into his strange blue eyes, which swirled intermittently with blood. She touched her fingers down the side of his face, "I love you, Keenan. I always have."

Keenan closed his eyes as if he savoured the words and turned his face into her hand and kissed her fingers. Then he reached down to her leg with his left hand and brought it upwards to widen her legs. His fingers ran along her intimate folds and she shuddered and sighed into his kiss.

Gently, he eased a finger inside and slid it carefully in and out in a slow, deliberate rhythm.

"Oh, Keenan, please," she whispered, next to his mouth.

He moved his forearms under her shoulders and let his heavy body edge down to lie between her open legs. His erection nudged at her in just the right place. Her heart thumped in anticipation and she held her breath.

He nipped her lips with his. "Breathe," he whispered.

She exhaled on a smile.

He began nudging his hips forward in a soft, slow rhythm. She gasped when she realized that he was penetrating her little by little with every gentle thrust of his hips. She found herself digging her heels into the bed to push herself up to meet him and tempt him further. His eyes closed with his concentration, and perspiration beaded on his forehead and top lip with the strain of holding back.

She knew it was killing him to be gentle, so she pushed herself onto him further. He pushed a little more and she stiffened. Her muscles held him in a vice-like grip and it was painful. She held her breath, then panted. He stopped moving and opened his eyes; their eyes locked while he waited. She knew if she told him to stop, he would. Instead, he pushed his tongue into her mouth and mimicked what he was doing. She sucked his tongue.

Gradually, her muscles relaxed and she tentatively moved her hips toward him again and so he pushed a little further. He stilled, looked into her eyes and whispered, "It's gonna hurt for a bit, babe. Tell me to stop if you want."

She nodded and felt a feeling of love wash over her so strong, she pulled his head down to kiss her wildly and deeply, the most sensual, meaningful kiss of her life. Then he plunged into her in a single thrust, to the hilt.

She cried out in pain and the overwhelming feeling of fullness. He breathed deeply to hold still. She panted. Then, as her breathing slowed, he began to move a little at a time and she closed her eyes and lost herself to sensation. Her heart beat wildly and she felt herself get swept up in the most wonderful feeling of togetherness.

Gradually, he moved more and more with harder thrusts, and she began to meet him with a mirroring force, until they both moaned and he pistonned into her with a ferocity that he needed.

Her face and body were aflame and so was his. A glimpse of their striped bodies moving erotically together as one nearly made her come apart. *Alien … Fuck*, she didn't care. This was what her whole life had led to.

Keenan pushed into her madly as he leaned up onto his elbows and looked at her face in ecstasy. She was the most beautiful thing in the world in that snapshot of time. He wanted to bind himself with her for ever.

He slowed his pace and she opened her eyes.

"What's the matter?" she breathed, her eyelids low.

He didn't know where the urge came from but he needed to speak the words. "Do you take me as yours?" he said, his face serious while he lifted his own wrist to his mouth.

"Oh god, yes. Always." Her eyes closed and he felt her grip her tight sheath around him.

Growling with approval, he scored his wrist with his razor-sharp teeth, held it over her face and watched as droplets of his dark blood dripped onto her lips. How he kept it together, he had no idea. Erotic was an understatement. Her little tongue licked her lips tentatively and when he lowered his wrist to her mouth, he groaned aloud when she swirled and licked around the wound and then latched on and sucked with long sexual pulls. His eyes were glued to the sexiest thing he had ever seen, and when her eyes went up into her head, *fuck* he wanted to bury himself deep inside her.

There was nothing left to do but thrust into her relentlessly, hard and fast after that. The bed creaked in rhythm and slammed against the wall. He found himself growling and she groaned until he felt her constrict around him. She pulsed and milked him over and over and she gasped his name in surprise.

The last of his control disintegrated with her orgasm, and he struck her neck and pulled hard. He came wave after wave. He pushed his seed as far into her as possible and drew her very soul into him through her neck into his mouth.

When at last the shudders of their orgasm abated, he relaxed heavily on top of her, breathing hard. His face tingled and his body hummed with a wonderful sense of wellbeing. When his breathing slowed enough to speak, he whispered, "You're mine now, Lacy Rain."

Keenan ran them a deep, cool bath to ease the tension of the night and to wash the blood from their faces and hair. He pulled her into the bath with him to sit between his legs, and lay back with her head on his chest. She gave a contented sigh when he scooped handfuls of the soothing water and trickled it over her shoulders and breasts.

Before long, they were both hooped in stripes again. He noticed Lacy's were black and his were grey. It was the first time in their lives they had given each other the chance to truly study each other's naked bodies fully transformed.

She voiced the words they'd skirted around for so long: "What are we?" and measured her arm up against his like you would a suntan.

"I'm not sure," he said, honestly, on a sigh. "But I think I'm different to you."

"No you're not," she said in dismay, turning her whole body to look at him.

Keenan put his head to the side and put his finger to her lips and felt her tiny teeth. "No fangs, Lace."

She swallowed and frowned sulkily, "Maybe it's a bloke thing."

He smiled ruefully, exhausted. "I think those blokes who came when we were kids know something about it."

She frowned while she thought about what he said.

He reached over the side of the bath to pull his jeans within reach, and pulled out his mobile phone with the piece of paper from the pocket.

He dialled the number.

"What is it?" she asked.

He shook his head and put his finger to his lips. He wasn't sure himself yet.

It rang a few times, then someone answered. "Hello … this is Keenan Santos … er Santalini."

An Italian-sounding male voice replied, "This is Alfonzo Bonaci … Is Lacy with you?"

"Yes, she's here." His hackles began to rise at the bloke's obvious interest in Lacy. "We need a flight." He cut in before the guy could say anything else. He wasn't up for idle chitchat. "I was told to ring you."

"You did the right thing," Alfonzo said. "I will arrange a flight to New York. You will be met at the airport and taken to your family residence."

His family? He frowned while he processed what the bloke was saying.

"You must guard my niece with your life. Do you understand?"

"Your niece?" Keenan balked.

"Everything will be explained in due course."

"Oh, and one more thing … my boys. I want them out of

there." He felt like he was taking the piss, but there was no way he'd leave them in the shit he'd left.

"The Protectors have a safe house they can go to. Their removal will be arranged."

Before Keenan could question him further about the strange things he was coming out with, he cut in forcefully with, "I will text you the flight details. Do not let Lacy out of your sight."

Keenan was starting to feel annoyed. "I won't," he snapped. And ended the call.

Protectors? Was the guy crazy? The call posed more questions than it had answered.

"What is it, Keenan?" Lacy said, interrupting his thoughts, looking intently at him.

"He said we are going to New York and will be met by my family. And he said he was your uncle," he said, shaking his head.

"I don't understand," Lacy said in confusion.

"Me neither." He began to stand up and picked her up with him. They stepped out of the bath and dried themselves. "We'd better get some sleep," he said, leading her back to the bed.

He wrapped her in his arms, and they fell into an exhausted, dreamless sleep in the rumpled bed and waited for the text that would change their lives for ever.

KEENAN ENJOYED WATCHING Lacy's excitement at being in First Class. *Fuck*, neither of them had been on a plane before. For Lacy, it was Christmas in a toy shop. Pressing buttons, ordering drinks and snacks. She was like a little kid. It saddened him that she'd had so little time to be a real kid. She, like him, had had to grow up really fast.

He would have enjoyed the flight as well if he weren't as

edgy as hell, seeing eyes on them everywhere. He had this niggly feeling that they were walking into a trap, but hadn't had much option but to take the flights. They were getting his boys out, or so they said. Even so, there was no way he was going to expose Lacy to a situation without checking it out first.

No, they would give their welcoming committee the slip until he could suss it out more on his terms. There was no fucking way he was going to walk into something where he wasn't in control.

After their plane landed, Keenan explained to Lacy what was going to happen. He told her to hang back through Customs and walk out close to someone else, after he'd already gone through.

He reminded her of what the blokes were likely to look like, judging by the visit they'd had when they were kids, and told her to avoid big army-looking blokes like the plague.

After years of mixing with street kids, ducking and diving, it was a simple thing to slip past while the guys were in conversation, and them running was the last thing they expected. They were obvious and stood out a mile off. Just too big to be anyone other than soldiers, way taller than the average person.

Briefly, his own height occurred to him, but that concern was squashed when he yanked Lacy into an airport shop and out another doorway. Then they were lost in a crowd, out of the building and into a cab.

Queens was the only place he could think of to tell the cab driver. He'd heard of it in a film. So he asked the cabbie to take them to an okay hotel in Queens. Luckily, he'd remembered to change some of the money he'd stolen into dollars. There was no way he could use the credit card yet.

.   .   .

Lacy sat on the bed, tired and a little bewildered in the budget hotel room. "Are you sure they are bad guys, Keenan?" she said, wearily.

"No, Lace, I'm not. That's the point. I wanna check them out first."

She nodded. Keenan was usually right in these things. She was probably getting tetchy and paranoid. She'd thought she'd seen the same bloke on their flight, and then again when they rushed through the airport. And when she'd looked out of the back window of their cab, he was getting into the cab behind them. Stupid, she knew, someone could have been on the flight and got into a cab near them, but, hey, her life had gone all 007 all of a sudden, so who could blame her.

"What are we gonna do for money? she asked, watching him pull their stuff out of the holdall.

"I've got a bit, but I reckon we should get jobs. Then I'll check out my so-called family."

"I could dance?" she said.

Keenan stopped what he was doing and looked at her as if he were weighing up what she'd said.

"I've known enough of them to blag it?" she continued.

He nodded, surprising her. "I suppose I could go for security … as long as we were at the same club," he said, resuming his unpacking.

She grinned and ran to him, knocking him over from his crouch onto the floor. He rolled with her till he had the dominant position on top. "What was that for? he said, smiling, flashing some fang.

"What have you done with the real Keenan?" she laughed. "I just never thought you'd go for it, that's all." She still hadn't got used to Boyfriend Keenan, as opposed to Brother Keenan. Her heart flipped. *God*, she felt so blessed.

"What?" he said, searching her face as her cogs worked and a stupid grin covered it.

"I love you," she whispered. And a tear escaped the corner of her eye. "I never want to lose you."

He frowned and caught it on a finger. "Never, babe."

Keenan nestled his lower body between her legs and kissed her slowly, then leaned back up again. The blood swirled in his eyes. "I stayed your brother, Lace, for our safety … until I just couldn't do it any more." A rueful smile crossed his lips. "I was gonna tell you that night."

Lacy remained quiet and stared at him. "I got him killed, didn't I?" she said, eventually.

"No … no," he said, concern creasing his brow. He sat up and scooped her up with him so she was sitting on his lap. "He stabbed Vince, Lace. If it weren't for that, I would have probably just given him a slap and a warning, and that's about it. He took it to the next level, not you." His face was earnest looking into her eyes.

He squinted, suspicious all of a sudden. "Were you trying to make me jealous?" he said, amusement playing on his lips.

"No," she said, shaking her head, deadly honest. "I just thought until you started to look at me like a grown-up, I was stuck being your little sister."

"Why Razz though … my rival?" he said, squinting again, as if he didn't fully believe her.

"He asked me," she said, matter-of-factly. "Nobody ever had the guts to ask me out before."

He barked a laugh, looked up, then shook his head.

"What?" she asked, laughing along with him.

"Nothing. I'm an idiot, that's all."

THE NEXT EVENING, they trawled the clubs looking for something suitable. It had to need a bouncer and a dancer.

Beefing up wasn't a problem to look the part, as since Keenan had finally got together with Lacy, he couldn't stop eating. He was now losing the tall, lanky look of a youth and becoming more like a bloke who worked out. Briefly, the size of the Santalinis popped into his head.

Eventually, after a couple of nights of looking, they found a place. Ironically, it was called 'Leather 'n' Lace'. Lacy squealed with delight, saying it was a sign. And, it wasn't a strip club, more a place for exotic dancing. So they presented themselves to the manager in their brother- sister guise, so he wasn't put off employing them.

After they'd been given the jobs, they laughed and chattered all the way home. Lacy wagged her finger at him as they walked together, "No punching the punters for ogling me," she ordered.

Shit. She knew him too well. Thank god he'd be out on the door and not in the club having to watch it.

On their third night in New York, they started their jobs and soon settled into a routine. They had to remember to keep their hands off each other till they got home so as not to blow their cover. Both slipped easily into their new roles and soon relaxed.

Keenan felt the most content he'd ever been, and began to think *Fuck it*, when he remembered he was supposed to go and see his family. No, they were fine on their own. Guilt pricked him about his boys, but he'd ring them soon and find a way of getting them to the States.

Lacy was a natural dancer. She told him she was building a small army of regulars. He avoided the main room as much as he could, but enlisted the eyes and ears of the other security men working inside, just to make sure no one took liberties. No, life felt too good at the moment to upset the apple cart.

They worked till three or four in the morning, then

hurried home and enjoyed getting to know each other till dawn. They slept most of the day, then started all over again the next night. Honeymoon didn't even come close. They'd wanted each other for so long, and finally getting their wish meant the rest of the world didn't exist. They wanted to stay in their private world for ever.

CHAPTER 6

*L*acy quickly became a favourite. She worked behind the bar till twelve, then did her slot on the runway or pole, and then did another at two.

She'd noticed a handful of men becoming regular faces. One had begun drinking at the bar at around ten and always watched her twelve o'clock performance, then left straight away.

After about a week, he introduced himself as Charles. He had a British accent and was sort of familiar to her. But then again, in her line of work, everyone started to look familiar. He was a nice-enough bloke. Good-looking, short blonde hair, unusual grey eyes, quite tall and toned. But her heart belonged to Keenan. And although she couldn't tell anyone, her stomach always flipped when she thought of him nearby, beautiful and fearless and hers. No one ever stood a chance in her eyes.

This particular night was the same as any other, fairly busy, same old same old, women dancing, and men leering. That was until the vibe suddenly changed like danger on the wind. Bouncers rushed from every corner of the club to the front doors– all talking into their headsets. *Keenan.*

Charles almost got knocked flying as he approached the bar.

She was about to abandon her post and rush to Keenan.

"Quickly, Lacy. You must come with me," Charles said.

"What?" she shrieked in horror. "No way … what's happening?"

"Listen. There isn't much time," and he began forcefully pushing her towards the back fire exit.

"No." She resisted. "I must go to Keenan."

He held her by the shoulders and looked her squarely in the eye; "Four men have just abducted your brother and will be coming for you once they realize you work here," Charles said.

"I don't know you … I'm not going with you," she said, beginning to struggle with her desperate need to get to Keenan.

Charles shook her forcefully. "I know you are not brother and sister. I am from Keenan's family. I've been watching you."

As he finished his words, her resistance slowed and she remembered where she had seen him. *He* was the guy on their plane and at the airport. *He* had followed them. "But …" she went to say.

"I'll explain on the way. Now quickly, before they come for you. Then you will be of no help to Keenan." And he pushed her out the back way and into a waiting car.

IT TOOK all four of Keenan's brothers to pin him down on the floor of the van that sped away from the club.

"Fuck! He's like a wild animal," one grit out.

"Keep out of the way of his teeth," another said, sucking blood off his hand.

Keenan had completely lost his mind.

Two of them had come up to him on the door of the club; one had a knife to his throat, another to his ribs. And when he fought them anyway, two more had jumped out of the van, bundled him in and sped him away. His vision had gone and the only response he could give was to lash out and bite.

"Where is she?" one kept saying to him.

"He has no control. Look at his eyes. It's useless till he calms down."

Keenan lay still, trying to focus. His breathing was ragged, but gradually he calmed himself enough and waited until one relaxed his grip so he could exploit a weakness.

When he struggled again, he was flipped onto his front and hogtied.

He concentrated on breathing, like Vince had taught him. He must think straight and he must get his vision back.

Eventually, he felt the van jerk to a halt and he was hauled out and shaken.

"Will you walk or be carried?" one shouted in his face.

After growling out the word 'walk', he went to kick the guy untying his feet in the head. Then someone put his lights out.

When Keenan woke up, he found himself sitting on a chair in what looked like a posh library. His hands and feet were bound to the chair and tape was across his mouth.

Four men of varying ages, all with a family resemblance, sat opposite him on a large desk, with fat grins across their faces. He would have spat if he could've.

One got down and went to walk toward him to remove the tape from his mouth.

"Watch his teeth," another said. "I'm nearly missing a digit."

They all laughed as the guy whipped the tape from his mouth with a searing sting.

Again, Keenan was forced to breathe to get a grip so he could think.

"He has no control. Look at his eyes," one said.

"Be fair," another said. "He's had no training whatsoever."

The one who looked the oldest walked towards him. He waited for the backhander and braced.

Instead, the bloke spoke. "I am Marius, your oldest brother." Then he half turned and pointed at the other three in turn. "This is Drago, Adriano and the youngest, Louis." He stood up straight, exasperated. "What on earth possessed you to run, Keenan? We were your safe place."

Keenan looked up at him, simmering through his eyebrows.

Marius crouched to his eye line and persisted, "Where is Lacy, Keenan? It is very important."

Now he could spit. "Fuck off!" he growled.

"Look …" Marius tutted, "we searched the club, Keenan. She wasn't there."

Keenan's mind went into overtime. Maybe she'd used her noddle and got out as soon as she knew there was trouble. *But fuck* … he shook his head to himself. Lacy would have come to where he was, no matter the danger. She was infuriating like that. Maybe she'd made her way home thinking he'd escape and meet her back there. *Yeah*, that was probably it.

"She is in great danger, Keenan. She is a Siren alone, with no one to protect her," Marius said.

Keenan was confused. He didn't know what the fuck he was going on about, but he understood she was on her own, though. "Why should I trust you?" Keenan accused.

Marius ignored the question. "Do you have a friend here, Keenan? She was seen leaving with someone."

That got his attention.

They must have noticed the change in his expression because they all stood up and looked deadly serious. "No … it's just us." He closed his eyes. *Fuck.*

"Give us the address. We'll check it out. Then, when we come back we'll fill in the blanks and explain everything to you," Marius said.

"I'll come with you." As hard as he tried, Keenan couldn't stop the red mist descending and totally squashing his ability for rational thought.

"No, Keenan. We can't trust you not to run."

His eyes churned and he hyperventilated as Marius put a steadying hand on his shoulder.

"We are trained soldiers, Keenan. Now. Give. Us. The. Fucking. Address. It is Lacy's only hope." Marius' face was the epitome of reason.

Keenan closed his eyes, cursed his stupidity and told them while he could still speak.

The Santalini brothers went to the address and it was quickly obvious that no one had been there. The club was checked again and the staff were questioned.

Lacy had simply vanished without a trace.

The most ominous information came from a vagrant who'd been asleep outside the back door. He'd described a girl getting into a car. It was taken seriously when his description of the bloke matched the bouncer's account of the man last seen talking to her.

Now they had the unenviable task of breaking the news to Keenan. A bound vampire prince, whose Siren female had been taken from him. It would be enough to send him mad.

. . .

KEENAN HAD HAD an hour and a half of agonizing wait in a locked bedroom. The shutters on the windows were locked and he had no idea where he was anyway.

He heard a crunch of keys in the lock, the door opened, and all four brothers walked into the room and locked the door behind them. His hackles rose with his sense of impending bad news immediately.

The one called Marius walked straight over to him.

"Did you find her?" Keenan found himself still having to ask.

"Turn," Marius ordered, and roughly turned him around and cuffed his hands behind his back again. "Sit." And he was plonked back into the stiff-backed chair.

"What the fuck?" Keenan said as he was pushed back into it and held there.

Another brother bound his ankles.

Keenan's anxiety was coming to an even, steady boil. He looked from face to face for any hint of an explanation. "What is this … where is she?"

Marius pulled over another chair and sat opposite him. He seemed to breathe for a moment as if to fortify himself. Then he shook his head. "I'm sorry, Keenan, she's gone … At the time we took you, she was seen leaving the club and getting into a car at the back entrance … she hasn't been back to your address, and no one has seen her since."

There was the bombshell he feared, come true. Keenan's vision zoomed to red like a rifle sight. His voice descended to a growl, "You've got to let me go. You've got to let me find her." In his madness that followed, he struggled to free himself and gnashed his teeth.

Marius stood and grabbed him by the throat. "Breathe!" he shouted. "Look… At… Me… Look at my eyes."

Keenan's mad eyes raced around in his head frantically and gradually slowed, along with his ragged breaths and he blinked. Eventually, he managed to focus on Marius's moving mouth, even if only to scowl at him with hatred.

"You are no use to her like this," Marius continued. "You would be killed just like that." And he clicked his fingers. "Then what would become of her?"

Keenan remained silent but was still breathing heavily.

"She is yours, bound in blood. As we Santalini are with our mates ... You are a Santalini – our brother. But she is special, and there are those who would seek her to use her ... Now, when you are calmer, we will teach you who and what you both truly are, and to fight properly so that you can take your rightful place as part of the Santalini, an ancient royal family; the first from the sea. In the meantime, we will scour the city for her. We won't give up until we find her." Marius let go of Keenan's throat with a push, leaving him staring up at him with cloudy, blooded eyes.

Marius walked slowly to the door and paused, "When you are ready to learn what you were meant to become, we will teach you and you will find your Siren." Then he left the room and the other three trooped out behind him.

The door was locked and he was left alone.

AFTER TWO DAYS of refusing food, trying to jump them at every opportunity without success, then smashing up his room, Keenan began to realise that the only thing he could do was go along with them, just till he found her. Then they were out of there. They'd been alone all their lives and that was the way they liked it.

So to gain their trust, he began to eat. Then he asked for showers and clean clothes. By the third day of his good behaviour, his door was unlocked and he was led down to a weight room.

"You can burn off some frustration here," Marius said. "Let me know when you are ready to learn." And the brother walked out and left him to it.

The wind out of his sails, he just stood in the room not knowing whether to try to run or what? *Fuck!* After long moments of indecision, his good sense won through and he began to train. In fact, from that moment, he pushed his body like a maniac. Eating and working out became his religion. His sole purpose was to be stronger, faster and fitter.

Rewarded for his efforts, Marius came to him at the end of every night and reported the areas they'd covered and where they would search the next day. Then, after one month, when Marius delivered his nightly debrief, Keenan blurted, "I'm ready."

Marius stopped mid-sentence and stared at him. "You wish to learn?'

"I'm ready to learn to obliterate whoever it was who took her." Keenan's eyes were low, his jaw clenched.

Satisfied, Marius nodded. "We'll start in the morning."

KEENAN BECAME A MAN POSSESSED. No one had ever seen such focus in a Santalini soldier. As well as working out in the gym, Drago taught him hand-to-hand fighting and wrestling. Adriano taught him martial arts, knives and swords. Louis covered all manner of firearms and Marius concentrated on his mental strength and concentration. Getting him to hold his volatile temper and use it to improve, rather than lose focus. This included learning to control his eyes and canines descending in public, a vital part of being a Santalini in the Human world.

The only time he wasn't expected to be able to control his

nature was in the vicinity of his bonded mate's blood, which no Santalini could control. The bond meant the very life force in the blood called them with such strength of compulsion as could never be ignored.

Days moved into weeks and he was becoming a formidable soldier, both in stature and expertise. So, on this particular day, it was nothing unusual to find him sparring with Samurai swords in the war room.

Keenan was aware of the door behind him opening; his senses and peripheral perception were razor sharp, but he was unaware of who it was. That was until he spoke. "Fuck me, he's enormous."

Keenan stopped dead. He dropped his sword and lifted his visor and turned slowly. Surely he was mistaken.

One black face and two brown ones grinned at him.

"Fucking hell!" he breathed. He blinked, then jogged towards them as fast as his cumbersome protective padding would allow and grabbed all three of them to him by their necks.

Vince, now completely healed, Rick and Dan, had made it to America. Never had Keenan been so pleased to see anyone in his miserable life before. It would only ever be topped by Lacy. He was choked up. Vince patted his back, feeling his emotion as the guy always did. "It's okay, man. We're pleased to be here an'all."

They all laughed, thrilled to be together again.

Keenan shook his head to get it back in the game and dispel his sappy tears. "She's gone, Vince." He bowed his head, his hands rested on his hips.

"I know, mate. We've been told."

Marius, who'd tactfully hung back, coughed, "Sorry to interrupt this little party, ladies, but it's time to learn some shit. Get showered, Keenan. We'll all meet in ten in the library.

They all patted backs and Keenan waddled off, still in all his padding, to the shower.

When he reached the library, showered and changed, ten minutes later, his friends were already there waiting. Marius was seated behind the desk. "Take a seat, Keenan."

He sat uneasily, looking at his friends' faces, then back at Marius. "You're more involved in this than you let on?" Keenan said, with a frown.

It was Vince who nodded.

Marius took over. "Perhaps if we started at the beginning, then you'll see how your friends fit into all this." He paused. You. Are. Not. Human …Well, hardly at all …"

Keenan's eyebrows popped, but he remained silent and waited.

"You are bigger, taller, your eyes fill with blood and you have canines which extend with intense emotion like lust or aggression."

Keenan kept his face blank but wasn't totally comfortable with the guy knowing all this shit about him.

Marius continued, "You develop dark bands on your skin when you spend any time in water." Marius paused and stared at Keenan.

Tell me something I don't know. Keenan shrugged; no point in denying it. "What am I then?"

"You are Atlantean, a descendant of Atlantis. Your forefathers were originally from another world, a world called Atlas."

Keenan listened, but it seemed too fantastic. He turned to his friends, but their faces were relaxed and attentive as if they knew the story already. He looked back at Marius in a daze.

"This world was colonized about ten thousand years ago, but the first pioneers were underwater dwellers and lived in the fabled city of Murrtaine. After a time, they gradually ventured on land. The Santalini were the first, legend says. Then, eventually, the city of Atlantis was built, as trade and communications with Humans grew. And so the hybrid race of Atlanteans was born."

Keenan rubbed a hand over his face. He wasn't sure what he should say. *Fuck.* He knew he and Lacy had always been different. "What about Lacy? She's different to me."

Marius nodded and sat back in his chair. "Yes, she is … she has purer blood than us: half Murr and half Atlantean."

Keenan felt confused.

"Murrs have pure Atlas blood and live in Murrtaine to this day. It still exists. It was them who first built Atlantis."

"They can breathe underwater?" Keenan asked.

Marius nodded, "Lacy can as well, but may not know that yet."

Keenan mulled over their time together. How their stripes came out in water. How Lacy, particularly, overheated and needed cold baths. It was plausible, he supposed. "What about these?" He pointed to his fangs.

"Even on Atlas, we were always the special forces of the race and so we went out of the water first to scout the land. We had genetically prominent canines, first bred as a deterrent for our enemies. We were given special dispensation from the king and quickly learned to use them to survive on a diet of blood from Human hosts, but this was only intended as a temporary measure. Over time, it just became a way of bonding with our females, allowing us to lower our body temperatures while on land. As well as a rite of passage into adulthood, triggering the rapid growth that you yourself have experienced and, of course, to dominate an enemy."

Keenan sniffed when the image of him shaking Razz's dead body in his mouth came to mind. *That was the truth.* "I still don't understand. What was living on our own all about?" he asked with more than a hint of annoyance.

Marius conceded a nod. "I know it doesn't seem fair, but you have to understand our society is made up of five royal families who are all related. The Santalini are one, there's the Bonaci, Lacy's family, then there are the Dubonnetti, the Florianna and the Borge, who we refer to as the Murrs. They all vie for prominence. And Lacy is one of five sisters."

Keenan's eyes went wide at that revelation.

"Each has immense power that, in the right hands, will make a great Atlantean king to unite us for the first time in millennia. So sadly, in order for it to be fair to all families, the five sisters had to be hidden in the world. I myself helped in this process."

Keenan's face hardened.

"As a special privilege to the Santalini, known as the Honourable Guard, you were permitted to be with your most compatible mate almost from birth. The princes from the other families search for theirs with no guarantee that they will find their most compatible mate before someone else does." Marius took out an old-looking oval white opaque ring, leaned forward and offered it to Keenan.

"You pushed one on my finger before. I remember it. It was a darker colour, though," Keenan said, examining it closely.

Marius inclined his head. "You have a good memory. It is a divining ring. All princes have one forged particularly for them at birth. This is yours."

Keenan looked at Marius' hand.

"I choose not to wear mine. Our family has their Siren … Unless I need it for divining purposes, of course."

This seemed logical. Keenan slipped his onto the middle finger of his left hand. The spike had long since dissolved in his skin. But the scar served as a reminder.

"It will tell you when you get near a Siren by turning

turquoise. And if she's yours, its colour will change to purple."

Keenan turned it on his finger and sighed. It had recognized Lacy before he did, and he swallowed down a lump in his throat before anyone noticed his emotion. "So it's another family who has her?" His face was now a suitable mask to cover his sadness and anger.

"It is the most likely scenario, but we have investigated extensively and can find no lead relating to any of the other families … but there are Human factions and indeed governments – this one included, who know of our existence and of the Sirens and their power."

Keenan exhaled noisily, suddenly feeling overcome with exhaustion. "So I am a prince?"

"You are."

"So any one of us could be king?"

"In theory yes … until recently. A Dubonnetti prince has already found his mate and married her, so, in accordance with Atlantean law, he is king. Our contract as the Honourable Guard means we sacrificed the kingship in return for guaranteeing we have our Siren."

It sort of made sense; he had no wish to be a king anyway. "So there is no reason for the other families to take Lacy then?"

"If only that were true." Marius smiled ruefully. "Past generations have slaughtered each other to steal the Sirens for power for themselves … it is a sad fact that unless this king secures all the Sirens, it is unlikely he will hold his crown."

"All? … That means Lacy … So it could be him who has her?" Keenan's eyes squinted and he grit his teeth as he tried to get a handle on what he was hearing.

Marius held up a placating hand. "It is my understanding that the other four sisters will pledge their power to the new king anyway. If he were to steal Lacy, he would be breaking the contract with our family that binds us to him as his guard, which would be madness when he has our pledge automatically. No, they will pledge to him but live with their chosen mates … In fact, his own mate no longer lives with him."

Fuck. Keenan frowned. He wouldn't want to be him. If he felt half of what he felt for Lacy, he must be in hell. He shook his head and the thought away.

He looked over at his three friends, "You knew all this?"

"Nah," they all said, shaking their heads.

"We knew bits," Vince said. "This is the first time it's been explained to us like this."

Keenan looked back at Marius, "Are they Atlantean as well?"

"Well, they have Atlantean markers in their DNA, so have it in their blood, so to speak … when we discovered their close bond with you and Lacy, we decided that if they proved to be one of us, they would make perfect Protectors."

"Protectors?" Keenan remembered the bloke on the phone had used that word.

"Sirens have lifelong Protectors. It's a great honour," Marius explained. "They have been given talismans to distinguish them in their task."

Then each of the friends pulled out St Christopher-like pendants, turquoise in colour, from inside their shirts and grinned.

Keenan grinned back at their goofy smiles.

"Now you are all out in the open, you can have your identifying tattoos," Marius said, smiling.

"Wicked," Vince said.

Keenan always loved a good excuse for a tattoo. "What will they be?" he asked.

"Yours will be the Santalini coat of arms and war tattoos,

in tradition with all Santalini princes. You can insist on the same for your Siren's Protectors if you wish … it's up to you." Marius said, concluding.

"What now?" Keenan asked, itching to get going in his search for Lacy; now his boys were with him.

"You will all continue to train, but I think you are ready to patrol areas of the city as we have been doing. We will continue to follow every lead."

Keenan nodded. He felt grateful for the trust finally being put in him.

Marius narrowed his eyes on Keenan, "When they took Lacy from you, they took her from this family. Do you understand that?"

He was beginning to. For the first time, he was starting to feel part of something, and not so totally on his own. It was still a small warmth, but it was growing day by day.

At least now he could start doing something constructive, except now he was trained. He could look and he could fight if need be. Except now he had his boys and his family with him.

CHAPTER 7

Keenan and his boys scoured the city relentlessly. Time was passing and Lacy was still missing.

It felt as though she had never been there now, but Keenan clung to those few special days when they had finally become a real couple and he used the time apart to mature and grow into the Santalini warrior he was meant to be.

He, Vince, Rick and Dan had gone from being petty villains to fighting machines at the peak of their fitness. Keenan had lost his boyish recklessness and had become quiet and serious. His control was so honed it was as though he had no emotion at all.

Another fruitless night ended and Keenan had just said goodnight to his boys when Marius caught him on the stairs, "No luck?" Marius asked.

Keenan shook his head. He was tired right down to the bone and was in no mood for chitchat.

"Get some sleep … we fly to Ireland in the morning," and Marius turned to go back down the staircase.

Keenan went to protest. He couldn't afford the time off from the search.

Sensing Keenan's misgivings, Marius paused again, "We are to meet with Alfonzo and Sebastian Bonaci, Lacy's uncle and father," he said.

Keenan's eyebrows rose with interest. This was what he needed right now. He wanted to know *everything* about Lacy. He felt she was slipping away from him, further and further every day.

KEENAN AND MARIUS were shown into the old sitting room at Ballygowen Castle, ancestral home of the Bonaci, in Galway, Ireland. There, two older gentlemen rose from their chairs and greeted them. One, a thinner, more austere-looking man, was introduced as Alfonzo, the other, plumper and a little less serious-looking, was Sebastian. Both had an abundance of greying hair to their shoulders and were obviously brothers.

Pleasantries were exchanged while Keenan just observed. He was still uncomfortable with all the fancy manners and finery reserved for the aristocracy in this new world he found himself in. He would be much happier kicking back with his mates, having a beer or two.

"You still have no news?" Alfonzo asked.

"Nothing," Marius answered. "Any whispers from your informants?"

Alfonzo shook his head. "All intelligence tells us that the families still scour the earth for their own Siren as expected – except the Dubonnetti, of course."

"That brings us to the purpose of our visit. You wish to assign us to the Dubonnetti Siren?" Marius asked.

Alfonzo didn't answer, but continued to study Keenan, making him feel a little uncomfortable. "Tia Storm married and pledged to Dante, the eldest of the Dubonnetti sons. She was his, according to his ring, but she has taken a lover in her Protector. He is a Human, and an adopted son of Dubonnetti and Dante's best friend. She has since moved away from Dante to Montana to live with her Protectors. In fact, the Human is an adopted son of this house, also. He runs the family business," Alfonzo said.

Keenan thought things were fucked up, but interesting. *And he thought his sitch was shit.*

"How many Protectors does she have?' Marius asked.

"Three – including the one she is in a relationship with."

"And she needs us?"

"That is what I want you to assess. Obviously, she would be better off with the Dubonnetti boy; both for her wellbeing and the state, but you know that Sirens are characteristically troublesome and wilful."

Keenan smiled to himself. *Troublesome and wilful, yep, that was Lacy all right.*

"Are you backing this boy as king?" Marius asked.

"He has reacted badly to the separation from his mate and is somewhat of a loose cannon at the moment, but we will tutor him when he is ready." Alfonzo gazed in Keenan's direction again. He averted his eyes. Weird, it was so like his own beginning with the Santalini and the bloke knew it. Then he spoke directly to him, snapping him to attention. "Are you prepared for her return?" Alfonzo asked.

"Of course," was all he could say, caught totally off guard.

"Her power will pass to the king and she will be married to him," Alfonzo continued.

Keenan realized then why he'd asked the question. No one said anything about Lacy marrying anyone other than him. He looked accusingly at Marius; he had certainly left that part out of his education.

Marius held up a hand to halt his thought process. "She will still be yours," he said, quietly. "It's just in name only."

Keenan worked methodically through the facts he'd learned before he could get angry, which in turn helped him get a handle on the control he needed. "How does Lacy marrying him benefit our family?" Keenan asked, directly to Alfonzo.

Alfonzo's eyes widened with surprise and he smiled as if pleased with the question, and nodded to Marius. "Our young king has decided that stability of the kingdom is paramount and intends to create a council on which all the princes mated to the Sirens will sit and have a share in government ... We were impressed with the wisdom of it."

Fuck. He'd learned enough of Atlantean history to know that every time the Sirens had been on earth, the royals had never got it together enough to make any kind of lasting kingdom. "Why does he need to marry them all, though? Why can't everyone be equal?" Keenan asked while his eyes narrowed.

"Good question ... but that has been tried before. One prince always sought prominence over another. The power of the five Sirens ensures the king's power over the other princes and his place as king."

Keenan had to see the sense in that. However, he still didn't like the idea of Lacy marrying anyone else.

Marius brought things to a close. "Very well. We will set off for Montana immediately."

Just as Marius and Keenan went to stand and leave, the door knocked and a liveried servant, like something out of Alice in Wonderland, came in and whispered something to Sebastian, who had remained quiet for practically the whole meeting. *Fuck, it was the twilight zone here.*

"The king is here," Sebastian announced. "We thought it a good idea to introduce you before you left to go to Montana."

Marius stood, so Keenan followed his lead. He wasn't good at this etiquette shit yet. But he was more than a little interested to meet the guy destined to be with Lacy's sister.

Dante Dubonnetti entered the room with a servant who bowed and left. Trying not to gawp too much, Keenan was struck by the overall appearance of the bloke. He looked like some sort of rock star, or something. Not what he was expecting as a king. Curly jet-black hair to his shoulders, olive skin, tall slim frame – around six three, black jacket and jeans, white shirt with large starched cuffs and collar, and a big ring like his own. But the thing that struck him most of all was that the guy looked very pissed or stoned or both. The bloke was wasted. Functioning like a man well practised in keeping up appearances.

Fuck, he was familiar. He may even have sold gear to him in his past life.

"Cuz!" Dante said. A slow blink followed, emphasising his pissedness. He reached out and Keenan shook his hand.

Keenan just nodded as they shook, but was watching him closely. He wasn't going to let the waster act fool him into underestimating him. Especially as the guy had designs on marrying Lacy, and he'd just remembered him.

"Do I know you?" Dante said, looking around him for a drink while he patted his pockets for a smoke. "I'm sure I'd remember a big fucker like you, though," he said, clearly giving up on the smoke idea.

"I think we may have met in my old life. I was smaller then." Keenan decided to give the guy a little dig. "You was always with a pretty boy, weren't you?"

Keenan knew his aim was sure and true when Dante laughed and squinted his eyes. "Must have been in a club," he replied with a very thick Irish accent.

"Not up West, you came over to East London, to a Blues. That was when it was."

Dante stared at him, trying to place him, shifting his weight and narrowing his eyes. Then he shook his head and gave up. "The pretty boy is with me wife," he said absently, patting his pockets again.

Sebastian and Alfonzo stood, signalling the meeting as over. "Marius and Keenan are heading to Montana to take charge of Tia," Alfonzo explained to Dante.

"Sweet … What happens when your woman returns?" Dante said directly to Keenan.

The guy was annoying him a bit now. "We'll cross that bridge when we come to it, shall we?" Keenan allowed a little blood to swirl into his eyes just as a warning.

Dante appeared to try his best not to smile, but inclined his head, "I look forward to meeting her," he said, a wide grin creeping across his face.

In his old life, he would have decked him just for the inference. Today, he bit down and went to follow Marius out of the room, who he could tell was getting nervous at the atmosphere between them.

Then, at the last minute, Dante added, "Do you still run in a Salt 'n' Pepper team?"

Keenan turned to hide his surprise, then smiled, but the smile didn't reach his eyes. "Always."

Dante nodded and smiled, but the point had been made and taken. He might be drunk, but his brain was very on the ball. He'd known exactly who Keenan was and where from. He'd just been toying with him.

Keenan just nodded back in a silent exchange. He would remember, though, when dealing with Dante in the future. *He was a slippery fucker.*

The whole experience had only heightened his interest in sussing out the 'Pretty Boy'.

· · ·

NOT LONG AFTER sending the Honourable Guard to take charge of the Siren Tia Storm, Sebastian and Alfonzo were requested to meet with the US Secretary of State in D.C.

It wasn't unusual for them to meet. Usually, once a year, both the US and the UK governments met to discuss issues relating to where Atlantean law, finance or property affected the Human world and so forth.

It was an alliance based on suspicion and paranoia, particularly from the Humans; after all, they were forced to share *their* planet with interlopers who seemed to dominate the world's wealth and privilege and kept equilibrium with them only until Atlas returned. So the Humans needed to be kept sweet.

Sebastian and Alfonzo had long been nominated and respected as spokesmen for the Atlantean race in the absence of a king. They were elder princes from the Bonaci, one of the five royal families. In fact, all members were referred to as princes, and some preferred to be known as dukes, but all had equal standing, which was why it was so hard to elevate a king above the rest.

The meeting had been brokered by the distinguished elder statesman, known in Human circles as the Ambassador of Central Atlantic Affairs, to the Atlanteans, who knew him, he was the Duke Ormond Delissi, the diplomat.

This meeting had come early, though, and it was with a little unease that they received intelligence from Delissi that the special meeting had been called to discuss the matter of Sirens appearing in this generation.

The two Bonaci princes entered the large meeting room, accompanied by Delissi, their kinsman and mediator. Those already gathered in the room stood as they entered. The rotund American Secretary of State sat at the head of the table, with four other officials, two on either side of him. One was a smart-looking woman and another was a hard-looking male in a military uniform. The other two were just suits in glasses. Delissi, Sebastian and Alfonzo sat at the opposite end of the board table, facing their opponents.

The SOS spoke when they were all settled in their seats. "I would like to extend my government's thanks for your willingness to meet with us at such short notice, and to convey the president's promise that what is to be discussed will be treated with the utmost secrecy and security."

Sebastian and Alfonzo both slowly bowed their heads in thanks.

"As you know," the SOS continued, "we call these extraordinary meetings when there is a need for us to confer with your nation on matters of national security."

The two princes just listened to the diplomatic claptrap and fixed their eyes on the SOS, who was already sweating profusely; clearly less than confident in what he had brought them there to discuss.

Sebastian leaned sideways and whispered to Delissi, who spoke up in beautiful Italian-accented English. "Perhaps we could go straight to item one on the agenda, sir?"

The SOS went red and blustered slightly while he gathered his thoughts and what he could say which wouldn't offend their guests, who, he was all too aware, were not Human. He swallowed and launched in. "The US government would like to know who you have appointed as king from your five families."

Alfonzo and Sebastian looked at each other, then Alfonzo spoke, "A king can only be appointed when a Siren has been found for him. We still await that happy occasion."

The hard-looking man in a military uniform threw his pen down loudly on the table and leaned back in his chair, annoyed.

"Dick!" the SOS reprimanded, before there was an interspecies incident that he would have to square with the president. "Forgive my colleague, gentlemen, but we have reliable intelligence to the contrary."

Duke Delissi sat forward, more than interested. "May I ask what information you have?" he asked, his Italian accent ringing out.

"We know for sure that Sirens are present," the SOS said.

"I assure you, you know more than us," the duke argued.

"Bullshit!" the military officer said loudly, flinging himself back in his chair again.

The Atlanteans bought some time by looking at each other and taking shelter in outrage.

"Our sources tell us that a king has, in fact, been identified," the SOS continued more reasonably, "and we would ask that he attend our next meeting so we can deal with him personally. That is all we ask."

Sebastian stood. "This meeting is over."

Alfonzo and Delissi stood with him, the latter promising to contact the SOS in the next few days.

When the three walked out into the fresh air, Alfonzo was concerned; nothing got the Humans tetchier than believing the Atlanteans had entered into the last days.

"They have bluffed before, Cousin, and we've ridden it out?" Delissi whispered.

Alfonzo shook his head, "No … this is more than that. The further along we are in the process, the more they fear Atlas' return and heaven knows what they could do to prevent it … Find out exactly what they know … and how they know it."

"Consider it done," Delissi replied. "But if that is the case, I don't think we will be able to hide our position for much longer."

"We must prepare Dante," Sebastian said. "And hope he is up to the task."

"For all our sakes," Alfonzo concluded.

CHAPTER 8

*K*eenan and Marius stood on the threshold of the Montana ranch house belonging to Tia's Protector: Cash Reynolds – a cowboy by all accounts.

They'd parked their hired SUV a way back from the house so they could scope the place a bit before they went inside.

"Exposed as fuck," Keenan said.

Marius nodded. "Yes, but you'd see anyone coming a mile off if it weren't for all these outbuildings."

"Is it workable?" Keenan asked.

"Let's find out whether we're taking her on first?"

On cue, the door opened.

Keenan kept his head down as they were asked into the large rustic hunting lodge with an open-plan living room.

The cowboy introduced them to everyone, one by one. He allowed himself a glance at Lacy's sister and the only word that immediately came to mind was: wow. He averted his eyes quickly so he didn't stare.

Then he was introduced to Jay. The guy who was obviously 'Pretty Boy'. Keenan gave a fleeting character assessment by the guy's eyes and handshake and Jay fixed him in the eye with such a challenge, it took him aback. Keenan almost laughed, but caught himself just in time. In fact, as the little tête-à-tête continued, the fucker was on such a short fuse, he thought he would go any minute. Never in all his days had anyone had the guts to do that, especially not a Human who was a fraction of his weight and a good five or six inches shorter than him.

It was as though the exterior didn't go with the real him – that there was more under the bonnet than met the eye. He wished he could meet him under different circumstances.

He'd remembered exactly where he'd seen him and Dante before now, though. It was at The Graveyard – a little illegal Blues in Mile End. Rough as houses it was. He remembered wondering then how they didn't get jumped – two little rich boys, reeking of money, a long way from home and way out of their depth. But having met Mr Blarney himself, Dante, and now glimpsing the tats on this little charmer, he sort of understood how they'd survived. Yeah, and thrived, judging by the stir they caused with the women – this one particularly.

Jay seemed protective of the Siren, as if she were his, though, which was curious – as if he were an Atlantean. Not like the Human he'd been informed he was.

His thoughts were interrupted when he heard the conversation refer to him.

What was a royal doing there, sporting a fucking fat divining ring, in the presence of a Royal Bonaci Siren? Jay was saying, obviously not big on diplomacy.

The fucker was really starting to piss him off. *What the ... what could be further from his fucking mind than getting hold of another bird – Siren or no Siren?* "You've got nothing to fear from me, I've got my own Siren," Keenan said low and deliberate, keeping a lid on his rising hackles. But as soon as he said it, he knew it would lead to inevitable questions about Lacy, which the girl bombarded him with. *Shit.*

IT WAS WEIRD. Originally, he'd thought his main focus of interest would be Lacy's sister Tia, and of course, he wanted to find out more about her, but this guy she was with was having a convo with no one else in the room but him, whether the words were aired or not.

Keenan watched him; he sort of admired his front, really. He wasn't fazed by him in the slightest – the days of building a reputation were long gone. But what interested him about this bloke was, he wasn't fazed by him either. Keenan could always smell fear, but what came off this guy was pure aggression. *Interesting.*

After taking an instant dislike to Dante, he was expecting to feel the same about this one. He'd heard they were supposed to be like brothers. Well, if they were anything like him and Vince? It just didn't fucking compute, him taking Dante's girl, asshole or not.

Thankfully, the mental game of tennis was halted when Marius asked to speak to the guy alone and suggested he take Tia outside to see the horses. He welcomed the breather and the opportunity to get to know her a bit.

Keenan studied her as she petted each horse they came to in the barn. She was so like Lacy in so many ways. With the same small features and smooth tanned skin. But this girl's eyes were weird. Same colour, but they were huge disks, like a neon fish. And her hair was several shades lighter than Lacy's.

She was beautiful in an otherworldly way, and he liked her, but she seemed to have an air of tragedy about her that Lacy didn't have. Lacy was upbeat and bubbly, but this one had the weight of the world on her shoulders and he felt sorry for her.

In fact, meeting Tia only kicked him in the gut with longing for his own Siren. They'd never been apart for a day in their lives before she was taken, and now it had been months.

He answered all her questions about Lacy and some comically naive ones about vampires and they found their way back to the stable barn entrance and went back inside the house. There, they were told that the Guard accepted her as their charge.

Keenan was itching to find out what had gone on between his brother and Jay, but Jay kept a low profile for the rest of the day and made sure he monopolized Tia's company. And all Marius said was that Cash had a lot of work on, and Jay had the Bonaci Corporation to run and was leaving for London the next day.

When the third Protector walked into the kitchen and introduced them to his wife, Sarah, a pretty, petite, blonde, it was plain to everyone that she was pregnant and so took him out of the game for a while as well. That meant he was stuck. *Fuck.*

THAT EVENING, he and Marius sat in the kitchen drinking a beer with Cash and Sean. Sarah had gone to bed, and he guessed that was where Tia and Jay were. But it gave them a chance to find out some good background stuff without getting the hairy eyeball from laughing boy.

"Do you have CCTV? Marius asked.

"No." Cash shook his head. "Never had a need for it before. Tia didn't know who she was, and I always had my eye on her, as well as most of the male ranch hands." He couldn't help a small laugh. "Hadn't even thought about it, to be honest."

"I'm going to get some tech guys down here, if that's okay with you?" Marius said.

Keenan had kept quiet pretty much the whole time they'd been there. He preferred it that way, but just then, the woman called Mrs Ross said goodnight to everyone. When she had left the room, "The housekeeper, has she been here long?" Keenan asked Cash directly. He'd seen her on her mobile a number of times since he'd been there.

Cash seemed to wake up slightly, taken unawares by his question. "Mrs Ross? Sure … let me see … two, three years maybe. As long as I've known Tia, for sure."

"So she can be trusted?" Marius added.

"Never put a foot wrong in the whole time I've known her," Cash said.

"We just need to make sure you understand. When security is installed, certain codes will have to be on a strictly need-to-know basis," Marius explained.

Cash nodded. He got it. Keenan really liked the bloke. He was his kind of man.

Sean was ex-military, he found out. *Handy.*

"Are you expecting something?" Sean asked. "Coz I can stay if she's in danger."

Keenan looked him dead in the eye. "A Siren will always be in danger. She was located and married as soon as she was fucking eighteen. She was lucky it was her mate and an Atlantean."

Keenan's words sobered the room to silence. None of them really understood the undertone to his meaning; that he was angry with himself.

"She's coming back with me now." Jay stalked into the kitchen, shirtless, to get a drink. He went to the fridge, took out the juice and poured a glass. Everyone stared at him as he leaned back against the counter.

An unfortunate set of words to enter the room on, Keenan thought, and closed his eyes momentarily. When he reopened them, he was drawn to Jay's numerous black lettered tats that covered his body. Jay sipped his drink, his expression remaining stony cold.

"She still should keep a guard with her now, wherever she goes," Marius informed him.

"She goes everywhere with me," Jay said.

Keenan wanted to smile, but decided not to provoke him. "I could do with getting back to New York?" Keenan said to Marius, deciding to use the situation to his advantage.

"So could I," Marius answered. "Okay. We'll go back." He turned back to Jay, "Guards are being sent to Ireland tomorrow. I will divert a couple to London. They can meet you there. Wherever you and Tia go, they go. Understand?" Marius said, offering him no choice and obviously starting to get pissed off at the guy's attitude.

Jay glugged the rest of his drink and shrugged. "No skin off my nose." He left the room.

Keenan watched him go, shirked off the insult, and turned back to the others, "I'm going to turn in." Tia going back to England with Jay was the out he was looking for; he needed to get back to New York and his boys to renew the search.

She was still out there somewhere; he could feel it. Jay could wait another day, and he knew that day would come.

CHAPTER 9

$\mathcal{M}$alleven followed his uncle into the Lanslow Gentleman's Club in London's Mayfair. Founded a couple of hundred years ago, it stunk of old money, which Malleven wasn't adverse to, except it was something he had only ever been on the fringes of, living on the goodwill of his uncle, Rodrigo Mancini. A confirmed bachelor all his life, he'd plucked Malleven from obscurity as a small child, sponsored his education and kept him under his wing ever since. Now he was twenty-five, they still met up periodically when Rodrigo wanted to keep tabs on him or advise him on a direction he should go.

Malleven didn't particularly like the man, but he was acutely aware that until he was where he wanted to be in the world, he needed his uncle to vouch for him and to open social doors, especially in his pursuit of the profound powers found in alchemy.

The two of them walked into a dark wood-panelled lounge, tastefully decorated in conservative blue.

"Christian!" Rodrigo said in surprise. "Come, Malleven, we will sit with our cousin."

Malleven followed his uncle to a group of small armchairs grouped around a low table already scattered with teacups and newspapers.

The tall, greying man stood as they approached and held out his arm to the vacant chair next to him. "Rodrigo, what a pleasure," Christian said, his voice crackled like a smoker.

His uncle shook hands with him.

"May I introduce you to my nephew, Malleven Mancini?"

As Malleven leaned forward and touched the skin of the older man's hand, he looked into his dark, crow-like eyes.

"I am hearing good things about the young man already," Christian said, smiling broadly.

Malleven shook his hand and took the opportunity to absorb some of his energy. Avarice hit him immediately.

Christian let go of Malleven's hand and touched his forehead absently, as if he had a pain there.

Malleven enjoyed honing his newly found skills by assessing new people he met by just drawing the smallest amount of their psychic energy.

The three of them sat down and a waiter quickly took their drinks order and disappeared.

"Congratulations, Christian, on your family's good fortune," Rodrigo said. "How proud you must be to have sired the king."

Christian bowed his head, "I always knew he was destined for great things."

Malleven almost laughed. It was a well-known fact that his eldest son, Dante, was nothing more than a playboy who neither worked nor studied, but preferred the company of women, his Human best friend and a bottle.

While Christian spoke about his son's attributes, real or otherwise, Malleven sent out a mental feeler, a new talent he was perfecting, and the man's aura was all wrong. It simply did not go with what he was saying. He did not feel love or pride when he spoke of his son, but he did feel ambition.

"What brings you to London, Rodrigo?" Christian was saying.

"Malleven has just graduated from Cambridge with honours. We are celebrating," he explained.

Christian nodded, smiling, "Admirable … Admirable."

Malleven knew he was thinking that having a son as a king trumped having a nephew who was bookish. He couldn't exactly read thoughts; it was more of a vibe. He was getting better at reading people every day. He smiled benignly, letting him drone on.

"You are fortunate to have been chosen as Rodrigo's protégé," Christian said.

And there was the undermining dig. He could have laughed aloud. "I am always aware of that." And Malleven bowed his head, allowing Christian to have his day. He already knew that the Dubonnetti house featured greatly in his future. Men like Christian were always so filled with their own self-importance that they never saw what was right under their noses. He would be useful.

He looked over at his uncle. He was no better. He sought prominence for the Florianna, but mainly for himself, and he recognized something in Malleven that was of use to him.

Malleven absently played with the large ring on his left hand. It was a divining ring, the same as that worn by any other prince, but this one had been bought with hard work and not given to him by a benevolent father. *He* sought to change the path of his destiny. For now, he just listened and learned and absorbed the secrets of the illuminated ones.

CHRISTIAN KEPT his eye on the boy. But he wasn't a boy at all, although he should be at just twenty-five. No, this one was as sharp as a dagger and in no time at all would be just as dangerous. "I understand you read Chemistry, Malleven?" he said.

Malleven just gave a small nod, not elaborating at all.

"Are you looking for a post … or will you be taking some time out?" he persisted.

Rodrigo butted in, leaning towards Malleven. "Christian is thinking of moving into gold."

Malleven smiled, "My favourite metal."

The three all laughed together at that.

Christian seized his opportunity and pulled a business card from his breast pocket. "Here. When you're ready to work together, contact me," and he handed it to Malleven, making sure he locked eyes with him. He wasn't sure how he knew, but he was convinced he was in tune with what he was thinking, that power was important at all costs. That Dante, although king now, would find it hard to hold the crown, and he, Christian Dubonnetti, would be there to catch it when it fell.

THEY ALL LEFT the ranch at the same time when Jay took Tia back with him to London. Except when Tia gave Keenan a shy smile of goodbye on the Tarmac at Billings, she followed Jay up the steps of the Bonaci royal jet, and he and Marius entered the small Santalini plane reserved for business trips.

His plane taxied and he wished her well, he really did. Not just because she was Lacy's sister and she would love her, but he genuinely liked her and hoped she found a way to be happy in this fucked-up world they'd found themselves in. None of them had asked for it.

So it was with relief that Keenan stepped into the large marble hallway of the Santalini mansion.

Vince came out of one of the reception rooms to greet him. "Hey, man." They clapped hands and hugged.

"What was she like?"

Keenan nodded and smiled, "As beautiful as you would expect Lacy's sister to be."

"Sweet." Vince nodded as if he'd guessed as much. "Listen. Me and the boys have been keeping up the club trawling, ears to the ground, and all that."

Keenan didn't look him in the eye but looked at the floor while he listened. "Any luck?"

Vince shook his head, "Not yet, mate."

They hugged again and Keenan went to bed, exhausted beyond measure.

THEY SIFTED, searched, scanned and probed the city for a lead for months. Some came up, but all led to dead ends. It was as if she'd disappeared from the face of the earth. Keenan never gave up, never rested and only ever allowed himself a break when his obligations as a Santalini soldier were required.

The day came when the Santalini were drafted and it was necessary for Keenan to leave New York with his four brothers and twenty first and second cousins. He was to accompany the king on his first diplomatic trip to meet with representatives from the US and UK governments in England. They were the king's private guard as well as a great PR exercise for an impressive show.

Vince had said a heartfelt farewell and promised to leave no stone unturned while he was away.

His heart still in New York, Keenan boarded the large Santalini troop carrier bound for a US base in Suffolk, England. Dante, Alfonzo and Sebastian were to meet them there. This was his world now, he reasoned. He owed it to himself and Lacy when he found her to see where they fit into it.

When they landed, they all waited on the plane for Dante's to land before they alighted together.

"Why didn't they come in the larger Bonaci plane?" Keenan asked Marius as they began to stand up to leave the plane.

"Jay has full use of it." His eyebrows went up as he spoke.

Proved his brother felt the same as he did. That it was a truly fucked-up situation.

Keenan had been briefed on the way. He and Marius were assigned to the king as his personal bodyguards. The other three brothers were to guard the princes, Alfonzo and Sebastian. Their cousins were there to make an impressive entrance, which they all did with their huge physiques in black uniforms with scarlet-red shoulders and gold buttons. Red and black were the Santalini colours – red for blood and a warning to their enemies. Keenan approved; they all looked awesome. They were met on the Tarmac by a convoy of army vehicles, which took them to the main building of the air force base.

Keenan was struck straight away by the difference in Dante. He looked older, more serious; he'd filled out a bit too. He was dressed in an expensive dark grey suit, with just a gold pin in his lapel showing the Dubonnetti colours of pale blue and yellow. His hair was loose to his shoulders. He looked every bit the European prince that he was.

However, the main thing was, the guy was stone cold sober. His eyes looked clear and shrewd and showed not an ounce of nervousness. Well, if he was, he hid it well.

They entered the building and he and Marius took their place at either side of the king and followed the three American soldiers, showing them to the meeting room.

Dante leaned his head in Keenan's direction, "Have you found Lacy yet, Keenan?"

Surprised at the enquiry, all he said was, "Not yet."

By then, they had reached the room. The bulk of the party stayed outside the meeting, but everyone else entered. Dante, Alfonzo and Sebastian were shown to seats at the end of a huge oval boardroom table. Keenan and his brothers stood behind them in a row.

Keenan thought they all looked really cool, like a royal delegation. He had to keep telling himself that's exactly what they were.

He looked to the other end of the table as they all introduced themselves. This was a big deal, he suddenly realized, when the British prime minister and the US vice-president identified themselves.

Marius leaned down to Alfonzo's ear, "Where is Delissi?"

"Working on something for us with the president."

No shit. Whoever this Delissi guy was, he must be important.

The US Secretary of State spoke first. "Your Royal Highness. We welcome you to this meeting. As you know, we already have a long working relationship with your cousins, the Princes Alfonzo and Sebastian, and hope that we can forge a similar relationship with you. We are honoured to meet the first Atlantean King in several hundred years."

Keenan glanced across to see Dante's reaction to all this. He was unreadable. He just bowed his head regally. Could he be the same bloke?

"You may feel free to dismiss your soldiers. We are all friends here," The SOS continued.

Keenan felt Marius stiffen next to him. He didn't mind going outside and relaxing for an hour until they were ready to go, but then he realized by the uncomfortable silence that some sort of blunder had been made.

Surprisingly, it was the king who spoke up first.

"Everyone here today, including those outside are royal princes. Any one of them could have been king. It just happened to be me."

Keenan inwardly laughed when he looked around at the embarrassed red faces, all blaming each other for not doing their homework.

"Bill, get their highnesses some seats," the SOS ordered.

There was a lot of scurrying around and five more chairs were arranged around the table.

Keenan had to admit it was all getting amusing. He was curious as to what the Humans knew. *Fuck,* he was even seeing them as the enemy now. Less than a year ago, he'd thought he was one of them. *What can happen in a year, eh?"*

After the disruption, the SOS continued, "We would like to congratulate you on your recent ascension as king ..." He trailed off as Dante held up a hand.

"Look, compliments and flannel are not necessary. I know why I'm here. Please ask your questions and I will try to answer them as best I can."

Dante was really going up in his estimation. They obviously thought a young bloke like him would be some sort of puppet. He was impressed. Maybe this was sober Dante and the guy he'd met before, the drunk.

There was a lot of shuffling of papers and conferring whispers at the other end of the table until an old skinny guy stood up and cleared his throat. "My name is Doctor Brunswick ... I have made it my life's work to study the history and literature from the ancient civilization of Atlantis, here at Cambridge University." The guy stuttered and coughed, clearly in awe of the company in the room.

Keenan checked Dante's expression, which remained impassive. His mind was working away though, he could tell.

"What do you want to know?" Dante asked again.

The professor looked over at the vice-president and

Prime Minister for some sort of permission, and after seeing a nod, he looked back at Dante again. "Have you located all the Sirens?"

Hallel, fucking lujah!

Dante smiled and leaned forward onto his elbows. "No, we have not."

No surprise there. Keenan looked at Sebastian and Alfonzo. They weren't cringing, so he must have said the right thing.

"Can you tell us how many you still seek?" the professor asked.

"One," Dante said.

Well, he was lying good.

"And the Orb … is it safe … and stable?"

"Very. Are we not still affluent?" Dante said, sitting back in his chair again.

The professor looked back at the dignitaries and reluctantly sat down as if his moment in the spotlight was too short.

"Well, gentleman," Dante said, beginning to stand up, "if I have answered all your questions, I suggest we reconvene in, shall we say, three months?"

The dignitaries were all looking at each other in consternation, obviously thinking more needed to be said, but Dante had effectively brought the meeting to a close like an old pro. Keenan had to hand it to him. The boy had done good.

Dante was already leaving the room, flanked by Sebastian and Alfonzo and followed by Keenan and his brothers.

Dante stopped and turned, "Doctor Brunswick?"

The old man stopped shoving his many papers into his worn briefcase. "Yes, your highness?"

"Do you understand written Atlantean?"

The professor looked surprised at the question. "Yes, your

highness … I can speak it as well, but we are unclear on the pronunciation."

"Do you have the time to accompany me to Ireland?" Dante asked in all seriousness.

"Yes … yes, your highness, I do." He began shoving his papers in, crumpling them all up in his haste.

He walked quickly over to Dante, who put his arm around the man's shoulders.

Keenan just heard, "I have been looking for a tutor …" and then the throng of the Santalini guards joined them and they all marched back to the waiting vehicles that took them to their planes.

Just before they separated and went into the Santalini plane, hands were shaken and promises made. Keenan was hovering, just waiting to go, when Dante spoke directly to him, "Keenan?"

Dante was about to go up the steps. "Let me know what I can do to help?"

Keenan stared at him and just gave a small nod. Maybe he had misjudged the guy. He didn't know what else to say.

Dante jogged up a few steps and then stopped again, with a huge grin on his face, "After all, your woman is my woman." And the fucker jogged up the remainder of the steps and disappeared into the plane.

Keenan was left with his mouth open, staring after him.

He was still replaying the comment in his mind as he strapped himself into his seat.

"He carried himself well, didn't he?" Marius said.

Keenan raised his eyebrows without answering the question. "Why did he say that four Sirens had been found?"

"Clever," Marius said, nodding and smiling.

"I don't get it … why not say he has them all?"

"They know more than they are letting on, so there's a strong possibility that they have procured one for themselves.

That would make our new king a liar. To say he only has one would make him weak. Four is powerful. Five … means a possible return for Atlas … major issue for the Humans."

Keenan nodded. *Shit was getting complicated.*

"What about the Orb being stable and safe?" Keenan had learned that the Orb had come from Atlas and was the source of all their power and riches.

"The Humans search for the Orb like some sort of Holy Grail. In fact, that was exactly what the crusaders were searching for, but it is more than a source of power. It is a beacon of communication between Atlas and us. It also affects the climate here."

Fuck, he didn't know all that.

He sat back in his seat for the long journey home.

That was twice he'd underestimated Dante now. He wouldn't do it again.

The idea that the bloke would marry Lacy before him did not sit well, not well at all.

VINCE POUNCED on Keenan as soon as his foot hit the marble at Santalini HQ.

Vince whispered in his ear, "A club barman came back to us and said a girl matching Lacy's description has been in asking for work."

Keenan's eyes snapped up to Vince's. This was the lead he'd been waiting for so long.

"What did he say to her?"

"He said he didn't have anything … thought she looked like a bit of a druggie," Vince said, shifting uncomfortably with the sensitive info. "But he felt sorry for her and told her to clean herself up and try tonight when the boss was in."

Keenan pushed his fingers through his overlong hair

while he thought straight. His eyes darted. "We'll get there early and have a drink at the bar … Fuck, Vince … it could be her."

Marius was walking past at that point to go into the library, looking down at some papers in his hand.

"Keep it under your hat," Keenan whispered.

"Oh, Keenan," Marius said, looking up from his papers. He nodded his head in the direction of the library. "Can I have a moment? I've got a job I want you to do tonight."

Keenan's heart sank. He rolled his head back, then looked at Vince.

"Something wrong?" Marius asked.

Fuck it. He'd have to tell him. "Vince and the boys have a lead … I wanted to follow it up with them tonight."

Marius stalked over to them and ordered Vince to tell him what he knew.

"Okay. But if it's her, you don't go off half-cocked and lift her on your own. You got it?" Marius was clearly annoyed, but Keenan agreed, relieved it was all still on and he wouldn't have to fight with his brother over it.

"This is politics now," Marius continued. "This is more than just a kidnapping, okay? We need to know who's behind it."

Fuck the politics, but Keenan went along with the plan laid out by Marius, his brothers and a few of his cousins. To be honest, he didn't give a fuck who was there. The president himself wouldn't stop him when he got his hands on whoever it was.

They were due to go out at six in case she turned up at the club early, which made sense. Marius had four guards on standby that he was to call when he'd located her. He was then to follow her home so the business could be cleared up in one swoop.

He paced and watched the clock. Six couldn't come quick enough.

CHAPTER 10

Their blacked-out SUV was parked across the road from the club with Keenan, Vince, Rick and Dan inside. They waited impatiently for the opening of business.

Keenan had sat for as long as he could. "Dan, you go round and mind the back. Rick, stay in the car in case we miss anything."

Both boys nodded and tested their ear-coms. Satisfied everything was working okay, Keenan radioed Marius and signalled 'the go'. They watched Dan go down the alley to the back exit, and then he and Vince got out the car to go for an early drink in the club.

When they got inside, the place was empty. The barman was still setting up.

"We too early for a beer?" Keenan asked.

"No … no girls on till eight though."

"I'll live."

The barman smirked and handed them their beers in the bottles. Keenan thanked him and both he and Vince got on stools to wait out the duration.

They waited the longest hour of Keenan's life. Three or four guys had come in wearing cheap suits, probably straight from boring office jobs. Girls had started showing up for work still in their everyday clothes. The bar tender knew them and put up his hand as they passed by to the dressing room. The wait was excruciating.

Keenan scanned the staff milling around and quickly identified the boss when he came out of a door to a corridor, spoke to the bouncers, and went back in again. He was the guy she would come to see.

He felt her before he saw her. The small hairs on the back of his neck began to rise, his heart fluttered and he felt woozy. He had always been aware of her when in her vicinity, but this was way more than he was used to. Marius had told him that he escaped much of the ill effects of his mate's pull mainly due to the fact that they'd been together since childhood and were blood-bonded. Well, he felt it now. He shook his head.

"You all right?" Vince asked.

"Yeah. Feel weird." Keenan looked around him and saw her walk through, then stop to ask a waitress something, who pointed to the door towards the back of the club.

At that moment, the smartly dressed man came out. Keenan got off his stool fast. His heart skipped several beats. Somehow he stayed rooted to the spot and watched the guy stop to speak with her.

Keenan took an unconscious step closer. He needed every ounce of willpower not to run and snatch her up. Vince followed his line of vision and locked onto what he was looking at. Something alerted her to them; she probably felt the pull as he did, and she looked straight at him, swooned and grabbed the manager's arm.

"Get outta here. You're drunk!" the manager sneered and

pushed her off him. He signalled to a bouncer to take her outside.

If Keenan had not been so intent on not losing her, he would have killed the guy for treating her like that. They followed her out to the street, far enough behind that the bouncer wouldn't notice them.

Keenan was glad that the bouncer was kinder to her. He escorted her outside the front doors and asked if she was okay. She nodded and wandered slowly up the street.

Keenan spoke into his ear-com. "Dan … we're following on foot. Get in the car and follow with Rick. Radio Marius and tell him what we're doing."

"Roger," came back in his ear.

They followed a safe distance behind so as not to spook her. Lacy knew how to lose someone because he had fucking taught her, so he had to pre-empt any move by her to shake them off.

God, she looked small, at least a stone lighter. Her clothes were tatty and not warm enough. Every instinct was screaming for him to run up to her, shake her and demand she explain where she'd been. Instead, he had to play this game of cat and mouse like he didn't know her.

Completely oblivious to them, she was walking like she was tired, not even aware of her surroundings. It was almost dark and she should be looking over her shoulder and being at least aware of strangers passing or walking behind her. It sliced his heart that she must be drugged or something. He'd be there and help her no matter what she was addicted to.

After twenty minutes of walking and several blocks, they entered a run-down street. Rick passed them and drove further on down, overtaking Lacy and then the second car arrived and did the same.

Keenan and Vince jumped back behind a dumpster when

she turned to walk up the steps to a run-down front door to a four-storey block. She looked over in their direction as if she sensed they were there, paused, and then entered the building.

"Quick," Keenan said, and he and Vince sprinted so the door didn't lock itself and they missed which apartment she went into. They bounded up the steps and found the door catch busted and slipped inside. There were probably eight small flats in the building. They waited in the first stairwell, breathing hard, more from nerves than anything. They listened to her shuffled footsteps as they went up the stairs.

"Back-up is here," Rick's voice said in his ear.

"Roger. I'm going up with Vince," Keenan said.

"We're coming in after you. Marius and the others are climbing the back fire escape."

Keenan pointed as a silent signal to Vince and they bounded silently up the three flights of stairs. They paused. "She must be at the top," Keenan whispered.

Vince nodded.

Marius's voice came over the ear-com, "When you identify the door, wait, Keenan."

"Roger. We think she's on the top floor." Keenan knew Marius would be getting his men in position on the fire escape at the back of the building.

Rick and Dan came up quietly and stood with them. Then they moved up the stairs as one unit. Whoever took her might be heavily armed and holed up in that apartment.

They all paused and held their breath when the crunch of keys could be heard going into the lock. Then a door opened and closed with a click.

They climbed the last few flights noiselessly and stood outside the door at the top. Keenan's heart was beating like a train. He felt sick, with waves of nausea hitting him hard.

Dizziness threatened to topple him as he struggled to get a grip. Blood surged into his eyes and his fangs descended. *Fuck, what was happening to him ... this couldn't be a mate's pull, could it?* "You're gonna have to pick the lock, Vince. I don't wanna scare her and my hands won't stop shaking."

Vince looked at his face, understood, and got to it, clicking the lock in seconds. They pushed the door ajar and listened. A TV busied itself in the background, and could that be kids' voices? *Shit.* Keenan and Vince frowned at each other. "We're in," Keenan whispered to Marius through his ear-com.

"We're in position at the back window," Marius answered. "Report the head count, then we're in."

"Roger. You should know there are kids in here. We're not sure how many yet."

"Ah, shit," Marius muttered.

Keenan pointed forward to his boys as he quickly poked his head in the first room he came to on his left. Scummy bathroom. Next came a tatty bedroom – two unmade beds on cold, bare floors and peeling walls. The place was a hovel. Nothing was making any sense to him. *Why would she stay here? Who would, in their right mind?*

He took a quick peek into the living room. There were two kids, a boy and a girl, watching an old, flickering TV from a dated, ripped sofa. Clattering coming from the kitchen, straight off the living room, told them where Lacy was.

"Come in," Keenan said. "Two kids and her ... that's all."

Keenan walked swiftly and quietly past the kids and opened the large, dirty window, giving access for Marius and the rest of the guards to pile into the room.

The kids' eyes went wide in fear when they saw them. Keenan put his index finger to his lips.

"Mommy," one whimpered.

Before Keenan could analyse that one word too deeply, he moved quickly towards the kitchen, while she was cut off from them. He stood in the doorway. Time seemed to slow down. She saw him and her eyes went wide with fright. She grabbed a carving knife. Then it was pandemonium.

CHAPTER 11

Keenan's vision went to zilch. His fangs shot down so fast he pierced his own lip and could no longer close his mouth.

Lacy began to scramble backwards as if a homicidal axe-wielding maniac were stalking her, knocking pots and pans and plates to crash to the floor.

Marius caught him by the arm before he stepped further into the room.

She began screaming the kids' names at the top of her voice, "Nicky … Pauly!"

The kids began to scream and wail for her behind him.

"Keenan! Keenan!" Marius shouted at him and shook him by the shoulders to snap him out of it. "There must be blood, Keenan … try to get a grip." Marius called Vince to take over from his hold on Keenan while he searched the room.

The girl cowered, crouching on the floor with a carving knife, ready to kill.

.   .   .

THE IMMENSE MAN in the doorway terrified Lacy. Never had she seen anything like him outside of a horror film. Eyes burning red like hot coals and huge canine teeth so large they forced his mouth open.

To cap it all, she wasn't feeling good at all. She wanted to be sick, she was being hit with nausea so strong her heart was beating and skipping and she was burning up with a fever. *Shit, the kids. She had to get to them. Maybe they were sick too.*

"Come any fucking closer and I'll kill you," she spat, not sounding like herself at all. She held the carving knife with two hands out in front of her. *Could he even fucking see?*

Then she saw him scan the kitchen like the Terminator. Another huge man appeared next to him. He was talking to him quietly. She couldn't hear what he was saying. All she could think of was that they had trapped her in the room away from her kids. "Nicky … Pauly!" She began to scream as she heard their cries become muffled as they were bundled out of the apartment.

Her mind raced in panic. She could lose them. In desperation, she threw herself at the monster. But before she could scream at him or plunge the knife anywhere near him, he'd knocked her arms to the side with such force that she was spun round so that her back was against him. And before she could get her bearings, he bit her neck in the soft part where it joined her shoulder and held her hard.

She could scarcely believe what was happening to her. *Was he eating her?* Absolute terror gave way to lethargy and she went limp. Her arms betrayed her and fell to her sides. Involuntarily, her hands opened and the knife clunked onto the floor. Her legs were next to give way and, as he caught her in his arms, she sagged against the front of his body. He made a sound like a groan. She suddenly felt completely relaxed, as if someone had pushed her pause button. Slack against him, she was vaguely aware of the other huge male walking away from them and searching the kitchen cupboards and drawers. Then he looked in the fridge.

He turned to face them and held up three red vials and a syringe and some small bottles of a clear liquid. She had no idea how they got there.

"These are your problem, Keenan," he said, indicating the red ones, then uncorked and sniffed one of the clear bottles. "We'll get these analysed … some sort of drug probably."

Then he walked back over to her and leaned down to her eyeline. "You are coming with us. You and the children will be safe … blink if you understand."

She wanted to scream at him that she wasn't stupid, that she could perfectly understand fucking English, but all that happened was she blinked like an idiot as no words were forthcoming.

"Come, Keenan. We'll leave a surveillance unit here. Whoever extracted her blood will be back."

Blood? Slowly, she felt his bite pressure lessen until she was released and he carefully removed his mouth from her neck. It was a caring gesture, as if he would kiss her, but he didn't let her go. Instead, he bent his huge body and picked her up like she weighed nothing and walked briskly out of the apartment. The black one who'd held him followed them, shutting the apartment door after them.

HE CARRIED her down every flight of stairs and didn't put her down until they reached a blacked-out SUV. The children's cries from inside the car ruled out any thought of running. The door was opened and he placed her down into the back seat. He pushed her over and got in behind her. Relief flooded her when the children flung themselves into her arms and she could soothe their cries. Both clung to her like limpets and sobbed into her chest. "There, there ... Shh," she whispered into their hair, and kissed each one lovingly

She flashed her eyes at the monster watching her as if she'd just committed an atrocity.

The car pulled away. Lacy sat between him and the black one. She thanked god, they had put the children with her and she hugged them to her possessively. Their crying had eased, but they still clung to her, not willing to give up the comfort.

She couldn't take her eyes off the one who'd bitten her. *What the fuck was he?* He stared at her and the children the whole time. His teeth had disappeared up into his gums, she assumed, but his eyes were constantly changing and swirling. They appeared to move between a blood red and purple, and then eventually they seemed to settle on the palest blue with an occasional burst of red, which quickly dispersed and disappeared.

He made her jump when he spoke. He was apparently English, with the same accent as her. "Whose are the children?" He said it bluntly, like an order.

Lacy frowned. *What a fucking stupid question.* "Mine." *You idiot.*

"They can't be yours. You've only been gone ten months. They are around five years old."

She didn't bother to answer him, but continued to scowl at him. He was talking like he knew her. She looked at the black one in the hope of some sense.

He just raised his eyebrows and nodded. Then he looked across her at the other one. "She don't know what's going on, mate."

The weird one spoke to her again, "Who else lives there?" he demanded.

"My boyfriend ... sometimes," she ended up finishing in a small voice, shrinking into the chair as she watched his face changing again.

"What. Is. His. Name?" he bit out slowly.

"Charlie," she whispered.

The kids were scared and snuggled into her all the more as they began to be freaked out by him again.

The black one spoke again, "Don't you know us, Lace?"

She turned her head to look at him. "No … should I?"

He looked shocked at her answer and looked across her at the other one again. "We were brought up with you," he said, looking at her again. "We've known you all your life."

What kind of sick mind game was this?

"She doesn't know us from Adam," the black one said. "I'm Vince, and he's Keenan," he said, pointing.

"I don't care who you are." And she sat back in her chair. The conversation was over as far as she was concerned.

She watched the other one staring out of the window with her peripheral vision. His chest was moving up and down like he'd been running.

Her mind began to race. She needed to get away from these men. She somehow knew that if she reached the end of this car journey, she'd never escape.

KEENAN MADE sure that when they reached their destination, Vince and Dan carried the kids to make sure she didn't try to run. Marius, who'd beaten them home, came up to them as they stood in the huge marble hall. "Bring them all to the sick room, Keenan. I've called a female doctor and a nurse to examine them."

Keenan gave Lacy a nudge to get her moving and they all walked in the direction of the sick room.

When she and the kids had disappeared inside, Marius pulled Keenan back into the hallway, "Give her some space, Keenan."

Keenan went to protest. He needed answers.

Then Marius completely took the wind out of his sails. "I've just got off the phone to her father."

That was logical. He would need to know she'd been found. *So?*

"He said it was quite possible that the kids could be hers ... and indeed yours, Keenan."

His heart stopped. He stared at Marius and blinked like a dumb fuck.

Marius didn't explain further. "Let's test their blood first. We'll know more then." Then he walked away.

KEENAN SAT with Vince in the corridor, traumatized, while they waited for Lacy and the kids to be examined. His head was reeling. Could it really be possible that the kids were his?

His blood boiled at the thought that someone had not only taken his mate but his children as well. He clenched his fists.

"Don't jump to conclusions yet, mate," Vince said.

Keenan looked at him menacingly, "When I find out who did this, Vince ..."

"I know, mate."

"How can she not know me?"

Vince slowly shook his head, "Beats me."

"Through all the shit ... through everything. It's always been me and her."

He was interrupted as the door opened and the doctor walked out.

Keenan and Vince both stood as if to receive bad news.

Marius came out and joined them.

"Is she okay?" Keenan asked, braced for whatever news was coming. He'd deal with whatever it was.

The doctor gave a half-smile. "Physically, she is fine. We've taken bloods from her and the children, toxicology and DNA. But I can tell you from my impression of the internal exam, she doesn't appear to have given birth. Of course, you can get a second opinion?"

Keenan stared at her and remained dumb. What was she saying? He was in shock. First, he wasn't a dad, then he was, then he wasn't again. Then she was a mum and now she's not? *Fuck!*

He stood looking at the floor with his hands on his hips while Marius showed the doctor to the door and thanked her.

Marius came back over. "Don't go off half-cocked, Keenan."

"I want some fucking answers," he said, beginning to pace up and down while his mind worked a mile a minute. "What the fuck's been going on?" Keenan said, looking at Marius for an answer.

Marius raised his eyebrows and shook his head. "I don't know. Hypnotism, brainwashing, drugs, probably all three … You need to give her some time, Keenan.

"Who could do something like that?" Keenan said, holding out his arms in exasperation.

Marius breathed out wearily, "Whoever it was wanted her blood. That's what I find so difficult to understand. The families want Sirens for power, if it's one of them, why not just take her?" Marius was clearly at a loss and shook his head. "I'm going to make some enquiries with the heads of families in New York. See if any children have gone missing in the last few months, matching their age. At least when the DNA results come back, we'll know which family they descend from. Could be a clue."

Before any more could be said, the door to the sick room opened and the nurse walked out slowly with her arm around Lacy's shoulders and the two kids huddled to her legs.

"I wanna talk to her alone," Keenan said, quietly.

"Do you think that's a good idea tonight?" Vince said.

Keenan turned on him, "I don't fucking care. I deserve ten minutes."

Lacy clung to the nurse, not wanting to come anywhere near him.

Marius walked over to the nurse and whispered something discreetly, then held the top of Lacy's arm so she couldn't follow. The nurse nodded, reached down for the kids' hands and walked off with them in the direction of the kitchen. "It's okay, Lacy. She's just taking them to give them some milk and cookies."

First, Lacy struggled, then when Marius released her, she stood all alone and fidgeted like a frightened little girl.

Keenan couldn't stand it any longer. "Come with me," he said forcefully. Not willing to have any argument, he quickly led her away by the elbow.

Vince followed them. "Go easy, mate!"

Keenan ignored him and carried on marching her along the corridor and up the huge, sweeping staircase. Then he pulled her with him along the landing and to his bedroom.

"Keenan … Keenan," Vince tried, but eventually slowed to a halt a few feet from his door.

Keenan opened his door and roughly pushed her inside. He paused before he followed her in. "She's mine, Vince. She stays with me." His voice was low and his temper was riding him. He wasn't fucking around and Vince needed to get the point for his own good. Vince nodded and walked away.

Lacy stood in the middle of the large, masculine bedroom with her arms folded and her eyes darting frantically around. The one who'd bitten her locked the door and stalked towards her. She felt a tremor of fear when she remembered how he changed into something else, something inhuman.

He didn't stop till they were mere inches apart and loomed over her. "I want some fucking answers," he demanded.

She shrugged to look nonchalant, but her fear intensified.

"What does he look like? he shouted, making her jump.

"Tall!" she shouted back.

"Tall?" Keenan said, disgusted with the non-answer to his question. "What else … hair … eye colour?"

Her head hurt. She touched her temples. Her thinking was fuzzy. She felt like crying. No matter how hard she tried, she couldn't bring him to mind. He was just a blur.

Frustrated, Keenan shook her by the shoulders.

"I don't know! I don't know!" She tugged at her hair with her fingers. Why couldn't she think? Then she snapped and pushed him away from her. "Who the fuck are you anyway to shout at me like that?" she screamed and went to turn away.

He grabbed her again to face him, taking her by the wrist and then yanking her arm up to her face. "What are these?"

She frowned and looked at her forearm, confused. "What are what? … I don't know."

"The scars … how did you get them?"

She looked again. She opened her mouth and then closed it again. Surely she would know they were there? Loads of round scars. Holes the size of knitting needles, in twos.

"I can't remember," she said. A lump was coming into her throat and she didn't want this pig to see her cry.

"I gave them to you," he said more softly. "When we were kids … you used to let me put my teeth in you." His voice began to crack with emotion and she looked up into his face. He continued to look at her arm lovingly. "You would let me drink from you … you were mine. You loved me." He looked into her eyes then.

For a moment, she locked eyes with him. Then she narrowed them in disgust. "I wouldn't have loved you, you're a monster," she said through gritted teeth.

No sooner had she registered the surprised look on his face than he grabbed her arm and pulled her along to the bathroom, where he turned the shower on to cold.

Lacy struggled, demanding what the hell he was doing, but he ignored her and shoved her under the spray fully clothed and followed her in, hemming her in under the spray with his big body. She was even more scared when he pulled his saturated T-shirt up over his head to reveal a large, muscled chest with every inch covered in black tattoos that danced in front of her vision, distorted by the spray.

She dragged her eyes from them and looked up into his eyes, swirling like a tempest. "Let me out." She meant to shout it, demand some fucking rights, but it just came out in a strangled whisper.

She tried to push past him, but it was a waste of time. He pulled her back to face him like a rag doll, pulled up her sleeve as high as it would go and put her arm next to his.

She watched in shocked amazement as his arms revealed thick dark bands so similar to her own emerging stripes. She gazed between them, over and over, transfixed.

"We are the same," Keenan said softly.

Absently, her hand came up to her mouth and she touched her teeth.

He answered her unspoken question: "You don't have the teeth. You're from a different family." His voice was so soothing, lulling her. "I'm not sure what's happened to you … drugs … hypnotism … probably both."

She snapped herself back to reality. "I don't believe you. Let me out!" She tried to shove past him with all her strength. "Where are my children?"

"They're not even your kids, Lace."

She stopped dead. "How dare you." She looked into his face with as much venom as she could muster and then snapped. Hitting, punching, screaming, crying, scratching, biting, she acted like a crazed animal.

He didn't retaliate; he just hugged her to his chest, hard. She struggled but was unable to move. She tried for a few more moments and then dissolved into huge, wracking, sobbing tears.

Slowly, when he wasn't letting her go, she relaxed into gentle, hiccupping sobs. Finally, she sagged into his warm chest and let his beating heart soothe her.

He wasn't crushing her, but stood and held her quietly.

Slowly, heat bloomed in her stomach and chest. It shocked her first of all with its strength and speed. The most marvellous scent entered her nose and her reasoning power became foggy. She found herself turning her mouth into his skin. Breathing deeply, she looked for the source of the smell. What was it? It lured her. *God*, she needed to find it.

She felt all his corded muscles tense around her as he froze. Then he groaned and his hand slowly moved up her back and threaded into her hair.

She found herself licking her lips and a coppery tang skated over her taste buds, and then kicked in like a fortified wine. She closed her eyes and groaned aloud.

He pulled back slightly and looked down into her face. Then he pulled out of her grip and out of the spray and turned the water off. The silence made her open her eyes, but her mind was still hooked on the wonderful taste in her mouth and she needed more. She wanted it badly.

Through bleary eyes, she looked at his chest and saw the marks she must have made with her nails; she'd scored his smooth skin, causing it to bleed. That must have been the source of the addictive smell and taste. She licked her lips. *God*, she wanted more. She moaned with want.

Keenan stepped into her space again and leaned his mouth down to her ear. "Did he give you his blood?" he whispered.

She closed her eyes, trying desperately to resist the pull towards him. "No," she whimpered, not sure how she knew that, but she did.

He leaned out of the shower, reached an arm over to the basin and grabbed his razor. "There is not enough for you," he said. He removed the blade and scored his skin along the line of the scratch she had already made. He made it deeper and she watched in drunken lust as the rivulets ran down onto the ridges of his hard stomach.

Somewhere deep inside, she knew she should be disgusted at her own reaction, but she couldn't help it. "No, I don't want to ..." But she was closing her eyes slowly. She felt his arms pull her slowly towards him, the flowing blood already tantalizing her senses.

As if he was hypnotizing her, he spoke softly, "Your mind has forgotten, but your body remembers ... It remembers me." And he pulled her tight up against him.

She shook her head and struggled weakly, but the scent overran her and her protests were half-hearted. Soon the smell was in her hair, in her skin, in her nose, and when she licked her lips, it was in her mouth. She groaned loudly and thought she had died and gone to heaven; the sensation was so strong. The blood blasted into her senses and she licked his skin in one long drag.

"Ah, Lacy ... it's been so long." And he buried his mouth in her hair.

She closed her mouth over the wound and gave herself over to lapping and sucking it hard. Her lips became frenzied in their demand for more and more. It made her heart pound and that feeling bloomed in her chest again like she would explode. Then it shot down into her groin and she thought she would die if she didn't have something satisfying between her legs, so she pushed the lower half of her body into him. He responded by pulling her into his hips.

His hot breath was next to her ear and he began to kiss lightly down to her shoulder in sensual nips, and then back up the side of her neck.

Suddenly, she remembered the bite from earlier and an image of what he became slammed into her consciousness. She fought to push him away from her, but a flood of warmth surged between her legs and she drew hard from the wound.

"Ah, that's it, babe," he groaned.

She felt his sharp teeth graze her neck. Somehow, she knew if he pierced her skin, she would be lost to him.

Her mind unclouded for a second; *what was she doing grinding on a complete stranger? He'd kidnapped her, for god's sake.*

She put her hands flat on his chest and pushed back with all her might, but only managed to push a couple of inches. "Stop!" she managed breathlessly. "Get away from me." She shook her head and rubbed her temples. "I can't think straight." Her accusing eyes looked up into his.

He looked down at her, eyes half closed and bleary with want. A stripe perfectly accentuated each cheekbone, making him look fierce and tribal. His tattoos and ear piercings made him all the more menacing.

She wondered what he would do next. But he stepped back, turned, and walked away from her and out into the bedroom. She was left breathing hard and her heart thumping in her ears. *God, what was he doing to have an effect on her like that? She was acting like she was drunk. She had a boyfriend, for god's sake.*

Taking a deep breath, she stepped out of the shower and looked at herself in the mirror. She hitched a breath in shock at the freaky striped reflection streaked with crimson blood staring back at her.

She put the palms of her hands to her cheeks as if to feel if she were awake. *Could she be hallucinating again?* She knew she had had several bouts; Charlie had helped her through them. Everything was so mixed-up and hazy. She grabbed the roots of her hair and pulled to wake herself up from this nightmare in which she was a striped, blood-drinking monster like him.

CHAPTER 12

Keenan had to get out of there before he said or did something he'd regret. He couldn't breathe when he staggered out into the hallway. Still dripping wet in just his fatigues, striped from head to foot and smeared with blood still oozing from his chest, he slid down the wall and sat on his haunches. His head fell into his hands and his elbows rested on his knees.

Vaguely, he was aware that someone slid down the wall and sat in the same position next to him. A slight glance sideways and a flash of black skin told him it was Vince. He was waiting for the 'I did tell you', but Vince remained quiet and he was grateful. Not a word – *but what was there to say?* When his soul mate, the person meant just for him, who had known him his whole life, who'd pursued him relentlessly until she won him so recently, didn't remember any of their sweet memories or meaningful moments together. *Fuck.*

He shook his head and got a grip on his spiralling emotions. Her body knew him, of that he was sure. He'd work on that. It was only a couple of hours after he'd gotten her back and she'd already almost given in to their physical pull. Within a few days, she'd be his for sure. Then he'd get to work on her memories, one step at a time. He'd enjoy getting her to remember him, bringing it all back, one milestone after another. He sat back against the wall, resolved in his plan of action.

THE SURVEILLANCE VAN remained outside Lacy's apartment for three days, but no one had gone there. It didn't make sense. Fresh blood had a shelf life. Someone had to be coming for it.

Baying for blood himself, Keenan made sure he took a shift in the van. He took the late afternoon to midnight slot. The one he felt most likely to be fruitful. Then, when he knew Lacy would be asleep, he would come and sit in the armchair in his room and watch her till morning.

Occasionally, she would open her eyes and see him sitting there. She would study him, not saying a word, until her lids fluttered and slowly closed. But he knew she didn't sleep. He could hear the quickening of her heart.

She had insisted on having the kids with her, and the three of them slept in Keenan's big bed. It was the one thing that Keenan had put his foot down about; that she was to stay in his room. She had agreed on the proviso that the kids stayed with her. And so he spent his nights brooding in the armchair.

After the first night, he was glad he'd allowed it.

Every night, at 1.30 a.m. on the dot, the little boy clambered out of bed, walked to the bottom of the bed, stopped abruptly, turned left, walked four paces, stopped again, and pointed his index finger in a stabbing motion eleven times. It was baffling.

After three nights, it was downright weird.

On the fourth night, Keenan sat with Vince in the

surveillance van and told him about the boy's nightly sleepwalk.

"And he does it at the same time every night? Vince asked.

"Yeah. It's fucking creepy. One-thirty, exactly."

Vince was quiet while he thought, fidgeting and frowning now and again.

"What are you thinking?" Keenan asked.

"When we get back, I've got an idea."

THE SHIFT DRAGGED – another no-show. Eventually, Vince and Keenan walked back into the hallway of Santalini HQ.

Vince turned to Keenan as soon as they were inside. "I'm just going to go and get something. I'll meet you at your room."

Keenan raised his eyebrows, shrugged, and then bounded up the stairs to change out of his fatigues.

A few moments later and Vince gently tapped on his door. Keenan padded over and quietly let him in. It was imperative they woke no one up.

Vince held out an old touch-tone phone. Keenan's eyes went wide. *Fuck.* That was it. The kid was fucking phoning someone in his sleep. He didn't even need to speak, just dial a number. Genius. No wonder no one had come back to the flat. The kid was fucking hypnotized to dial him up every night, and when it stopped, he knew there was something wrong.

The two of them sat an agonizing wait till one-thirty. Then they held their breath when the boy sat bolt upright, slipped off the bed, walked to the end, turned left and walked four paces.

Vince had put the phone on a pedestal table at the approximate height of the sideboard he'd remembered the phone to be on, back at Lacy's flat.

The boy reached out his hand like he'd done on every other occasion and poked at the numbers while Vince wrote them down – eleven in all.

Keenan and Vince looked at each other and grinned. The boy turned on his heel, retraced his steps exactly and got back into bed.

Keenan motioned for Vince to come outside into the hall-way. He took out his mobile phone with slightly shaking hands and a thumping heart and dialled the number. He looked at Vince and put it to his ear.

After three rings, a childish jingle played, like the theme tune to some kids' program. Then it clicked off. *Fuck. What an anti-climax.* Keenan shook his head on a deep sigh and explained to Vince what he'd heard.

"So he gets the boy to ring into an answerphone, which he checks every day. Clever." Vince said. "The question is: will he go to the flat after a break of three days?"

"And, how badly does he need the blood?" Keenan nodded.

"How long does blood last?" Vince asked.

"Human blood's about three weeks, I think, I dunno about ours."

They agreed the next night would be crucial. Keenan informed the guards on the rest of the night shift to be extra vigilant, said goodnight to Vince and went back into his room. He needed some sleep tonight so he was on the ball when he finally got to rip the bastard up who fucked with his woman.

LACY WOKE at the click of the door when he must have left the room. Quietly as she could, she slipped out of the bed and padded over to his heavy jacket, slung over the back of the chair he always slept in.

Hurriedly, she went through all the pockets. Not sure what she was looking for, a phone, a weapon, anything. *Shit. Nothing.*

She nearly jumped out of her skin when a voice spoke from right behind her.

"Looking for this?"

She turned slowly and saw him standing there holding out his mobile phone to her. "Go ahead. Use it. In fact, I'd be interested to know who you would phone?"

Gradually getting her breathing back to normal after the shock of him catching her out, she frowned when she thought about what he said. It was true, she couldn't for the life of her think of a single person to ring. She rubbed her fingers anxiously across her forehead. "Oh fuck off!" she yelled, then stomped past him, making sure she shoved him as she went.

Too wired for bed, she took herself off to the bathroom, having nowhere else to flounce off to. No lock. *Bollocks.*

Putting the loo seat down, she sat on it with her forehead in her hand.

The door snicked open, and she knew he'd followed her into the bathroom. "Didn't you hear me? I said, fuck off!" She flashed her eyes at him, towering above her. But even in her temper, she noticed the V-shape of his torso neatly tapering down into narrow hips and the way his powerful legs touched the fabric of his trousers.

She felt his eyes rake over her body with interest and then saw the flush in his cheeks. Then the tips of those fangs pushed his mouth open slightly like a bloody invitation. *Shit.* Her own body responded with a blast of heat that shot up from her toes and flamed up to her cheeks. Pissed off at her reaction to him, she pulled the oversized T-shirt – belonging to him – down over her knees.

He seemed amused and folded his arms across his chest.

He leaned on the wall next to him as if he had all the time in the world.

"Don't you have somewhere to be?" she spat.

"This is my room," he said, infuriatingly reasonable.

She looked away from him in annoyance. *What could she say to that?* She could scream with frustration, but didn't want to wake the kids.

He smiled at her and she caught it out of the corner of her eye. "I'm glad you find this funny."

"Not funny … ironic."

She looked up at him, frowning.

"Ever since I can remember, you followed me around like a puppy – was a pain in the arse, most of the time. And now …" He let out a sigh and smiled ruefully. "Shoe's on the other foot."

She stared at him for a long moment. She never knew whether he was telling the truth or not. She didn't know him. She didn't trust him, just because she fancied him … "If what you're saying is true, why would someone do that? Take me away, give me kids to believe are my own?" She shook her head, dismissing the thoughts as ludicrous.

"We thought it was one of the royal families, to make you marry into their family; it's always a risk till you're married, but it seems he kept you to take your blood. We're not sure why … and the kids, well, they appear to be the cleverest part of all."

She searched his sad face as he spoke. "What do you mean by clever?"

He looked at her, his head tilted at an angle as if he was curious why she didn't get it. "They kept you tied down to that flat and they reported to him unknowingly that the coast was clear … or not," he added.

Her head ached with all the conflicting information. She felt tired and overwhelmed by it all.

"What reason did he give for taking your blood?" Keenan asked.

Her heart sank the minute she brought the answer to mind and how it would sound aloud. She didn't believe the words herself as she said them: "I'm sick. I have to have regular tests." She bowed her head.

Thankfully, he didn't laugh. He was quiet and tactful, actually.

"Look, we'll get the results of the blood and drug tests any day now. We'll know more then. But I'm not the one lying to you, Lacy." He held out his left hand to her with a large, oval purple ring on the middle finger. "This is a divining ring. All princes have them. It is purple because you are mine. That's why you react to me the way you do. You can't fight it. You can't change it. It's just the way it is for as long as we live."

She stared at it and her heart began to thump. "What does it mean when it's a bluey-green colour?"

He was very quiet for a minute. "You've seen one that colour?"

She looked deep into his eyes, "My boyfriend ..." She shook her head and swallowed hard. "The bloke ... Charlie ... he had one the same, but green."

Keenan stood up straight and stared out ahead of him while his brain whirred. "He's a prince," he muttered, more to himself than to her.

She studied his face as he worked through all the ramifications of what she'd told him. Then he turned and went out of the room and left her alone.

Confused, she sagged. She didn't know what way was up anymore. Maybe she was going mad.

MARCO DUBONNETTI HAD TAKEN a swish rented apartment in Kensington, London. Not only did it go with his jet set 'actor' lifestyle, it was central for his needs and away from the ears of Dante the king, his elder brother.

He had never been a great fan of his and the feeling was mutual. Dante had disappointingly gone from strength to strength since being king, instead of crumbling into a drunken, broken-down mess, as his father had said he would when his Siren, Tia Storm, had gone off and shacked up with his best friend.

Life sucked at times. Even though he had thousands of willing, adoring female fans, he longed to be king and have a Siren of his own as he was initially promised. That was the credibility he sought.

He wasn't the only disgruntled Dubonnetti son, either. Dante had not made friends with any of his brothers when he had gone back on the plan for them each to have a Siren. He'd gone all sanctimonious about doing everything for the good of the crown and bullshit like that. They all felt cheated.

Stephan, the youngest, hated Dante with a vengeance for taking the woman he loved as a wife, then discarding her when he'd made her go blind. Mind you, she wasn't even a Siren in the end, but Marco enjoyed having Stephan on his side, so he fanned the flames of Stephan's hatred.

His brothers, Paulo and Antonio, had also been overlooked and had chosen him as the winning side. He was sure that loyalty didn't come into it; they just knew where their bread was buttered. So they looked to him now to secure their futures, and that he had vowed to do.

He'd started by seeking out friends and relatives from the other royal families who had next to no chance of ever making it into Dante's government, with or without a Siren. A word in the right ear, a commiserating shoulder to cry on, you name it, he'd done it, until he was sure he had a tight group of friends.

Tonight he had invited likely candidates to a little house-warming party. Just his brothers and a few budding starlets to make up the numbers and some well-chosen 'friends'.

The first to arrive was Ruby Santalini. She was sister to the five Santalini brothers. And by her sex alone was doomed to being a decoration, and nothing more.

Her brother, Keenan, had proved to be every bit of a no-hoper as Dante, given that he was brought up with his Siren and still managed to lose her. It was galling for her to have her brains overlooked for nothing but an oaf. Being brought up in a garrison of soldiers like him, it didn't take much for Marco to win her over and into his bed.

She was in love with him. He smirked. And would do anything for him. *Good shag too.* The rest of the Santalini bunch were too damn honourable to bother with.

The next to turn up were two of the Florianna princes. He'd had to invite Cesarè for appearances. He was a playboy from the main, silver-spoon branch of the family, but the person he was really interested in this whole evening was his cousin, Malleven Mancini.

He'd heard he was a member of the sacred Magi organization, and rumoured to be one of the most talented alchemists and magicians in the world – Human or Atlantean.

His brother, Antonio, was certainly taken with him. Not that he gave two shits whether Antonio was gay or straight, it was quite normal in Atlantean society for the love of a person to be valued irrespective of gender. He was more bothered that he was monopolizing his time.

Finally, the Bonaci brothers arrived. He wasn't sure about these two at all. They fit his criteria completely, being born from a different mother to the Sirens and sharing a father. But they had only ever seemed loyal to the Bonaci family. Still, it would be a coup to make a friend of Luca and Dino Bonaci.

Marco began to work the room, making sure he chatted to everyone and making them feel the most important guests there.

He pulled Ruby to him. "So, Keenan has his Siren back … do you think he can keep her this time?"

She giggled and circled her arms around him.

Marco thought her really striking with her raven-black hair, 1950s figure and startling blue eyes.

She threaded her arms around his neck and into his blond bed-head hair and kissed him wantonly.

Marco allowed it to a point, and then extracted himself as quickly as he could. "Later," he said, putting a finger to her lips, which she kissed.

He wanted to get to Malleven before he made his excuses and left. He was very much aware of how rarely Malleven put in an appearance at private gatherings.

As he came nearer, he could see his brother, Antonio, flirting with him outrageously. "Malleven?" Marco said and kissed his cheek on both sides.

"Marco," Malleven replied, in beautifully accented English. All the Florianna were permanently based in Italy.

Marco gave his brother Antonio a "fuck off" look, and he scowled and disappeared into the kitchen to get another drink.

Malleven didn't mince his words: "What do you want, Marco? There must be a purpose to your invitation." He took a gold lighter out of the breast pocket of his beautifully tailored light-grey suit and a thin cigar from a gold case. "Do you mind?"

Marco, a little stunned by the guy, blabbered, "Not at all." All he could do was watch him light his cigar hypnotically with his long, dark-brown, slender fingers and run his spare hand through his jet-black, shiny hair.

He really was a startlingly good-looking bloke. Around

six feet three and slim, his grey suit and crisp white shirt just accentuated perfectly his dark coffee skin and beautiful chiselled features. He should have been a model.

"Thank you," Malleven said, looking deeply into Marco's eyes.

Marco's eyes widened when it dawned on him that the guy had just read his thoughts.

Malleven laughed easily and took a seductive drag on his cigar. "Don't worry, your secret is safe with me. I only have room for one Dubonnetti in my bed."

Marco blinked in astonishment, *to have his innermost fantasies exposed like that – never acted on, of course.*

Malleven smiled knowingly.

Marco was now convinced the guy was as powerful as his father had said he was. He knew that despite the guy making him feel all kinds of uncomfortable, he wanted him on his side.

"I am sure we can come to an arrangement," Malleven said, reading him exactly again. "But what you have in mind is treason, Marco Dubonnetti." He smiled, showing his perfectly shaped white teeth.

Marco's face fell, as he suddenly feared he'd made a huge blunder in inviting this man into his circle.

His discomfort was interrupted when his brother returned with two glasses of champagne and passed one to Malleven, who gracefully reached for the glass, flashing a gold watch and a black Atlantean hieroglyph tattoo on the inside of his wrist depicting an owl – the insignia of the Magi. His father had told him that the owl hunts at night and the mouse doesn't know he's coming until it is too late. It made him aroused just thinking about it.

Malleven put his cigar in his glass hand, stroked along Antonio's jaw and pulled him in close to kiss his lips gently.

Then he looked Marco in the eye with mischief. They

were the colour of deepest midnight blue. "Don't worry, Marco, it is okay to dream. It is through our dreams that we get what we want." And he flashed his startling smile again. "Come, Antonio. I am not in London for long. I want to make the most of it."

Marco was left with his mouth gaping and watched as Malleven steered his brother towards the door. Then he opened it for him to go through first and stopped and took one last glance back at Marco, "I will contact you when the time is right."

Marco swallowed. He wasn't sure who recruited who tonight. He felt exposed, like the guy had seen every part of him. Mentally violated … that was how he felt.

Shit, with that guy on side, it was only a matter of time before he was king.

CHAPTER 13

Keenan waited in the dark, in Lacy's old flat. Vince, Dan and Rick were listening in from the SUV parked in the street.

He'd taken the precaution of swapping the blood for the common Human variety so it was no use to the kidnapper and wouldn't trigger his physical reaction to it.

"Keenan," he heard in his ear. "Man coming up … scruffy … woolly hat on."

"Roger that … I'm more than ready. Stay put unless I say so."

"Will do."

Keenan couldn't help it; as soon as the key went into the door, his vision went to night predator instantly. However, with the lights off, he had the advantage – *all the better for tracking the fucker.*

As soon as the guy crept in, he knew he wasn't the one, too short for a start. And he reeked of drugs; his hunter's sense of smell couldn't miss it.

Coming to a quick decision, Keenan decided to let the thing play out and follow him to see where he went.

He went straight to the fridge, so he knew what he was coming for. Then, like a typical druggie, he did a quick shifty around the place, looking in drawers and the usual hiding places for money and valuables.

Satisfied there was nothing worth pinching, he left the way he'd come in.

"I've let him leave, Vince. It's not him; it's just a gofer. I'm going to follow him on foot.

"Okay, mate," Vince said. We'll stay close, but out of sight."

Keenan followed him for a couple of blocks until they came to a more industrial part of town.

The guy turned into an alley, looked all around him and dumped the blood in a bin, then turned around and ran back out and away down the street.

"Dan! Follow him just in case. I'm staying here, see who turns up."

It didn't take long.

The guy was tall and hunched over as he sidled into the alley.

Keenan peeped around the corner and watched as he stopped in front of the dumpster, lifted the lid, and leaned inside. Then he flew at him.

While the guy's head and shoulders were under the lid, Keenan slammed it down on him over and over, smashing it into him with all his considerable strength. He kept it up until the body went limp. Keenan stopped himself from killing him and leaned on the bin, breathing heavily. Then he allowed the body to slide down the outside of the dumpster to a heap on the floor.

He tried to get a hold on himself to speak, "Vince ... I need a pick-up. I've got him."

After they bundled the unconscious body into the back of the SUV, they went to pick up Dan, who'd followed the first guy back to a squat full of no-hopers.

"Do you want this one lifted?" Dan asked.

"He ain't goin' nowhere," Vince said. "We know where he is."

So they left him and Dan jumped in.

Keenan was quiet, brooding over the hunched-over body between him and Rick on the back seat.

MARIUS MET them as soon as they returned to the Santalini mansion. Vince had radioed ahead that they were coming in with the possible abductor.

"I've got a doctor to check him over before we question him," Marius said, giving Keenan the evil eye.

Keenan went to protest. "I want to …"

"This is politics now, Keenan; it has to be handled carefully. Fuck. Look at the state of him."

Keenan's answer was to drop the suspect in a heap at Marius' feet, then walk away. But he stopped next to Marius' shoulder as he passed. "Question him if you want, but nothing will keep him alive when I get the chance."

Marius didn't bother to answer him. He motioned for the other three men to pick the suspect up and follow him to the sick room.

KEENAN WALKED INTO HIS ROOM, threw down his jacket and found the room empty. *Thank fuck.* He began stripping off. Shucking weapons, taking off shirt, boots and trousers and then walked into the bathroom and turned the shower on to cold.

He hadn't calmed down. His blood was just on a slow simmer. His vision was impaired and his teeth were tender.

He stopped moving when his keen predator hearing

heard Lacy enter the bedroom and close the door. No kids' voices. She was alone.

He switched off the shower and reached for a towel, tied it around his waist and walked back into the bedroom.

She appeared to be sitting on the bed waiting for him.

"It's probably not a good idea for you to be around me at the moment. I just brought your boyfriend in."

Her face froze, her eyes wide like a deer. "You sure?"

Then, a moment later, her eyes tracked down his torso and back up to his face. He had to question whether he'd really watched her do it, given what he'd just said.

"How do you know it's him? she said, narrowing her eyes.

"We don't."

Lacy looked down at her hands fidgeting in her lap. Keenan slowly lowered himself onto the bed next to her.

"Where are the kids?" Keenan asked, more gently. Something was wrong.

She looked up and tears brimmed in her eyes. "The nurse is getting them ready. Their real parents are coming for them." Tears rolled down her cheeks.

Keenan resisted the overwhelming urge to pull her into his arms. *Fuck*, he didn't know what to do.

"The bloods came back. They are not mine." She began to cry properly, not able to hold it back any longer. "They also found drugs in my system ... not the usual," she sobbed. "To make me suggestible."

Keenan reached a tentative hand up to touch her cheek. "I'm sorry, Lace."

She leaned into his touch and closed her eyes. "I feel so alone ... like I'm going crazy."

Keenan saw real fear in her eyes when she opened them. "No, you're not mad. Someone has fucked with your head." He said the last part through gritted teeth. The thought that the guy could possibly be downstairs made him want to tear down there and rip him to shreds.

But nothing could have dissipated his anger more than her moving closer to him and leaning into him for comfort. He took the cue and put his large arms around her. "And he'll pay. Don't worry." He felt her sob in his arms. He rocked her quietly and rested his mouth on her head.

The phone rang and he reluctantly released her to answer it. "I'll be right down."

ALREADY A POWDER KEG waiting to go off, Keenan felt murderous for the pain and anguish Lacy had been forced to endure. Even though she was softening towards him, he would give anything to stop her hurting.

The phone call was from Marius, informing him that the prisoner was now conscious and able to be questioned. Lacy was to go with him down into the sick room to see if she could identify him. If she could see beyond the bruising, Marius had added sarcastically. Any sign of aggression from Keenan would not be tolerated and he would be slung out of the room.

Keenan walked in step with Lacy down the grand staircase and through the marble hallway towards the back of the mansion where the gym, pool and sick bay were located. They didn't speak.

Keenan's blood was on a rolling boil all the way to the room where the prisoner was being held. Marius had taken no chances and had Vince, Rick and Dan on the door, knowing they were the only people liable to get through to him.

Vince put his hands out flat on Keenan's chest as he arrived. "Simmer down, man."

Keenan bowled straight into Vince's hands and looked

with deadly intent into his friend's eyes. "Let me in, Vince," Keenan said quietly and evenly.

Vince held his ground and stared him back dead in the eye. "We cool, Keenan?" he said, stepping in front of him each time Keenan went to step around him. "Think … see if she knows him."

Keenan blinked as if he were waking up. *Yeah, if he killed the wrong bloke, he'd never know.*

He nodded and turned to Lacy, who was looking scared next to him.

LACY FOLLOWED CLOSELY behind Keenan when they walked into the sick room that she herself had been examined in when she first came to the mansion. With frightened eyes, she scanned the room and found him propped up on pillows in the bed.

He had cuts and bruises on his face. His arms and torso were heavily bandaged.

Marius walked towards her. "Lacy, please look at him closely and tell us if you know him?"

Warily, she edged closer to the bed.

Despite the heavy bruising, she knew he was a stranger to her and shook her head, "No, I don't know him."

Keenan, who had kept a lid on his temper so far, strode forward, past Lacy, towards the man on the bed. Everyone leapt forward to bar his way and hold him. Lacy jumped out of the way.

He grappled with their hands. "Leave off me," he growled. "Did he have a ring?" he said, trying to get a look at the man's hands. Then he looked at Marius for an answer.

Marius shook his head, "No … no divining ring. He says he was given fifty dollars just to go and look in the dumpster."

Keenan spoke directly to the suspect. "What else did he say to you … what did he look like?"

The man looked terrified of Keenan.

"It's okay, you can speak," Marius reassured him.

"He asked me how tall I was … I can't remember what he looked like."

Keenan went to lunge at him again.

Vince grabbed him from behind with both arms. "Taking it out on him ain't gonna change nothing … think about it. He's probably telling the truth … Lacy can't even remember the bloke."

Keenan took a last hate-filled glance at the man on the bed. His eyes were staring and glassy. Then he began to speak in a strange and far-off voice, as if he were remembering something long gone. "I have a message for the Santalini prince …"

The room went silent. Everyone froze.

"I have no more use for the girl … Let it go, if you want to live." The man put his fingers to his temples and rubbed them as if he had a nasty headache coming on.

They all looked at each other in shock.

Keenan scowled at them all and pointed at the prisoner, words failing him. "You see that? … He's fucking playing with us." And he turned and marched out of the room.

Eventually, everyone came back to life, and Marius walked over to Lacy and touched her shoulder gently, "Are you sure you can't think of anything that can help us … anything at all?"

She looked back over at the man on the bed, who had turned his head away from everyone. "I'm sorry … nothing."

Marius sighed, "Not to worry, Lacy," and he nodded at Vince.

"Take her back to her room, Vince. It's been a hell of a day for her. Here …" Marius handed her a little cup with a couple of blue and yellow capsules in it. "A little something just to help you sleep … Insomnia is not surprising after the drugs you've had pumped into you."

She looked into Marius' compassionate face and took the cup. After staring into it, she knocked it back into her mouth, washed them down with some water Vince passed her and walked slowly towards the door. She stopped and turned. "What will happen to him?" she said, looking over at the man on the bed.

"We'll patch him up and send him on his way," Marius said, smiling kindly.

She nodded and walked out.

When Lacy entered the bedroom some time later, Keenan was sitting in the armchair with his head in his hands. She didn't say anything but sat on the bed opposite him.

Miserable didn't even cover the way she felt; guess he felt the same way. Lost, bereft, alone, *god*, she couldn't think of a good enough word to describe it. She brought her legs up and hugged her knees.

Keenan looked over to her, still cradling his head. "You have a sister, you know … Well, four actually. But I have only met one of them. She is really nice," he said, breaking the silence.

She looked at him, surprised. "Really?"

"She's beautiful like you, but with lighter hair and more Atlantean looking."

A tear escaped the corner of her eye. *How did he know how she felt?*

"You have two half-brothers, a mother and father, an uncle and, to my knowledge, loads of cousins.

A sob escaped her.

He stood up restless, not knowing whether to cuddle her or keep his distance.

When she looked up and saw the pain in his face, she ran to the bathroom, not able to bear any comfort from him. With the door shut, she sobbed her heart out. It was for her children, her memories, her lost love that didn't exist, and the forgotten love that probably did. She wailed, giving vent to it all and was grateful Keenan left her to it.

After a while, her sobs lessened and she breathed easier, having run out of steam, lapsing into the pathetic exhaustion that followed a good cry. She took a quick shower and decided the sleeping pills must be working.

She ventured into the bedroom, clutching her towel around her, but the room was empty. Thankful for the privacy, she put one of Keenan's T-shirts on and clambered into the bed. She wanted to sleep for a hundred years.

KEENAN COULDN'T BEAR to sit and listen to Lacy's heart break. She'd lost her children today and her whole life was a big hole of nothingness. She didn't know who to trust. *Fuck*, he felt the worst kind of helplessness. He knew if he tried to comfort her, he could only make things worse. She needed some time. So he took himself off to the gym like he'd done all those months before when he wanted to take the edge off his frustration.

The treadmill was the machine he chose to kill himself with exhaustion on. He'd been running flat out for ages when Vince found him.

"You'll burn the motor out at that rate," Vince said.

"The machine can take it," Keenan grit out.

"I wasn't talking about the machine," Vince said, looking up at him from a weights bench next to him.

Keenan looked at his old friend and allowed a small smile to steal across his face. He sagged with defeat, pressed the stop button and the belt gradually slowed to a halt. He glugged some water, stepped off the treadmill and sat on it opposite Vince. He wiped his sweat from his neck with a small towel. "I want to kill something, Vince," he said, crushing the empty water bottle in his hands and throwing it across the room into a bin.

"I know, mate." Vince shook his head.

"The stupid thing is, I fucking knew deep down that he wasn't the guy. He's too clever for that … I just …"

"Don't beat yourself up … it's me, remember. I know how much she means to you …" He shook his head and looked at the floor, then back at Keenan a moment later. "I can't imagine what you're going through, what that bastard has done to her. Fuck, I can remember you knocking Jason Hargreaves' front teeth out just for making her cry when she was seven years old," Vince said, grinning at the memory.

Keenan cracked a smile, as if it were a sweet memory for him too, but wiped it away quickly, "For the first time in my life, Vince, I'm at a loss what to do. If it were only that simple."

Vince sighed and looked up at the ceiling for inspiration. "Maybe you're trying too hard. Just … you know, be there for her.

Keenan looked at his old friend and smiled, "How did you get so wise?"

"It's the old cockney charm, I guess."

They stood together and Keenan pulled Vince into a sweaty hug. When Vince complained, he put him away from him again, but held his shoulders. "When I catch the bastard, I don't care how royal Marius says he is." He shook his head with a promise. "No mercy, Vince."

"And I'll be there with you."

Keenan squeezed his friend's shoulders and returned to his room.

Lacy was sound asleep when he got back.

Keenan showered quickly, grabbed a throw and settled in his usual chair opposite the bed. He'd only coiled up for a few minutes when he heard Lacy tossing and turning in the bed. He lifted his head to look.

She must be dreaming. Mumbling gibberish, she threw off the thin sheet and thrashed and scissored her legs.

Frowning, he stood up, concerned. *Did he wake her or leave her be?*

He decided to try calming her without waking her up. He went over to the bed and, gently as he could, lay down next to her. He stroked her fevered face and pushed the curls away from her eyes and mouth. *God, it must be an anxious dream.*

"No ... no, Charlie ..."

CHAPTER 14

Keenan's blood ran cold. *Fuck*. His brain raced. He just lay still to see what else she said.

"Don't … don't," she shouted, and sat up.

He sat up quickly with her and held her, trapping her arms at her sides.

Lacy pulled slightly away from him and looked into his eyes. She appeared to be awake, but her eyes were glazed and weird. "Charlie … Thank God," and hugged him tight.

Keenan's mind reeled and was repulsed as she held him. She thought he was *him*. Every fibre in him revolted at the idea, but he needed to see where this took him. "Shh!" he said gently and lay her back down.

She pulled him to her and put her mouth on his and kissed him gently. It built in strength till it was urgent and passionate. *Fuck*. He couldn't help himself; he rolled on top of her and kissed her back and groaned. He pushed his tongue deep into her mouth like he hadn't been able to do in ages.

Shit, he wanted to bury himself deep in her and worry about the morality of it later. Grinding his hips, deeper, harder. "No!" He stopped himself and leaned up on his elbows, breathing hard. "No, Lace … not like this."

His fangs were protruding and he couldn't close his mouth. He must look terrifying to her.

Then she shocked him rigid. "Are you thirsty?" she asked, in the small voice she used like when they were kids. It was spine-chilling. She was looking straight at him, but he could tell she wasn't seeing. She must still be asleep.

Oh god, fuck! She put her arm across her face so he could have access to her wrist like she'd done so many times before. *He needed to get off her. He needed to get away. Oh sweet mother …*

All the while, his mind played thought after thought of what he should do, his head came lower and lower till he could kiss her delicate arm and graze her skin with his aching, straining teeth.

As he looked into her eyes, he knew his had swamped with blood and must look hideous, but when she didn't flinch away from him, his lust overtook him and he struck fast. "Mmm," he groaned and took great, long pulls of the nectar he'd been starved of so long. He closed his eyes and gave himself over to his thirst.

Responding as she used to, she pushed her pelvis up into his and gyrated in small circles, inviting him to take her completely. He knew it was wrong. He knew he should stop. But he could feel her breathing hard, and smell her body wanting him as much as he wanted her. She panted and ran her spare hand all over his back. *Oh, Lace, Babe.*

Something made him open his eyes. Hers flashed at the same time. Then she screamed and pushed him off, ripping her wrist away from his mouth and tearing her delicate skin.

"Fuck off!" she screamed and scurried away from him, off the bed and onto the floor, hugging herself in a ball next to the wall.

"Ah fuck, Lace, I'm so sorry." His voice was a barely audible growl, transformed into the animal he knew he was. His eyes were still glued to the blood running down her arm. "You must let me seal the holes.

"Keep away from me, you animal."

"Animal?" He got up and stalked towards her menacingly. He glowered down at her with his burning red eyes. "You knew me in your sleep, Lace. You called me Charlie, but you knew it was me."

She shook her head, not willing to believe anything he said. She shut her eyes and tried to cover her head like a small child. Then yelped as he pulled her gently to standing by the elbows.

He turned her to face him and held her fast.

"Leave… Me… Alone," she spat.

Slowly, he pulled her injured wrist up level with his mouth. She hitched a breath and held it as he put it to his lips and licked the wound shut, holding it for a long moment in his mouth to make sure it was closed.

Then he put her away from him, grabbed his jeans and left the room.

WHEN LACY AWOKE, she was alone.

The first thing she did was to check her wrist and saw the jagged, healing scars on her pulse point. It wasn't a dream.

She was fuzzy and confused. She knew she'd been seriously turned on, and then everything became a jumble. She remembered what Keenan had said. She'd called him Charlie, but knew who he was. Then she remembered the feeling of lust and it hit her so hard that she clutched her lower abdomen just at the thought of it.

Shaking her head, she got up and dressed quickly and went downstairs. She looked for him, but found out he had already left. And not just for the day either. An emergency with one of her sisters' Protectors, she was told. Keenan was delivering a booster supply of Elixir. Everything sounded like riddles.

The feeling of being cheated out of another showdown with him gave way to relief when she decided the break from him was probably a good idea. He affected her in ways she didn't understand, and it made her feel uncomfortable.

And so she relaxed over the next few days. Keenan had left Vince, Rick and Dan with her. Marius had explained that they were *her* Protectors. It made her smile as they seemed so proud of the role, but honestly, she didn't remember them being in her past life any more than she did Keenan.

Then she'd sought out Marius and he'd kindly answered a lot of her questions, like who she was for a start: Ligeie Anatolia Etain Bonaci, apparently. *Who knew?*

So, what Keenan had touched on was all true and she would meet her family soon. She felt a stab of guilt at the way things had been left with him, then reminded herself that he had been chewing on her arm in her sleep. Warmth flooded her core and the guilt returned.

She went to browse the extensive Santalini library to try to learn more and shake off the disturbing feeling that she was actually missing Keenan. Her head was in a large volume when she heard the door click closed behind her.

When she turned, there stood an incredibly beautiful girl like an old-fashioned movie star. She had raven-black hair, startling blue eyes and a tall, curvy frame wrapped in a scarlet dress. Stunning was the only word to describe her.

"Hello, Lacy," she said. "I am Ruby, Keenan's sister."

Of course, she must be a Santalini. Her colouring could be nothing else.

Lacy said a wary 'hello', unsure of everyone these days.

"My brother Marius thought it would be nice for us to

spend some time together while Keenan is away?" she continued.

Lacy nodded and smiled weakly, not sure of what to say. "I'm not very good company, I'm afraid," she said eventually, as she exhaled.

"Perhaps I could find you some clothes to wear ... something a bit more feminine?"

Liking that idea, Lacy smiled and nodded. "Thank you."

Ruby held out her hand for her to take and led her out of the library and up the great staircase to her room.

Ruby managed to find her some trousers and a couple of tops that didn't drown her. All Atlanteans were so tall, she realised. "Why aren't I tall?" she asked.

Ruby stood still and thought for a minute. "Do you know, I'm not sure. I'll find out for you if you like?"

Lacy smiled.

"Sit for a minute," Ruby said, patting the bed next to her.

Lacy sat down.

"Are you okay, Lacy ... really?"

Lacy smiled a wan smile, "I don't know what to tell you, Ruby ... I don't know anything anymore.

"Give it time," Ruby said. "I'd love to tell you that Keenan's a good guy, but I don't really know him. He was brought up away from us."

"With me," Lacy added with a sigh.

Ruby reached over to her dressing table and passed Lacy a beautifully carved, highly polished wooden box.

Lacy took it. "What's this?"

"Open it."

Lacy lifted the lid and it revealed a beautiful dancing lady on a spring, which turned as a pretty tune tinkled. It delighted her.

"It's like you," Ruby said. "I want you to have it. When I

was a little girl and felt lonely, living in an army barracks for a house, I would open it and it made me feel better."

Lacy leaned over and hugged her. "Thank you, Ruby. It's lovely."

"You're welcome. I want you to think of me as a friend from now on."

Lacy put her head on an angle while she thought for a moment. "You know, I think you are my first one."

A WHISTLE MADE Keenan turn his head away from the CCTV unit the tech guy was working on in the basement. "Keenan … come and see this," Reeve, his guard-mate said.

Keenan stood and followed Reeve up the staircase and out through the kitchen into the yard. "What is it?" Keenan asked.

"They're sparring in the barn. That Human is fast."

Keenan perked up. This he wanted to see.

Reeve whistled and nodded his head in the direction they were going, for two more guards to join them. They quickly jogged over and marched along with them to the barn.

Keenan hauled the sliding door across and they all filed in. They stayed near the edge and Keenan leaned against the wall with his arms folded, watching the fight closely.

Jay was fighting the big cowboy, Cash, and he guessed he'd already fought with the soldier, Sean. Reeve was right, the guy had moves, lightning fast, he ducked, weaved, punched and kicked. He had flair too, rolling back onto his feet like a cat whenever he was thrown.

It was weird because the guy was plastered in the ancient lettering of Atlantis. His whole upper body was smothered, yet he had the face of a model. If he kept covered up, you would just assume he was some kind of office bod.

It was hard to tell that not more than twenty-four hours

ago, he was on death's door either. Brought on by Lacy's sister binding him to her with her Siren's breath, Keenan had been sent on an urgent mission by Alfonzo to deliver Elixir, a potion to lessen its effects, to save his life. The thanks he got was the fucker threatening him to keep away from Tia with a smashed glass in his hand. He still shook his head in amazement at the guy's madness or guts. The guy had anger issues similar to his own, Keenan chuckled to himself.

The fight came to an end as a draw. Jay and Cash touched knuckles, smiling, and leaned down with their hands on their knees, catching their breath. Jay stood back up and stared over at Keenan, "You wanna have a go?"

Keenan raised his eyebrows. As usual, the bloke had shocked him with his front. "You've fought already; it wouldn't be fair."

Jay just shrugged. "I don't mind if you don't?"

That was it. It was on. Keenan whipped his tight black T-shirt up over his head and gave his watch to Reeve. The other guards grinned. Things were getting good. The only way to stop all this bollocks with the guy was to have it out.

Tia came running over from some makeshift record decks and shouted, "No!"

"Your woman has no faith in you, Jay?" Keenan said, just to rile him up.

He knew Jay was handy; he'd just witnessed it, but he had at least eighty pounds in weight and around five inches in height on him, and the guy wasn't put off at all. So he had to give him his dues.

"What say we change it up a bit and use a weapon?" Keenan said, grinning.

"Okay," Jay said without a trace of fear.

Cash threw over a couple of broomsticks. Keenan laughed but agreed. A bit different from samurai swords, but they'd do. Cash didn't want to see his guy hurt. He'd only rough him up a little bit.

They began to circle each other, crouching low. Keenan tested him a couple of times with some fast jabs, but Jay spun away each time.

Keenan continued to toy with him with a few lunges, but Jay used his stick to block him, holding it wide above his head, then turning and striking at his side to get his ribs super-fast. Keenan blocked expertly, but Reeve was right; Jay was lightning fast. Everywhere Keenan went to strike, Jay pre-empted him and countered quickly to try and catch him off guard. Keenan had to admit that Jay was a worthy opponent.

Having seen enough, Keenan decided playtime was over and used his greater weight to pin Jay against the wall with his stick across his windpipe. "What about something a bit more close quarters?" Keenan said next to Jay's ear.

Still not fazed, despite being beaten, Jay grit out, "Anytime."

Keenan smiled and released him.

Reeve pulled out two daggers from a holster around his ribs and passed one to each of them. The others with Tia went to protest, but the guards were enjoying themselves too much and they all knew Jay had it coming to him. "Let them continue," Reeve said, pushing them back out of the way.

Keenan grinned at Jay. *Oh yeah ... Let's see what you got, Human.* Jay was focused, flipping the knife from hand to hand to feel its weight.

They began to circle each other again, crouching low, looking each other in the eye. One lapse in concentration could be disastrous. Keenan was sorely tempted to intimidate Jay by dropping his fangs and flooding his eyes, but resisted the urge in the spirit of fairness. He wanted to see what the guy had. So when he went for Jay and he put out his leg and tripped him over, he realized that he was a slippery fighter with a quick mind as well as fast reflexes. They rolled around in the dirt until they sprang to their feet again.

Again, Jay surprised him by dropping to the floor when Keenan came for him and putting his flat foot in his stomach and throwing him over his head. Keenan rolled and came back up onto his feet. Jay was waiting for him.

Fuck this, Keenan had seen enough and quickly unbalanced him and pinned him to the floor with his weight and his dagger to his throat.

Nobody around them made a sound. Even his guard mates didn't know what he'd do. Jay needed putting in his place.

"I could have killed you in the hospital and I could kill you now," Keenan whispered, and allowed a swirl of blood to enter his irises mere inches from Jay's face.

Jay's eyes widened, but Keenan could tell his brain still whirred, working on a way out. He was immobilised but not beaten, not by a long shot.

Keenan had to smile at the guy's gumption. He was either very brave or a complete nutter; he suspected it was the latter. "You don't give up, do you, even when you're pinned?" Keenan said.

When Jay said nothing, Keenan knelt back up, then stood and reached down with his hand. Jay took it and sprang to his feet, then walked back over to his group, where the two blokes patted his back in consolation.

Keenan pulled his T-shirt back over his head and walked over to him. "Have you sparred with daggers before?

Jay shook his head, "Would you teach me?"

Keenan nodded. Again, the bloke surprised him. Humble in defeat, he wasn't mouthing off or making excuses, just a simple request to show him how.

· · ·

THE LETTER SEALED with the royal crest arrived later that day and shocked them all. It said Dante was no longer Dubonnetti and Marco was assuming the throne, being the eldest, which was ridiculous as he had no Siren. It ordered Keenan to bring *his* Siren, along with Tia, to Ireland to pledge to Marco.

There was no fucking way he'd even entertain Marco getting his mitts on Lacy. He didn't like Dante, but the shock stunned them all and everyone disappeared to bed early, leaving him and Jay alone on the porch.

The silence gaped between them like the Grand Canyon.

"Do you want something stronger?" Jay said eventually.

"Sure," Keenan said.

Jay returned with a bottle of Jack Daniel's. "You know I won't let you take her to that prick?"

Keenan had to laugh; the guy was so confrontational, but he fascinated him. How he managed to survive in the Atlantean world, bag himself a Siren, and keep Dante in his place, he had no idea.

"You know I remembered you and Dante from before I came into this world?" Keenan said.

Jay's eyes shot to his in obvious surprise.

"You wouldn't remember me. I was tall, but I wasn't built back then."

Jay shook his head for him to elaborate.

"It was in a Blues – you know, an illegal club, in Mile End?"

Jay thought for a minute and nodded, falling in when it must have been.

"So you've known Dante all your life?"

"Pretty much."

"And you're fucking his wife?"

Jay gave him one of his dagger looks again. "What is this … you trying to pick a fight now?"

Keenan couldn't help laughing. "There you go again. I'm just trying to understand."

Jay breathed out loudly and sat back in his chair …

"I met her briefly when she was only sixteen, over your way, in East London. Even then, she was stunning," Jay said wistfully. "Then she just showed up out of the blue at my hotel a few months ago. We got together … neither of us knew what she was. Course, I knew she was different. Anyway … Marco found her, took her home … they found out she was Dante's," he said, pointing at Keenan's ring. "And instead of telling his brother straight away she was with me, the bastard kept it quiet, Dante married her and they became bound. The rest is history … nothing any of us could do about it."

Keenan sat back in his chair. It all made sense now, how they all put up with each other. None of them could help the situation they were in. "Lacy, that's my Siren, was my best friend; the closest person to me. We had no family growing up, just each other."

"Was?" Jay said.

"She doesn't know who I am … not a clue."

"Fuck."

Keenan felt his anger rising as he explained his sorry state of affairs. How it looked as though someone had wiped her mind and left her vulnerable to the likes of Marco. But Jay reminded him that you could force a Siren into the water, but no one could force them to accept anyone because she was a dangerous creature, even if she wasn't aware of it yet.

Strangely, Jay had made him feel better. Then the thought struck him, as Jay tried to allay some of his fears, reminding him of the bond, he could never have that with Tia. That had been the whole reason for the urgent delivery of elixir to his bedside. *Fuck*, she had nearly killed him by breathing her life's essence into him outside of the water. She'd kill him for sure if she ever got him in it.

When he clinked glasses with Jay and thanked him for the reminder, he decided that the bloke was all right; a fighter by nature just like himself, in a killer of a situation just like he was. And there was nothing the pair of them could do about it.

LACY BEGAN to unwind over the next few days. She passed the time in the library and learned as much as she could about her Atlantean heritage. And Ruby helped her order some clothes of her own from the Internet so she felt good about herself.

However, despite outward appearances, her longing for her lost love loomed over her constantly. It was always just out of reach in her thoughts. *Charlie.* No matter how hard she tried, she could never remember his face. She would then think of Keenan and her pulse would race, then in the guilt would tumble. It tore at her and robbed her of any peace.

She was mulling such thoughts while she sat and listened to the little musical box in her room, when there was a tap on the door.

"Come in," she called.

Ruby put her head around the door. "Hey, sorry to disturb you, but Marius asked me to come and get you for one last round of blood tests."

A pang of unease hit her stomach, but then anything pertaining to blood did that these days. "Really, I thought they were all done?" she said.

"No, just one more DNA to do with your sisters, or something?"

"Oh, okay," Lacy said, getting off the bed and she followed Ruby out of the room.

When they reached the sick room, there was just a nurse she'd never seen before and no one else around.

"Marius had to be somewhere. Don't worry, I said we could get it out of the way," Ruby said, smiling brightly.

The nurse extracted four vials of blood, wrote her name on each and then popped them into a little plastic box and placed them in the fridge.

"Come on, Lacy, let's go and get changed. We've got visitors in a while."

Lacy followed lethargically. Pretty soon, she was dressed in a pretty green blouse and navy-blue slacks.

Ruby wore her customary red in the form of a sweater and teamed it with jeans.

A loud bell announced there was someone was at the door. It was early evening.

"Come on," Ruby said, excited.

"Who's coming?" Lacy asked. Strangely, the only person she felt like seeing was Keenan.

"The Dubonnettis," Ruby said, pulling her quickly down the staircase.

When they reached the hall, a servant told them their guests were waiting in the drawing room. Ruby continued to pull her along. *Like, what was the rush?* She started to wonder if Ruby was romantically involved with one of them; she seemed so excited.

Ruby burst into the room and four men stood up.

Lacy stood in the doorway, scared to go in. Glancing around quickly, she saw three of the most beautiful men she'd ever seen. Weird, as Keenan popped into her head with that thought. And with them was an older gentleman who she assumed was their father.

The three younger men were all blond with a mop of hair the colour of straw and eyes the colour of the sea on a winter's day. And the way they stood was as if they knew they were 'all that', which, of course, they were.

Running a quick glance over them, she noticed each had on a ring the same as Keenan's, except theirs were green, *like Charlie's. Could she never escape it?*

"Ligeie," the older gentleman said. He pronounced it 'lee-shey', which was better than 'Liggy', which was how she'd tried to say it. He walked towards her. "I am Christian Dubonnetti."

She stood wide-eyed as he bowed over her hand and kissed it. Then he presented her to each of his sons, one by one: Stephan, Paulo and, lastly, Marco, the tallest of the three. They all kissed her hand; Marco lingered over it the most.

Lacy couldn't help taking a sideways glance at Ruby, who, for a second, looked like she wanted to kill her. Then she seemed to snap herself out of it when they all greeted her. She told them to make themselves comfortable and ordered them some drinks.

Lacy sat quietly as far away from everyone as possible, just spectating. It still amazed her to think they were all from another species. Then she chided herself that she was, in fact, more alien than them, if what she had learned was true.

She blinked and turned her head when she realized she was being spoken to. She was about to ramble some random reply when the door burst open and Marius marched into the room, accompanied by Drago and Louis, and the eldest member of the Santalini family, Andreas.

"What are you doing here, Dubonnetti? How dare you question our Siren without a designated chaperone?" Marius bellowed.

The older man, Christian, laughed sarcastically, "Come, Marius, is that any way to greet an old friend and cousin?"

Lacy looked from one to the other as if she were watching a good soap opera.

"This is a long way from Ireland for a social call, so please spit out the reason for your visit?"

Christian seemed to ignore Marius and turned in his chair to face Lacy again.

Shit, don't involve me.

"We understand that, as yet, you have not pledged to a prince or aligned to a family, Lacy?" He glanced slyly at Marius as he said the word 'family'.

She shifted uncomfortably in her seat and would rather she were invisible. *Fuck, what did she say to that?*

"You know as well as I do, she belongs to my brother," Marius said, glowering at him.

Then she found herself shouting angrily: "I don't belong to anyone!"

"Quite," Christian agreed, smiling at her. "You are your own person, with your own mind."

Marius looked at the ceiling, exasperated.

The tallest one, Marco, spoke up, "We would like to invite you to come home to Ireland with us and consider pledging to the Dubonnetti family?"

She was confused; she was under the impression that she was already going to pledge to a Dubonnetti – her sister's husband, Dante. *Bloody hell,* she found herself wishing Keenan were there for the umpteenth time that day.

"You have no right to invite any Siren, unless it is to pledge to your brother," Andreas said, speaking for the first time directly to Marco.

Then Marco dropped the bomb: "Dante's claim is void … I am the eldest now."

After a beat of silence, Marius thankfully bought some time; "But you have no pledges as yet, and as far as I am aware, your brother still has one backed by the Bonaci, so has a stronger claim than yours."

Go Marius. She wasn't sure why she was so glad Marius had stuck it to them. She had never met the brother, but she supposed it all boiled down to Keenan, as per usual.

Christian stood angrily, signalling that the meeting was over. The sons followed his lead. "We do not wish to force you, Lacy, but should you wish to align yourself to a family, we strongly advise you choose wisely and for the good of the Atlantean nation."

Although she felt like saying, 'thanks but no thanks', she inclined her head demurely, figuring she would avoid them at all costs after this.

Marius lost patience at Dubonnetti's impertinence and called for a servant to show them all out.

Lacy had forgotten all about Ruby throughout the whole drama and watched her follow the Dubonnettis out to the hall. She was curious to find out why she didn't share her brother's dislike of the Dubonnetti family, but realizing the attention was off her, she shot up to her room to escape.

There, she locked her door and ran to her window. She peered around the edge of the curtain down to the drive below.

She watched them all getting into their waiting limousine. She was about to move away from the window when she saw Ruby run outside and down the main steps to catch them before they went. Then Ruby took something from beneath her jumper and passed it to the tallest one, who put it under his jacket before the others could see. He then kissed Ruby. It was the kiss of intimate familiarity, the kiss of lovers.

The box was treated like it was precious. Whatever it was.

. . .

LACY HAD BEEN in bed for a couple of hours, unable to sleep, when she heard the echo of raised voices in the hallway downstairs. Curious, she crept out of bed, out of her room and to the balustrade that overlooked the hall.

She felt him before she saw him. A swoon, a flip of the stomach and she homed in on Keenan, flanked by two guards. He was in heated conversation with Marius, Vince, Dan and Rick. Keenan seemed to loom over them all.

Straining to hear what was being said, she held her breath when Keenan looked straight up into her eyes. He knew she'd been there the whole time. Their eyes locked for a moment, until his lowered and he resumed what he was saying to Marius.

Absently, she touched her throat. Her palms were sweaty and her heart pounded. She suddenly became conscious of how she must look and glanced to either side of her for witnesses. There was Ruby, standing in the shadows, her face blank and unreadable. Lacy stared at her, feeling she'd been caught out like a naughty child.

"I came to hear what was going on," she found herself explaining.

"So have I," Ruby replied quietly, her face unreadable.

Feeling uncomfortable, Lacy turned and went back to her room. Ruby didn't move.

CHAPTER 15

*A*fter checking that the immediate danger of Marco's visit had passed, Keenan went up to his room. He'd welcomed the excuse of going to help Lacy's sister's Protector as a way of giving them some needed space, but when Marius had phoned him in Montana to tell him that the Dubonnettis were sniffing around HQ, he'd hot-footed it home.

The Dubonnettis were already spreading rumours throughout the Atlantean world that Dante had been deposed as king and they were putting Marco forward as his replacement. But he'd checked out the info with Alfonzo Bonaci and found out that Dante was still king and backed by them. Also, having no Siren meant they couldn't hope to make a claim. So he'd torn home and was relieved to find Lacy where he'd left her.

It wasn't the only disturbing news. Some CCTV footage of the sick bay had revealed that the prisoner he'd brought in as Lacy's abductor had searched the room before he had been released. Keenan was convinced he was looking for the blood that was stored at the apartment. Thankfully it had been destroyed. His own stupidity in not seeing the full extent of his purpose made his blood boil.

He walked back into the dark bedroom and took off all his weapons and went to take a shower. Even with the shower turned to cold, it did nothing to lower his ramping temperature. The animal need to claim Lacy after the threat rode him hard. Especially when he knew she was awake and her blood would be surging through her rapidly beating heart. *Fuck,* he was almost hyperventilating.

Shit. He had to come out of the shower sometime. This was going to kill him, living like this. He walked back into the bedroom and brazened out his feelings and knife-edge nerves.

He rubbed himself dry and pulled on some sweatpants and moved towards his chair.

"Don't you get backache in that chair?" Lacy's small voice came from the bed.

He stopped dead. *Did he hear right?* He turned to face her.

She was facing the wall away from him. "I don't bite."

"But I do …"

"Tell me about it."

Keenan frowned, puzzled by what seemed to be … banter? *Was she flirting with him?*

Gingerly, he moved to the bed and lay on top of the covers, as far away from her as possible, with his legs crossed at the ankles.

"You weren't away long?" she said.

"I came back when I heard the Dubonnettis were here."

She turned over to face him. "Why … what's bad about that? Your sister seems to like them – Marco particularly?"

Keenan just grunted, "She would. They are trying to depose the king, Marco's own brother – your sister's husband. They need you to do it."

That explained a lot; how angry the Santalinis were, but not Ruby?

"Why doesn't Ruby share your opinion?" she asked.

Keenan turned onto his side to face her. "I don't really know her, Lace. She seems to be a bit wild." He searched her face for a few moments. "It was just me and you growing up."

Lacy found herself looking deep into his eyes and watching the now-familiar blood seep into them, swirl and disappear again.

"Why do your eyes do that?" She reached up her hand and touched her finger gently on the corner of his eye.

He flinched a little, then moved slightly into her touch. "Strong emotion; particularly anger."

She trailed a finger down to his mouth. "Are you angry now?" she whispered.

He didn't answer, but parted his mouth slightly so she could touch the exposed tip of his canine, which elongated in front of her eyes.

"Amazing," she said in wonder.

She edged herself closer to him in the bed so she was just a few inches apart and on the same pillow as him. Feeling brave, she leaned forward and brushed her lips against his, and felt heat pulse through her body, from her chest outwards. A hot bolt sent a pool of wetness between her legs. *God*, this man had such a physical effect on her.

She brushed her lips on his again. This time, his tongue gently stroked the seam of hers. Another wave of heat surged through her body and she opened her mouth and tentatively met his tongue with hers. She gently stroked and swirled her tongue and his wonderful taste entered her senses. She moaned her appreciation.

Her chest ached with a pain she was growing accustomed to when she got anywhere near him. It was something she didn't understand. The pain went down to her womb and throbbed with an overwhelming need to fill it – with him. She began to pant.

Keenan rolled on top of her in one smooth, fluid move and, without permission, kissed her fully and deeply. He pushed his weight against her hips so she had to open her legs to relieve the pressure. He was then free to nudge at her core.

Ah, bloody hell. With him this close to her, she was filled with an all-consuming need for him. Her hands flew up to his back and she scored the smooth skin with her nails to urge him onward. Her eyes rolled up into her head when he answered her by undulating his hips and nudging further.

Driven mad, she began to meet his hips with hers, creating more friction.

Suddenly, he leaned up on his elbows and stopped.

Confused, she opened her eyes to stare up at him and frowned.

He was staring down at her, eyes narrowed. "What is this?" He shook his head slowly as if he didn't trust her.

She continued to frown but didn't say anything. *What had she done wrong?*

He touched her temple with his head at an angle, "What's in here … Do you think I'm like some school boy who can't control himself?"

She was shocked, not understanding what he was getting at all. She was just going with how she felt, plain and simple. Sick of questioning her impulses continually, she'd wanted him.

Apparently, that was the wrong thing to do.

"You wanted me to touch you since you were an underage little girl, Lace. I didn't take you until early this year."

Still confused, she was at a loss for what to say.

He sprang off her.

She sat up, shocked, feeling foolish and vulnerable.

Keenan dragged a T-shirt over his head. "The next time you want to scratch an itch, have the decency to admit it … and don't try to instigate a situation which takes away your guilt."

He stormed into the bathroom and slammed the door.

Her jaw was still open. She felt slapped. *Shit.*

She looked about the room for help, processing what he'd said. He was totally right about her, *wasn't he?* How could he possibly know how guilty she always felt around him?

She slid out of bed, padded over and tapped on the bathroom door.

"What?" she heard quietly from the other side.

She pushed the door wide without walking into the room. He was leaning over the sink, grasping the edges as if he'd just splashed his face. He turned to look at her with a blank 'what now?' expression.

"You're right … and I'm sorry, I really am."

She expected some sort of reply, but he stayed in the same position and blinked, willing her on.

"I don't understand my body's reaction to you … but in my head, he's still there. And my heart … I miss him so much.

He looked back down at the water in the sink, took a deep breath and looked like he was getting a hold on himself, and when he looked back at her, the amount of blood in his eyes scared her for a second. "What does he look like?" He asked the question like he was sick of asking it.

"That's just it … I start at his feet, I look upwards. He is big, strong and tall, like you, but when I get to his face … it's just not there. I try so hard. I can't …" She began to tear up, in frustration more than anything.

Keenan didn't listen to her any more. He pushed past her and out of the bedroom.

· · ·

KEENAN BARGED into Vince's room, which was in darkness. He paced up and down on the carpet a few times and then sat on the end of the bed, stirring Vince as the mattress dipped.

Vince raised his head, bleary-eyed. "Come on in, why don't cha?" Vince said, lifting his head up. "She turn you down again?"

"No she didn't, funnily enough," Keenan said with his head in his hands and his elbows on his knees.

Vince pushed his elbows underneath him and leaned up. "Excuse me for being thick, but what are you doing here?"

"She fucking loves him, Vince," Keenan said, turning his pained face to his friend. *Fuck*, he wanted to punch something.

"But she fancies you?" Vince said in confusion.

Keenan dropped his hands, "Well … yeah."

Vince shook his head in disbelief, "What you doin' here then, mate? If it was me, I'd give her such a good seeing to she'd forget what day it was, let alone some bloke completely off the scene."

Keenan stared at Vince, then looked around. Then looked at Vince again. Then stood up while his brain whirred over what his friend had said.

Then he strode back out of the room.

Vince lay back down on his pillow and chuckled.

KEENAN BARGED BACK into his room and found it empty. The sound of running water told him she was in the bathroom.

He knocked.

"What?"

He pushed the door open to find her standing naked, testing the temperature of the water with her hand.

Lacy gasped and her eyes went wide when she saw him. She didn't move when he reached her in two strides, grabbed her and spun her so her back slammed into his chest and his forearm went across her neck, he held her to him by the opposite shoulder.

He positioned them so they could see themselves in the large mirror above the sink. He towered above her. She looked tiny in comparison.

He ran his free hand down the front of her body and parted her legs with his foot. He tilted her forward slightly, and brought his hand up the inside of her thigh until it glided through her wetness.

Pleased, he heard her gasp.

She closed her eyes and leaned back into him.

He brought the hand up and pushed her head roughly off his body. "Open your eyes," he demanded. "You keep your eyes open when I fuck you. Do you hear me?"

A look of fear and shock covered her face. Her eyes were wild, but she remained quiet, breathing hard.

"Do you hear me?" he demanded again. She had to understand where he was coming from.

He gave her neck a rough squeeze to answer.

"Y…yes," she managed

"You will know it's *me* fucking you." And he pulled his sweatpants down and out of the way, bent her forward over the sink, making sure he held her face up by her hair, and plunged into her hard.

Keenan fucked her relentlessly and mercilessly. All his pent-up frustration came pouring out of him and into her. With every cry that came out of her mouth, it only caused him to bury himself deeper and faster.

He pushed her into the shower and flat against the wall and bombarded her small body under the cooling spray. But every time she went to close her eyes and moan in ecstasy, he would grab her head and demand she open her eyes, and say his name as she cried out when she came.

Over and over he made her shout it, and as a last mark of complete domination, he bit her neck savagely when his own release overtook him.

He drew her blood deeply within him as he pushed his seed deeply within her, to mark her psyche clearly, and to leave her in no shadow of a doubt that she had been well and truly fucked by Keenan Santalini. And if she didn't love him, she was going to bloody well love to fuck him, and need him like no one else.

LACY FELT BONELESS, exhausted and strangely cold in the shower when she came back to her senses after the sex of her life. Not that she remembered having much sex before, but if she had, this would have topped it, for sure.

Her teeth began to chatter.

"You're cold. Come on, I'll dry you and warm you up in bed … I've taken too much of your blood." And gentle Keenan replaced stern Keenan.

She allowed him to lead her from the shower, wrap her in two large fluffy white towels, and lay her on the bed.

Keenan rested half next to her and half on top of her to warm but not squash her. She lay there, still and quiet, staring up into his eyes while he brushed the hair from her face. She studied him, trying to work him out.

That she was madly attracted to him, she was in no doubt, but he still felt like a stranger and scared her a lot of the time.

He interrupted her thoughts. "Do you have a bond with him, Lace?"

She frowned, not fully understanding what he meant.

"Did you swim with him?"

She shook her head, puzzled. *What did swimming have to do with anything?*

"Did you swap blood?'

"God, no," she said. As if the thought was disgusting to her.

"You have one with me," he said, his voice gone husky with emotion. A flicker of blood crossed his irises.

Strangely, she wasn't repulsed by that revelation and trailed a finger down his face. "What does it do … the blood bond?"

"On a practical level, it allows us to keep our body temperature lower than other Atlanteans," he said, kissing her finger, "during sex," he added.

Then he smiled to himself as if remembering a beautiful memory; "It's the closest thing between two people … like an aphrodisiac." He closed his eyes. "You can feel them whenever they are near." He opened his eyes again. "We Santalini are lucky to have it. The only thing closer is the Siren's bond."

She narrowed her eyes and waited for him to explain.

Keenan shook his head, "It's one of the things I'm not allowed to tell you, but soon you will be married to your sister's mate." His face hardened, his eyes went distant, then he looked at her again, "Then, if you choose, you can bind me to you in the same way … that is, bind me or kill me," he said, going to push away from her.

She gripped his arm to stop him, "Wait. What are you saying?"

"That is your power, Lace, to bind or to kill." He pushed off her and swung his legs round over the edge of the bed. Not letting him off the hook, she followed him and sat next to him.

"That first night, when you pushed me under the shower and I scratched you … your blood … it was like …"

He looked at her and nodded.

Her eyes became heavy at the memory. "That feeling …"

"You've been bonded to me since you were a small baby, Lace," he said, watching her face intently.

Lacy couldn't help but watch the rhythmical tick of his pulse at the side of his neck.

"You want to drink from me?" he asked, quietly.

She swallowed hard and looked into his eyes. Her heart was thumping and the heat was pooling between her thighs at the mere thought of it.

Briefly, Charlie – or rather the association of him– popped into her head, slamming a pang of guilt into her and she closed her eyes with the pain. *But oh, she wanted this.*

Keenan gave her no chance to talk herself out of it and reached over to grab one of his knives from the holster he'd left on the chair. He knelt on the floor in front of her until his body pushed between her knees and his eyes were level with hers; just a few inches from her face.

He took the knife and slowly scored a downward cut on his neck and her eyes zoomed in on it. His eyelids lowered as if he knew what it did to her. Her breath sped up. Her chest hurt with the strength of her beating heart. And there was something other–something big, clambering to escape.

She looked from his neck to his eyes and then back again. She was almost hyperventilating; she was breathing so fast. *Shit ... she mustn't.*

"Take it," Keenan whispered. "Take blood from me ... you need it."

She wailed in fury, frustration and then need. She grabbed his shoulders and latched onto his neck hard, with her mouth open wide, and groaned with the heady satisfaction of the earthy, fragrant taste.

The noise that came from Keenan's chest was a growl, "Fuck, Lace, yes." He tugged the towels away from her body so she was naked, and pulled her over the edge of the bed to his kneeling lap, where his waiting erection strained for her.

She felt him pull her slowly down until he nudged at her. Already needing him and aroused, she sucked harder as she realized what he was going to do. Then he pulled her down onto him, all the way. She would have thrown her head back if the fantastic taste hadn't got her totally hooked.

God, yes ... she wanted all of him, inside her in every way. She ground onto him until he groaned next to her ear. She nearly let go as the sensation of fullness almost overwhelmed her completely and she bit him with her teeth to stay joined to his neck.

"Ah fuck, yeah ..." Keenan moaned.

He seemed to love that she was using him in this way, giving her everything. He lifted her, taking her weight in his arms easily and laying her on the floor without leaving her body or breaking the seal of her blissful bite.

Once he had leverage, he pounded into her over and over until she was forced to let go with her mouth to cry out with him with their release. The crescendo blew her brain and both of them came apart in a heap on the floor.

They were left panting for breath and sweating, with the heat of their bodies dangerously high.

Keenan fell off her onto his back. They were both blissfully sated and looked up at the ceiling while they gradually cooled.

Feelings and jumbled thoughts vied for attention: Charlie, Keenan, sex and want. It was bewildering. She turned her head to face him. "Why do you bother with me, Keenan?"

He turned his head to face her, and a red blush still lingered on his cheeks. "You are my most compatible mate in the world, Lace. I've loved you ever since I can remember."

My god, such vulnerability and honesty ... She touched his face and wished with all her heart that she could remember him.

CHAPTER 16

That night, Lacy drifted off into a comfy, blissful sleep easier than she had in a long while. The glut she had taken of Keenan's blood fortified her from the loss of her own, and made her drowsy and warm in the way of a good wine.

For the first time in memory, she lay with Keenan intertwined like lovers amongst the sheets. It seemed pointless, Keenan now sleeping on the chair and she welcomed his body next to hers.

Everything felt so right – so in tune.

Keenan told her that they often crept into each other's bed in the dead of night when they were small children to innocently hold hands, and sometimes she would let him drink from her when his teeth hurt or he needed comfort.

Yes, she could really fall for this man. If it wasn't for the spectre of Charlie always in her mind like a dark shadow – a shadow that she pushed to the back of her mind repeatedly over the following hours. The house seemed to know and left them alone despite their not venturing out of the room the whole of the following day and into the night.

The beautiful minutes of half wakefulness, when she delighted in the feel of him next to her, were then ruined by an incessant knocking at their door.

"Keenan … Keenan!"

She opened her eyes fully when she became aware, and gently rocked Keenan's shoulder. "Keenan," she whispered. "Vince is at the door."

He opened his eyes drowsily and rolled onto his back to listen, then rolled to face her, looking sleepily into her eyes and smiling the most beautiful smile of recognition – fangs and all. *Wow.*

"What, Vince?" Keenan answered, not taking his eyes from hers.

Vince opened the door and came into the room a little at a time, with his hands covering his eyes dramatically in case they weren't decent. "Sorry, guys."

"What's up, Vince?" Keenan's amusement at his friend's discomfort fell away immediately when he realised that it must be something serious.

"It's Lacy's sister. She's been taken. We're all going to Montana." Vince turned and left Keenan to get ready.

Keenan turned back to face her. His eyes showed regret. Their period of closeness was being abruptly brought to an end.

Then he seemed to come to a decision: "I'm not leaving you here, Lace. Get ready, you're coming."

JUST FIVE HOURS later and they were leaving the large Santalini plane, which was more like a US troop carrier than a private passenger jet. They transferred to a convoy of three SUVs to take them from Billings Airport to Cash Reynolds' ranch, around two hours east.

Keenan held her hand throughout the whole journey. She

didn't mind, she kind of liked it. He didn't seem so moody and angry around her any more. As if he'd accepted that she didn't remember him and what she was able to give him, which took the pressure off her.

They pulled into the long, flat drive to the ranch just as the sun was rising. There was beautiful pasture on either side of the road, dotted by all different colour horses.

"Are you okay?" Keenan asked.

She realised she must have been frowning when she turned to face him and smiled, "I just realised that I could be meeting my sister, my first real relative, for the first time."

A look of sadness flashed across Keenan's face. She was about to ask why when he interrupted her, "Let's pray we can get her back for you then." Then he smiled and kissed her forehead.

LACY STUCK CLOSE to Keenan as they trooped into the ranch house.

She was introduced to Cash and Sean immediately and told they were two of her sister's Protectors. She liked them.

Marius had told her that Protectors were Atlanteans destined for the job of protecting a Siren, like a lifelong bodyguard.

Vince, Rick and Dan were hers, but the honour had been bestowed on them, and she thought of them more as Keenan's friends than hers. *But hey, what did she know.*

The house was filling up with Santalini soldiers who had travelled from all destinations to prepare for whatever rescue operation was arranged for them.

Lacy stuck close to Keenan's side, not sure what good she was doing there, really.

Activity seemed to be happening in the kitchen and soon whispers reached their ears that the king had arrived.

Shit. It suddenly occurred to her that he was her sister's husband, the one she was supposed to marry herself any day now. She must have betrayed her nerves as Keenan gave her hand a little squeeze.

Two men walked into the large lounge and she was physically struck by how good-looking they were. However, when she glanced around her, there wasn't a bad-looking male in the room. The Santalini were a good-looking bunch, *or was it the Atlantean genes?* Those two weren't Santalini.

Lacy watched Keenan as he reached out and shook the tall dark one's hand and then the blond one with startling blue eyes, and thought he was every bit as beautiful as the two of them, but he was lethal as well, like a warrior. Butterflies tickled her stomach.

Someone was speaking to her. She stopped staring at Keenan and blinked herself awake. The dark one was being introduced to her as Dante.

He smiled warmly and looked deep into her eyes. She thought his eyes looked mischievous and found him unsettling.

"You can tell she's her sister," he said, and all three of them agreed.

The blond, incredibly handsome one, seemed much more serious. He said hello and was introduced to her as Jay, then he looked straight back to Keenan, his mind clearly elsewhere.

Lacy felt a little lost and sheltered behind Keenan's big body. She longed to be on her own. The last forty-eight hours had been overwhelming and she'd had very little sleep. Thankfully, it didn't take long for Cash to tell them he had a room made up for them.

Keenan told Jay to call him if any news came in and nudged her towards the stairs, telling her they needed some sleep. He didn't know when he'd be called to action.

Cash led the way, showed them into a comfortable, large room and explained where all the facilities were. She thanked him and he left them alone.

Keenan walked into the bathroom and began to run her a deep bubble bath. "You always preferred baths to showers," he explained.

She raised her eyebrows in acknowledgement. The thought of soaking her aching muscles was really appealing. Her nerves felt shot to pieces; she was as jumpy as hell, probably because she'd had so little sleep. "Do you want to bathe with me?" she asked, cautiously.

He stopped sloshing the water around, making bubbles and stared at her for a bit. "Yeah … I'd love it," he said quietly and resumed stirring the water.

When it was ready, they both stripped off and he helped her in and cradled her between his knees. Then he settled her back against his chest so he could look over her shoulder and cup the cool water in his hands and trickle it over her chest and shoulders. It was wonderful.

"Do you remember we bathed like this after the very first time we made love on the way to America?" he asked.

She racked her brains – nothing. She couldn't remember past the dingy flat she'd spent the last year in. "No." She grabbed onto his hand. "I'm sorry, Keenan. I don't remember anything, even the last year is a haze."

He nodded quietly next to her shoulder. "It'll come, don't worry," he said, dismissing his sadness, and grabbed a washcloth and soap to gently wash her. "What did you think of Dante and Jay?" he asked.

"They seemed okay," she said warily, not sure where the conversation was going.

"Your sister is bound to both of them," he said, running the flannel over her legs.

"Is that like what you were saying last night about marrying Dante but having your own partner?"

"Sort of, but their situation is more complicated … Dante is her mate, you know, like you're mine."

"His ring, you mean?"

"Yeah, but she'd already met and fallen for Jay, who happens to be Dante's best friend."

"But she is with Jay, though?" she said, not seeing the problem.

"Yeah, but imagine how hard it would be for us not to touch each other … nigh on impossible."

She thought about her situation with Charlie and, strangely, hearing about her sister's predicament made her feel a bit better about her own. "So she can't help herself with Dante then?"

Keenan sighed and shook his head, "I don't think so. It's a bastard for Jay, though. He's Human as well."

"So he's the one you took the medicine to the other day?"

"Yeah, she nearly killed him."

"Oh," she said, shocked. *And she thought her life was complicated.* It was probably a good thing that Charlie was not on the scene. She didn't think Keenan would be as lenient toward anything like that. "Will you be okay with me bonding with this Dante?"

Keenan thought about it for a moment, "Not really, but at least you're not attracted to him."

"I dunno… he's very good-looking."

Keenan stiffened and looked sideways at her for a second. Then pinched her sides as she giggled. "That was so like the old you, Lace … You have no idea, do you."

She shrugged.

"You tortured me unmercifully for years, trying to make me jealous."

"Really … why?"

He sank lower in the water and turned her to face him so she lay on top of him. "So I would lose my control and make you mine."

"And did you?"

He nodded and smiled a wicked smile. "Oh yeah … you won in the end … I had to have you." He pulled her up to his mouth and kissed her thoroughly. "You were always mine, though Lace," he whispered.

Her worries drifted away momentarily as he crushed her in his arms and she pushed her tongue wantonly into his mouth. "Were you always mine?" she whispered between kisses.

"Always."

THEY SLEPT most of the day and into the evening. Hunger then got the better of them, so Keenan made her get up and took her down to the kitchen.

Santalini guards were still hanging around everywhere, awaiting news on when they were to pull out. Those who didn't have bedrooms bunked in with the stable staff and some were even in the outbuildings.

Lacy was amazed at how many there were; at least thirty or forty, it was hard to tell.

Cash welcomed them warmly and clapped Keenan on the back. "Just tell Mrs Ross what you want to eat and she'll rustle you something up," he said.

"Where's Jay?" Keenan asked.

"Out on the porch. I think he got a call from Dante … he's on his way back from D.C."

Mrs Ross made them a sandwich and gave them both a cold beer and they took it outside to join Jay.

He was just clicking off his phone when they got there.

"All right?" Keenan said.

"All right," Jay replied.

Lacy managed a small smile.

"What did he find out?" Keenan asked.

"We're out of here as soon as he gets back. They're holding her at an airbase a couple of hours north of here."

Keenan nodded and swigged his beer.

Jay fascinated her. He was all simmering, intense broodiness. She wondered how her sister could possibly get close to someone like that.

"We'll get her back, mate," Keenan said.

She could see that Keenan really felt for him and her heart melted further at his compassion.

"Yeah ... we will," Jay said. There was no smile, just a steely, ice-cold determination.

It made her shiver.

Jay pushed his fingers through his hair like he didn't know what else to do with himself.

"You wanna drink?" Keenan asked and got up to go back inside.

Don't leave me here, she silently pleaded.

"Go on then," Jay said, exhaling loudly.

Lacy began to bite her nails. She wasn't sure if she usually bit her nails, but it seemed a good idea at the time.

She needn't have bothered, Jay just looked ahead of him, a million miles away.

Thankfully, Keenan soon came back with a bottle of Bourbon and three glasses. He poured them each a glass and passed them round. She didn't even know if she liked the stuff.

She pulled a face when she took a gulp, and Keenan grinned at her. "Yuk!" She coughed and spluttered.

Keenan laughed out loud and Jay looked over at them. "Just testing," Keenan said. "You never liked whiskey."

She playfully hit him in the shoulder.

"Tia doesn't drink anything else," Jay said, silencing them and drawing their attention to him.

Lacy looked into his eyes and for a split second she was sure she saw despair. Then he snapped himself out of it and downed his drink in one.

"Tell Lacy about her Jay. I've not been much use," Keenan said, trying to cheer him up.

Jay poured himself another drink and sat back in his chair, deep in thought. As he creased his brow and secretly smiled to himself, she realized how deeply he loved her, although she was sure he must rarely show it.

"Well ..." he started. "She loves music ... She's a brilliant DJ. She's a good laugh ... She's tough in a lot of ways ... except," and he trailed off and frowned, "she's not always confident, but she hides it well."

Lacy looked at Keenan, who was enraptured by Jay's description of her. It wasn't really what he said, but more the strength of feeling behind it that was so evident.

She wondered how he must feel about the king, his best friend, sharing the woman he loved? It must be devastating. "What's the bond like?" *Shit, had she spoken out loud?*

Both men looked at her, surprised for a few beats, until Jay eventually answered, "It's the closest thing you'll ever have with another person ... I was gonna say Human?" he laughed, but his eyes held a hopelessness that she couldn't miss. Then he drained his glass again. "Course, mine is only one-sided." He stood up. "Dante will be back in a couple of hours," he said directly to Keenan. "I'm going to have a rest for a bit."

"I'll be ready," Keenan said.

Jay nodded and walked back inside.

Keenan shook his head after he'd disappeared.

Lacy put her hand up and touched Keenan's hair.

"I don't know how he's holding it together, Lace?"

"Were you like that? I mean, when I went?"

He looked at her in amazement. "Fuck, Lace. I was like a rabid animal for weeks. We hadn't been apart since we were babies, and suddenly you were ripped away from me."

She swallowed hard; the thought that she could have been the cause of such pain, and having no knowledge of it, was heartbreaking.

"God, Keenan, I'm so sorry."

He pulled her to him. She nuzzled and breathed in his wonderful smell at the crook of his neck.

"It's not your fault, babe," he said, holding her tight.

She felt the tension in his jaw and knew he was thinking about what he was going to do to Charlie.

CHAPTER 17

It was in the small hours of the morning that the door was rapped loudly. "Keenan. Be ready to leave in ten," someone shouted.

Keenan rolled off the bed immediately, and Lacy went to rouse herself as well. "Stay," he said, placing a gentle hand on her side.

"No, I'll come down and see you off."

The lights were switched on and she hurriedly dressed in what she'd worn previously.

Keenan had a two-minute shower and dressed quickly in his black T-shirt and fatigues and then meticulously placed weapon after weapon around his body, various knives in holsters at his back, chest and at his calves. Then he pulled out a long chunky case, flipped the catches and took out black metal pieces, which he clipped and assembled into a submachine gun with ease. Finally, he shoved rounds of ammunition in the array of pockets in the tough-looking jacket that he put on last.

He stood up and faced her. "Ready," he said.

He looked savage and beautiful. The water from his

shower still clung to his hair and glistened in the light, and his eyes swirled with blood in readiness for the fight.

He looked devastatingly hot, but the reality of what he actually did for a living scared her for the first time. She touched her throat in fear that he might not come home. She shook herself and walked over to him. "Be careful." She didn't know whether to touch him or not.

He had no such qualms and pulled her to him. He kissed her gently but sensually. She gave herself over to it for the briefest moment. He smelled delicious and clean. Her stomach fluttered. She pushed herself away from him before she betrayed her sissy fear by deepening their kiss when he had to go.

He smiled as if he was pleased with her. *Did he know?* He held her hand and led her out of the room and down towards the assembled men below.

When they reached the bottom of the stairs, Vince, Rick and Dan greeted them. Keenan was pleased, as always, to see them, but looked at them with a query as to why they weren't dressed for fighting.

"Marius ordered us to stay with Lace while you go off playing soldiers."

Keenan laughed and pulled all three into his big arms. "Nice," he said.

Lacy was starting to learn just how deep Keenan's bond was with his boys.

Everyone stopped chattering and turned towards the large fireplace when Dante started speaking. He outlined the plan. He was taking a small unit of Cash, Jay, Sean, Keenan and around eight of the best Santalini Guards.

There would be a second standby unit on hand should things go wrong and the remainder of the soldiers would guard the royal Siren left at the ranch.

Lacy blushed when she felt all eyes on her.

"We'll take three SUVs to the helicopter point and from there go straight into the base. Any questions?" Dante asked as he looked around the room.

"Yeah," Keenan piped up, "how long do we have when we're in there?"

"Ten minutes. That's all. We're in and out."

She saw Keenan curse at the small window of time and her unease intensified. She wanted to ask him not to go but she knew that would be wrong of her.

Everyone started to grab their weapons and move out. Keenan gave some last-minute instructions to his boys.

Lacy stiffened when she saw Dante and Jay make their way over to where she and Keenan stood. Jay nodded at her, but remained aloof and quiet as usual. Dante looked drawn and tired. Then again, he probably hadn't slept much over the last few hours, spending most of it on a plane.

He still managed a rakish grin as he passed her and stopped. "Be ready to come to Ireland, Lacy, when we get back," he said in his rich Irish accent. Then he winked at her and glanced at Keenan, who clenched his jaw and wasn't laughing.

Then Jay touched Dante's arm to get his attention. "You should stay here, Dante. It's too dodgy for you to be there," he said.

Lacy supposed it was dodgy because he was king.

"I have the link, Jay. I have to be there." Dante touched his temple with his finger.

"No, let him go, Jay," Keenan said with a humourless grin.

Dante barked a laugh and turned to Lacy. "Your man doesn't want me here with you, Lacy." Then he looked sideways at Keenan. "Come on, Keenan. Use some of that pent-up aggression on someone who needs it." Then he walked out with Jay, Cash and Sean following him closely.

Keenan stopped in front of her and picked up both of her hands. "I'll be back tomorrow … later today now, I guess."

She felt her eyes misting up. "Be careful."

"Stick close to the boys … You hear me?" he ordered. Then he rushed out to join the others.

THEN CAME THE AGONIZING WAIT.

The house still seemed full of soldiers. All were passing the time texting on their phones, chatting, drinking and having a laugh. Vince, Rick and Dan were with a bunch, playing cards.

Lacy realized there were two other women in the house: Mrs Ross, the housekeeper, and Sarah, Sean's wife, who hadn't long had a baby. She hadn't come out of her room at all while Lacy had been there. Apparently, she'd been there when her sister had been taken and was upset and shaken.

Wandering around aimlessly, Lacy found herself in the kitchen in the hope of offering some help with anything. Mrs Ross was jiggling the baby in her arms while she was warming up some formula. She smiled at Lacy warmly.

"Is there anything I can do? The wait is killing me."

"You could take the baby for a second while I make up his bottle."

She reached out and took the impatient bundle. "What's his name?" she asked.

"Ronnie," Mrs Ross said.

"Is his mum okay?"

"Yes, she's fine. Just a bit shook up."

Then everything became a bit of a blur. It was like one of those creepy thriller movies where everything slows down. One minute Mrs Ross was busying herself rattling pots and pans, then her mobile phone rang. She took it out of her apron pocket and began a conversation while she worked.

"Hi … yes, she's here … she won't … I have the baby … don't worry … okay. I'll pass you to her." Then she stopped speaking and looked over at Lacy, stony-faced. "He wants to speak to you."

Despite her haze, she was shocked. Lacy looked at the woman and frowned. *Who on earth would want to speak to her?* But as she had the thought, ice started to creep through her veins. Slowly, she moved towards the phone being held out to her and took it gingerly. She put it to her ear and remained quiet.

Beautiful music tinkled like an old-fashioned piano. "Charlie, is that you?" she said, in a small childlike voice, so unlike her.

Her heart stopped.

"Hello, Lacy … where did you go? I came home from work and the place was empty, our beautiful children gone." The Italian accent purred.

Everything seemed to grind to a halt like a freeze frame on a film.

After a moment, Mrs Ross took the baby but smiled benignly at her.

"I … I … didn't have a choice," she blabbered.

"My beautiful Leeshay … don't worry. I forgive you. In a moment, you will forget you spoke to me. Mrs Ross is your best friend. You trust her implicitly … say yes if you agree?"

"Yes, Charlie," Lacy said.

"You will go up and befriend Sarah, but when you are alone with her, you will tell her that she has nothing to fear, because you know Malleven. Say the name, Lacy."

"Malleven," she repeated.

"Again."

"Malleven … Malleven … Malleven … Malleven."

The beautiful music sounded again, then she looked at Mrs Ross. She touched her head; a bad headache had crept over her. "There is no one there," Lacy said, handing her back her phone.

"Oh, maybe it was your lovely Santalini. Probably lost his signal." Mrs Ross smiled brightly. She passed Lacy some Advil. "Take a couple … Do you want to come up with me and see Sarah? She'll be glad of the company."

Vince wandered into the kitchen, "There you are, Lace … You okay?"

Lacy smiled and nodded.

"She's got a headache," Mrs Ross said. "I'm taking her up to meet Sarah, okay? … Then I'll make you boys some breakfast."

Vince smiled broadly, "You're a diamond, Mrs Ross."

LACY FOLLOWED Mrs Ross into Sarah's room and they found her asleep. She soon became aware that someone was there and began to rouse herself. She beamed a smile when her eyes lit upon little Ronnie. He held his arms out and chugged an impatient cry.

Lacy blinked in shock when she watched Sarah snatch him from Mrs Ross' arms and cling to him as if she hadn't seen him in ages. Probably delayed shock, she guessed.

Then Sarah looked accusingly at Mrs Ross and screamed, "Get out!" It made the baby cry. Her eyes pinned the woman with venom.

Lacy's eyes went wide. *Bloody hell, what was she meant to do?*

Mrs Ross just seemed to ignore the whole thing and buzzed around the room picking up washing, baby toys and some glasses for washing up. Lacy just stared at her in disbelief.

"She's overwrought … I'll be right downstairs."

'Shall I? …" Lacy said, and went to follow her.

"No … No … stay and keep her company." Then Mrs Ross left the room.

Lacy stood frozen, not knowing what to say or do.

Sarah busied herself feeding the baby and rocking him in her arms.

"Are you okay?" Lacy asked, thinking her actions were a little manic.

"I saw them … you know … take her … I saw … they kept Ronnie so I went … I had no choice in the end."

Lacy listened to her ramblings sympathetically. "You're safe now."

"I am now I have my son, and that bitch is gone."

For a minute, she thought she was referring to her sister, Tia, but realized she must mean Mrs Ross. "I'm sure she is only trying to help?"

Sarah narrowed her eyes on her, "What do you know, anyway?"

"I would like to be friends … that's all. I'm the only other girl here."

Then Lacy was struck with absolute horror as Sarah began crying and calling for help and crawling with her son to the furthest point in the room. She was screeching over and over, "Get away … get away from me and my baby."

Lacy stood up and stepped closer, then stopped and turned to the door. *Fuck, what should she do?* "Sarah, what's the matter?"

The door flew open and Vince stood in the doorway. Then his body sagged in relief when he saw Lacy standing there in one piece. Sarah was whimpering next to the wall and the baby was crying his lungs out.

"I don't know what happened, Vince," Lacy spluttered. "One minute I was chatting to her, the next she started screaming."

Vince bundled her out of the room, and another guard

passed them and went in. She heard him ask Sarah if she wanted Mrs Ross?

Then Sarah began screaming again. "No … no, she knows Malleven. They all know Malleven."

The door closed sharply and Lacy allowed Vince to lead her to her own room. "I don't know what I did, Vince?"

"Don't worry, Lace, she's had a nasty shock, that's all."

She was still shaking when she reached her room. She longed for Keenan to wrap her in his big arms, as only he seemed to be able to do.

It wasn't until some time later, when she'd got back into bed, that she thought of Charlie. She wasn't sure what sparked the thoughts, but into her head they tumbled, along with the usual guilt. It seemed that the closer she got to Keenan, the worse she felt about betraying Charlie. *Was she going mad?* After everything that Keenan and Marius had told her, he was still a ghost haunting her.

Slowly, she drifted off into a troubled sleep. Her dreams were disturbed visions of Keenan leaving her, Sarah screaming, a baby crying, and the name Malleven repeated over and over.

It was lunchtime when she heard the sound of cars coming into the yard, then men's voices and the slam of car doors. They were back.

Lacy jumped out of bed and ran to the window. Her heart thumped when she saw Keenan, unhurt, looking as lethally handsome as ever. *No! She mustn't keep thinking like that.* She must resist him. She mustn't allow herself to weaken where he was concerned. She must stop whatever it was between them to lessen the damage. If she could just assure Charlie that she was confused and weak, then maybe he would forgive her.

Then her eyes moved to Dante helping a girl out of the back seat of the first vehicle in what looked like a lab coat, sunglasses and little else.

Lacy put a hand to her mouth when she saw the state of her hair and the pallor of her skin. Then the girl struggled and ran into the arms of Jay, who was unloading a bag from the car behind.

He was stiff and wooden when the girl clung to him. *What was wrong with him?*

Her eyes tracked back to Dante, who was watching in sad resignation. She felt for him then, a witness to his heartbreak. He walked slowly over to the couple and said something to Jay and bent down to speak to the girl clinging to his chest. Then he touched Jay's arm affectionately, turned and walked slowly back to his car and got back inside.

She found herself welling up, and decided that Dante wasn't a bad guy; he probably just hid behind a lot of bravado. She would try to get to know him, she decided. Perhaps her own situation was not too dissimilar to her sister's, after all; they were both stuck between two men.

With a sad heart, she moved away from the window and made her way towards the door. She had to see Keenan sometime, and decided to get it over with.

Lacy was standing at the top of the stairs, mustering the courage to go down when Keenan came bounding up. He stopped on the first landing and stared up at her.

She stared back but didn't say anything.

"What's wrong?" he asked, his face cautious.

"Nothing ... did everything go okay?"

He climbed the last few stairs slowly until he stopped right in front and loomed over her, "We got her, but she's a bit of a mess."

Lacy nodded but didn't meet his eyes.

"She'll be okay in a few days," he continued.

Lacy still said nothing and wouldn't look at him.

"Lace?"

She allowed her eyes to finally meet his. He looked at her for a beat, then, as if he sensed she'd gone cold on him, his face hardened. "We have to go straight away. Dante wants us to travel back with him."

"Okay," she said, and turned on her heel and went back to their room to pack.

Keenan packed quickly, then grabbed both of their bags and walked past her out the door. "Come on," he said.

He stopped and spoke briefly to his boys when they got downstairs and they all looked at her. She knew they must have been talking about her. *Oh bloody hell*, Vince must have told him about Sarah flipping out.

Then Keenan nodded his head in the direction of the back way out and she followed him.

As they walked into the kitchen, Jay was walking in with her sister. Lacy frowned. The girl's eyes were the weirdest she'd ever seen, and her hair appeared to have been hacked off.

When they stopped in front of each other, the girl said, "Hello, Lacy. I can't see you that well today."

Lacy wanted to cry. It was a reality check into how dangerous their world was. She wanted to run away, but instead, she looked up at Keenan next to her. He smiled weakly down at her as if reading her thoughts.

"I'll see you in Ireland though?" Lacy said, looking at Keenan again for reassurance.

All too quickly, the meeting was over. Keenan shook Jay's hand with real warmth and shuffled her out past all the guards trying to come in, and past the ones trying to go out, until they were outside.

Keenan nudged her past Dante's car to the one behind and told her to get in. She obeyed and watched while he spoke quietly with his boys. Then they all joined her in the car.

KEENAN PULLED his boys into a close circle so they couldn't be overheard. "I want us to watch her like a hawk now, okay?"

They all nodded in agreement at the heightened risk after Tia's abduction.

"I don't know what's happened, but something has while I've been away … Apart from Sean's bird freaking out at her, can you think of anything else?"

Vince leaned in close to Keenan's ear, "She was on the phone to someone earlier today."

Keenan frowned and stood up straight while he thought. "I thought all the phones were monitored?"

"No," Vince continued, "this one was a cell phone that belonged to the housekeeper … I walked into the kitchen after I heard her talking, and they both acted all innocent."

Keenan took a deep breath and nodded thanks, then touched Vince's shoulder. "Okay, don't say anything to her about it. But if she speaks to anyone … anyone at all, I wanna know about it."

They all murmured their agreement and got in the car with Lacy. Three other guards got in with Dante and another four in the car behind, and they all set off for the airport and Dante's private plane.

THE KING WAS quiet and broody all the way to Ireland. He'd suddenly become really interesting to her since she realized the difficult position he was in.

Then her eyes skated over to Keenan, who'd fallen asleep in the chair next to her. Her heart sped up just looking at his savagely beautiful face, relaxed and infinitely kissable. She didn't know how she resisted snuggling up to him and feeling those big tattooed arms around her.

"You can lay your head on me if you're tired?" he said, making her jump.

"No, it's okay," she said, completely taken aback.

He opened his eyes and they swirled with blood as if to remind her how close to the surface the feral animal in him was. "You have nothing to fear from me, Lacy. I won't touch you unless you want me to . . ." and he turned in his seat to face the other way. "And you'll want me to."

Her cheeks flushed with embarrassment. *How did he always know how she felt?* He was infuriating, the bloody sod, but hot as hell.

CHAPTER 18

$\mathcal{I}$t was almost dark at the Milestorm US Air Force base, Montana. The wind was howling and buffeting the two lonely figures waiting on the Tarmac. A small private plane had just had a rough landing and was taxiing to an available parking spot. Its large Florianna crest was just visible in the darkness on its tail. Rain now joined the wind in spatters.

The door on the side of the plane was flung open and steps joined to the side. One tall, dark male descended the stairs and stalked toward them in graceful, predatory steps. He stopped right in front of them.

"Malleven Mancini?"

The new arrival bowed. "Duke Ormond Delissi. A long-awaited pleasure."

The duke inclined his head.

Malleven's eyes rested on the prize he'd coveted so long. "The Siren Isla Snow?" he asked.

"This is she," Ormond replied.

Isla stared blankly in front of her, neither looking left nor right, as if she were in a daze. She had only recently woken from her induced sleep in an observation tank in the lab.

Malleven needn't look down at his ring. It vibrated from his pocket, revealing her authenticity. However, even if he hadn't procured one, he, being too minor a prince, would have known her. He remembered every curve of her body, every shadow on her sad face and the feel of her soft, petal-red lips.

Malleven dragged his eyes back to Ormond, "Her handler?"

"Disposed of, as promised."

"I cannot afford to be linked with her in any way."

"And nor I," Ormond replied.

"And the Dubonnetti Siren, Tia Storm?"

"Already safely back with her husband, the king … And the Dubonnettis … they bargained with their own Siren, Tia Storm, for Isla Snow in return?"

"Yes, unthinkable but true. They think they can merely swap one for another to pledge to the lesser son, Marco," Malleven said.

And what of Lacy Rain … is she back where she belongs?" Delissi probed.

Malleven bowed his head slightly, a smile playing on his lips. "It is my understanding that she is."

Delissi's shrewd eyes narrowed on Malleven. "I don't have to tell you the importance of Isla reaching the Florianna House, and that House only; the consequences should she not, would be catastrophic. The exchange was facilitated only as a necessary evil to free Isla from under the Americans' noses."

"You have no need to worry, Ormond. I have no intention of handing over Isla Snow to the soulless Dubonnetti traitors. She is destined for my House."

"You are absolutely sure?"

"Have no fear, I have consulted the stars. There is no doubt." The corners of Malleven's mouth twitched with amusement as he glanced over at Isla.

"Good … The US Government received their replacement Siren –Tia Storm, as agreed, for this one, albeit for a very short time, so my hands are clean, so to speak … Farewell, Malleven, guard Isla well … Oh, and one more thing."

Malleven paused as he was about to turn toward the plane, his face to the wind. "Say nothing of this to the king … He knows nothing yet of this transaction. It is better that he learns of Isla through your House in the way that is right and proper."

Malleven bowed his head and touched his heart. "He will not find out from me." Malleven straightened and inclined his head to Delissi in a way of goodbye. "Come, Isla. It is time for you to come home." And he turned and led her towards the steps of the plane, with his hand at the small of her back. The rain lashed them, but she seemed oblivious. She didn't even blink as it pelted her face and flattened her lustrous blonde hair.

When they reached the shelter of the inside of the plane, Malleven took off his raincoat and asked the steward, "Please bring Miss Snow a towel." Meanwhile, the door was shut, and they began their way to the runway to beat the worsening weather.

"Sit," he said, and sat in the seat next to her. He could barely wait to savour her taste and sink into her beautiful body. To make his that which was never meant for him. He'd worked so long and hard for this, perfecting and experimenting on the Santalini Siren; Lacy Rain. At last he'd secured his own House's Siren, and he could now affect his or anyone else's divining ring to turn the purple required to be a Siren's mate.

"Buckle up, Isla. It's going to be a bumpy ride." He laughed out loud and ordered a whiskey to warm himself.

The steward brought it quickly, along with some water for Isla, which Malleven passed her with his left hand. He wasn't sure what made him look, a jolt of the plane, or a slip of the eye; he wasn't sure, but something made him look at his ring for the first time.

There, as deep and as rich as could be, his purple ring shone.

He held it up to his face to marvel at it, not believing his eyes. Laughter bubbled and escaped him. He laughed louder and louder. "After all these years, Isla … the plotting, the magic, the manipulating. The ring is fucking purple … purple." He threw his head back and looked heavenwards.

She didn't say a word.

It was only a few days after they'd landed in Ireland that Lacy's sister arrived and she had a chance to meet her.

She decided that she liked her instantly. They'd put their foot down to get some alone time together and realized that they were really alike in a lot of ways.

Tia's eyes had healed, thanks to some ingenious cure from the Murrs, and they spent a wonderful couple of hours together. Her decks had been set up in the corner of the great hall and she switched them on to show Lacy what a talented DJ she was. Lacy had danced on a pole Dante had installed and shown Tia her strength in movement to music.

That was the key they found, that they were completely attuned when they got into the music together. They had a true sisterly bond that was only visible to fellow Atlanteans when their power pulsated in time to the music.

After their meeting, Lacy wasn't ready to face Keenan, so

she followed Tia back to the room she shared with Jay. He made himself scarce.

Lacy sat on a wicker chair in the corner and watched as Tia rummaged in her wardrobe for clothes, throwing them over her shoulder as she went. Lacy had to laugh; she was so messy, totally reminding her of herself. Their similarities were piling up.

"Come on then?" Tia said, mid-rummage, turning to face her.

"What?"

"Spill."

Lacy was quiet for a beat and then went for it. "Are you okay with this … You know, me marrying him?" Lacy kept her gaze down, not able to look her sister in the eye. "I mean, we don't even know each other."

Tia balked. "What difference does that make? You wouldn't remember me anyway."

Lacy looked at her, shocked for a second, then they both laughed. "True," she conceded. She was really starting to like her sister.

Tia flopped on the edge of the bed and sighed as if exhausted. "Look, the situation with me and Dante … Well, it's hard, you know? Especially for him."

"So you love him then?" She was pleased for Dante to know that, but the comparison to Keenan was never far from Lacy's mind. When Lacy focused on what Tia was saying, tears had welled in her sister's eyes until she closed them and then they brimmed over and ran down her cheeks. Lacy felt terrible for making her cry.

"I close my eyes, Lace, and he's with me all the time … inside, loving me, adoring me … wanting me. It's the bond, you know?"

"And Jay?" Lacy couldn't help asking. She just had to know.

Tia stood up as if she was annoyed and busied herself again. "I can't live without him, Lace, I refuse to live without him."

Lacy stared at her sister, trying to understand. The way Tia felt about Jay was a substantial, strong, real love. She tried to liken it to how she felt for Charlie, but, as usual, the feeling was fleeting and always tinged with disquiet. *That wasn't love, was it? Bloody hell*, she changed her mind hourly.

She decided not to press her sister any more after that. She was in no doubt as to her turmoil and didn't see the point of burdening her with her own, real or imagined. Nevertheless, the fact remained that the gap between her and Keenan was getting wider than ever.

She had put off going back to her room as long as she could, but she had to get ready for the wedding ceremony that evening; *her* wedding, *for god's sake. Could life get more insane?*

The truth was, she didn't want to be alone with Keenan, but she knew she had run out of time and so bit the bullet, kissed her sister goodbye and went back to her room.

She really should have a nap, but she was just too wired. She had just met her sister, Charlie preoccupied her thoughts most of the time, and she had to go into the water with Dante that evening and she couldn't even swim. There just wasn't much need for swimming as a child growing up in East London, and nobody had suggested she learn. Of course, being smothered in stripes when she got wet kind of put her off asking for lessons.

While her head was in her bag, raking around for make-up that wouldn't run in the water, Keenan came into the room.

He sat down on the edge of the bed. "Sit with me a minute?"

The time avoiding him had come to an end, so she sighed and did as he asked.

"You gonna tell me what happened while I was away?"

"Nothing … nothing at all."

"Don't lie to me, Lacy … I thought we were making progress."

He sounded worn out.

She was trying to work out in her head what she needed to say to him; *she was killing him for Christ's sake.* "I let myself weaken with you. I shouldn't have. I don't love you, Keenan." There it was … she'd put it out there at last.

The only clue to any emotion in the whole of Keenan's body was the wash of blood that surged through his eyes.

"I'm sorry," she said, swallowing hard. "I don't want to string you along."

"Have you forgotten that the man took you from me, held you for almost a year, gave you fake children to keep you prisoner, drugged you and took your fucking memory?" He ended up shouting and standing menacingly over her.

"You don't know that for sure," she said, not able to look at him.

"The. Kids. Weren't. Yours."

Her body sagged, utterly deflated. He was right, of course. *Why, oh why, did she feel the way she did?* The confusion alone was killing her.

He pulled her up with him to standing and hugged her into his huge chest. He whispered into her hair, "Whatever you think … whatever you decide, Lace, know that I never lied to you. Everything I have told you is the truth. Okay?"

She nodded and breathed his wonderful smell from his chest, which felt like coming home.

A knock at the door interrupted them. Keenan tutted and went to answer it.

A servant spoke quietly to him and he shut the door again and turned to face her. "Dante wants to see you alone."

Her eyes opened wide, "Why?"

Keenan shrugged, "I'll take you to him. He's in the great hall."

They walked into the large room that was the centrepiece of the castle. It was a huge cave of black rock beneath the castle, with black chandeliers and lights twinkling in the ceiling. The space was filled with soft leather and velvet seating in reds, russets, and browns. All arranged around the large circular fountain in the middle of the floor, which served as the gateway to the castle by sea.

A shudder rippled through her at the thought of when she would next see it, made even worse when her eyes were drawn to the dominating feature of the room—the magnificent underwater window to the sea. Lit from outside, it looked like a gigantic aquarium.

Dante was sitting in a high-backed armchair in the corner of the room, reading some papers. He looked up when he heard them approach. "Give us a minute, Keenan. I won't be long."

Keenan didn't move for a moment, looking unsure.

"Wait over there, Keenan," Dante said, pointing to the other side of the room. "I just want to speak to Lacy before tonight."

There was no joking with Dante this time; he was all business. Lacy realized that the two sides to his character existed simultaneously. She was beginning to see what her sister saw in him.

Keenan wasn't happy about it, but he walked away from them and out the servants' entrance at the other side of the hall.

"Sit down, Lacy," Dante said, indicating a chair. "Is everything okay?"

She nodded. When she finally let her eyes meet his, he was smiling in that roguish way of his. She couldn't help but grin back at him. *He was such a contradiction.*

"So, wife number two. How do you feel about that?"

She smiled and shrugged. "I don't know … but thanks for asking. You are the first to bother."

He laughed easily. "Yes, it's a bastard all this, isn't it? But necessary, I'm afraid."

Dante studied her like he was building up to something. "I wanted a chance to speak to you before tonight to put your mind at rest … You know that I love your sister, right?"

She nodded. "I know."

"But all this is necessary for the strength of the crown and our two Houses."

"I understand," she said, looking down at her hands.

They were quiet for a few moments while Dante just watched her. "Say what's on your mind, Lacy. I'll be able to feel your feelings anyway, after we're married."

"Really?" Her eyes shot to his.

Dante leant forward and poured a glass of red wine for each of them. "Come now, you can speak to me. Even though we are not lovers, we should be friends."

"My sister," she began cautiously. "She loves two men." She allowed what she'd said to sink in.

His eyes narrowed on her, "You love Keenan," he said eventually. "That is how it should be."

She felt uncomfortable continuing, and fidgeted until a tear trickled down her cheek. She wiped it away on her fingertips. "It's like a heavy weight bearing down on me … I can't shake it off. But when I'm with Keenan …" she trailed off.

"You can't help yourself …" he finished for her.

She nodded. "Exactly … I feel so guilty all of the time."

Dante sat back in his chair and sipped his wine. "Look,

Lacy, I'll be straight with you. I know the circumstances of your abduction, and you have to know that there are those who would do anything to get control of a Siren."

"But why do I love him so?"

"Can you tell me anything at all about him, Lacy?"

She looked hopelessly at him and shook her head. How could she convince him of anything when she didn't know herself?

Dante rested his elbows on his knees. "Don't worry ... it will all work out, you'll see. But one thing I will say to you: don't trust anyone. Do you hear me?"

She nodded, but in a world where she had no memory, the warning was redundant.

"The only people you can truly trust after today are Keenan, me and your sister, okay?"

She frowned, not convinced she would trust ever again.

"We are all family and our lives depend on one another."

"But, Keenan ..."

"Would die for you, Lacy. I know that because that's how I feel about your sister."

She looked at him sadly. She was confused and wanted to ask him a thousand questions.

"In a couple of hours," he continued, "you'll know what the bond is, and you will be able to offer that bond to a partner of your choice ... My situation with your sister is fucked up; don't make that mistake ... You and Keenan are already bound tightly. That will only get stronger with time."

She knew he spoke the truth when she sensed Keenan come back into the room and begin to pace by the entrance.

Dante stood and took a step towards her, then pulled her up into his arms. "I'll see you in the water," he whispered. "Don't be scared. We'll all be there for you."

She nodded, already pulling away from him with emotion

welling up in her, and Keenan growing anxious behind her. "Thank you, Dante … My sister is a lucky woman."

"So are you, Lacy. Remember what I said."

She walked away, but continued to look back at him.

THE TIME CAME for Lacy to be tested and married in accordance with Atlantean law and tradition.

Everyone was gathered in the great hall of Ballygowan Castle, but it was to be officially witnessed by Lacy's father, Sebastian, her Uncle Alfonzo, and Keenan as her mate, as dictated by divining ring.

Her mother, Naomi – a full-blooded Murr - was to enter the water with her to help support her through the terrifying process. Tia, her sister, had to go into the water as well, as she needed to reaffirm her own pledge afterwards.

The two Sirens waited nervously next to the fountain, dressed in nothing but their bikinis. Lacy watched Jay pull Tia aside and into his arms, the biggest show of affection she'd seen from him.

It only made her more conscious of Keenan standing next to her. She longed to bask in his body heat, but things were still strained between them. She had listened to Dante, but a black cloud hung over them, threatening to burst at any moment.

Logic told her that someone had messed with her head, but every time she almost weakened and went to Keenan, she had such a feeling of foreboding she couldn't explain it. She had not one piece of Charlie in reality to cling to, but she clung to him anyway. Yet Keenan waited and she sensed it.

"Are you okay?" he said, leaning down to her ear.

She nodded but wouldn't look at him; her resolve was too weak. She found herself wishing to get on with it just so she could get away from him, which was madness, as the water was terrifying. It didn't help with the animosity he was emitting in Dante's direction. It was making her really nervous, especially when Dante winked at him before he disappeared into the depths of the fountain first.

Tia and her mother, Naomi, were next. They grabbed her hands as they stepped over the wall and guided her to the deepest part in the centre of the fountain. They explained that it went down into a tunnel, under the great hall and out to the sea in front of the window. If they didn't hold her fast, she would have run in the opposite direction; her fear was so great.

The witnesses would all be stationed in front of the panoramic window. That meant Keenan would watch the whole thing. *God, could things get any worse?*

Finally, it was time for her to submerge beneath the water and absolute panic robbed her of oxygen.

Do not be afraid. Take a deep breath, child. It will give you plenty of time to become accustomed to the water, her mother explained.

Forgetting herself, Lacy looked at her mother in astonishment. Her words were spoken straight to her head, making her fear subside. She wanted to ask her so many things, but was prompted to step into the fountain.

Taking a moment to gather herself, she took a deep lungful of air. The world fell silent and a split second lasted an eternity when she glanced back over her shoulder straight into Keenan's eyes. *Oh god,* he looked ruined. Then he seemed to know he had to be strong for the both of them. He took a breath, straightened up and gave her the smallest of nods to tell her everything was okay.

She turned back and slipped beneath the water with Tia and her mother.

Thankfully, the tunnel was lit. It was circular like a large drain, but the rocks were roughly hewn and jagged.

Keep going, child, her mother urged. *Don't be scared. We are both here for you.*

Lacy looked at the mother she hardly knew, who was as graceful as a mermaid. She supposed that was exactly what she was. Then her sister who smiled in encouragement. Her eyes had already dilated into huge black disks, making her look otherworldly.

Eventually, they reached the sea and the temperature of the water plummeted. She was still holding her breath but very conscious of not being able to hold it for much longer.

There, in the rough rocks of the castle, was the shiny black surface that she guessed was the window of the great hall. It was unnerving to know that Keenan looked straight at her.

Suddenly, the weight of the water was overwhelming, and she went to turn back the way she came. She didn't want to play this game anymore; she wanted out. She tried to snatch her hands from Tia and her mother's grip, but they held on tightly.

Shh, her mother projected immediately, *please don't struggle, Lacy. This is natural for you. When you let the water in, you will be able to breathe and then you will no longer need to worry.*

That may be true, but every time she poised herself to do it, panic would rise, and she would change her mind. Pretty soon, she was fighting them to get away.

Let go, she willed over and over, knowing her mother could hear her thoughts.

She shook her head. Her heart was palpitating, and her head pounded. She fought until the last millisecond of her air supply and then drowsiness overtook her.

elcome back, her mother projected straight to her mind.

Her sister hugged her. *Congratulations.*

Lacy couldn't believe it, she had survived and she wasn't breathing air. She put her hand to the tickling sensation behind her ears and felt the bubbles.

She looked at her sister and mother, bewildered, but they were moving backwards away from her. She didn't realize what was happening until she noticed Dante a way off, waiting, and then remembered she wasn't finished yet.

He looked awesome. He seemed to have grown in height; his skin was lighter, which showed off his vivid stripes all the more. He even had them on his face.

When he saw her studying him, he grinned and beckoned her to him with a finger. *Shit. What was she meant to do?* Her sister mimed for her to go to him. She slowly swam towards him with trepidation until she looked up into his savagely handsome face. She was very close to him now.

He slowly moved his arms towards her and held her by

the shoulders, then pulled her gently towards him. *Was he going to kiss her? No one said anything about snogging.*

Her eyes went wide as he slanted his mouth over hers. *What was she meant to do?*

His mouth stayed on hers for ages, but he didn't move or try to kiss her. It was as though he was waiting.

He pulled away, looked into her eyes and smiled slightly, then moved in again. It must be something to do with the bond.

Her heart was thumping for fear of doing something wrong. *What if she was a dud and couldn't do it?* She felt herself start to panic.

Then Dante passed his tongue over her lips in an incredibly sensual way. His eyes were steady when she looked into them. He was trying to tell her something. *What?* Her mind raced over what she'd learned. *This was a marriage ceremony, wasn't it?* That meant it was to bind partners together.

Without bidding, an erotic image of Keenan slammed into her head, and Dante's tongue stroked her mouth again. Between the two of them, it shot her temperature sky high. Dante seemed to sense it in her and held her tighter. The familiar weight appeared in her chest; the one that always came when she was hot with Keenan. Except this time, it was unbearable, as if she needed to expel it. It had never felt so strong. Maybe it was because she was under water, where she was meant to be.

Dante pushed his tongue into her mouth to bring her mind back to him. It shocked her as with it came an image of Keenan aroused in the shower. Bursting heat immediately bloomed in her chest. *Wow.* For a split second, she felt faint. Then something flew out of her like a pot boiling over, and a huge pressure was released.

Whatever it was, Dante felt it because he let go of her and

floated backwards. His chest and face were glowing orange. He appeared to be stunned.

She stared at him in horror. *What had she done to him?* She sagged in relief when he shook his head and grinned at her and beckoned her again.

She took a nervous glance at the window and wondered what Keenan was making of all this, then she swam to him slowly again.

He repeated the whole thing. Holding her by the shoulders, putting his mouth over hers, just as before. He coaxed her to open her mouth just like the first time. Just as she was starting to worry that Keenan would kill him, she felt the most amazing heat enter her mouth. It made her cheeks burn and travelled down to the centre of her until it reached her heart. Then it exploded.

THE NEXT THING SHE KNEW, she felt Tia's and Naomi's arms come around her. Then Dante approached them all. *How do you feel, wife number two?*

Lacy felt fuzzy and warm and a bit shaky. *Okay, I guess.*

He laughed. *Take her back, Naomi.* Then he looked at her seriously for a moment, *Thank you for your gift, Lacy.*

She didn't know what to say. She just smiled weakly, then made her way back to the tunnel with her mother. However, she couldn't resist one last glance back at Dante, who took her sister's hand and pulled her to him. Then they disappeared out to sea.

She wasn't sure how she knew, but she knew for sure, there was no room for anyone else in that male's heart other than Tia.

.   .   .

WHEN SHE EMERGED and stood up in the fountain, it felt as though she would cough up her insides. Her mother had warned her that she wouldn't be able to speak for a while because her throat would be painful, but no one mentioned feeling like she'd swallowed razor blades.

Keenan quickly wrapped a towel around her. As he did it, she looked straight at Jay. In that moment, his look was unguarded, like a wound before it was dressed. Then in a split second, his mask came over his face and he was hard and back to normal. He touched Keenan on the shoulder and said he was going to bed.

Lacy studied Keenan's face as he helped her out of the fountain. He wasn't faring much better. As if he assumed there was something between her and Dante as well. *Bloody men. Why did they have to bloody own everything about you?*

They arrived at their bedroom in silence. Keenan still looked like he had the weight of the world on his shoulders. Her heart sank. She knew it was hard on him. Even if she could speak, what could she say to him? *Well, it was done now.*

She grabbed some things out of her wash bag, went to the adjoining bathroom and switched on the shower. She quickly stepped in and took off the bikini, letting it fall onto the wet floor at her feet. Then she shampooed her hair to wash out the seawater.

Her head was a jumbled mess of hurt and confusion. It was filled with the sad eyes and aching hearts of Keenan, Dante and now Jay. *God*, it was as though everyone was doomed to be cursed in this life. She wanted to cry with the weight of sadness.

She threw her shampoo bottle at the opposite wall in her temper. She wanted to scream her lungs out, but it hurt too much.

The door opened and Keenan stood dominating the doorway. "Are you okay?"

She gave him her most thunderous look and croaked, "No." Then turned her back on him. She couldn't bear to look at him for fear of what she would do.

Lacy closed her eyes and her heart thrashed when she felt him approach. He didn't stop until he stood right behind her. She was holding her breath. He was so close his clothes must be getting wet, but he wasn't touching. She stole a look at him over her shoulder and saw his eyes burning red and then cooling to glacier blue.

He turned her gently, even though she resisted, and pulled her slowly into his body. He held her silently. He just stood there fully clothed, holding her, getting soaked and she let him.

"I'm sorry, Lacy."

She lifted her head from his chest and frowned up at him.

"For not being able to protect you ... today, or before ... when that bastard ..." he grit his teeth.

She watched his strange, turbulent eyes. They really were the windows to the soul, and he was in turmoil. The familiar pull was so strong she just couldn't help herself. She reached up into his tousled hair and pulled his mouth down to hers. Her mouth joined with his forcefully. He didn't need asking twice and groaned, lifting her easily so she could clamp her legs around him.

She pulled at his T-shirt, pulling the sopping fabric over his head and pushing the waistband of his jeans down, but he was way ahead of her, and unzipped himself so he could spring free and nudge at her backside.

She pulled him to her and kissed him hard, then put her open mouth and tongue next to the skin of his cheek and tasted him mixed with the water from the shower. Feeling helpless and breathing hard, she lifted her head and stared into his eyes and felt so clearly the need deep within the swirl of his eyes. She slowly turned her head to expose her slender neck to him.

She didn't understand the urge in her, only that she felt the power in him fighting for control, trying to stop the feral animal in him pouncing and devouring. But that was what *she* needed. She wanted him hot and fierce and out of control and she had no idea where it came from.

No one knew how much self-control it took for Keenan not to pounce on Lacy the minute she came out of the sea after binding herself to another man, Dante of all people.

Because that was what it fucking was. No wonder the bastard was so smug. In the way a tomcat needs to piss on its territory, he needed to dominate Lacy in every way possible. So that she and every other bugger knew she was his.

Instead, he'd breathed and counted, recited the Lord's Prayer backwards. Anything to give her the space to go into the bathroom and away from him, out of harm's way, because if he took her now, she would probably hate him for ever.

His nerves were already in shreds when he heard the loud bang in the bathroom. *Shit.* He had to check to see if she was okay.

When he went in, fighting to keep the blood out of his eyes, she looked at him as if she would kill him. Nothing like a challenge when you're on a short fuse. She stood buck-naked with soapsuds travelling over the soft curves of her body, where he wanted to be.

Like a child, she turned her back on him angrily, and he stepped in closer, into the shower space. Then he turned her to face him and pulled her tight to his chest. All he could think of doing was to hold her.

When she reached up and kissed him hard, he scooped her up and almost lost himself when she exposed her beautiful neck to him as an offering. So like the old Lacy, he wondered for a second if he had her back.

His fangs strained to penetrate her. His breathing was ragged. Somehow, he managed to pause. "What do you want, Lacy?"

She turned her head back to him, looking confused.

"Because I can't play these games any more. You are playing with fire with me …"

Her eyes filled with bewildered embarrassment, which he could have kicked himself for, but he couldn't go on. He slowly let her down to stand on her feet. Even though everything in him screamed for him to take her anyway.

He turned and went to walk out of the room. "Let me know."

"Let you know what?" she croaked painfully, holding her throat.

"When you know what the fuck you want." And he left her alone in the room.

LACY DIDN'T KNOW where Keenan went for the rest of the night, but he appeared again in the morning.

Naomi, her mother, had asked for some time with her as they barely knew each other, and Lacy welcomed the break from the intense atmosphere between her and Keenan. So she had sent her a message to meet that morning.

Keenan said he would take her to the library, to show her where it was in the above-ground part of the house, but she suspected that he was keeping an eye on her.

They entered the old wood-panelled room and her father Sebastian embraced her, followed by her mother. Then her father shook Keenan's hand. It all struck her as so absurd, like parents meeting a daughter's intended, when she didn't know any of them, including Keenan.

Out of water, her mother still looked weird. She guessed being Murr meant you didn't transform as much as a land-dwelling Atlantean. Her hair was long and lustrous, but her bones were stark and angular and she was tall like a super-model. Her large, soulful eyes had far too much iris and not enough white to them.

Hello, child.

Lacy looked at Keenan to see if he heard it, but he looked at her quizzically, proving he didn't.

No, only you hear the thoughts I want you to hear, her mother explained.

Keenan looked between them. "What?" he asked.

"Do not worry, Keenan," her father said, kindly. "Let us leave mother and daughter to finally get to know each other."

Lacy looked at Keenan with a trace of fear but nodded to say it was okay.

Her father led the way and Keenan followed haltingly.

Sit, child.

They sat in two armchairs that faced each other next to the fireplace. Lacy studied the pale skin and dark shadows of her mother's face that made her look so alien. She broke the silence first, "You can talk straight to my head?"

Her mother nodded. *We don't talk the way humans do, handy for under the water, no?* And she smiled at the reference to Lacy's pledging the evening before.

"Can you read my mind?" Lacy wasn't sure if she liked that.

Yes, she nodded slowly again. *But manners dictate only to do so when invited. It can be a painful experience if not.*

Lacy looked down at her hands, a habit of hers when she couldn't put into words what she wanted to say.

What is the matter, Lacy? Do you wish to confide in me?

Lacy looked up, her eyes full of tears. "Do you know what happened to me?"

I know you were taken from your life mate and no longer remember him.

Lacy nodded and continued to fiddle with her fingers. "They think I was brainwashed or something … I can't remember his face … the one who took me."

Her mother stared at her for a few moments, as if she was deciding on something.

Lacy looked at her mother and frowned.

"What is it … tell me?"

What if I were permitted to look?

"Look in my head?"

Yes, perhaps I can see or feel something you cannot.

Lacy's heart quickened with hope. Perhaps her mother could unlock her lost memories. "Okay."

Are you sure, Lacy … we don't know what we will find?

"Do it … Quickly, before Keenan comes back and stops us."

Very well. Breathe slowly and evenly and try to relax.

That was easier said than done. Her mind was suddenly racing with the possibilities and her heart was beating wildly.

Relax, her mother repeated, but her voice was closer. Like a caress, as if her hand were stretching inside her, gently stroking her to calm her. It was the strangest feeling, like a ghost was inside her, possessing her.

She felt her mother hold her hand, not a real hand, a psychic one. *Come, child, show me the way.*

Lacy walked ahead as if exploring her own mind, like the corridors of an empty hospital or institution. They came to a door with a gold doorknob.

Open it, Lacy. I am just a spectator; I can't affect anything.

Lacy pushed the door open and heard the happy laughter

of children. The two children she'd believed were her own came running to her.

"Mom! Mom! We missed you."

She scooped them up and hugged them fiercely to her, closing her eyes. They felt so real she could even smell them. When she spun around with them and opened her eyes, she found her arms were empty and was forced to lean on a wall to steady herself.

It was just a memory, Lacy.

She fought back the tears in her eyes and walked back into the corridor. *She could do this*; she had to, however hard it was.

Let us try another. Perhaps if we go way down the corridor, we can see a memory from before you were abducted, Naomi said, leading her by the hand again.

It felt as though they glided without legs, down, down, down the dark corridor, to where just a single light flickered. There they came to a dark wooden door with a silver handle, very different to the others.

Try it, Naomi said.

Slowly, Lacy reached out a hand. But fear made her snatch it back again. Something significant was behind this door. She looked at her mother and shook her head, "I'm scared."

You may never know unless you try.

Lacy tentatively reached out a hand again. She gripped the handle, pulled it down and pushed open the door. It creaked open wide.

She saw a small girl, no more than around ten or eleven years old, sitting on a bench alone in a school playground. She had grazed knees and grey socks rucked down to her ankles. Her school uniform was worn and her jumper had holes in the elbows. Somehow, she knew it was her.

Some boys were nearby, sniggering. They came closer, gathering round her.

"That's the girl," one said.

The others laughed

"Yeah, that's the one."

They gathered around her closely. "Do you snog your brother?"

"Fuck off!" she shouted, but her heart was beating with fear.

"Is it true?"

"I'll snog yah ..." another said.

The others all chimed in with laughter.

"Oi!" came the shout from the opposite side of the playground.

They all turned to look.

A tall, lanky kid with a mop of wayward black hair strode across the Tarmac, eating up the ground, with one black and two brown boys walking briskly with him.

Her heart skipped. It was Keenan. She knew it then and she knew it now. Her stomach flipped and love flooded her. The others must have been Vince, Rick and Dan.

A few of her tormentors ran off at the first hint of trouble, but three stayed frozen to the spot. One actually wet himself.

When Keenan arrived, he didn't even give them time for excuses, but punched the ring-leader square in the face and dropped him to the floor.

Vince went over and pointed down to the boy, "I'd stay down if I were you."

A teacher must have seen the commotion and came running over. "Get out of here, Keenan Santos, this instant. You don't go to this school and I will call the police," she said, going red in the face.

Little girl Lacy stood up and put her hand in Keenan's, looking up adoringly into his boyish face, but his eyes were the same: strong and fearless, startling in their blue and flashing red with blood. "We must go, Keenan, they'll see your eyes."

Vince, Rick and Dan closed ranks behind them and they trooped out of the schoolyard together.

Keenan stopped at the gate and whispered in the ear of a boy who thought he'd got away with it, "I'll find you and kill you, you go near my sister again … you 'ear me?" He didn't sound angry, but the intent was there, and the boy got it and nodded his head vigorously.

Lacy put her nose in the air with pride. Everyone was scared of her brother.

Then, just as before, the vision evaporated and they were back in the corridor.

Are you okay? her mother asked.

She felt shell-shocked. "I remembered something. Did you see? It was Keenan."

Her mother nodded happily and hugged her.

"I can't believe it. He saved me. Did you see?"

Yes, my child, I did. Her mother put her away from her slowly, but her face had become serious. *Shall we try another nearer to the present ... maybe we can see who took you?*

Lacy stilled while she thought. This was massive. "Yeah. We've got to try, haven't we?"

Her mother led her back the way they'd come. *Stop at the one that calls to you, child.*

They carried on walking till the light became brighter again, almost to where they'd begun.

"This one," Lacy said.

"You feel something?

Lacy took a deep breath and nodded. The door they had stopped at was old with a latch, like an old cottage. It swung open with a creak. She took a step into the room, gripping her mother's hand tightly.

She was back in the grotty bedroom of the flat Keenan had taken her from. The TV was on as it always was in the other room, and it smelled of dampness and mildew. She looked over at the rumpled bed and there was a woman lying on it. Her arms and legs were carelessly wide and her head was to the side.

Lacy held her breath. She recognized the pitiful sight as her, but she looked drugged or inebriated or something. She couldn't lift her head and her eyes rolled about in her head.

"Look at me, Lacy," the voice said, from across the room.

Tentacles of ice crossed her heart as she listened to the chilling voice. "Charlie." Then her thoughts felt jumbled when two pale hands from the opposite direction pulled out her arm and smacked her vein at the crook of her elbow. Then a syringe went in, the plunger went back and the vial filled with blood. It was one of her blood tests. No wonder she never remembered them.

She watched the hands. They were refined with long fingers – aristocratic and feminine. Then she saw the ring she knew so well. "Charlie," she whispered again.

Lips brushed hers and kissed her gently.

"Come. That is enough," the disturbingly familiar voice said from the shadows. Two people were in that room with her. *Two were Charlie?* She shuddered with the sordid realization.

The bed sagged as Charlie leaned back up onto his legs and off the bed. Using all her energy, she struggled to look at him. Her eyes tracked up his long legs, to his chest and neck, then his face, but a light flashed and blinded her for a second.

Lacy shook her head to clear her vision. She desperately wanted to see. She must see him. Her heart would burst if she didn't. Everything rested on it. Whether she ever let this go and had a chance to make a go of it with Keenan. This was so, so important.

She sat up and crawled closer and grabbed onto his arm. She pulled herself up his body, but everything felt like a lead weight, like some terrible nightmare. She was almost level with his face, and then she looked, opened her eyes wide, and screamed.

CHAPTER 20

Keenan was on his way back to the library when he heard Lacy's scream. He broke into a run and bashed the door open and barged into the room.

Naomi was standing, cuddling her while she sobbed into her shoulder. Sebastian grabbed his arm before he could intervene.

"What happened, Lacy?" he said, desperate to rip her away from the woman who didn't even know her, and get her the fuck away from everyone.

Naomi put Lacy away from her slightly while she thought something to Sebastian. He then walked forward and took her from Naomi. Before Keenan could say anything else, Naomi projected straight to him, *Let her father take her, Keenan. Please stay so I can talk to you.*

He went to argue, but there was something in her expression that told him he needed to hear what she had to say. The door closed and he and Naomi were left alone. "You gonna tell me what happened now?"

I know you love Lacy very much, Keenan. But she is very troubled.

You don't say ... for fuck's sake. He was exasperated. As if he didn't know how his own woman felt.

She needs to remember, Keenan. She needs to find out who took her.

"You don't think I know that?"

In order to make sense of her feelings for you, she needs to make sense of what happened to her.

That hit home. He'd all but told her to sort herself out. He gathered himself and tried to calm down. "What upset her then ... why was she screaming?"

She put up a hand to slow him down. *Lacy asked me to walk through her mind with her to see if I could help her to remember something.*

Keenan's eyebrows went up, "And?"

She remembered a day in her childhood when you came to her school playground and protected her from some nasty boys, and took her from school.

"She remembered that?" Hope rose in his chest. He swallowed a lump in his throat, remembering the day like it was yesterday. He was only about thirteen or fourteen and still a hot-head. He couldn't believe it. This was good news, the best in a long time. It was such a breakthrough, he could kiss her.

Then he stopped his train of thought. "Why did she scream like that?"

Well, Naomi continued in her slow, calm way. *She felt excited, as you did, about remembering something and so it gave her the confidence to look at her more recent memories to see what the man who took her looked like.*

"And?" Keenan urged again, his face darkening and his fists clenching.

It was a day he was taking her blood. She couldn't see his face at first. There was a blinding light, but when the light faded, she saw his face.

"Whose?" Keenan said, his face dripping with hatred.

Yours.

THANKFULLY, Naomi never thought for a minute that Keenan could be in any way involved with Lacy's disappearance, so as soon as Keenan had recovered from the shock, they sought out Dante in his study. There, they relayed the events of the afternoon.

There was another voice giving the orders in the shadows. I don't think the man she believed was her boyfriend was the one making the decisions, Naomi explained.

"And she saw his face, you say? And it was Keenan's?" Dante asked again, needing to clarify events. He was truly baffled, but Keenan and Naomi looked to him expectantly. Dante got up and walked around the room and then sat back behind his desk. He took a deep breath and looked at Keenan. "When I spoke to her yesterday, she seemed to think she is torn between two men, in a similar situation to her sister, myself and Jay."

Keenan frowned but waited for him to elaborate.

"What if the hypnosis was so good, he just transposed the love she felt for you onto him?"

Keenan looked at Naomi, who was nodding sagely. *That would explain why her love is so deep for this man; she would be fighting her own love for the same man.*

"Enough to send you mad … but quite brilliant when you think about it," Dante said.

Keenan didn't see the brilliance in it, only the evil, and he simmered.

Naomi tried to offer comfort. *His arms and body definitely weren't yours, Keenan. So there must be a face in her mind somewhere.*

"Can't you keep looking?" Keenan said, flopping into a chair and running his fingers through his hair.

Naomi shook her head. *I'm not powerful enough to break through his failsafe's. What she saw terrified her enough.*

Keenan looked up and closed his eyes. He could punch a wall with frustration.

"Unless ..." Dante interrupted, "you let me?"

Keenan scowled. He just didn't trust the fucker. "What can you do that she can't?" he said, pointing his thumb sideways at Naomi.

Dante gave him his aggravating grin. The one reserved for him, he was realising.

"Now we are married, I have a link with both sisters – the power of two. It could be I have enough power to get through the barriers he left in her mind." He sat back in his chair to let what he'd said sink in. "It depends how badly you want to find out, and whether you can handle me inside her head?" Dante said, grinning again.

Shit. He hated that he was right and waited for Dante to say some other smartass comment, but he didn't.

"It's up to you, man. But whoever did this to her was more powerful than a Siren, and he's clever."

The one who I saw taking her blood was definitely a prince. I saw his ring, Naomi said.

"Okay," Keenan said, sitting up and making a decision. "When?"

"Let's get the presentation out of the way ... then we'll do it," Dante said.

Now Dante had married two Sirens, it was necessary to present them to all the leaders and royal family heads. Those who came to the royal presentation would sign a charter accepting Dante as king and witness the authenticity of the Sirens by divining ring, so all could be in no shadow of doubt.

The huge bash was a Who's Who of the Atlantean world. A representative from each family would meet Dante and the sisters in his study, sign the charter, and then come down to the great hall where Keenan and Jay waited, propping up a specially erected bar. All Keenan's boys were with him and Tia's Protectors were with Jay.

It was a relief for Keenan to be in his own crowd. Looking around at the quickly filling room, he would have felt totally out of his comfort zone.

Dante had come down with the girls at last, to circulate with his guests, and the fucker was clearly really enjoying having one on each arm. *Let the bastard have his day.*

"How are things with you?" Jay asked, interrupting his thoughts, referring to the aftermath of the pledging the night before.

"Strained ... you?"

Jay shook his head; "I was smashed by the time she got back last night ... not a lot of point getting the hump when she leaves tonight."

Keenan raised his eyebrows, "You're a better man than me."

Jay could never stand pity when it came to his relationship with Tia and quickly changed the subject. "Listen ... I'm fucking off in a minute ... why don't you bring Lacy to The Bluebell after all this ... get away for a while?"

Keenan understood that Jay wouldn't want to wait around to see Tia leave and thought about it for a moment. "Yeah, why not."

That reminded him and he looked around. It was a while since he had seen Tia and Lacy. "Where the fuck are they?" he said, getting off his stool. Then he strode off through the crowds towards the bathrooms at the furthest part of the hall. He felt Jay's presence behind him.

When he reached the bathroom allocated to the ladies and sensing she was inside, he just barged in without thinking. Lacy and Tia were in each other's arms and Lacy had been crying. He was momentarily stunned. It was not what he was expecting, seeing Lacy comforted by anyone other than him. Tia was her sister; she had to go away, and this was her goodbye. *Fuck!*

Tia shouted at him. He stormed out again and paced the hallway outside. Jay just leaned against a wall, watching him. "Look, you've got to chill out …" Jay said, quietly.

Keenan stopped and looked at him, worn out. "You don't understand, Jay. Dante has to get inside her head to see if he can unlock her memories. Her mother tried and the bastard has left booby traps everywhere, now she's terrified of me like *I'm* the fucking bad guy. I feel so useless."

Jay closed his eyes to think about what he'd said; that's what he liked about Jay, he never fucking wasted words.

The girls came out. Lacy's eyes were red from crying. Keenan decided he'd had enough. He promised Tia he would look after Lacy, wished her luck on whatever little adventure she was going on, and dragged Lacy off through the crowds with him.

Ah, fuck. Just as he came up to the bar to say he was off to Vince and the boys, he realized Dante was standing there laughing with a group of poncey rich blokes, probably princes from the other families. He couldn't care less; he didn't have the slightest interest in them.

"Keenan," Dante said, calling him over.

Keenan looked to the heavens. Lacy was quiet and brooding next to him.

"Let me introduce you to some cousins," Dante said. "This is Sandro, Roberto, Mario and David Florianna."

Keenan reluctantly shook all their hands. They varied in age, but Sandro looked the oldest and most serious.

"Ah, and this is Mall, a cousin from another branch of the Florianna family," Dante continued. Then Dante got distracted by one of the Borge brothers, who were even taller than Keenan.

Which left him facing Mall. The guy was dark and fucking good-looking, like he didn't swing that way, but credit where it was due. Impeccably dressed and filling out his bespoke suit, he wasn't puny either. "Pleased to meet you at last, Keenan."

The guy was looking deep into his eyes; it was eerie. Like he expected to see something there, or for him to recognize him. "I'm sorry, have we met?" Keenan asked, feeling a bit uncomfortable with the bloke.

"No, but I have heard of you, of course, being the fortunate Santalini to be brought up with his Siren." And he cast his deep black – or were they dark-blue eyes – on Lacy? He felt like he should protect her from his gaze; the man just emanated power.

Lacy was oblivious to him. Strange that she didn't even glance his way.

"Excuse me, mate," Vince said, butting straight in.

Mall bowed his head slightly and moved away.

"Well timed, Vince," Keenan said, smiling at his old friend. "He was giving me the creeps."

"Who was he, then?"

"I dunno, some cousin from another family."

"What's his name?" Vince said, creasing his brow.

Keenan shrugged, "Dante called him Mall, or something … why?"

"Ah, nothing, your brother said that lot was all wizards or something," Vince laughed.

Keenan laughed as well, but what was funny in the Human world was all too real in this one. And you never knew who your enemies were.

LACY RODE the lift up from the hall with Keenan and Vince in silence. She'd agreed to Dante's psychic walk in her head. What did she have to lose? Her life was in tatters anyway. However, Keenan was torn, she could tell, between wanting her to remember him and hating Dante anywhere near her. He'd just have to grow up.

Tia had told her she had to go away to Murrtaine with her mother. It couldn't have come at a worse time; she could really do with both of them now she'd got to know them a bit. Although she realized that whatever was going on was something major, as Tia probably wouldn't have left Jay. He'd sodded off back to London and Dante was pining for her already.

So whoop-di-doo for her, she had her serious Uncle Alfonzo there in case anything 'legal' came to light, Dante moping about like a wet weekend and Keenan, who wanted to kill everything in sight.

As she was feeling so optimistic as to what direction this little meet was going to go, she asked Vince to come as well to keep Keenan in check, just in case.

When they arrived at the library, Dante told them to come in and for Lacy to sit in the armchair he'd placed next to him. She sat down and he reached into her lap and picked up her fidgeting hand. "It's more effective if I can touch skin, I'm not a Murr where it's second nature and I'm not used to finding my way with you yet, Lacy." A smile played on his lips.

Lacy saw a muscle tick in Keenan's jaw and a swirl of blood whip through his eyes, but he was holding it together … just.

For her part, she was grateful that Dante explained things to her rather than to Keenan. It made her feel more her own person, which she was finding harder and harder these days. She was beginning to understand why her sister rebelled so much.

"How's this gonna work?" Keenan said.

"I think whoever used Lacy covered their tracks well," Dante explained. "They expect us to look over the last year for memories, so that's where I believe most of the failsafes are." He looked directly at Lacy. "Like you saw last time. This time, I want to go further, but not too far, and try to get in a back door, like a computer."

Lacy got what he was driving at. Everyone else was quiet, absorbing what he'd said.

"Plus, a fresh pair of eyes might see something that Lacy doesn't," Dante added.

Lacy nodded, "Let's get it over with."

Keenan still stood rooted to the spot.

"You may as well sit down, man. This could take a while," Dante said, pointing at some vacant chairs.

Vince pulled them over, and he and Keenan sat opposite them. Alfonzo had stationed himself behind a desk, slightly apart from everyone.

"Ready?" Dante said.

Lacy nodded.

Dante took her hand and rested both their forearms on the arm of her chair. Lacy watched Keenan's face for any reaction – *so far, so good*. She studied the savagely beautiful face with the palest-blue eyes she'd ever seen, the creamy skin in contrast to the unruly black hair – bed hair, even his gunmetal piercings in his ears and the warlike tattoos peeping out from his shirt. She wanted to remember every part of him so she could conjure up that strength of love she felt in the memory of him; her mother helped her find. The one where she was a little girl. Yes, she wanted that. She had to learn who Charlie was.

"*L*acy ... Lacy," a voice said.

She was in the dark. Beginning to get anxious, she looked around her. This was nothing like the time her mother had joined her in her head. All she could see was an inky-blackness. It was claustrophobic.

"I'm here."

She immediately felt Dante's presence behind her and turned suddenly in shock.

"Shh," he soothed, and held her gently by the shoulders.

Then gradually she could see, as if a single lightbulb lit them from overhead. Everywhere else was still in darkness. Dante stood before her, naked from the waist up, covered in his vivid Atlantean stripes and tattoos. At least he had his trousers on.

He looked down at himself and chuckled, "Well, whad'ya know, I'm only half naked in your head, Lacy, I'm stark-ass in your sister's ..." He narrowed his eyes, "Does this mean you fancy me a bit?"

Her eyes widened at his audacity, which appealed to his sense of humour even more. Thankfully, she had clothes on;

skimpy club clothes, but still clothes. Maybe there was a little something in what he said. They were just psychic representations of themselves after all. "What now?" she asked, shaking off that troubling notion.

"We're just waiting for your sister," Dante said, smiling.

Lacy was genuinely surprised. Her sister was coming to help her after all. She didn't know why she didn't think of it; it just never occurred to her that she could be here psychically.

"I can feel her." Dante rolled his head back and closed his eyes as if he were summoning a spirit.

Lacy watched as two stripey arms came around him from behind and then he turned into Tia's arms. He kissed her tenderly. "I won't keep you long. I don't want to tire you." Then his eyes raked over her sister's body, which was only covered by the tiniest of bikinis. *That must be Dante's idea, surely.*

She coughed.

Dante turned back to her, smiling. "Forgive me, Lacy." He held out his ring hand for her to take. "Let's walk." And they walked through the expanse of inky-black nothingness.

"It wasn't like this last time … why is that?" Lacy said.

"I'm not sure … all I know is through me we stand more of a chance with this." Dante led the way onwards.

Pretty soon, they began to feel soft, wet grass under their bare feet. "What the—?" Dante said, lifting one foot at a time.

"Why grass … I don't get it?" Tia said.

The other two remained silent, as no one knew the answer. They continued walking.

Then they all paused and listened to the muffled sounds of music, as if they were in the cloakroom of a club. They all looked at each other.

"I know this song," Lacy said. "And I know that smell."

Dante laughed, "I expect you do. It's marijuana … fuck, this is so trippy."

"I'm feeling a little freaked-out, Dante," Tia said quietly from the other side of him. "What are we looking for exactly?"

"I'm not sure … some sort of door or way into a memory. I think this is the place the memories used to be."

"It's so empty," Lacy said.

The moment she said the words, an old-fashioned black telephone appeared on a pedestal in front of them and began to ring. The bell tringed, over and over. Lacy looked at Dante, terrified. "Who's going to pick it up … should I?" She looked at it nervously.

"I don't think it will matter, we're all joined, remember? We should all hear it," Dante said. "Go ahead."

Lacy reached out a cautious hand as ice clutched her heart, then snatched it to her ear, "Hello?"

"Hello, Dante, or should I say, Your Highness?"

Lacy looked at Dante in horror.

Dante frowned but was listening intently to the voice.

"Sadly, you will not hold the crown."

Dante began to walk slowly around the pedestal.

"Even if you secure five pledges, only one will be legitimately yours."

Dante looked across at the girls, his arms out, at a loss.

"They will all come to me one by one, willingly and turn against you."

Tia had heard enough. She strode over to Lacy, frozen in fear, snatched the receiver from her hand with the rest of the phone and threw it with all her might into the blackness. "Fuck off, asshole," Tia shouted. A smash, like breaking glass, echoed in the distance.

"Fucking hell, Tia. What did you do that for?" Lacy said, more than a little angry with her.

"He was taunting us, Lacy. He gets off on it," Tia argued back.

"Was that him?" Dante asked, walking back over to Lacy.

"No … yes … I think so. It's weird. I can't explain how I know, but he's not called Charlie."

Dante tutted in frustration, then he was thoughtful for a moment. "Listen. We aren't going to find out any more like this. You go back, Tia. I can call you if we need you."

"You sure? I am getting a bit worn out."

Dante pulled her into his arms and kissed her then and lovingly touched her stomach.

Lacy's eyes went wide at the gesture and what it meant.

"Sorry, Lacy, if I blew it for you," Tia said, still in Dante's arms.

Lacy sighed, "It's okay. You were probably right anyway. He wasn't exactly going to tell us anything, was he?" She watched as Tia pulled reluctantly out of Dante's arms and walked off into the blackness until she completely disappeared.

Dante watched her go. He took a minute as if gathering himself, then turned his attention back to Lacy and smiled. He picked up Lacy's hand and pulled her to him sharply so she was flush against his body. It happened so fast she didn't have time to protest.

"Shh, don't be scared. I want to try something now we're alone."

Lacy was stiff as a board. "Like what?" she said warily, trying to extract herself.

"Relax. While we have the privacy, I want you to imagine a time you were up close with Charlie. But when you think of it, I want you to breathe for me. It's a long shot, but maybe I can share your experience and see something."

"Why couldn't you do it while Tia was here?" Lacy said, knowing how ridiculously obvious the answer was.

Dante smiled indulgently down at her. "Lacy, Lacy ... for the same reason we couldn't do it in the flesh in front of Keenan. I assure you, this is purely in the interest of science."

A crafty grin crept over his face so that she didn't know if he was serious or taking the piss – knowing him, it was probably both. She couldn't help but laugh at him. "You want my sister to kill me?"

"No of course not ..." Dante said, dramatically. Then he tried to keep the smile off his face. "Now, look into my eyes ... look deeply and try to cast your mind back to a time you were with Charlie."

Lacy was very aware how close Dante was to her – mere inches. But she did as he asked and before long, she was back in the dingy flat.

It was really weird because for the first time she noticed that just before her feeling of strong craving for Charlie, came a spine-chilling feeling of dread. That didn't make sense. Well, she supposed it did, if she had been brainwashed, and her body knew she wasn't with the man she loved, even if her brain didn't.

"Can you see what he looks like?" Dante's voice filtered through to her subconscious.

No, she wasn't seeing him. There was a man in front of her, but he was faceless. It was the same as the time before, the time she had seen Keenan's face, but now she knew it wasn't Keenan. His skin was fairer and he was slimmer and not as tall.

"Breathe for me, Lacy. Show me what you see," Dante's voice echoed.

However, she wasn't looking at Dante; she was lost in her vision. Dante's lips gently rested on hers. Hers parted and she began a steady flow.

When Dante pulled apart from her, the man in her vision was doing the same. She saw his chest and his tattoos. There was one she particularly noticed over his heart, and there were several others down his arm. All of them definitely did not belong to Keenan. There was his ring, turquoise, on his left hand. Then he put on an expensive shirt and walked away from her, doing up the buttons.

She opened her eyes. Dante followed a few seconds later. His face was deadpan and unreadable. "Well?" she asked. "Could you see him … could you see what I saw?"

He nodded but was cagey. "Come … I've seen enough."

They returned to consciousness, to their fleshly bodies, moments later. They were bleary-eyed and blinking when they looked around them, while their eyes focused properly.

"Well?" Keenan said. "You were out for ages."

Dante stood, stretching out his arms and legs. Then he turned to Alfonzo, "He had a distinctive tattoo over his heart."

"What did it look like?" Alfonzo asked.

"Give me a pen … it's easier if I draw it."

Alfonzo pushed a notepad and pen across the desk toward him. Dante quickly drew an old-fashioned looking letter M with two strokes, one under each of the arches.

Keenan and Vince looked over his shoulders. "What is it … Atlantean writing?" Keenan asked.

"I don't know … but I've seen it before," Dante said.

Keenan's eyes narrowed, "Where?"

Dante's expression was incredulous. "My brother … my brother Antonio."

KEENAN TURNED ANGRILY on his heel.

"No!" Lacy shrieked and threw herself to cling to his arm. She recoiled when he stopped and sneered at her.

"You won't save him, Lacy, so don't waste your energy." He turned back to the door.

Vince jumped in his way. "Wait, man, steady up."

"Don't you get tired of saying that, Vince? You've been saying that your whole fucking life."

"Keenan!" Dante reprimanded.

Keenan turned to face him slowly. "No one's gonna stop me … not even you."

Dante spoke evenly and clearly. "Look, just because I saw my brother there doesn't mean he's the one behind this." Dante shook his head, still not quite believing it himself. "I've known him all my life … this is too big for him."

Alfonzo spoke for the first time directly to Keenan. "How many Santalini guards are here at the castle?"

"Ten permanent guards, plus me and my boys," Keenan said.

Then Alfonzo looked at Dante. "You can't put off the inevitable any longer, Dante. You must arrest your father and brothers; they seek to cause you nothing but harm."

Keenan pulled out of Vince's grip to speak. "You wanna take away my right to make him pay?" he said angrily to Dante and Alfonzo.

Lacy watched a very different Dante saunter up to Keenan and into his face, even though Keenan was bigger and taller. Gone was the frivolous, light-hearted man she thought she'd got to know. He spoke low and deliberately, "You are not yet bound to your Siren."

Lacy could just about hear what he said. Her heart was in her mouth.

Keenan's eyes looked into Dante's churning indigo and red. "I am bound in blood."

"As you could be with any woman, Atlantean or Human. Only a Siren can bind you to her." After hitting home, Dante walked slowly away, then stopped again, "You'd do well to concentrate on securing her for your family and leave dealing with my family to me … Then you can be in the government that sentences him."

"You expect me to sit idly by while you bring him in?" Keenan said, in disbelief. "For fuck's sake!"

Vince held his arms again.

"No, I don't … Take Lacy to London. Jay said he'd invited you. Take your boys and go … now!" It was an order. "I'll keep you informed."

Keenan looked around the room for back-up, and when none was forthcoming, he stormed from the room.

MALLEVEN LAY languid and sated in the silk-covered bed, his smooth dark-brown skin a perfect contrast to the red sheets. His features were beautifully chiselled, his nose straight and perfectly proportioned between shrewd eyes that were like eternal pools of midnight blue.

Antonio ran a loving finger from his shaven chin along his jaw and down his neck to his hairless, well-muscled chest, all the while leaning up on an elbow, still recovering from their energetic lovemaking. And that was what it was for Antonio; he loved this man to distraction, so much so that he would do anything for him, including double-crossing his own family. That included both Dante and his father and brothers.

Malleven jabbed a sharp fingernail into Antonio's pectoral, just above his heart. There in black ink was the tattoo symbol of Malleven's name. "I thought I told you to disguise or remove this."

"No one knows what it means." Antonio picked up Malleven's hand and kissed the finger that poked him. "I couldn't exactly wear your coat of arms?"

"So a text speak symbol with an M and the number eleven is testament of your undying love for me?" Malleven's laughter bubbled over and he sat up and threw his legs over the side of the bed.

Antonio lay back against the pillows with his hands behind his head. "What I don't understand is why you don't just take one of the Sirens for yourself? That's what Dante's fucking doing after all."

Malleven pinned Antonio with his deepest-blue eyes, "Your brother has one, proven by divining ring, and the other has pledged willingly." Then he turned back and closed his eyes momentarily. "As will I, when I am finished. Then all the Soul Breathers will come to me … willingly." Then he cocked a brow and faced Antonio again. "Well, almost." He leaped on top of Antonio and held him tightly by the throat so he could barely breathe. He slowly lowered his head and gave him the gentlest of kisses to his bluing lips.

Antonio lay limp, not fighting him at all.

"Did the Santalini Siren see you at the ranch?"

Even though Malleven's influence on Lacy was powerful, Antonio would always be the physical representation of Charlie, and no amount of hypnotism could eradicate it. If she ever came face to face with him, she would remember him.

Antonio shook his head as much as Malleven's grip would allow.

Malleven lowered his ear to Antonio's mouth.

"I escaped as she got there," Antonio said, in a whispered rasp.

"You gave the king's Siren the pills?

Antonio managed to swallow with difficulty. Malleven released his throat but shifted his grip to his arms above his head and pinned his body with his full weight.

"Yes," Antonio said, breathily. "Whether she will take them or not, I'm not sure … she wasn't that keen … I don't get it, I thought you wanted her power?"

"I do," Malleven said, still pinning him with his eyes. "For all intents and purposes, they will do exactly as they are meant to – suppress Murr characteristics, but there is a little something added; a gift from me, shall we say."

"What?" Antonio asked, cautiously aware of Malleven's fine line between genius and madness.

Malleven trailed a finger down Antonio's cheek as if the previous act of violence never happened. "The more of the pills she takes, the less of her own willpower shall remain. Gradually, she will become more and more suggestible, ready for when I call her to me." Malleven paused and appeared to study him. "You did well, Antonio."

"Someone set the barn alight and almost got me lynched," he accused.

Malleven didn't answer but kissed him hard and savagely bit his neck. He pressed his lips to Antonio's ear and pulled his hair. "You mean much to me, Antonio, but if you ever betray me, know that I will show you no mercy."

Antonio's chest rose and fell in fear and anticipation. He never knew what would come next, pain or pleasure, but it was always profoundly satisfying.

Antonio's phone buzzed on the bedside table and broke the electric atmosphere. Both of their eyes went to it. Malleven released Antonio's hair, picked it up, and listened. "One moment," he said, and passed the phone to Antonio, "A Mrs McNally, for you," and he allowed his captive to escape to answer it. Malleven's face was amused and questioning. After sitting up, he reached for a cigar from his case and watched Antonio's worried expression until he clicked off the phone.

Malleven flicked his ash into a glass bowl. "Whatever could your old nurse possibly want?"

"My family … they've all been arrested."

Malleven rolled his eyes and crossed his legs. "It was only a matter of time. They were sloppy."

"They were looking for me?"

Malleven's eyes narrowed and face hardened while his brain worked.

"I thought you said ..." Antonio went to whine.

"Silence!" Malleven snapped and stood up.

Antonio sheepishly watched Malleven's tall predator's body pace the room. His heartbeat thumped in his ears with fear. "What will you do?" he had to ask eventually.

"A Santalini warrior knows you have something to do with the abduction of his Siren." Malleven stopped pacing and glared at Antonio. "You are as good as dead."

Antonio swallowed hard, *fuck*. "I don't get it ... how could they know anything about me?"

Malleven stalked towards the bed and threatened his chest with his cigar. "I should fucking kill you myself."

Antonio looked down at the tattoo and could hear the lit end of the cigar singeing his hairs. "My god, I'm sorry ... I had no idea ... I never dreamed ..." Antonio's eyes looked up hopelessly at Malleven's cold face.

"You are fortunate, Antonio, that I have a soft spot for you ... and it suits me to strike first." He pressed the lit cigar into Antonio's flesh.

CHAPTER 22

$\mathcal{I}$t was begrudgingly that Keenan went to Jay's hotel in London, along with Lacy and his boys. The atmosphere was frosty, to say the least. Jay, however, greeted them warmly in the bar when they got there, shaking all their hands and kissing Lacy on the cheek.

It seemed Lacy couldn't wait to get away from Keenan and quickly made her excuses to go up to their room. Keenan nodded to Vince and the boys, who made their excuses as well. Their room was adjoining Lacy's; Keenan was taking no chances with her any more.

Keenan ordered vodka for himself and a Jack Daniel's for Jay. As soon as they were alone, he wasted no time, "I wanted to ask you to do me a favour, Jay."

Jay sat on the stool next to him and gave him a sardonic look as if he knew what was coming.

"What?" Keenan said, all innocence.

"No, mate."

"You don't know what I'm going to ask yet."

"Don't I?"

"Who told you?"

Jay gave a mirthless laugh and raised his eyebrows. "The downside of the bond is you get Dante, twenty-four/seven."

"Surely you, above all people, understand?"

"Yes, I can … but I've known Antonio a long fucking time … and kidnap?" He shook his head. "Not his style."

"Dante saw him, though."

"I know, he told me," Jay sighed, and took a slug of his drink. "The safest thing for you to do is to get spliced with Lacy, you know that."

Keenan put a foot up on the rail under the bar. "I feel we are a long way off that yet."

"Look, why don't you go up, get changed, and we'll go out for a few jars … loosen up a bit with her. See what happens … There's a pool in the basement?" he said, with raised eyebrows, smiling, "out of bounds between ten and six?"

Keenan cracked a smile. "Okay, man … a few beers."

FROM THE MOMENT Lacy stepped out of The Bluebell on her way out with Keenan, the evening felt tinged with danger and made her nerves on high alert. The cold air was hung with a fine mist. It made a change from the extreme rain and wind they seemed to be having all the time lately, but it still didn't help shake off her feelings of dread.

Jay was taking them out for a night out on the town, but her thoughts were in Ireland, where the man who had kidnapped her was being arrested. How could she relax and have fun knowing all that was going on? She had so many questions she needed answering. Well, at least Keenan was out of harm's way. He would undoubtedly kill the man before she could find anything out. That thought made her feel slightly better.

One bar quickly merged into another and everything

began to feel like a blur as she was beginning to feel quite drunk.

She was hoping the night was coming to an end when Jay said he just wanted to stop at one last place, 'The Kats Wiska's'. She saw Vince whisper to Rick and chuckle, and she guessed what sort of place it was. Not that she was a snob, *but could the evening get any worse?*

"You're quiet?" Keenan said, bending his head next to her ear.

The place was dark and crowded, so she was forced up close with him. "Can you blame me?" she said, looking up at him bleakly.

"Come on," Keenan said, pulling her to the other side of the club, where it was darker and away from the others. An old reggae record came on: 'Silly Games'. She recalled it, but she wasn't sure where from. Keenan pulled her close to dance. Her heart fluttered at his close proximity. He started to move with her and she found herself pressed up close against him with his leg moving between hers, and his head bowed low next to her ear.

She felt him smile next to her cheek. "What's funny?" she said, suddenly self-conscious. "Am I doing it wrong?"

He broke into a laugh. "No," he said and shook his head, "it's just that I realized I've known you all your life and it's the first time I've danced with you."

She stared up into his eyes, amazed. "Really, why?"

His head came down to her ear again and he continued to move with her to the music. He moved exceptionally well for such a big bloke. "I could never get this close to you when we were young."

Understanding dawned on her. "Oh yeah, you were my brother."

"That … and I couldn't have kept my hands off you," he said, taking a sideways glance at her.

Her heart sped up at the implied words, which he emphasised by nipping her earlobe with his lips. Her legs turned to jelly and an ache went from her womb to the juncture of her thighs.

The music moved seamlessly into a lovely Lovers Rock tune that Keenan obviously knew. "Relax," he whispered.

"I am," she lied.

"I can feel your heart racing. It makes me want to bite."

Her head snapped up to look at him. She was shocked, as a rod of pure lust shot to her stomach. A swirl of blood entered his irises. Then her eyes dropped to his mouth as he parted them slightly, grinning so she could see his distending canines. *Could he get any sexier?*

Keenan laughed at her expression.

"Someone will see," she whispered, looking around her the whole time.

"Kiss me then," he said, bending and gently putting his lips on hers.

Her heart raced as she tentatively kissed him. He simply was too sexy to resist. She was grateful for their dark corner and she would have totally lost herself in the kiss if the pungent smell of marijuana hadn't filtered its way to her nose.

She pulled apart from him. "What's that smell?"

"Weed," he said, looking at her, confused at what the big deal was.

Something was really unsettling her though; she couldn't put her finger on it, but it had been building all night. "I need a drink," she said, more for a distraction than genuine thirst.

Keenan took her hand, but she could feel he was concerned as to what was bothering her. *Shit,* he was getting under her skin again.

As they neared the bar, Jay was standing with a scantily clad blonde and brunette draped on either side of him. It wouldn't have bothered her if he weren't supposed to be in love with her sister. She wasn't sure what she made of him anyway, as he was such a closed-off person.

Keenan immediately clocked the scene and was aware of what she was thinking; it was all over his face. "Don't read too much into it, Lace."

She looked into his eyes but didn't answer him. The girls left as soon as they came up to Jay, as if prompted.

"All right?" Keenan said, trying to defuse an awkward atmosphere. "Wanna drink, Jay?"

"I'll get 'em … I just heard from Dante."

"Oh yeah?" Keenan said.

Lacy's ears pricked immediately.

The barman fixed an excruciatingly long round of drinks for everyone, but took no money from Jay, Lacy noticed.

"Antonio wasn't there," Jay said, eventually.

"So they didn't get him," Keenan said, his body deflating with disappointment.

"No … they've taken in Christian and the others for questioning."

Keenan shifted from foot to foot with impatience, like a caged animal.

Jay tried to calm him; "It wouldn't have made any difference if you had been there. They reckon he hadn't been there for days."

Keenan knocked back his drink, fuming.

KEENAN WAS furious that the first real lead in months had evaporated. He went to turn away from the bar to hide his disgust when he caught sight of Lacy staring into space, shell-shocked. *Fuck.* He was so wrapped up in his own anger that he hadn't given much thought to how Lacy must be feeling.

The best thing to do was to make their excuses and go. He was just about to tell Jay when a tall, leggy blonde came over to him.

"Hey, babe," she said, and kissed Jay on the mouth with the ease of someone very familiar with him. Jay looked Keenan square in the eye, which spoke reams. "Kat … let me introduce you to some friends of mine."

Keenan smiled at her, careful not to show any teeth extended with his anger. Her eyes widened while she took a full visual sweep of his body.

"Wow!" she said, turning to Jay, "where have you been hiding this one?"

Keenan reached his hand across to take Lacy's, to send a clear message to Kat and reassure Lacy that he wasn't interested. Kat got the point and turned her attention back to Jay.

"How's Chantelle?" Jay asked, bending his head down to hear the answer. Then he took a wad of money from his wallet and pushed it into her hand.

Keenan knew this whole situation was fucked-up, but he had too much of his own shit to deal with to fathom it now. "We're going to go, mate," Keenan said, butting in on Jay's conversation.

Vince, Rick and Dan, sensing they were going, downed their drinks and hovered, ready to leave.

"I'll come with you," Jay said, and kissed Kat on the mouth quickly.

Keenan led the way up the stairs and onto the street. He made sure he tucked Lacy under his arm and out of the rain that had started up again. She was so quiet and subdued.

Jay's face remained closed as they walked along. No explanation was offered. Keenan had lived on the streets long enough to witness all kinds of working girls, patrons and sponsors and that was definitely the deal back there. It was absolutely none of his business, though. The problem would be convincing Lacy of that. *Yeah, he had his own fucking worries.*

From the time Lacy had descended the stairs into the Kats Wiska's, she had the feeling of dread. The same feeling she always got before she had any dealings with Charlie; the smell of the weed, and the throb of the music like it was underwater, only served to compound the feeling. She just couldn't shift it.

Keenan squeezed her hand from time to time on the walk back to The Bluebell. She smiled half-heartedly back at him.

They walked back into their room and she sagged in relief. Keenan, as drained as she was, threw the key card down on the table and flopped onto the bed. Sitting back up, he beckoned her over with his hands. "Come here."

Lacy went over to him and he pulled her between his legs at the edge of the bed. He linked his arms around her waist and lay his head on her breasts. "I'll get him, Lace," he said, simply.

"I need to find out why, Keenan."

"I know." He pulled her to him tighter.

She ran her fingers through his messy hair. *God,* just touching his hair did things to her.

"Did Jay upset you tonight?" he asked.

She was quiet for a moment and Keenan looked up at her with soulful eyes. "Not upset … I just can't work him out."

"He does love her. I know he does," Keenan said earnestly.

She nodded and sighed. "He'll hurt her, though, won't he," she said, with resignation.

Keenan pulled her around to sit on his lap. "We'll be there for her, whatever … okay?"

Her heart melted a little more for him then.

"Anything else bothering you?

"No ... only ..."

He gave her a little shake to continue.

"It sounds silly when I try to say it."

"No, go on ... you can tell me anything."

She wondered if he was aware she was going through a major defrost here ... "I kept on having a weird feeling tonight."

Keenan just frowned and waited. The phone rang. They both looked at it. She hitched a breath with fright.

"What?" Keenan asked, starting to get really concerned.

"Don't answer it."

"Why?" he said, standing up.

"That's it ... it was in my head ... everything." She was terrified.

Keenan continued walking to the phone next to the bed, but it rang off before he got there. He shook his head, then turned back to her. "It was just a wrong number, that's all, Lace."

He must have read the horror on her face because he marched back over and held her by the shoulders. "What's the matter, Lace ... tell me?"

"It was in my head ... tonight, when Dante ..."

"Look, slow down, talk me through it." He sat and held her hand.

"When Dante and Tia tried to look for my memories, we went to a space where Dante said the memories used to be."

Keenan frowned, trying to get a handle on what she was saying. "Yeah?"

"Well, it was so black, and so empty, it was scary ... oppressive ... claustrophobic," she said, imagining it all over again.

He nodded, willing her on.

"First of all, we felt wet grass under our feet, then we heard muffled club music, then I smelled weed."

"I don't understand, Lace. That could have happened hundreds of times in your life?"

"Then the phone rang, and it was him. I know it was him."

Keenan's eyes went to the phone in the room. "Who? Antonio?" His eyes were starting to flash red with anger.

"No, it wasn't. Dante may have *seen* Antonio there as Charlie, but that's not him … Antonio's not the one … not on the phone, I just know it."

"And you thought that was him?" Keenan said, nodding towards the phone in their room.

"What if …?"

"What?"

"What if it wasn't the past, but the future?"

"What did he say, exactly, the man on the phone?"

"That Dante couldn't win. That he'd take us all from him, and we would go willingly … I've just got this horrible feeling, Keenan, that something terrible is going to happen."

Keenan searched her eyes for a moment, then pulled her to him and hugged her tight. Whether he believed her or not, he knew it was important to her and she appreciated that.

The phone rang again.

CHAPTER 23

They both looked at each other, stock still for a moment. Then Keenan got up, refusing to be rattled, walked around to the phone, looked at her, and picked it up. He sagged with relief. "Dante … Yeah, Jay told us … a bit on edge … okay, mate." He put down the phone.

"What did he say?" Lacy asked, anxiously.

"Same as Jay, basically," and he walked back round to her and pulled her into his arms. "Look, you're bound to be nervy."

The phone rang again, making her jump.

"Hey, come on," he said, gently, and went to move towards the phone again.

She held onto his arm to stop him. It stopped ringing. *Thank god.*

"It's all a coincidence, that's all," he said, walking back towards her. "Get into bed. I just need to have a quick word with the boys and while I'm at it, I'll speak to Jay about what's up with the phone, okay?" He kissed her on the forehead.

She nodded and he released her and went to the connecting door to the next room.

Not more than a minute after he'd left the room, the phone rang again. She battled with the looming feeling of dread and chided herself for being so silly.

When it didn't ring off, she edged towards it, hoping it would stop before she got there. It didn't. She stood over it, then reached out one of her hands and touched it with the tips of her fingers. *Stupid cow*, and she snatched it up. "Hello!" she almost shouted.

The line was quiet for a beat, then a tinkling tune eased her, and a familiar voice spoke. "Lacy, can you hear me?"

The rich, accented voice caressed her ears. "Yes," she said, in a breathy whisper.

"It is time for you to come to me; it has been too long."

"Too long," she copied.

"Tell me, Lacy, why are they looking for Antonio?"

"They think he's Charlie … the tattoo … Dante was in my head."

"I see." The voice hardened. "Do you have the little musical box with you?"

"Yes. I take it everywhere, like you told me."

"Good … You will wake early, when you hear the music from the box, you will make your way out to the street outside your hotel. A car will be waiting. Do you understand?"

"Yes."

"You will not remember speaking to me; it was just a night porter."

The door opened and Keenan walked back into the room. He frowned when he saw her on the phone. She returned the receiver and pinched the bridge of her nose with her thumb and finger.

"Who was that?" Keenan asked.

"Oh, just a night porter, testing the phone."

Keenan nodded. "Come on, bed. You look knackered."

She obediently allowed him to strip off her clothes and got into bed like a tired child.

DANTE COULD HAVE DELEGATED the task, but needed to know how deeply his father – and he used the term loosely – and his brothers were involved with the kidnapping and imprisonment of Lacy.

Alfonzo and Sebastian sat in the room as well, as legal witnesses. A secretary noted everything that was said, verbatim.

"How many more times do I have to tell you, I have no idea where Antonio is," Christian spat.

"There is a warrant out for his arrest," Dante said, feeling a curious detachment from the man who had bullied and tormented him for most of his life. How the tables had turned, the man meant nothing to him, and he was glad of it.

"What for ... he is no threat to you?" Christian protested.

Dante stood and stalked towards the pathetic excuse of a man. "That is a matter of opinion. Where shall I start? ... He set fire to Tia's Protector's barn to isolate her. He then took her away from her Protectors – a crime in itself, to meet with Marco, who handed her over to Humans, of all people. We now have evidence that says he was complicit in the abduction of her sister, already blood-bound to the Santalini Prince – another crime."

Dante studied his father's face closely as he spoke. He saw a definite discomfort when he spoke of Tia, but saw confusion, then indignation when he mentioned the part about Lacy. Whether Antonio was guilty in that or not, he was sure his father was in the dark about it. He could have proved his suspicion without any doubt, his power was such now that he could have just touched skin and read his father's thought patterns, but it was a card he wasn't willing to show yet. Besides, his father was an open book.

"Rubbish," Christian said. "I know my son. I would know if anything untoward was going on with him."

"Maybe you're losing your grip," Dante taunted. "After all, Marco has been trying to oust me as king, Stephan has carried out one attempt to kill me, why not go for yet another Siren … even a third?"

Christian's face blasted red.

Interesting. The mention of a third definitely struck a chord.

Christian pinned Dante with eyes of absolute hatred. "All princes have a right to vie for the crown. If you have evidence implicating your brothers, then charge them, but you have nothing on me." He sat back in his chair and smirked.

DESPITE BEING DOG-TIRED, sleep evaded Lacy. "I need to speak to Jay … it's no good." She pulled out of Keenan's arms, slipped out of bed and quickly put her jeans and sweater back on. Then she stomped from the room.

She knew Keenan was dressing quickly to follow her, but she didn't care and rapped on Jay's door. No answer.

"He's probably still down in the bar, Lace," Keenan said from behind her.

She huffed and pushed him out of the way, then marched to the lift and hit ground floor. Keenan followed, sockless in just his jeans and T-shirt. When they entered the lift, he turned her to face him and searched her eyes.

"I need to speak with him, Keenan … Alone."

He was silent for a beat. 'Okay, I'll wait outside. I won't let you go anywhere by yourself, though."

She huffed again and turned away from him. Then, as soon as the lift pinged, she could barely wait till the doors opened to get out.

She halted at the entrance to the bar. There was Jay, sitting all alone at the bar, drinking coffee, looking over paperwork. It stunned her for a second. She wasn't sure what she expected him to be doing, but working, she did not.

Jay looked up as he sensed her there. Keenan paused behind her. "I'll wait out here," he said, and pulled back the wooden doors, closing them in together.

Lacy stood nervously. Jay's face was as unreadable as ever, but he smiled at her slightly and pulled the stool next to him out for her to sit on. She walked over to him and climbed on it, allowing her eyes to glance at him for a second.

"Wanna drink?" he said, sipping his coffee.

"No thanks."

"What's up?"

Her heart and mind were racing. She'd come here on such a whim that now she was here she didn't have a clue what to say to him. There were a hundred things she wanted to say to him – scratch – accuse him of, but her sister loved him, she was sure of that. Nevertheless, there was something about him that made her feel uneasy. She supposed the truth of the matter was, she didn't trust him and tonight hadn't helped convince her otherwise.

She remained quiet while Jay got off his stool and went to the other side of the bar to busy himself with an impressive-looking coffee machine. He pushed a cup at her. She looked up at him.

"Hot chocolate, to help you sleep," he said, and walked back around and sat next to her again.

"Thank you," she said quietly.

She sipped the drink. Strangely, he didn't question her, but carried on looking at his figures, as if her sitting next to him in the middle of the night was the most natural thing in the world. It was weirdly comforting. "What's Antonio like?" she said, breaking the silence eventually.

Jay put his pen down and turned to face her on his stool. "He was an okay kind of guy growing up, kept himself to himself. Not a big-head." He continued to watch her absorb the information.

"What does he look like?"

"Nothing like Dante. All the other brothers are blonde with light-grey eyes, tall, good-looking, medium frame – but you met them, didn't you? – in New York?" he said, frowning as he picked up his coffee cup.

That's right, she remembered now, when Ruby had invited them, and Keenan's brother had been furious. "Antonio wasn't with them, though." She wondered if she was the reason why.

"No, it seems he was very busy,"

"With my sister?"

"Look, for what it's worth … taking you? I just can't see it – not for himself anyway. Mind you, I would never have thought he'd be involved in taking your sister either." He shook his head, at a loss, and sipped his coffee.

She was quiet again, not sure how to phrase her next question. Jay watched her, seeming to know she was in turmoil and she saw the corners of his mouth twitch as if he wanted to smile.

"Are you going to hurt my sister?" she blurted, but looked him dead in the eye for any evidence of discomfort.

His eyebrows went up. "That's not my intention, Lacy."

She fidgeted with her fingers.

"Look," he said, trying to help her a bit. "You don't know me. You shouldn't judge me, not on what you think you've seen tonight." His face was just as unreadable.

"I don't trust you … does anyone really know you?"

Jay tried to cover up his amusement, which was really starting to piss her off.

"Only one person … probably." He was trying to look earnest, like he knew he was infuriating her.

"Does he trust you?" she asked.

"You'd have to ask him, I guess … but you should know … you can feel what he feels?" He raised his eyebrows like a question.

Was he mocking her? She felt outwitted. She'd come down here to get some answers, but he'd told her very little. She went to get down from the stool to go. He touched her gently on the arm. "Don't you want to bind Keenan to you?" he asked, quietly.

She stopped and froze, half off the stool and got back up again slowly. Did she really want to go into this with him? "I'm not sure … I don't think I'm ready for that yet."

She let her eyes track up to his face and was surprised to see genuine concern there. She felt tears welling up. *Bloody hell.* She dragged an impatient forearm across her eyes, angry with herself.

Jay gently let go of her arm and sat back. "Imagine how you would feel if Keenan wasn't with you. How would you feel about that?"

"That's never going to happen," she said, as if he'd physically struck her.

"If not him, it will be someone else."

Shit. She'd never thought about it like that. She'd kind of taken him for granted since she'd been back. She shook her head, "I'd hate it."

"And you're attracted to him in the way a Siren is for their mate?" he said, with heavy hooded eyes, hiding the emotion she knew he felt when he thought of Tia and Dante.

She swallowed and nodded. "I can't imagine ever being attracted to anyone more." *Shit,* she really felt like she was stabbing him with every word, but he showed not one ounce of what he felt. A tear brimmed and ran down her cheek.

Jay stood down from his stool and pulled her towards him to do the same. He held her somewhat stiffly, as if he wasn't used to comforting anyone in that way. "Then I think it's a no-brainer," he whispered next to her ear.

The heart that had been sticky-taped together up until that point broke, and the tears flowed. It was for her confusion, for the pain she knew she caused Keenan, for her lost year, but most of all, it was for the hopelessness she instinctively knew ran through the veins of this man, who held and comforted her more than anyone had in her short, miserable memory.

The door clicked and she felt Jay's voice rumble in his chest. "She's okay."

Keenan walked cautiously over to them and put his hand on her back. "Lace?"

Jay loosened his grip, but she continued to sob. "Take her to the pool," he said, softly.

Keenan stared at him, not comprehending at all.

"Don't waste any time. Go!" Jay said, more forcefully.

Keenan led her away, tucked into his body, still not taking his eyes off Jay as if they were having a silent conversation.

They got in the lift and he pressed the button to the basement, and she allowed him to take her to the pool.

Keenan put a broom between the handles of the doors leading into the pool as soon as they reached the basement. Lacy, rooted to the spot, watched him as he gathered towels and threw them on a sun lounger next to her. The silence was deafening while he stalked the perimeter, looking for any other entrances that meant they could be disturbed.

Lacy was shaking, she realized. She'd slept with him many times since she'd been back, but the anticipation for this felt different. It was premeditated and solemn. It meant something. Not like the spur-of-the-moment desperation she always felt to pull him to her.

When he'd finished preparing the room, he approached until he towered over her. She wasn't scared of him any more, but she was scared of how he made her feel, and how out of control she became. She gazed up into his eyes, churning indigo, purple and red. It was hypnotic.

"Are you sure you want this, Lacy?" His face was concerned and puzzled. "What did Jay say to you?"

She found she had to look away from his molten eyes, but

he pulled her chin back up, not willing to let her off the hook. "No more running, Lacy."

"He just asked me how I would feel if you weren't always with me."

She saw him visibly relax with relief.

"And what did you say?"

"I couldn't bear it," she whispered, but her eyes bored into his with a conviction so strong he couldn't doubt her.

He swallowed and picked up her hand. "Let's get into the water," he said, quietly.

She nodded and allowed him to pull her sweater over her head. She was naked underneath. His cheeks burned. She pushed his T-shirt up and he pulled it off, so they both stood in just their jeans.

Lacy ran her flat palms over his washboard stomach up to his chest and stroked over his warrior tattoos and the Santalini crest. He stood still and allowed her to study him, but his chest rose and fell and his erection bulged in his jeans.

Her eyes rested on his parted mouth, the tips of his fangs were just visible and she ached for him to sink them into her. She stepped out of her jeans and popped the button on his, until he took over and they both stood naked.

She held his hand and led him to the pool's edge, where they both slipped in off the side. Keenan pulled her to the middle, where the water was waist-height on him and almost chest-height on her.

The muted lights and the slight mist from the heated water gave the place the feel of a lake, magical and remote. She reached up and touched his cheek. His whiskers were starting to grow through, but he was beautiful, dangerously beautiful, if there were such a thing. He leaned into her touch.

"It can't be a full bond yet, Keenan. You know that, don't you?"

Keenan nodded and closed his eyes. He was no expert on the legalities of it, but he'd learned enough from his short time in the Atlantean world to know that only a prince could truly bond with a Siren, because it had to be under water. And the full bond could only occur when it was tested to the point of him drowning. Then only she had the choice to either allow him to die or breathe her life's essence into him, saving his life, opening his gills and joining their spirits for ever. And it was supposed to be a two-way thing and totally irreversible.

"I wouldn't be strong enough to hold you," Lacy explained, feeling terrible.

"Shh." Keenan touched her lips with his finger. "It's enough that you want to bind me to you." He slipped his arms behind her, dipped in the water and pulled her up close. He kissed her gently. She nipped at him with her lips and ventured with her tongue, taking his piercings around his ear into her mouth and kissing his neck until he groaned. She pushed her tongue into his mouth and tempted him to do the same, where she met, matched him and sucked to let him know what she wanted from him.

Keenan pulled her legs around his waist and locked his lips and fell with her into the deeper water, ringing the deepest of kisses while they rolled over and over. Their lips remained joined and their eyes closed until she allowed him to the surface to take a breath, many minutes later, when she released him.

They were totally transformed, as if their complete arousal were a catalyst to send all their markings to the surface to complete the mating dance. Zigzagged in stripes, he glided towards her again. He couldn't stop himself much longer. He'd take her with or without a bond if he didn't calm himself down. His heart raced and his chest hurt like a medicine ball rested in its centre.

"It's time, I can feel it ... oh, Keenan, it hurts."

He was on her in an instant with his mouth on hers. First he felt warmth on his lips, then a tingle, and bubbles went over his tongue and down his throat. A burn like the best scotch went down and soldered his chest to his heart, where it felt like it blasted him into tiny pieces, making him cough.

It was an alarm bell of sensations to his nervous system. Everywhere vibrated and exploded like a million little fireworks, each one a minor orgasm of joy. They were coming so thick and fast, he thought he would pass out, as he just couldn't breathe. He felt paralyzed. Then, as it began to subside, it was as though he was floating on a cloud of bliss.

"Are you okay, Keenan?" Lacy asked. She was frantically shaking him as he lay suspended in the water like he'd been stunned. "Have I killed you, Keenan?"

Gradually, his legs came under him and he began to get his motor skills back. His arms came around her back and he pushed her to the side of the pool.

"Keenan?"

He still hadn't spoken and his eyes were still almost closed, like he was stoned on the best drug. A soppy smile crept over his face.

Talk to me, she projected straight to his head.

His eyes widened when he realized what had just happened and he gave her his full, befanged grin. "Come here." He pulled her tight to him and kissed her hard. She jolted when his hand went straight between her legs. "I'm sorry, Lace. I can't stop," he mumbled next to her lips. He yanked her up out of the water as if she were a doll and placed her on the edge. Her eyes were wide with shock when he widened her knees and plunged his head to her core. She gasped his name and held his hair, but he was merciless and lapped and circled her beautiful bud with his tongue.

He hovered over her groin where her pulse kicked so near to the surface. He licked and he panted, but he couldn't move. His fangs grazed the skin, asking a silent permission.

"Ah, yes, Keenan, yes."

His elongated fangs, razor-sharp, sank deep and she jolted and screamed out his name. In response he growled deep within his chest. Something primeval took hold of him as he drew deep and touched her intimately with loving strokes until she shouted his name again with her release. Before her heart rate could return to normal, he licked the puncture wounds closed and pulled her off the side onto his lap.

His huge waiting erection nudged at her until he gripped it, placed it, and sank it home. She gasped loudly, but he gave her no time to acclimatise. He wedged her into the tiled edge of the pool and thrust over and over, holding her hips still while he pounded relentlessly.

The water lapped noisily against the sides, their panting and groans built and echoed in the cavernous room. Keenan moaned her name as he came over and over and she kissed him and pulled him under the water with her. While she scored his back with her nails, she breathed her essence into him once more. She felt him pulse and gyrate into her and sink his teeth into her shoulder. She breathed for him again for what seemed like an age until he lay limp in the water.

Frightened she'd kept him submerged too long this time, she pulled his face out of the water. He coughed and spluttered and his eyelids fluttered open.

"Are you okay, Keenan?"

"Ah fuck, Lacy," and he grabbed her again and plunged with her into the deeper water. This time, she opened her gills. His control had snapped for the first time, and he grabbed her waist from behind and pushed into her again, slamming into her harder than he'd ever been.

It seemed the rougher he was, the better she liked it. *Ah, Keenan ... don't stop,* and when he realized she was talking to him telepathically, it seemed to push him up a gear. Her light was building in her chest and she knew it needed to come out. Could he take more? He was a prince, wasn't he built for it? *Ah fuck, yes.*

She managed to scramble away from him for enough time to turn around. He grabbed her quickly and pulled her back onto him. Then, while he took a breath at the surface, "I'm sorry, Lace ... I can't help myself," he gasped.

Come here. She breathed a blast of her spirit and he sank in the water as if he'd been shot, but they stayed joined. She released his mouth and put her teeth on his neck and bit him hard, then sucked his blood through his skin. Quickly, his arms came to life again and he thrust upwards into her until she became lost to sensation. Her womb clenched and her muscles bunched and retracted. *Love ... you.* And she bit his lip hard enough to draw blood. The mixture of water and blood in their mouths sent him over the edge again. As he groaned into her mouth, she streamed a slow flow of her essence on and on, down into his heart and the two of them came apart into a thousand pieces, and those pieces went into him in a jumbled torrent, binding them for ever.

KEENAN MADE love to Lacy over and over, as if he'd been starved of her his whole life. Eventually dawn was approaching and early swimmers would want to use the pool, so the pair, just wrapped in towels, crept into the lift and back up to the top floor to their room.

They got straight into bed and Keenan hugged her into his body. He spooned her, fitting her perfectly as he hugged her from behind, and it wasn't long before Lacy felt his breath on her shoulder lengthen and deepen as he fell into the heavy sleep of a contented, replete male.

Lacy dozed in his arms, waking often and saw the gradual grey light of dawn steal between the curtains, which hadn't been closed properly the night before. Her mind meandered and she was about to slip off to sleep again when she heard the pretty little tune from her musical box, given to her by Ruby. It was of such sentimental value that she took it everywhere with her. *Was she dreaming?*

She carefully lifted Keenan's heavy arm from her waist and slithered out from under it and out of the bed, careful not to wake him. She moved cautiously towards the dressing table. The little bell tinkled in her ears. She looked over her shoulder; Keenan was impervious to it, and slept soundly. Weird, the lid was closed. She must be asleep, she concluded. There could be no other explanation.

She reached forward and pressed the little flower at the front and a tiny drawer sprang open. Inside was a wrap of paper, about an inch wide and a couple of inches long. Like half a gram of coke, she mused and looked at Keenan again.

Carefully, she unwrapped the corners to reveal a fine powder. The granules were too fine for coke, though. Something, she wasn't sure what, made it suddenly really necessary for her to leave the hotel. She padded over to Keenan's sleeping body, leaned over him so she was only inches away from his face, and gently blew on the paper. She blew softly until all the powder had gone. Like a cloud of flour, it floated down onto Keenan's face, his pillow and on the bed around him.

Quickly, she grabbed her things and pushed them into her bag. Somehow, she knew Keenan wouldn't wake up and stop her, but she needed to hurry. She threw on her sweater and jeans, and when she had all her belongings, including the music box, she slunk from the room.

She breezed out of the hotel, saying a cheery good morning to the night porter, still on duty in reception, and out to a waiting car. The door slammed and the expensive car glided away.

Panic ensued as soon as Vince managed to wake Keenan up around lunchtime.

It didn't take long for the remnants of the powder on his face to be noticed and what had happened, deduced.

"Fuck!" Keenan punched the door. Then he held his head in his hands. "I don't understand. Why would she bind me to her then run?" He looked at Vince for the answer. He was in misery, his eyes churning.

The door opened and Jay walked in. "I just heard. I've alerted Dante."

Keenan closed his eyes as if shit couldn't get any worse.

"Sorry, mate, I had to."

He knew Jay didn't have a choice and struggled to get a grip. Dante had to know, not only because she was so important to the state, but because he had a complete bond with her and was the best person to help in the search.

Jay's eyes were sympathetic. He'd been in his shoes many times. Keenan just grit his teeth and tried to hide his absolute jealousy. *Fuck*, how Jay got through each day he had no idea. "What did he say?" he managed to ask eventually, although his voice was like gravel with the effort.

"He'll be here in an hour ... hour and a half tops."

Keenan looked to the heavens. He was beside himself with worry. He couldn't go through the months of agony again. *Why? Why?* was all that kept going through his mind.

The phone rang. Dan snatched it up. "What?" He put it to

his shoulder. "Some bloke asking for you?" he said, looking intently at Keenan.

Keenan walked slowly towards Dan, staring him in the eye before taking the phone from him. Then his heart sank so low with dread that his head swam. He knew that voice. His stomach clenched and he forgot to breathe. "Frank," came out, barely a whisper.

"Yes. I'm glad you remember me at last. Took a detour did you … with my fucking money? Go off on yer holidays, did ya? Well listen, good, boy. You wanna see that pretty little sister of yours, then you bring my ten K, plus another ninety for my trouble, and maybe I won't let Razz's boys have a go. Know what I mean?"

Keenan was incandescent with rage. The receiver began to crack under his fingers. "Where?"

"I'm over your way. Make it Number Eleven, in an hour. Leave your cronies behind and come alone and unarmed, and you might just see her again." The phone clicked and the call was over.

In shock, Keenan replaced the receiver slowly, and then looked into Vince's eyes; who knew, he could tell, that one of the worst people he could imagine had Lacy.

Vince stared cautiously back. "Who is it, mate?"

"Big Frank, Vince … Big Frank's got her … He wants his money. I've got to take a hundred grand to the Number Eleven in an hour, otherwise …" He squeezed his eyes shut with a shudder. "Otherwise he's handing her over to Razz's boys." He sank heavily onto the edge of the bed.

"Shit!" and every other expletive were mumbled around the room. "How the fuck did he get her?" someone said.

Keenan shook his head in hopelessness. "How am I gonna get that sort of money together and get it there in an hour?"

"I'll give it to you," Jay said quietly.

Keenan stood up. Words escaped him. The guy hadn't

even asked any 'whys and hows', just offered it. *Fuck*, he was humbled. "Thank you."

"I'll come with you. You'll need backup." Jay said.

All the boys nodded and agreed with that.

Keenan shook his head, "I've got to go alone, and unarmed."

Vince pushed away from him in disgust. "That's suicide, mate."

Keenan shook his head again, not willing to be moved on this. "I can't take chances with her life, Vince … He wants his money back, that's all. It's a pride thing. Besides, he'll under-estimate me anyway. I'm not the skinny nutter I was back then."

Vince turned to look at Jay for some assistance. "Won't make no difference to a shotgun, how fucking big you are."

Jay made no comment, but kept his own counsel.

Keenan could have kissed him. "Jay … I need to get going. I haven't got time to argue with everyone."

Jay let out a deep breath, "Come on … It's in the safe."

Ten minutes later, Keenan was packing a rucksack with the notes Jay had given him. He said a hasty goodbye to everyone, but pointed a finger at Vince as he left. "Don't fucking follow me, Vince. D'you hear. Don't follow me!" And he was gone.

CHAPTER 25

Keenan pulled up outside the Number Eleven club and let the engine idle while he thought for a minute. It was undoubtedly a trap he was walking into, but he couldn't sneak into the place any other way, as the front way was the only way in to the basement club. It broke all kinds of health and safety regulations, which is why it was illegal and never likely to get a license. And he knew the owners weren't going to have seen the light in the year or so he'd been away.

No, this he was going to have to brazen out, and hope to god his reflexes and training were good enough to carry him and Lacy out in one piece.

He got out of the car, crossed the busy road, and descended the stairs at a jog. He ran straight into the barrel of a gun, and four others were trained on him. Big Frank sat casually at the bar, one butt cheek on the stool he precariously perched on, his huge gut, which gave him his nickname, resting halfway down his thigh and his heel on the rung of the stool.

"That's more like it," Frank chuckled. "About a year late,

but better late than never, eh, lads?" The others all took the cue and laughed along with him. He gestured with a finger for one of his men to take the rucksack from Keenan.

Keenan passed it over slowly, then held his hands up in front of him. "Lacy … where is she?"

Frank looked over at one of his men who was checking its contents and nodded. Frank smiled, "Who else did you piss off, Keenan? Some foreign mush wants you hurt bad, boy?"

Keenan didn't answer; not sure who else was in the frame to get back at him and, to be honest, he didn't have the will or the inclination to work it out now. He wanted to get Lacy and get out.

"Still, a deal's a deal," Frank continued, "she's in the office out back. I'll leave you two to it then. Boys?" And Frank slid off the stool like a walrus and waddled up the steps to the street, followed by his four men.

Keenan, aware that it had been far too easy, ran to the office at the end of a corridor to the left of the bar. He stopped. Breathed. Then barged in and stopped in the doorway and did a quick sweep of the room.

His vision zoomed to red while his breathing became ragged and uneasy. He could make out a warm orange glow on a chair facing away from the door. She had a paper bag over her head. Her hands were moving as she was trying to loosen the knots.

Fuck, he was nauseous and his head began to pound.

He moved haltingly towards the shape. Something was way off. Even before the Sirens' bond her blood would have called to him, but not like this. This was spilled blood; spilled blood belonging to Lacy.

He went to grab the bag, but he knew what he would find. It wasn't her. Before his hand had a chance to make contact, the Taser hit his leg.

He let out a roar as he turned to rip apart whoever was in the room, but as he swung around to face his attacker, the baseball bat connected with his skull.

DANTE WAS ALREADY HALFWAY to London on his private jet when Jay brought him up to speed with the latest developments with Keenan. He cursed as memories of Tia's abduction came flooding back.

His plane landed and he quickly transferred to his waiting car and sped off in the direction of Jay's hotel. He was almost there when he heard a frightened voice in the recesses of his mind. *Dante, Tia, Naomi, help me ... anyone ... I don't know where I am.*

Lacy? Dante projected back. *Is that you? Are you okay? Keenan is on his way to you.*

I'm okay, but I don't have a clue where I am.

Dante started to feel uneasy. Something was off. *Describe to me where you are, Lacy?*

I'm walking along a road. Hang on, I can see a sign. South Circular, it says.

Dante stopped breathing for a second. *Fuck,* this wasn't right. *How did you get there, Lacy?*

She started to cry. *I don't know ... I don't know what I'm doing here,* she wailed.

Shh! Dante said to soothe her. *Look, I'm on my way to you. I know roughly where you are. Go to the nearest pub, okay? Then tell me the name of it. I shouldn't be long finding you.*

Thank you ... thank you so much, she sobbed.

Dante advised the driver to change direction and they drove southward. He took out his phone and hit Jay.

"Dante?" Jay answered immediately.

"We've got trouble," Dante relayed the conversation he'd just had with Lacy.

"That means …"

"Yeah … Keenan's walking into an ambush."

"Shit."

"Take his boys and get over there," Dante said. "I'll go pick up Lacy and meet you there … who is this bloke?"

"Some villain he crossed before he came in."

"Okay, get going then, Jay."

Dante clicked off the phone, but he was troubled. Keenan could very easily have pissed a few people off over the years. *God knows* he pissed him off, but getting Lacy away like that to make him a sitting duck? No, this was bigger than South London villains. This had Atlantean written all over it, and a powerful one.

KEENAN SLOWLY BECAME aware of his surroundings; he was strapped tightly to the chair the girl had been tied up in. As he tried to look around, he became aware that one of his eyes was useless. What he could see revealed that they had moved him while he'd been out. He was in some damp old shed on an allotment or garden somewhere. It smelt of newly dug earth and rotting vegetables or compost nearby, and it had rained recently.

His vision cleared a little, and he noticed four nervous-looking men standing around him, waiting for him to make a move. He grimaced as he tried to straighten up and realized he wasn't escaping any time soon; he was hurt bad. They were Razz's crew; he recognized them more from their voices than his sight, which was blurring and zeroing to red. They would have been there the night he'd ripped Razz to shreds with his teeth, and now they wanted payback. "Where's Lacy?" Keenan rasped through his injured mouth.

One of them lunged forward and punched him in the jaw, nearly knocking him off the chair.

Another spoke. "How would we fucking know? Now shut the fuck up, freak!"

"Mind you, she was a sort." They all laughed.

Keenan's mind raced. He ran through the day and the implications of what they had just said to him. Relief was beginning to creep over him as he started to think there was a chance that Lacy wasn't involved in this situation at all. "Frank ... has he got her?"

The first one laughed, then shrugged. "I doubt it. He just said you pissed someone else off and som'ink about your chickens coming home, anyway. Said you would turn up with his money. Not that that makes any difference to you, mate ... not now."

"Come on, show us the teeth?" another said.

"Come and see for yourself," Keenan grinned, gave them the full dental show, and allowed blood to engulf the whole of his eyes.

"Fuckin 'ell," they all said in awe. Then the Taser hit his chest and the lights went out again.

"As soon as it's dark, we'll dump him in the canal."

LACY'S HEART raced faster than the car they were speeding along in. As hard as she tried, she couldn't account for around eight hours. She'd remembered being in the pool with Keenan, and totally giving herself over to binding him to her. Her womb clenched at the memory.

She remembered the exhaustion she'd felt in Keenan's sheltering arms when he'd all but had to carry her to bed. It was the last thing she remembered. Nothing made sense. She'd given in to her feelings for Keenan. *Why would she go then?* The next thing she knew, she was walking along a road in Forest Hill, south London.

She'd never thought she'd say it, but she was thankful for

the bond she shared with Dante. Without it she would have been lost and alone, and who knows what could have happened to her.

It all made her realize that, despite not having her memory back, she would complete the bond with Keenan. Not just for their mutual safety, and that was a huge factor, but last night had made her know for sure that she loved him anyway, whether or not she ever remembered their time before. *Wait!*

Half the bond was complete, so that meant she could speak to Keenan in his head; he just couldn't reply. She began to concentrate, *Keenan. I know you can't speak back, but I want you to know that I know what I want at last. I know now that I love you. I've grown to love you since we met again. Even though I know I must have loved you my whole life, and I may never remember that time, and if I don't ... Well, I fell in love with you all over again. Just like you said, I can't help it. I want you, Keenan. I'm coming to you. Please hang on ...*

"Lacy!" Dante said, interrupting her thoughts.

"What?" she said, shaking her head.

"You okay?"

He must have felt her anguish as she tried to reach Keenan. She nodded. "I was trying to speak to him ... you know ... like I do to you." A tear ran down her cheek as she realized the injustice of the bond she had with Dante and not Keenan. "I never really got to tell him how I felt."

Dante must have known what she was thinking. Perhaps he felt it. *Shit*, didn't that make her feel worse? He pulled her to him and put his arm around her shoulders. "Ah, babe ... he would have known, even as I know how you feel ... Listen, Lacy, we do what we must to survive this poxy world, okay? That's all. When you bond with him fully, you will be a real husband and wife."

"Really?" she said, pulling her head up to look at him.

He looked into her eyes and nodded. "You and me joined purely for the crown. And, for what it's worth, I only really feel married to your sister."

She swallowed, sobered instantly. She knew how Dante felt about her sister because when he breathed for her, there were no hiding feelings. "I hope Keenan feels like that for me."

"You'll know for sure soon, won't you?"

She nodded and sat back in her seat, *if she got to him in time*. She had a dark cloud over her heart that she couldn't shift.

They pulled up at some traffic lights and Dante's phone rang. It was Jay. "We're almost there," Dante said. "Two minutes." He clicked off his phone.

She felt a shift in his mood. He was trying to shield her from something. "What is it?"

He turned in his seat to face her squarely. His eyes were soulful and loving.

"What is it?" she repeated, her panic rising, dreading what he might say.

"He's not at the club, Lacy. But I'm going to take you inside, and I need you to be strong for me, okay?"

Her heart was thumping. "Why?"

He took a deep breath. "There is blood. I need you to tell me if it's his." He said it forthright and honest and she was glad of it.

"I'll know." She nodded.

He gave her one firm nod and sat back as the driver pulled into a space on the opposite side of the road to the rough-looking street door of the Number Eleven club.

LACY FOLLOWED Dante down the concrete steps that led into the club. The two burly Santalini guards who had accompanied them followed them down. Jay, Vince and the boys were waiting for them at the bottom.

Dante pulled Jay into his body and the pair embraced. She was always surprised at their closeness, but when she analysed that part of her that Dante now occupied, she recognized the love as brotherly, and she understood.

"Anything new?" Dante asked.

"Not much," Jay said. "Looks as though he was met here, sent out back and then jumped." Jay looked directly at Lacy and thankfully didn't sugar-coat his words. "There is blood on the floor."

Vince had been walking around the room while Jay spoke and came back over to them. "Do you remember this place at all, Lace?"

"No," she replied.

Vince just raised his eyebrows.

"Just show me the blood, Vince," she said, losing patience.

He nodded and turned in the direction of the office and she followed him. Her breath quickened as she neared it and she began to perspire. She didn't need to ask, but walked straight over to the corner of the room where the tiny spatters of blood peppered the wall and the floor.

The others watched intently and waited for her to speak. She turned to face them, her eyes closed. "It's his."

Jay walked to the centre of the room. "You walked straight past this blood, Lacy?" he said, frowning.

Lacy was confused for a second. She looked where Jay was pointing. There was a much higher concentration of blood and she hadn't even sensed it. "It can't be his," she said in a small voice.

"Maybe he got one of them?" Vince said.

Dante walked forward, shaking his head. "No. Look at the spatters Lacy sensed. He was hit with something … this? This was deliberately put there."

Jay got up from his crouch. "Why would someone do that?"

"It's mine, isn't it?" Lacy said, verging on tears.

Dante nodded, "I reckon it is."

Jay looked at both of them, needing an explanation.

"The one thing a Santalini has no control over is his reaction in the presence of his mate's blood," Dante explained.

Jay frowned, then looked back at Dante when he understood what it meant.

"Yeah, it would have probably incapacitated him," Dante voiced for him.

The memory of the effect her blood had had on Keenan when he had found her in the dingy flat came flooding back. Lacy had heard enough. She pushed between them and out of the room. "I need to get out."

The boys separated and allowed her through, but when she reached the street, Dan and Rick were right with her.

It was starting to get dark as the days were short and the rain clouds were gathering ominously, making it feel like nighttime. She glanced back at the club and paced a few steps. *Where on earth did they begin to search?*

The others joined them and they stood in a group on the pavement. Dante was looking up and down the road as if deciding on which way to go.

"Listen, they probably won't have taken him far," Vince said, looking furtively at Lacy. "Especially if Razz's boys are involved."

She swallowed a lump. She wasn't stupid. She knew he meant that if they were going to kill him, they'd do it close and soon, as they'd be less likely to get caught.

"Yeah," Dan said in agreement, "and if they were going to move him anywhere, they would probably take Commercial Road or Whitechapel sometime." Dante looked at both men and nodded as if weighing up what they were saying, but his deliberations were halted when his phone rang. Lacy watched him take it out, look at the number, frown and put the phone to his ear. "Who is it?" His face paled. "Who is this?"

Lacy felt the familiar feeling of dread that accompanied every phone call these days, but this was stronger than ever. It was as if the devil himself were on the phone.

Dante took the phone away from his ear, clicked it off and began to walk towards his car. "Let's drive," he shouted back to them.

"Where?" Jay shouted back.

"Fuck knows. Just follow."

Lacy ran to catch up with him and they jumped back in the car with the two guards they'd come with. "Who was it, Dante?" Lacy asked.

He stared ahead of him, preoccupied, like he was working through something in his mind.

"It was him, wasn't it?" she said, quietly. He looked sideways at her, neither confirming nor denying it. "It wasn't Antonio," he said.

"I saw the future, Dante, didn't I?"

Still, he didn't answer.

It was almost dark, and they'd driven around east London for what felt like hours. Around all the areas and housing estates Vince said they'd grown up in. To lock ups and garages and up and down Commercial and Whitechapel roads countless times.

Lacy despaired at their total lack of progress while the car slowed to a halt and purred at a junction of lights. Dante wound down his window and apologized to her as he took out a cigarette. "I only smoke now when I'm stressed," he explained.

A white van pulled up next to them, bass pounded and dub-step vibrated and ricocheted from inside. The windows were shut, so the music was muffled. She looked over at Dante. He looked back at her and twigged what she was thinking.

"Do you think?" she whispered.

Dante quickly concentrated and the van next to them stalled. They heard Jay's car rev behind them, overtake the van at a screech into oncoming traffic and stop next to the van on the driver's side.

"It's them," the guard driving said, after listening to an ear-com.

The lights went green and the van started its engine and sped away.

"Follow them until we get somewhere quiet and stop them … I don't care how," Dante said.

"What's going on, Dante?" Lacy asked, beginning to panic as everything seemed to go frantic. The van had got faster realising it was being followed and their two cars matched its speed.

"Vince recognised them, Lacy. It's them," Dante explained.

The van shot into an estate in an effort to lose them, taking several fast left and right turns. This carried on for some minutes until Dante had had enough. Lacy felt him centre his energy and the van drove up a small bank and flipped over, sliding on its roof.

The two cars screeched to a halt on either side of the van, which was still rocking upside down. They all got out and one of their guards walked around the van and bent right down to see the state of the occupants. "Two in the back are unconscious and beaten up bad. Passenger and driver conscious," he said.

"Get the van upright," Dante ordered.

The two huge guards, Jay and the boys all began to rock the van until they gave one last heft and it creaked and complained back onto its wheels.

They heard the driver groan in pain. The passenger was drifting in and out of consciousness.

"Get the driver out," Dante said. "Take Lacy with you, Jay. Vince, bring him with us in my car. He will take us to Keenan."

Lacy went to protest when Jay touched her gently on the

back and moved her towards his car. She knew he would allow no argument. She stamped her foot and got in his car with the hump. He got in the driver's seat.

"I need to be there when they find him," she protested.

"You will," Jay said. "It's just safer this way, that's all." He looked at her in the rear-view mirror, giving her his straight no-nonsense look, and she huffed and looked back towards the other car. She saw Vince and one of the guards virtually carrying the injured man into the back of Dante's car. He got in beside the man and the door was slammed.

Jay pulled away and they quickly joined the busy evening traffic.

"I need to know where he is, Jay," Lacy complained. "I should be in that car."

Jay appeared to ignore her. He was infuriating. "Do you have your ear-com, Dan?" Jay asked.

"Yeah."

"Keep it on. Speak to the other car. Get them to talk us through what's going on," Jay said calmly, driving as if they were on a journey to the shops.

"For fuck's sake, Jay!" she screamed.

A smile played on his lips. She saw it distinctly in the rear-view mirror. "You sound like Tia," he said, and a beautiful smile transformed his face.

THE MAN VINCE recognized as Hassan was screaming at the top of his lungs, although croaky and ragged due to the cracked ribs he'd sustained in the crash. A little mental pressure on his chest from Dante was all it took for the perfect persuasion.

"Look, mate," Vince continued, "just tell us where Keenan is and we'll drop you out the car and it'll all be over."

The young man groaned as if speech was difficult.

"You can't take much more before your lung punctures and fills with blood, then it's curtains, okay? Where. Is. Keenan?" Vince spoke calmly, the epitome of reason.

Dante kept up the pressure. Then, deciding he'd lost patience, he turned slowly in his chair to face Hassan, not much more than a youth really. He grabbed Hassan's hand and closed his eyes to summon more power, then spoke directly to Hassan's mind. *Look at me.*

Hassan blinked in shock and looked at Dante in the eyes in absolute terror.

Dante's mental voice was strong and authoritative. *You have taken my cousin and I want him back. Do you understand? We are the same.*

Hassan's eyes were wide with fear, but he nodded.

Dante knew Hassan was fully aware that Keenan wasn't Human, judging by his reaction and his eyes darting to his mouth. It was a blag, but a calculated one. *Now, first of all, who told you where Keenan was?*

Hassan became agitated with panic and his breathing became more ragged and laboured.

Easy. If you cooperate, I won't hurt you. Speak slowly, Dante said, calmly.

"Frank … Frank contacted us," Hassan whispered, breathing between words. "Some foreign bloke … contacted him … said he would give Keenan … to us on a plate."

Dante addressed Vince on the other side of Hassan. "Who's Frank?"

"South London villain Keenan crossed the night he left London. Took his money," Vince explained.

Dante spoke to Hassan telepathically again. *What about Lacy? Where did she fit into all this?*

Hassan shook his head, beginning to hyperventilate. "Bloke said to make out like we 'ad 'er … 'e'd do the rest … We never saw 'er … I swear."

Now, I'm going to ask you this once and once only. Where. Is. Keenan. Now?

Hassan swallowed, "The canal."

Which canal?

"Regent's," Hassan spluttered, and began to cough uncontrollably.

Vince, unaware of the internal conversation Dante was having with him, began to shake him, "Fucking where is he?"

"Vince!" Dante said, holding up an arm to stop him. Hassan was weakening fast.

"Near … to the Islington … tunnel." He began to slip in and out of consciousness.

"Regent's Canal, Islington tunnel," Dante repeated aloud to Vince.

Vince nodded and sat back in his seat. He knew where that was.

"Drop him outside Mile End Hospital," Dante said to the driver.

"Drop him here," Vince said, annoyed. "There ain't much time."

"He won't last five minutes," Dante said, calmly and deliberately.

Vince gave him the look that said he didn't give two shits. "Ah, for fuck's sake … Keenan could be . . . ?" Vince shook his head, not believing what was happening.

"Mile End Hospital," Dante ordered the driver. "I'm not a murderer, Vince. It won't take much time." He turned back to the driver, "Be quick."

THE CONVERSATION in Dante's car was relayed via Dan in Jay's earpiece, so they knew the instant Dante knew where they were headed.

"The canal," Lacy shrieked. "Does that mean…?"

"Don't jump to conclusions, Lacy. He's Atlantean, isn't he?" Jay said.

"He doesn't breathe the water … It's my fault," Lacy began to cry.

"Shh," Jay said calmly, looking at her in the mirror. "Speak to him. Let him know we know where he is. It could be what keeps him going. Okay?"

Lacy nodded with conviction and rubbed her tears away. Then she closed her eyes and reached out with her mind as she'd done earlier.

Jay switched on the car radio. The news was finishing and the weather report began. The constant wind and rain were worsening. It was going to be another atrocious night.

THE RAIN HAD REALLY STARTED to come down again as they pulled up near the Regent's Canal. All of them got out of their cars and pulled up their hoods or collars to protect them against the gale and lashing rain. One of the guards quickly found a spare jacket for Lacy. All she had on were the jeans, jumper and shoes she'd worn when she'd left The Bluebell.

Dante quickly began to organize them. "Right, go over the bridge with Rick and Dan, Vince, and see if you can see anything in or around the canal … Jay, you take the guards and do the same on this side."

Dante started to take off his shoes, then his jacket. "We'll have to go in, Lacy," he said, squinting in the rain. "We know roughly where he is, but not the exact spot. So go with your gut, okay? If you feel anything … anything at all, you tell me."

Lacy agreed and began taking off her own shoes and jacket, anything that would weigh her down. This was no time for modesty.

They all spread out and followed Dante's orders. Dante

and Lacy walked across a grassy bank that led towards the edge of the tunnel where the canal passed underneath. Lacy felt the wet grass squelch beneath her feet and froze.

"What?" Dante said.

"Wet grass."

Dante paused for a beat.

"Wet grass, muffled music, the phone call?" She began to walk faster.

"Careful," Dante shouted. He'd spotted broken glass around the steps that led down to the canal.

"We heard broken glass," Lacy shouted over the wind, "when Tia threw the phone.'

Dante came up alongside her. "This must be the place. We'll go in here." He crouched down to slip in off the side. I'm not sure what the visibility will be like. Stay talking, okay?"

She nodded, peeled out of her jeans and they both jumped in, submerged immediately into the inky-blackness of the water, black like the space in her mind. *Oh my god.*

Thankfully, she heard Dante quickly, *Lacy, can you hear me?*

Yes.

Swim close to the bottom. Hold my hand and we'll zigzag across. We'll feel as we go. He must be here somewhere.

Lacy opened her lungs. She did exactly as Dante said, as she couldn't see a damn thing. *Please be here, Keenan. Please be okay.*

ANTONIO HADN'T BEEN BACK to see his family in Ireland in ages. He found he wanted to be with them less and less these days. Instead, he'd been holed up in their New York residence, unable to bear being too far from Malleven, who'd now made the Big Apple his home.

Malleven had relocated to America, telling Antonio it was more central to his plans than London or Milan. Antonio understood while Malleven kept Lacy for his experiments, but she had long gone back to her true mate, Keenan Santalini. *What the bloody hell was he up to?* Malleven was a drug to Antonio that he couldn't get enough of, and so he waited anxiously for him to call so he could meet with him again.

He was also aware that he was too keen and too available, but whenever he made a plan to play hard to get, it all went out the window when Malleven first said a sexy hello.

Everything had gone quiet between them since the handing over of Tia Storm to the Americans. It had quickly become apparent that she would never pledge to anyone other than Dante, and Lacy Rain had been bonded from babyhood into the Santalini House. That had only left a third and previously undiscovered Siren – a much more attractive prospect in that she was unknown. It had occurred to Antonio that it was strange how Malleven knew of her.

She had been given to the American government ten years previously as collateral when just a small girl, in some diplomatic deal, but after enlisting Malleven's help for the exchange, the Dubonnettis had been duped. No replacement Siren had arrived at the meeting point and they'd in fact lost both – Tia and the mystery Siren.

Antonio hadn't heard much from Malleven since. He desperately wanted to see him but wasn't sure whether it was safe to contact him, knowing how volatile he was.

He paced the floor in front of the phone and was just about to make a grab for it when he heard a commotion in the hall, a mixture of men's voices. *Damn it.*

Wandering out into the large vaulted hallway, his heart sank. His father and brothers were ordering the driver and servants about where to put their luggage and taking off their coats.

Before he could slope off, his father caught sight of him. "Stay there, Antonio," Christian said, pointing a finger at him. "Take my bags up to my room," he said to a servant already laden with luggage. "My study now, boy," he bellowed, addressing Antonio directly.

Shit. He rolled his eyes and huffed, but followed his father's tall, brittle-looking body striding into the study.

Christian turned on him the minute the door closed, and he smacked him up against it with his cane wedged under his chin. "What happened at the ranch, Antonio? You were supposed to come with us to convince the Santalini Siren to pledge to Marco? … What the bloody hell went on?" he spat.

Antonio blinked as his father enunciated his words and spittle flicked at his face.

When he realized his grip was too restrictive for Antonio to speak, Christian let him go and prowled in front of him, his cane still gripped tightly.

Antonio never took his eyes off it. "I got a call, they needed help. I had to help get Tia Storm to the café; Marco took her from there … I was lucky to get her away at all considering someone set the bloody barn alight." He couldn't tell his father why there was no way he could go with them to the Santalini HQ for fear of Lacy recognizing him as the face of Charlie.

Instead, he continued to watch the cane; he couldn't help remembering how it was always reserved for Dante, but he'd long since got away, and now it was clear that it would be his turn.

Christian turned and narrowed his eyes at him. "We waited at the arranged point and the Americans didn't show. We haven't seen or heard from Malleven Since."

Neither had he. Not daring to answer back, Antonio tried

to inch away from his father's reach, but his progress was halted when he stabbed the wall next to him suddenly with the cane. "What is Malleven to you, boy?" Christian snarled.

Antonio shrank his eyes down to the floor and remained silent.

Christian smacked the cane at his mouth to chivvy him along. "Answer me!"

Antonio's hands came up in defence of his face. "What, Father … what do you want me to say?" Antonio screamed. "We're friends … we see each other socially."

Christian grabbed Antonio by the shirt collar and threw him across the room with remarkable strength for an aged man. Antonio rolled across the desk and over the other side, onto the floor and scrambled to his feet.

Christian stalked towards him. "I know you are rather more than friends, boy." And he backhanded him in the mouth, sending him flying onto his back. "Which I don't give a fuck about." He dragged Antonio back onto his feet with a painful grip to the shoulder. "What I do fucking care about is getting arrested by that runt of Delissi's and treated like a common criminal, because you've been conspiring against me with your fucking lover!" Christian screamed into his face. "Your loyalties seem to be askew." He punched him hard in the solar plexus.

Antonio collapsed forward, winded. Christian stopped him from falling by yanking his head back by the hair. "You will continue to be *friends* with Malleven, but you will report everything to me. Do you hear me?" he said very calmly through gritted teeth.

Antonio managed the smallest movement of his head. Christian threw him away from him like discarded dirty washing.

Antonio clawed his way back up to standing using a chair next to him. His face was throbbing, swollen and bleeding.

He put the back of his hand to his mouth and pulled it away to look at the blood that had printed onto it. Then something finally cracked or broke or just plain ended. "Never," he said, flatly.

His father narrowed his eyes and grit his teeth in the way that would normally make his knees quake. "What did you say?" he snarled.

Antonio felt remarkably calm. It was as if a weight had gone from him. "Never," he repeated, a bit louder. "I will never betray Malleven to you, and you will never beat him. He is stronger than you." Antonio was smiling, although his lip stung to buggery.

Christian's face moved from a grimace to a grin. "You're sure of that, are you? Do you think someone like you truly matters to him? You're a fool." The grin on Christians face evaporated and his eyes became vacant as if he were dreaming. "Soon, my darkly begotten son will come home. He is the strongest of all, and no one, not even the powerful wizardry of the Florianna, can beat him." Christian sighed wistfully and his consciousness came back to the room. "Get out!" he snapped. "Never darken my doorstep again … I have no need of you … go!" and he threw his cane at Antonio, which struck him viciously on the side of the head.

All Antonio could think of was fleet-footing it out of the room, out of the house, and out of the Dubonnetti family forever. He ran through the hall, vaguely aware that Paulo, Stephan and Marco lurked at the foot of the staircase. He went to pass them to grab his coat, but Paulo and Stephan stepped out and barred his way. "Let me pass."

They grabbed his arms and Marco came right up into his face, gritting his teeth with his nose almost touching his. "Where's lover boy, eh?" Marco said, grabbing his hair.

"Fuck off, Marco," Antonio spat, trying to wriggle free.

"We had a deal, Antonio, your boyfriend and me.

Santalini Siren Blood and inside information in exchange for a Siren … I held up my side of the deal, and where the fuck was he?" Marco pulled his head further back by the hair.

"I haven't seen him either."

Marco stared at Antonio for a few moments and realised that was probably the truth. He nodded at his two brothers and stepped to the side as they pushed him away from them. Antonio stumbled. "Tell him he'd better watch his back now," Marco said.

Antonio turned and wiped the oozing blood from the corner of his mouth. "He's quaking in his fucking boots, Marco." Antonio looked at each of them in disgust and then turned back for the door. He could feel their eyes on his back. *Fuck them all.* No more would he be anybody's whipping post. To hell with the lot of them, and he slammed the door behind him.

CHAPTER 27

Keenan had been knocked out several times with the Taser during the course of that afternoon. They were so scared of him, they couldn't handle him awake, *the shitters*. He would have laughed if every part of him didn't scream out in pain.

He knew his time was up when he realized he was in an old shed and it was dark, just before they outed his lights again.

He wasn't sure if you dreamed when you lost consciousness or not, but the memory of the dreams, imagined or otherwise, warmed him like nothing else could have in his miserable short life. Because in them, Lacy spoke lovingly to him, and she hadn't done that since before she was taken.

She told him she loved him, even though she couldn't remember their childhood together. She said she loved him anyway and that he had won her love all over again.

As he made another bumpy journey in the dirty, smelly van, face down in the grime on the metal floor, he heard her tell him she was coming for him. She would join with him and make him her husband, as he was always meant to be.

He liked that dream. He could die happy, and he was sure he wasn't far from that now. His right eye was half closed and his left couldn't open at all. He was sure he had a cracked skull, and judging by his breathing, his ribs were broken as well. Being the cowards that they were, they always kicked him after the Taser disabled him. *Fuck,* if he'd been Human, he'd probably be dead already. Now they were going to throw him in the canal to get rid of his body. A drowned Atlantean prince, he laughed at the irony.

"You won't be laughing in a minute," the one in the passenger seat said.

The van stopped abruptly. They had reached their destination.

This was probably it.

"Get out the sacks and the chains."

"Fuck, they're heavy."

"He's a big fucker."

"Why couldn't we use rope?"

"Coz he'd bite it off, you div."

"Oh yeah."

Keenan was pulled roughly to his feet. He used the last ounce of his strength to try to kick them away from him, but a kick to the side of his knee collapsed his leg and he fell to the ground like a ton of bricks.

"Nice one, Phazer… now we've gotta fucking carry him."

"Shit."

They dragged him more than carried him, his dead weight was so great. The fog in his head lifted a couple of times and he saw the rain, smelled the stale water and heard a glass bottle being kicked and smashed. They dumped him on his back with his arms painfully tied underneath him while two of them ran back for the sacks and the chains.

. . .

KEENAN LAY FEELING the rain wash his face. He came round to them, pulling his injured leg.

"Wrap the chain around his ankles and through the loops on the sacks."

The rain pelted down on them the whole time.

Keenan's last thought before they rolled him off the bridge was: *I'll always love you, Lacy.* Then he hit the chilled water.

Bubbles rushed around his head and his legs were yanked downwards. His arms were useless, still cuffed behind his back. Initially, reason left him, and he fought and thrashed his legs, but the chains bit into the bare flesh of his ankles, so he concentrated on calming himself down. He'd never been so thankful for the self-control training Marius and Vince had taught him.

Blessed with the Atlantean longer-than-Human capacity for holding his breath, he slowed down his heart rate and curled into a ball on the canal bed. Logic told him that the slower everything ran, the longer he would have. Of course, that same logic told him, no one would find him here, but being a fighter by nature, he would try to the bitter end.

His mind wandered through old memories of him and Lacy. The times they'd shared together. The laughs, the stolen kisses. The final bond they'd had. No one could have been closer, no one. That was a comfort, he realized. A good note to go on. No two people could have loved each other more. And although she had been stolen from him and forgotten him, she'd loved him again from scratch. So she'd been his twice. So wherever they ended up, in heaven or somewhere like that, he'd find her and win her again, he was sure of it.

His mind began to fog. His good eye closed. He'd finally run out of oxygen and time. He smiled when he thought of the welcoming oblivion of a Siren's kiss in the dingy, murky canal in East London – the warmth on his mouth and the glow that filled him with absolute joy.

Malleven was dressed in nothing but a silk robe, left undone and flowing behind him, as he sauntered through his hallway to the large lounge of his Manhattan apartment.

A buzz sounded on the wall by the archway leading to where he was heading. He paused and picked up the receiver to the concierge downstairs. He took a deep breath. "Send him up." He pinched the bridge of his nose, composing himself for the inevitable unpleasantness.

A few moments and a loud banging echoed from the door and through the apartment. Malleven unhurriedly walked the large marble hall to the front door, flipped the latch and swung the door wide. "Why, Antonio, what a surprise."

Although he always observed the smallest of details, he made no comment on Antonio's split lip, bloody nose and black eye.

"Stop fucking around," Antonio said, pushing past him into the apartment. He walked straight along the hall and into the living room. "I need a drink," he said immediately.

Malleven followed him noiselessly and pointed to a bottle of red, opened and breathing on the coffee table. "What brings you at this hour, Antonio? I thought I told you to always call ahead?"

Oblivious to the question, Antonio downed a glass of wine, wincing as the pain registered when it dribbled into his split lip. "You gonna ask me who did this?" Antonio said, pointing an index finger upwards at his own face. Then he stopped dead and did a double-take at his sudden awareness of Malleven's dress, or rather the lack of it, as he sank down into an armchair, not caring as the robe he wore landed on either side of his muscled, naked, hairless body, leaving his cock out on full show.

Antonio blinked, then frowned, then looked around the room.

A smile crept slowly across Malleven's face as he saw realization dawning.

"You're not alone, are you?" Antonio said, eventually.

"No, I am not." No excuse, no apology, no frantic backpedalling.

Antonio began to walk around the room, agitated, until he stood infuriated with his hands on his hips. "At least get him out here and introduce him to me," he said, angrily.

Malleven was smiling broadly by this point, enjoying Antonio's hurt immensely. Then he sighed, relented and got up, poured himself a wine and refilled Antonio's glass. "Relax, Antonio … Isla."

"I thought … I mean, I thought …" It was then that Antonio first saw her. She was a vision, like an alabaster statue, with soft waves of blond hair and peaches and cream skin. Eyes the colour of a crystal-clear pool that stared straight in front of her, appearing to register nothing. Her lithe body floated into the room, every curve kissed with the silk robe she wore.

Malleven made him jump when he laughed out loud at his reaction to her. "Close your mouth, Antonio, your jaw is on the floor."

Antonio turned to face him in disbelief. "My father just beat the shit out of me, not that you appear to care," Antonio flapped his arms to his sides, exasperated. "And what for? I'll tell you … my disloyalty to my family, with you, Malleven. I came here as my first port of call, and I find you shacked up with some … some—" Antonio became lost for words as he gestured with his hand up and down at Isla, who had neither moved nor sat. "Who the fuck is she?' he said, exasperated.

"Sit, Isla," Malleven said calmly. "Please stop shouting, Antonio. I want the two of you to be friends."

"Friends?" Antonio shrieked.

At last Malleven's patience came to an end, which he knew it would and he simply held up a hand, closed his eyes and silenced Antonio. Not a muscle in his body twitched and not a further sound came from Antonio's mouth. Bliss.

Malleven stalked around him and completed a full circle of him as he spoke. "I will release you, Antonio, but you will be silent or I will not be so patient next time, and with that, he waved his hand and Antonio sagged and panted, grabbing his throat.

He searched for the nearest chair and perched on the edge of it when he found one, as if his legs would buckle. Although he didn't talk, his eyes tracked up Malleven's body warily.

"Isla Snow, this is Antonio Dubonnetti ... a close friend of mine."

Isla moved her eyes for the first time, rested them briefly on Antonio and gave a slight bow of the head.

"Antonio?" Malleven continued, "Meet Isla Snow ... or should I say Bonaci ... my mate?" Then he threw his head back and laughed loudly. The twist of fate still hadn't got old. "I still can't fucking believe it."

Antonio's face was a rainbow of emotions, ranging from incomprehension to disbelief, to realisation and finally to pain. "But ..." was all he could manage to say. He said it several times.

"Look at your ring, Antonio," Malleven pointed.

Antonio glanced down, still bewildered, and saw that it was turquoise. "But ... which one is she?"

"She is the third ... the Florianna Siren and she is mine." Malleven held out his ring for Antonio to see.

Antonio frowned. "Your experiments have concluded … you managed to make it work?"

Malleven shook his head, smiling. "That was the most astounding thing of all. This ring has not been tampered with. It is pure." He looked back over at Isla. "She is indeed mine … who'd have thought it? Fate has smiled on the poorest branch of the Florianna family. I wouldn't have had a ring at all unless I had bought one for myself." And he looked back at Antonio, whose colour had completely drained from his face.

"So you will make a legitimate claim now?" Antonio said, quietly, eyes filled with disappointment.

Malleven pushed out his lower lip and shrugged in a very Italian gesture. "Eventually." He sat again.

"No wonder my father was so angry," Antonio said. "This was the one they were supposed to get for Tia from the Americans; he'll be gunning for you now, Malleven."

Malleven wiped away the comment with a hand. "Your father is no match for me and Marco is no Dante. He would never unite the princes."

"They will say you couldn't have done it without them."

Malleven shrugged again. "Maybe it would have taken a little longer," he conceded.

"Don't you realise? He has disowned me, Malleven. Said he had no need of me. Kept going on about having the Darkly Begotten and bringing him home," Antonio said, stuttering his words.

Malleven looked deeply into Antonio's eyes and summoned all the darkness in his soul to bore into him. The look alone was enough to stop him mid-sentence. "Do you have any idea what the Darkly Begotten is, Antonio?" Malleven asked, quietly.

Antonio's face had become fearful. He knew all too well how unpredictable Malleven could be, but today, he terrified him. "My father says he will ruin Dante's reign from within, like a virus, going unnoticed until it's too late."

Malleven bobbed his head and his bottom lip protruded again in a 'kind of' gesture. "It's not who, Antonio, more of a what."

Antonio frowned, not understanding at all.

"The Darkly Begotten is something conjured, something summoned from the depths of the darkest pit of despair. It is not a spirit, a life force, an entity of its own, but it can be wielded and guided to do its harbourer's bidding. It can never be detected nor can it ever be captured."

"And who is its harbourer?" Antonio asked a little uneasily, dreading and knowing the answer already.

Malleven grinned. "What did you think, Antonio, that I'm going to get him out of a box and show you?" And he walked towards Antonio, still perched on his chair and touched the tendrils of his hair that had fallen into his face. "I am strong, but with the Darkly Begotten, I will be the most powerful magician of all times." Then he pulled Antonio to his feet and led him over to where Isla sat, and gently guided her to her feet as well. Then he joined their hands and touched them both on the cheek. "I want the two of you to grow to love each other as you love me ... so with my mate," and he caressed her along her jaw, "and her sisters, the power I now wield will be magnified five times and I will be invincible." Nothing had been clearer to him.

"What of Atlas ... what of the Orb?" Antonio said, trying to keep the desperation out of his voice. "My father said the Orb destabilizes if the Fates are tampered with in any way."

Malleven sneered with contempt. "The Atlasians haven't been here for ten thousand years. We are a very different race from the one they left behind ... let them come. When you treat a race harshly, Antonio, you can't blame them for learning their lesson well. The Orb will know who the true king is. When it feels the power I wield, it will get behind me."

Antonio gazed at Malleven, overwhelmed. Secretly hoping that the fact that Malleven thought one thing and his father another meant that neither of them knew who or what the Darkly Begotten really was.

He shuddered. It wasn't that he felt cold or that his body was in shock after being physically assaulted; it was that for the first time, he was truly frightened of Malleven. Scared stiff that he could actually be right, and in just a short time, he could be in charge of them all.

CHAPTER 28

*L*acy would have missed it if her foot hadn't got caught underneath. "Dante, my foot."

"What is it?"

She curled herself around to reach whatever it was and felt a chain. She followed it, hand over hand, in one direction and felt a rough material. She tried to move it, but it weighed a ton. Her heart sank. *It's a chain attached to a sack.*

Dante was soon where she was. *It's him, Lacy. Follow the chain the other way; it's on his leg*, Dante projected.

Oh no! she wailed. Her hands travelled over the mound of flesh. He wasn't moving. She could feel his leg, then up his body and a strong arm. He was huddled in a ball. *He's so cold*, she said. Her grief was leeching into her mind, making it difficult to think straight.

Calm down, Lace. We may not be too late. Try to breathe for him like you did for me. Maybe you can open his gills.

She cleared her mind quickly and felt her way to his face. She put her mouth to his ice-cold lips. *Keenan, I'm here. I accept you as mine*, and gently prised his lips apart with her fingers and blew gently at first. There was no difficulty in summoning it. The light built within her, lighting the water all around them like a welding arc.

Nothing, no movement at all.

She tried again, concentrating from the depths of her soul. Dante held her hand. *I give you my strength, Lacy.* When she dug again from her toes, she felt Dante with her. She blew with such depth and such love that the light became blinding around them. She counted as she blew. *One, two, three – damn you, Keenan fucking Santalini. You fucking leave me and I swear I'll fuck Dante. I will, so help me god, I will.* She blew and smacked him in the shoulder so hard you could hear the thud.

Exhausted, she leaned back away from him to see. His exposed skin glowed like a soft light bulb. One of his eyes opened very slightly and the gloriously welcome bubbles rose in a thin trickle from behind his ear. He smiled an enigmatic smile.

She hugged him to her hard. *Thank god, Keenan. Thank god.*

However, his eye closed again, and he lay still as a corpse.

As soon as Dante saw the bubbles, he swam to the surface to get help from the others to get Keenan out.

With the two Santalini guards, Dante concentrated and broke the links to the chains. He didn't have time to mess about. He didn't want to scare Lacy, but he knew that although Keenan was now breathing underwater, he was hurt bad, and still might not make it.

They hauled him to the surface. Chains were still wound round his torso and legs. It took all of them to pull him out onto the concrete towpath. Jay sent a guard to bring the car as close as possible.

Dante and Lacy expelled their lungs, freed Keenan's

wrists and pummelled his back to release the water from his. Eventually, Keenan began to cough, and they began the arduous task of carrying him up the steep incline to the top of the bridge to the running, waiting car.

They thought they would never make it with his weight, the pouring rain making everything slippery beyond belief and the howling wind almost blowing them off their feet, but after using every ounce of strength, they managed to pull him into the back seat of Dante's car.

Lacy insisted on cradling his head on her lap. His breaths were laboured and uneven. She anxiously waited for everyone to squeeze in, willing them to hurry. It was tight, but they all managed to fit into the two cars and were soon on the move, *thank god!*

Jay knew immediately what Dante wanted when he looked him in the eye and passed him his phone. "Alfonzo? Yes, we have him … but he's hurt." Jay looked at Lacy as he spoke. "No, he's not conscious … Dante wants a Murr Doctor to meet us there … Thank you." Jay looked at Lacy for a meaningful moment and sat back in his chair. *Isn't a hospital better?* Lacy projected frantically.

A Human hospital is no good, Lacy. Dante wasn't willing to take that chance. Keenan was too important now. He was an Atlantean prince bound to a royal Bonaci Siren and a member of his new government.

Lacy's tears blurred her vision and she cried, her heart in bits

They can do more for him than any Human doctor, Lacy, Dante projected. *Alfonzo will inform Keenan's family in case they want to be at his bedside.*

Her head snapped round to him. *You're talking like he's dying.*

Dante didn't answer. In fact, all eyes averted themselves from hers.

Lacy stroked the wet hair from Keenan's battered face all the way to the airport. She spoke telepathically to him, telling him to hold on, otherwise she'd kill him herself.

The doctor met them with a gurney and they transferred Keenan to it and onto Dante's private jet. He listened to Keenan's heart and gave him a preliminary examination during the journey. Keenan remained unconscious throughout.

The doctor gave him oxygen and diagnosed broken ribs, a shattered knee, a broken orbital bone around the eye, a possible fractured skull and stitches needed to his eyebrow. Internal bleeding was probable.

Dante thanked him and promised him that Keenan would get first-class medical treatment on landing. When they did, Dante put the doctor straight back on the plane to England.

LACY SAT with Keenan for a week. The strange Murr medical team had met them as soon as they reached Ballygowan Castle. They were dressed completely in white to the floor, making them look even taller. They looked more like monks than doctors. Their heads were covered with a white cap, showing the smallest glimpse of blonde hair. Their eyes were covered by black goggles, probably to shield their eyes from the glowing machine they'd already set up that looked just like a CAT Scanner.

They gave Keenan various drugs, then placed him in the chamber for twenty-four hours, which was supposed to fix his bones. It also pinpointed any internal bleeding, stopped it and fused it.

Lacy was told that he wasn't in a coma, but merely in an induced sleep to aid the accelerated healing and the knitting of his newly set bones.

Now he just slept peacefully. His chest rose up and down

hypnotically and before she knew it, she had dropped off in the chair next to him.

WHEN KEENAN AWOKE in the brilliant-white room, he thought he was dead.

He blinked a few times and both of his eyes were now okay. He wasn't underwater, and the pain was gone from his head. He moved his fingers and wiggled his toes; nothing hurt. *He must be dead.*

Then he managed to turn his head to the left and saw Lacy's sleeping body curled into the armchair next to the bed.

She can't be dead, he reasoned. Then he lay back and remembered the warm glow he felt as he was about to die. He smiled and looked back at her. She had saved him, he was sure of it.

He felt behind his ears and ran a finger over the raised ridges. *Fuck.* She'd opened his gills.

He moved his hand weakly and touched the tips of his fingers along her leg.

Lacy stirred and moved her hand absently to push away the curls that had tumbled into her face. She groaned and slowly opened her eyes.

He smiled when her eyes focused and widened in surprise at him watching her.

"Keenan," she whispered. Then she flew off her chair to his bed and the arms that came around her slowly. He felt her wracking sobs. "I'm sorry, Keenan … It was all my fault."

He tried to talk, but his throat wouldn't work. He pointed to the water jug next to the bed. She quickly poured him a glass and passed it to him. Then she fell into his welcoming arms again.

"No, babe, don't cry," he croaked and pulled her away

from him so he could look into her eyes. "You opened my gills?" His voice was barely audible.

She wiped her eyes on the back of her arm. "I'm so sorry, Keenan. I should have done it before. Then you would have already been able to breathe the water … I'm so sorry."

He touched her tears with his thumb. "You saved my life … that means you accept me forever?" He looked at her with wonder, like she'd done the most amazing thing in the world.

"I do, Keenan. I love you. I know that now."

"Your memories?" he rasped.

She shook her head sadly. "I love you anyway."

The door opened and a tall, strange-looking nurse entered the room. Keenan looked at Lacy.

"Murr," she whispered.

The nurse floated into the room and smiled her enigmatic smile. She glided to the bed and touched his forehead gently.

Keenan felt a warm vibration tingle across his skin.

I will inform His Highness you are awake, she projected to him, and she turned gracefully and glided back out of the room.

Keenan took a second to recover from the strange encounter. Then he turned his attention back to Lacy. "How long have I been out?"

"A week."

He felt his eye, the one he thought he'd lost for sure. "But I'm completely healed?"

"The Murrs," she said simply. "Dante called them."

"Ah, fuck. Does that mean I've got to get along with him now?"

She giggled. "You should try."

The door opened and Dante strolled in, accompanied by Jay and his boys. All shook hands with him warmly, even Dante.

Lacy went to slide off the bed away from him, but he stopped her. "No. Stay."

"Glad to see you better," Dante said.

"Thank you," Keenan said solemnly, looking Dante square in the eye and holding out a hand. Dante shook it and nodded slightly back, realising it was an olive branch. "That goes for all of you … I owe you." His eyes swirled with blood and he felt choked at the part they all must have played in his rescue.

"I don't understand, though …" Keenan frowned. "Why didn't they take Lacy … why me?"

"We're not absolutely sure yet, but a new enemy has shown himself," Dante said. The room fell silent as the bomb dropped. They all looked at him, waiting.

"A guy named Malleven."

They searched each other's faces, looking for a clue.

"I got Alfonzo to do some digging and he found out some worrying facts … He's Florianna, but not from the principal branch of the family."

"We'll just take him out," Vince said. "No problem."

"Well, it's tricky. It's not exactly against the law to vie for a Siren."

"Ah, come on," Vince said. "He fucking brainwashed her. That's hardly winning her."

"Agreed," Dante said, holding up a placatory hand. "And attempting to murder another prince is as well, but we don't have the proof yet, and he knows it." The room went silent, digesting the news. "Alfonzo also found out that he is a master alchemist from an ancient order of Magi, said to be steeped in the occult and the black arts."

Keenan tried to sit up. "What I don't get is why he wants me gone? He seems to just take Lacy when he wants?"

Lacy went red.

Keenan touched her leg in an apology. "I'm not angry at you," he whispered.

"I dunno yet, but I know my brother is involved with him. I'm still not sure about the rest of my family," Dante continued. "I need to get Delissi involved. See what he can dig up … but I think he wants to smash my council before it's begun … you would have been the first," he said, pointing at Keenan.

"Sarah," Lacy said quietly.

"What about Sarah?" Keenan asked when the room fell silent and all eyes were on her.

She looked around, unsure all of a sudden. "When I was at Cash's ranch, when you went to save Tia, she kept screaming that name over and over, Malleven, everyone knows Malleven."

"Shit!" Vince said. "She did, I was there."

Dante exchanged a look with Jay. "Leave that with us, we'll look into it … But now, to more pressing matters. You have accepted Keenan as your bonded mate, Lacy?"

She blushed next to Keenan and he squeezed her hand. "Yes," she said.

"I've spoken to Alfonzo, and he agrees with me that you will have to repeat it with witnesses. Not only for Keenan to complete the bond, but all Atlanteans need to know that he is very much alive and that a Santalini prince and I are in accord and will sit on my council."

Keenan looked up at Lacy sitting next to him. "Do you mind doing it again, in front of people?"

They locked eyes for a moment, and then she looked around at all those assembled. "No. It's long overdue." She leaned down to Keenan's mouth and kissed him solemnly, which soon grew into a private moment between mates.

Everyone else filed out of the room, and they didn't notice them leave.

· · ·

While Keenan recuperated, and he had Jay with him, Dante called Sean and Cash to Ireland for the informal chat he wanted to have with Sarah, Sean's wife. Cash had been invited as well, to put Sean a little more at ease about the whole thing and also because the subject affected him since it had all happened at his ranch.

He kept the meeting secret from Keenan and Lacy. He didn't want to ruin their reunion and he wanted to question Sarah without her feeling intimidated.

Dante had pitched it as a kind of get-together while Tia was away. Beer and wine were ordered in abundance and delivered to the great hall of the castle. They all sat around in the comfy sofa's laughing and chatting.

The only person completely in on the reason for the party was Jay. Dante knew Jay needed to know who their enemies were as much as he did, as well as the fact that he always valued his oldest friend's shrewd opinion.

And so they chitchatted and drank, well into the evening, until Dante broached the subject on his mind. "Tell me, Sarah, how are you feeling after your nasty experience with Tia back in the summer?"

Sarah's face fell immediately and she looked decidedly uncomfortable with the question. Everyone else went quiet.

"Do we have to talk about that, mate? She had to see a doctor and everything afterwards. She still has anxiety attacks now," Sean said, taking the baby from her while he spoke.

Dante put up both his hands. "I totally understand and I don't want to upset Sarah. That's the last thing I want to do, but a name has come to light, who could be my greatest enemy to date, and I need to know who I'm dealing with … I think Sarah knows who I'm talking about." Dante looked intently at her and let his words sink in.

Sarah looked down at her hands guiltily.

Sean looked over at her, frowning while he shifted the baby in his arms. "Sarah?" Sean said, beginning to look infuriated. He looked at Dante, then back at Sarah.

Sarah, unable to stand it, put her head in her hands. Then she looked up at Dante and tears filled her eyes. "He will kill my baby if I talk to you."

Sean jumped up out of his seat, quickly followed by Cash, who took the baby from him. Sean fell to his knees in front of his wife. "Sarah ... baby ... you must tell me. How can I protect you unless I know what happened? Now. Tell. Me." Sean struggled to keep his voice calm.

Sarah looked into Sean's eyes. "He's too strong, Sean. I can't ..."

"Did he make you help when they took Tia, Sarah?" Dante said, cutting to the chase.

She looked at Dante, Cash, and lastly, Sean, nodded, then burst into tears. Sean moved closer to her on his knees so he could pull her into his arms. "Shh, babe. Tell us everything. Nothing's gonna happen, I promise."

Huge sobs racked her body with the secret she'd carried for so long. "You'll hate me," she sobbed into Sean's shoulder.

"No I won't," Sean soothed. "Come on, love. It's really important now. Lots of lives are at stake."

Dante looked at Jay. Jay returned the look in the way they had with each other since they were kids, way before the Sirens' bond, but Jay remained silent and let Dante do all the talking.

"I hated her ... I really hated her," Sarah continued.

"Who?" Sean said, confused.

"Tia, of course. Every time she clicked her fingers, you'd go running. It got so I couldn't stand it."

Sean leaned back, still kneeling, and started to seem a little annoyed, like they'd been over it a thousand times. "It's never been anything like that, babe." He stood up and walked away from her.

"So who approached you?" Dante said, getting the conversation back on track.

"The housekeeper – Mrs Ross."

Dante looked straight at Cash, who now held the baby. He closed his eyes as if the bottom just fell out of his world.

Sarah sobbed anew.

"So she said for you to get Tia away from the house?" Dante said.

"Yes, but by that point I was beginning to get cold feet, I swear. I knew Sean would hate me for it, and Tia was being so nice to me, wanting me to come with her to the presentation and buy a dress and everything." She looked up at Cash, a plea already in her eyes. "So I set the barn alight."

Dante and Jay both sat forward in their seats. "Wasn't that Antonio?" Dante said.

Sarah shook her head sadly. "No, it was me. I'm so sorry, Cash, but I thought after something like that, there would be no way we could go shopping."

"And yet you went?" Dante said.

"Antonio offered to go with us. Mrs Ross took the baby and said that she couldn't guarantee his safety unless I made sure Tia still went."

There was silence while they all digested the latest information. Sean still stood a way off from them, looking back at her with something resembling disgust.

"Where does Malleven fit into all this?" Jay said, speaking for the first time. It wasn't clear whether Malleven worked for the Dubonnettis or the other way round.

Sarah looked over at him. "Mrs Ross said she knew him and that he was the most powerful man in the world. And that if I told anyone anything, he could get to my baby, no matter how far away I was. Like he could get to anyone, even Tia and her sister."

"So why did you get so upset when Lacy was keeping you company in the bedroom?" Dante asked.

Sarah began to cry again.

Sean was looking over in disbelief, his hands on his hips.

"Mrs Ross brought her up to my room when she brought the baby back to me. I told her where to go once I had the baby back and she left Lacy and me on our own. She was okay at first, just girl chat … then she gets all weird."

"What do you mean by 'all weird'?"

"She said that Mrs Ross was her best friend. As far as I was aware, she hardly knew her. And that I had better listen to her, and she told me she knew Malleven … it was the way she said it."

Dante frowned and looked at Jay, who raised his eyebrows.

"I lost it after that. I felt like there was no one I could trust."

By now, Sean had his head in his hands. Cash went over to him and put a comforting hand on his back.

Dante stood and walked over to the two of them. "Don't be too hard on her, mate," Dante said quietly. "She was just used."

Sean looked up at the ceiling. "Fuck. How could I not have known? I'm a Protector, for fuck's sake. I didn't know what was going on with my own fucking wife." He shook his head and walked off towards the corridor to the living quarters.

Cash came over and pulled Sarah up onto her feet. "I'll walk her back," Cash said to Dante and Jay. "They got a lot to talk about."

Dante nodded, grateful for Cash's fatherly influence. He

watched him walk her slowly towards the bedrooms, leaving him and Jay alone.

"We'd better tell Keenan," Jay said.

Dante nodded and sighed, "Not yet, though … let them have their wedding."

Jay agreed. "Do you think Antonio was innocent?" Jay asked.

Dante shook his head. "Nah, I know what I saw and it was definitely him with Lacy. He's involved somehow … probably being used as much as she was," Dante said, nodding his head in the direction Sarah had just gone. "No, it sounds as though this Malleven guy has had them all dancing to his tune, and probably Marco and Christian as well."

"Do you ever wonder if Sean … you know … women have a sixth sense with these things?" Jay said.

Dante smiled sardonically at his old friend. "Of course he's in love with Tia, Jay. It's obvious. But there is no bond, I would know."

Jay accepted what Dante had said and they were quiet for a moment. Their thoughts were interrupted when the lift doors opened and Alfonzo descended the stairs to the hall. "Good, I have news for you."

Dante looked at Jay. "Yeah, so do we."

"The Americans have called another meeting. Their concern is growing with the worsening weather. They are also pressing for information regarding the last Siren and whether we have found her yet?"

"Wouldn't that be the one they already had … the one that Tia saw?" Dante said, remembering the awful lab they had taken Tia to, where she was convinced they held another Siren.

Alfonzo raised his shoulders in a way that said, 'You would have thought so'. "They must have bargained her for

Tia, as we suspected, and now they have neither. They are fishing to see whose hands she has fallen into. Delissi will brief you before you meet with them."

"Shall I come with you?" Jay said.

Dante shook his head. "I don't want you politically involved. At the moment, you are the business face for Bonaci, and that's how I want to keep it." Jay didn't argue, seeing the sense in his logic.

Alfonzo went to walk off in the direction of the living quarters.

"How can Delissi be sure they have lost one; apart from them asking questions … it may be just a double bluff?" Dante called after him.

Alfonzo stopped and turned back to face him. "Because Delissi works tirelessly for the Atlantean nation and makes it his business to know." Then he walked on, but paused again. "He delivered her, in person, to a member of the Florianna House where she is destined to belong." And with that bombshell, he turned back and continued towards the corridor to the bedchambers.

Dante was left stunned, churning the information over and over in his head.

Duke Ormond Delissi was his real father. He'd pledged allegiance to him as king. And now he finds out that he was directly involved in a transaction with the third Siren. *Did that mean he was involved in Tia's abduction?*

Rage blazed through him as he remembered what Tia had been through. Then, on top of that, to hand another Siren, that he himself needed, over to another House, one that could be his enemy, he could spit blood.

"You sure you don't want me with you?" Jay asked again, reminding Dante he was there.

Dante put his hand on his shoulder. As usual, he had read

his mind. "No, man. But thanks. I want you to bring Keenan up to speed while I'm away. He needs to watch Lacy closer than ever. It seems this Malleven guy controls her whenever he feels like it."

*D*ante arrived in Washington, D.C. the next day. He itched to meet with his father. It really grated on him because his first impression of the guy was that he liked him, and now this: *he was turning out to be a devious fuck*. Then he raised his eyebrows … *just like he was.*

Still deep in thought, he transferred to the diplomats' car that was sent to meet him. Max, the professor he'd hired, was waiting for him in the car. He'd proved invaluable to him, teaching him his own language, history and writing.

"Here's today's agenda, sir," Max said, passing him the sheet of paper.

Dante smiled to himself briefly. He'd come a long way from the pisshead he used to be, falling out of clubs at 4 a.m. with Jay. What a lot can happen in a little over a year.

Now he was even being trusted to handle this trip alone. Alfonzo usually sat with him, prompting him. Today, he would be accompanied by his father, who would guide him, should he need it. *Well*, he'd see what he had to say for himself first. Thankfully, the Americans had no idea of his family connection with the Duke Ormond Delissi.

"What's with their constant preoccupation with the weather, Max?"

"Yes, good question, your highness. I have researched the subject extensively for this meeting. It seems that the Orb dictates the earth's weather."

Dante raised his eyebrows; he knew the orb had great power and brought them wealth, but this was news to him.

"It came here, as you know, with your forefathers. At that time, the Earth had a tropical climate, rather like a greenhouse. Then, according to the writings in the ancient tomes, the appearance of the Orb caused the great flood, the one documented by all earth's civilizations. Then, following that period, the climate shifted into the weather patterns we are familiar with today."

"I don't get what the problem is … so we've had a bit of rain?" Dante said, losing interest fast.

"From speaking to several of my colleagues at the university, they have been documenting some pretty extreme weather shifts and a rise in overall global temperature over the last few years."

Dante turned, slightly bored, towards Max. "That's all well and good, but what does all that mean as far as we're concerned today. What do they want?"

Max remained patient. "Well, as far as the ancient writings go, sir, it points to the presence of the Sirens, as we know, but the Orb is an entity that likes everything in its place, so to speak."

Dante smiled slightly. "So you're saying it has a mind of its own?"

"More like, when the natural order of things gets tampered with, it reacts."

Dante pondered for a moment. "Could it be my regime it doesn't like?"

Max sat back in his chair and breathed out noisily. "I

rather feel it is more to do with a foretold influence which is mentioned that will follow the last generation of Sirens."

Unease crept over Dante. He had a feeling he knew what Max was referring to. He remembered Christian, the man he believed was his father for most of his life, mentioning it with some sort of reverence when he was a kid. "Are you talking about the Darkly Begotten, the fucking Antichrist or something?"

"It is referred to several times in the ancient tomes."

"So, who is it … Do the Americans think I know?" Dante asked, shaking his head and looking out the window.

"I'm not sure yet, sir … Ah, we're here."

The car had pulled up in front of a military-type building with no windows.

"I want some time to speak to Delissi alone, before we go in," Dante said.

"Be careful, sir. Here, the walls very definitely have ears."

"It won't be a problem," Dante responded as he got out of the car.

Max exited the car as well and they walked into the building together, flanked, as always, by four impressive Santalini guards in full uniform.

"Your highness," Delissi said, meeting them as soon as they entered the building. He bowed over the hand that wore his divining ring and the king's ring that bore five precious stones around a larger central stone, depicting Atlas and its five moons.

Dante no longer felt young and unsure of himself doing the king stuff. A little over a year as king, and the power of two Sirens, had made him stronger and more self-assured. He wasn't taken in by any sycophantic bollocks from courtiers either, and that included the father he barely knew.

A curt "Delissi" was all he said in greeting.

Delissi swallowed the obvious cold shoulder and led the

way into a small anteroom off the large chamber where they were to meet the Americans in a few moments.

"Careful, Dante, nowhere is private here."

Dante stood still and closed his eyes. He imagined a beautiful waterfall, cool, refreshing and really noisy. Then he slowly opened his eyes and wasted no time. "What do you know of Malleven Mancini?"

Delissi looked left and right, then whispered, "This is not the place, Dante."

"No one can hear." It was a little side effect he'd discovered purely by accident at home. If he amplified his power through Tia and Lacy, it tampered with radios and satellite TV, and he was using it today to play havoc with any listening devices.

Still sensing his father's reserve, he grabbed Delissi's hand. *Or do you prefer the Murr way, Father?* he projected straight to his mind.

Delissi jolted in shock when he realized Dante was in his mind.

Yes, I am very powerful already. Now answer my bloody question: What do you know of Malleven Mancini?" He watched as his father stood straighter and pretence fell away from him.

He is Florianna, Delissi thought. He couldn't project, but he carefully arranged his thought patterns so Dante could read them.

Yes, yes ... I know all the surface bollocks ... I mean, what do you know of my enemy Malleven Mancini? Dante thought forcefully.

The process was obviously painful to Delissi and he touched his forehead to gather his thoughts. *So you know I delivered the third Siren to him?*

Who the fuck's side are you on anyway? You know I need all five, and you give one to him ... do you know he was the one who took Lacy?

Delissi shrugged slightly. *I suspected.*

Dante shifted with frustration. Having a two-way conversation in his father's head was killing him in its restrictiveness. *He is powerful and he has promised to take all five.*

I cannot affect the outcome, Dante. He can only do that if he is a bound prince by reason of divining ring. And that is unlikely given the branch of Florianna he comes from, Delissi reasoned. *He vowed to take her to his family.*

Dante pulled his father in closer to him with a sharp yank, freeing his hand and grasping his forearm. His face was mere inches away. *I will scan your mind if I think you are against me,* Dante threatened.

You sail close to the wind as it is, Dante. Your plans for all five Sirens and a council for their mates are admirable, but you must listen to the Orb. It dictates one Siren for each House. You must give each of the Houses a chance; otherwise you are fixing the outcome. The Orb destabilizes already.

Dante focused his anger in his father's head, making him wince. *What of the Darkly Begotten?*

Delissi went to pull away, but Dante held him fast.

No one knows who or what the Darkly Begotten is.

Or what?

Yes, it may or may not be a person at all. The fact is, there is very little written in Atlantean books on it. You'd be better served searching Human texts for it.

Dante listened to that. He'd get Max on it right away.

Just when Delissi relaxed, thinking their briefing was over, Dante grabbed him hard again. *Did you deliver up Tia in return for the Florianna Siren?*

Delissi looked Dante in the eye. *Grow up, Dante; this is politics with the big boys now. You had your mate back within twenty-four hours; I myself saw to it, and we got another back into the bargain.*

Dante narrowed his eyes on his father. *Fuck,* he had no

clue what kind of man this was. They were complete strangers. After their last meeting, he sort of thought there was some biological bond that linked them. What a sap, but no more. *I am your king. You acknowledged me yourself at my own presentation.*

That I did and still see you as such, Delissi answered.

I will know everything from now on. As you speak to Alfonzo, you will speak to me. I accept you have to be underground, but I want all intelligence to be fed to me. Do you understand?

Delissi bowed his head. *I work for the good of the Atlantean nation, as I have ever done.*

Dante saw fervent passion in his father's eyes. *Then allow me to lead it,* Dante answered.

Delissi nodded, understanding him perfectly. Dante had done with pussy-footing around him. *If I have cause to distrust you from today, Delissi, I will scan your brain for intent and motive, and it will not be a pleasant experience. Do I make myself clear?*

Perfectly, Delissi thought.

THE MEETING that followed was pretty unremarkable. Dante promised them faithfully that every care to comply with ancient directives and regulations would be adhered to for the stability of the Orb. However, craftily, he pointed out that any intervention on their part with a Siren's path to their mate would also greatly have an affect.

What made him laugh was that they thought he had so much knowledge about the damn thing. He honestly didn't have a clue where the bloody Orb was in the earth, and he was pretty sure that most Atlanteans didn't either. But they had to believe he did at all costs. They were getting seriously worried; he just hoped they didn't get trigger-happy before he could assure them that it was in all their interests to work together. The threat of Atlas returning was just as much a threat to the Atlanteans and their way of life as it was to the Humans. After all, they'd almost been wiped out the last time.

He made sure he caught their attention by mentioning the Darkly Begotten and that he couldn't be responsible for its actions and its effect on the Orb. He used this to request their continued cooperation in intelligence gathering for any conspiracy to destroy the newly forming council, which he was convinced would ensure the health and prosperity of the whole earth.

The American Secretary of State finally asked Dante the question he knew was coming since he'd lied at their first meeting, when he'd said he had four of the five Sirens, when in fact he had only two: "Have you located the final Siren?" (*In other words, did the Atlanteans steal the one the American government had back?*)

Dante answered in all sincerity, "No. I myself have no knowledge of her whereabouts ... but, as always, we search all the time."

Dante inconspicuously touched his finger on Delissi's hand. *Did the SOS know of the lab where Tia was held?*

No, Delissi answered. *Most of the time, the government here doesn't let its right hand know what its left hand is doing.*

Did the president know? Dante asked.

Not until recently ... it was he who enabled the escape.

Dante breathed easier and sat back in his chair. He'd learned all he wanted from today.

The meeting was quickly concluded and Dante left, accompanied by Max, eager to get on the case to find out more about the Darkly Begotten.

Delissi turned back to pressing matters, weighed down with sadness and regret.

· · ·

KEENAN WAS UP and about and impatient to complete the bond as soon as Dante returned from his business trip. There was no way he was going to let Lacy slip through his fingers again. He'd had too many narrow escapes.

So just a few days after he'd regained consciousness, Dante arranged for Sebastian, Alfonzo, Marius, a Murr and a Florianna representative to attend their official wedding. Even Naomi was making a special visit from Murrtaine, sending ahead a message that she would never miss anything as important as her daughter's marriage of her heart – as Murrs called it.

The time came, and both he and Lacy fidgeted at the edge of the fountain in the great hall, waiting to get in the water.

"I hope I remember how to do it," Keenan said, picking up Lacy's hands. "I wasn't exactly with it the last time."

Lacy reached up and touched his face. "You'll be fine … it's natural for us."

Dante walked over and coughed. "Ready?"

Keenan took a deep breath and nodded. "As I'll ever be."

Dante averted his eyes. "Just do a quick exchange in front of the window and then … go wherever you like." But he couldn't help grinning.

Keenan didn't bother to reply. It pissed him off that nothing in his personal life was personal, but now was not the time or the place.

Jay came over and joined them, and shook Keenan's hand. "I'm off, mate. I wanted to wish you all the best … I'll catch you later."

Jay's eyes met his with a strength that said he meant every word. Keenan knew damn well why he was making himself scarce. Jay would never complete the bond with Tia and it killed him. Nevertheless, he wished it for him, and Keenan was gutted for his friend. "No worries, mate."

"Oh yeah, I almost forgot," Dante interrupted. "Come see

me anytime you two have a row, okay, Lacy?" He laughed to himself and walked away.

Jay looked between Lacy and Keenan, puzzled. "I'm not going to ask, I can guess."

Keenan's face looked like thunder. "What was that supposed to mean?" He wasn't really angry, more pissed off that Dante had one over on him with something.

Lacy couldn't help grinning. "He's such a sod," she said, shaking her head.

Keenan continued to give her the evil eye.

"Okay," she said, on a sigh. "When I was trying to revive you in the canal and you wouldn't wake up … I kinda … threatened to shag Dante if you didn't."

Jay took that as his cue, raised his eyebrows and a hand and barely contained a smile. "Good luck, mate."

Keenan scowled a warning at him, which made Jay chuckle and he walked towards the exit with his hands in his pockets.

All was in friendly banter, though, and he pulled Lacy to him. "Yeah, that would do it, you minx. I probably revived from that threat alone," he said, kissing the top of her head.

She looked up and gave him a goofy grin.

"Come on," he said. "It's about time I made an honest woman of you."

He looked over at Dante, who nodded, signalling it was time. They both stepped over the wall of the fountain and jumped together into the deep hole in its centre. They went straight down and swam into the rough tunnel that took them outside.

The temperature dropped as soon as they reached the open sea. It took a few moments to get accustomed to it, so they trod water in front of the huge polished flat stone that must be the window. They studied each other closely. Their skin began to rapidly change, and their true form began to show. It was mesmerizing, and they soon forgot they were being watched.

Keenan was still holding his breath. He wasn't sure what he was meant to do to open his gills. It still scared the life out of him if he was honest.

Don't worry, Keenan; I'll help you ... they should open by themselves now. But if you get in trouble, I'll breathe for you again.

He smiled at her, speaking directly to his head. He remembered what her breathing for him felt like and heated up instantly. *Shit.* They'd better get a move on so they could get away from this poxy window before something embarrassing started noticing in his shorts.

He pulled her to him and nodded, signalling he was ready. She looked into his eyes.

He couldn't help but rake his eyes over the whole of her body. From the black stripes now emblazoning her arms and legs and body, the slashes along her cheekbones and forehead, to her expanding pupils and hair fanning out around her like a mermaid. *Fuck*, she was the most beautiful creature he'd ever seen. And she was his. His heart leapt.

As if she'd read his mind, she said, *You look beautiful too, Keenan. We are the same. Look?*

He looked down at his own stomach and legs. The patterns of the stripes were different and lighter than hers, and his skin tone around them was darker, but he looked back at her and smiled. They were the same.

Just let the water in, Keenan. Your gills will open.

His heart started to beat wildly. He knew it was fear; something he wasn't used to. *Shit*, he didn't know he was such a coward. He kept telling himself it was impossible to drown now. He closed his eyes. *Fuck*. He couldn't do it and shook his head.

Just keep your eyes closed and slowly breathe in, Lacy said, soothingly.

Fuck, this was it. He had to do it. He was acting like a wuss. He stared her in the eye and pulled her in closer to him. Then he slowly closed them, sent up a silent prayer and let the water into his mouth.

He wanted to cough at first. His instinct was to fight it, but before he could, he felt Lacy's lips cover his. A warm memory flooded back to him: his dying thoughts. The wonderful glow that entered the small gap between his lips slipped into his being and down into his racing heart. He thought he would pass out from the speed of it.

Quickly, the palpitations turned into a whirl of excitement and joy. He latched onto Lacy's mouth and kissed her thoroughly and deeply. His face tingled then, the feeling catapulted to his nerve endings, which exploded throughout his body, and he found himself blanketed in a feeling of well-being and Lacy's beautiful loving nature.

When the euphoria subsided slightly, he knew he must return the bond for it to be a true marriage. It was the thing they were destined for from babyhood and never questioned; he had never wanted anyone else.

Dig deep, Keenan. I want all of you, Lacy whispered seductively in his head.

God, she was doing things to him with mere words. He wanted her here and now but was all too aware that, until they completed the exchange, they had an audience.

He pulled her into his body tightly and concentrated hard. He tried to imagine the root of his love for this woman. It was soul deep and that was what he wanted to share.

It had always bubbled and become uncomfortable in his chest at times of lust and need for Lacy, right since he was a youth. He had always managed to tamp it down when he drank her blood. There would be no need for that after today. It would pale in comparison, he was sure of it. It was bubbling now, stronger than ever. It was like the worst kind of heartburn. Through his oesophagus and up to his throat it came. Then he pulled her lips to his hard and invaded her mouth with his tongue. When she probed into his with hers, he caught it between his canines to hold it and blew softly into her mouth in a single long stream that went on forever.

When he eventually opened his eyes, she was shimmering, glowing gold and iridescent. Her eyes were closed and she drifted backwards with a look of complete ecstatic bliss on her face. The most sexy, beautiful thing he'd ever seen. She was his and he needed to claim her now.

Before she could open her eyes, he locked lips with hers and swam away from the window. Now their time was their own and didn't belong to the state.

WHEN KEENAN BREATHED his essence into her, she thought she'd touched heaven. It was an orgasm, plus the blood bond, times a thousand, with a much slower float down to earth afterwards. She'd had no idea before, the depth of physical pleasure you got from breathing the spiritual essence of the person who loves you totally.

The love she now knew he felt for her was overwhelming and all-consuming. She'd had no idea. *Keenan!* she yelped in his head as he yanked her bikini bottoms from her and pulled her legs roughly around him.

I need you now, he groaned in her head. She held his face on each side of his cheeks and looked at him in wonder. *I heard you, Keenan ... I heard you.*

He grinned, realising what she meant. It was the first time he'd ever been able to do that. Slowly, he brought his head down and covered her mouth with his again and breathed for her. She absorbed him willingly and wantonly until she thought her heart would explode from it.

Before she had time to process what was happening, he

plunged deeply into her and rhythmically stroked her stimulated nerve endings. As his essence joined with every neuron, serotonin flooded her brain and she came over and over. She gripped and pulsed around him, lost to all reason.

Everything happened so quickly; she was in a sensual overload. She wanted to come apart into a million pieces. Desperate, she grabbed onto the sides of his face to slow his pace for a few moments. *I take you as my mate, Keenan Santalini.* Then she breathed for him slowly and tantalizingly.

He clutched her to him so tight a whisker couldn't pass between them and he pushed into her so he touched her soul. They held each other on and on and breathed for each other intermittently, until they lay languid and drowsy, intertwined on the seabed. Fish swam close, seeing no danger as if they were their own.

CHAPTER 30

Sean didn't get much sleep after the bomb Sarah had dropped the night before. He'd tried to hammer it out with her afterwards to understand, but he wasn't even sure if they could come back after something as massive as this.

Unable to sleep, he was already up and about when there was a knock at his door. He stood still for a beat, closed his eyes, then walked over and opened it wide, knowing exactly who it would be. "Jay," he said, without surprise.

"Get your trainers on, we're going for a run," Jay said, his face as serious as ever.

Sean sighed, nodded, and went to change his shoes. He had known this was coming ever since he had answered Tia's phone to Jay in the middle of the night, all those months ago. "Come on then," Sean said, jogging past Jay in the direction of the lifts to the surface in the great hall.

They pounded the windy lanes in silence for ten minutes at a punishing speed, as both men were super-fit, and neither was willing to slow the pace.

"Let's go off-road," Jay said, breaking the silence.

"We gonna have a 'conversation', Jay?" Sean said, looking at Jay jogging alongside him.

"I dunno … do we need to?"

Sean didn't answer, but jogged left and leaped up over a stile onto the farmer's fields and Jay followed.

They jogged along a footpath for a few more minutes until they reached a grassy clearing.

"Hold up," Jay said, slowing down.

Sean slowed as well until they both stopped and caught their breath. He kept his eyes on Jay the whole time, breathing hard with his hands resting on his hips. He still wasn't sure whether they were going to fight or talk. He decided to start things off. "What d'ya wanna know, Jay?"

Jay walked over to him until they were face-to-face. "I wanna know why Sarah's got such a problem with Tia that she would do something like that?"

Sean shook his head, "She's the possessive type, that's all," and went to walk away.

Jay put a hand on his arm to stop him.

Sean looked at the hand, then into Jay's face. "We gonna have that 'conversation', Jay?"

Jay narrowed his eyes. "Why don't you start from the beginning and tell me how you met?" Jay's face changed from holding the threat of aggression to one of a reasonable question.

Sean stared at him for a few seconds and decided it was time he just laid it all bare. He turned and went and sat down on a log. "I met her in Ibiza. I was on leave from the army with a few mates. Only had a few days left …

I WAS WALKING along the rocks next to the sea, just wanting to get away from everyone. It was early evening. The beaches were emptying, everyone getting ready to party for the night.

I came across her all on her own, lying face down on a towel, earphones plugged in her ears. She floored me; she was so beautiful. I stood there staring at her like an idiot until she pulled the earphones out of her ears, sat up and looked back at me.

I said something really idiotic, like, "Your hair is beautiful."

She pushed her sunglasses up on top of her head. I thought her eyes were contacts; they were so unusual. She laughed at me and said, "I like your tats."

I just stood there like a dumb fuck. "What's the water like?" I asked when the silence got too long.

"I don't know. I haven't been in," she said.

A loud whistle and a shout from my mates and the meeting was over. "I gotta go," I said, holding up a hand.

"Are you out tonight?" she said, rummaging in her bag.

I stopped and turned back to her, "Yeah."

Give me your name and the names of your mates and I'll put them on the door of the club I work at if you like?" she said, taking out a pen and a scrap of paper.

I smiled at her, gave her the names and went. It was a weird meeting, one that stays with you ... you know?

We turned up at the club. We were on the list, just like she said and we got straight in. We got drinks and I looked around to see if I could see her, behind the bar or as one of the waitresses. In the end, I had to ask a waiter to see if he knew her. He pointed at the DJ booth and there she was, in a world of her own, lost in the music. She was so beautiful I couldn't take my eyes off her. Now, of course, I would have known because she had the whole place jumping.

When she finished her set, she walked through the crowd and I touched her on the arm as she passed.

"Sean!" she said, pushing her sunglasses up.

I was bowled over by her eyes close up. I'd never seen anything like them.

"Come on, buy me a drink," she said, laughing at me being dumbstruck and gawping at her like a sap.

We sat down in the chill-out lounge with our drinks and everyone seemed to know her, she was so cool. She asked me what I did and I told her that I'd just done a tour of Afghanistan, was on holiday with my mates and only had a few days left.

I went to the club to see her every night after that …

Jay sat on the grass opposite Sean, leaning back on his arms. "That's it?"

"That's how we met," Sean said.

Jay looked away impatiently then back at him. "How did you get to know her personally?" Jay said, more deliberately.

Sean nodded and continued …

Well, a few nights after we met, it was her night off. She invited me round to her villa – beautiful place, single storey, built around a courtyard with a pool in the middle.

We sat drinking all evening and got really drunk.

"Do you fancy a swim?" I said.

"I'm not really meant to."

It struck me as a weird thing to say at the time, but because I'd had a few, I just tried to convince her. "Ah, come on. It's only me."

We went in holding hands to the middle and turned to face each other. I pulled her in close and we kissed. Before I knew it, she'd pulled me into the deep water with her and kissed me on and on under the water. I thought I was going to drown.

When she came to her senses, she let me up to the surface. It took me a few minutes to right myself and get back to normal with the coughing and spluttering. When I stood still and looked at her, she was smothered, head to foot in stripes.

Even though I was pissed, the suspicion that I knew what she was crept over me. I led her out of the water and we lay down on a sun lounger together. "What are you?" I said.

"I don't know," she whispered back. I felt bad about asking her like that.

I travelled back to England the next day…

"AND THAT WAS ALL THAT HAPPENED?" Jay said, frowning.

"Well, yeah … She'd only just got out of prison after her sentence for killing Dannyl was quashed. She did the summer in Ibiza, then went to Cash's after the closing party, a couple of weeks after I left."

"I spoke to my dad about her as soon as I got back. He got the parchment out that he'd shown me as a kid and I knew then without a doubt what she was."

"So how often did you meet with her after you got back?"

"She would come to my barracks on her bike whenever she was in England, just like the time when you phoned," Sean said, giving Jay a meaningful look.

Jay gave a small nod of understanding. "So why did Sarah get the hump over it so much?"

Sean sighed. "We were childhood sweethearts. Been together forever. She wanted us to get married, but me being in the army … I was putting it off. Then she got pregnant."

"Don't get me wrong, I did fancy Tia. Of course I did. But knowing what she was and what she was meant to become, it scared the shit out of me."

Jay stared at him, willing him on.

"I knew when she came into her own, she would make mincemeat out of me," Sean said, smiling.

Jay smiled back and nodded, "Yeah, she does that."

"She would just turn up on her bike and wait for me outside the barracks, and I'd run out and jump on the bike and we'd go somewhere and talk. That's how I kept an eye on her; that is, until Cash contacted me. The rest you know."

"So how did Sarah find out?"

"Pretty soon, all the lads cottoned on and ribbed me. That meant their wives soon knew and so it wasn't long before Sarah got to hear. I explained how we were just friends, but suspicion and insecurity did the rest."

"Does she know what Tia is?"

"No. I've only ever told her that Tia is royal. She thinks she's queen of some small European kingdom."

"Maybe you need to tell her so she knows what's at stake."

Sarah had no idea that he himself and therefore their own son had Atlantean blood in them. Jay was right; she had a right to know. He just never looked at himself like that, like an alien, which of course he was.

Jay looked at him a long while. "Will you work it out ... with Sarah, I mean?"

Sean shook his head, "I don't know if we can."

After a minute of studying him, Jay said, "She didn't have a lot of choice in the end, mate."

"I know."

And just like that, Jay got up as if everything were forgotten. "Let's go back," he said.

They fell into an easy jog back towards the castle.

CHAPTER 31

The spectre of Keenan's close shave with death disappeared quickly. Lacy had made up her mind to enjoy the here and now and not keep harking on the past.

Dante had given them the option of living at Ballygowan Castle with him, explaining that all the Sirens should live with the king, according to Atlantean tradition. However, when Lacy looked sideways at him and he had his devilish grin, she could never tell whether he was being serious or just winding Keenan up.

Keenan simply replied that his reign would be the shortest in history if they did, making Dante roar with laughter. He really was a sod, but he did give them his blessing to make a home in New York with the Santalini family. He figured it was more like an army barracks anyway, and therefore safe enough to house a Siren.

He did warn them that the idea of them all living together wasn't as far-fetched as it sounded, and he hadn't ruled it out for the future if things got too dangerous. The threats around them were all too real. The British and American governments were champing at the bit. He wasn't sure if he could totally trust Delissi. Dante's own family had failed this time, but wouldn't give up. And, of course, there was Malleven. Lacy shuddered. She never knew when he would click his fingers and summon her again, and of that she was truly terrified. And they were only the threats they knew about.

So eventually she and Keenan made the exciting trip to the US, just as they had done a little over a year before, for their new start, but this time it was as truly bonded mates.

They still got sad at times, as so much was lost to them; childhood games and secrets, stolen moments from the time when their love was taboo, even when they finally got together. However, Lacy was thrilled when Keenan learned to use their bond to project their strongest memories to her, meaning they could relive them all over again together, like watching a reel-to-reel film. She couldn't help falling deeper in love with him every day.

After a while, wonderful news reached them. Tia had returned, having had three beautiful children, making Lacy an auntie. Strangely, two were Dante's and one was Jay's. She hadn't got to the bottom of how that was possible yet. *Way to go, Sis*, she giggled when she heard, liking her sister's style. Much to Keenan's look of disapproval!

Lacy was truly thrilled and happier than she had ever been. Everyone's life seemed to really be coming together. Well, everyone except Dante's. Despite being a father to two of the children, Tia was trying to make a go of it with Jay. Lacy could totally understand it, but couldn't help feeling sorry for Dante. Tia hadn't even gone to Ireland when she got back to officially present his children to him, and the word was that Dante was losing patience.

He had insisted that they leave Barbados and at least go to New York, as it was safer. So Tia and Jay had come to stay with them for a while, which Lacy was really enjoying. Although trouble was afoot, she just knew it.

She shrugged off the gloomy thoughts. She was so glad that her heart belonged to Keenan. She knew now without any shadow of a doubt that he was the one for her, and that whoever had stolen a large chunk of her life was to be despised and not pined for or confused over. She'd wasted enough time on that.

Tia, on the other hand, was genuinely caught between two men. Jay was the man of her heart, but Lacy couldn't help liking Dante and often rooted for him on the quiet, and his dastardly acts of trying to steal her from Jay. *But, hey, what did she know?*

Tonight, Tia and Jay had dragged them out to a bar with them. There was something desperate about their interaction with each other lately, as if they knew their time together was short.

Keenan's arms came around her waist from behind, as she stood watching them canoodle at the bar, unaware they were being spied on. The whole place was full of Santalini guardsmen and their mates.

"Are you okay? he asked as he nibbled on her earlobe and then kissed down her neck.

She covered his arms with her own, "Mmm," she moaned into the embrace.

"Yeah?" he said, pulling her tighter into his body.

She nodded towards Jay and Tia just as Jay passed an ice cube from his mouth to Tia's and her face blazed just as hers did with Keenan. They were oblivious to everyone around them.

Lacy was overcome with an overwhelming feeling of sadness. Keenan felt it instantly. "Babe, what's up?" He moved her to face him and enveloped her in his strong arms.

She turned her face and continued to look at her sister

and Jay. "Storm clouds are brewing." She battled back her tears.

Keenan nodded above her head. She could feel his chin moving.

"You feel it?" he said. He totally trusted her gift of foresight now.

"Yeah … he'll be here soon."

EPILOGUE

*G*overnment Basement Control Room, Washington, D.C.

THE AMERICAN SECRETARY of State was summoned to the small control room in the basement of the building.

"What have you dragged me down here for?" he asked, impatient to move on to more pressing things.

"We were going through old stuff to be deleted and came across this, sir," the soldier answered. "It's from just before the last meeting with the Atlanteans."

The SOS rolled his eyes. "Get on with it, boy … whad'ya have?"

"Watch." The soldier played back the CCTV recording from the afternoon of the meeting from the small anteroom, just before the meeting had started. A small device had been secreted into a wall fitting and several small radio receivers were dotted around the room, capable of picking up the smallest of sounds.

As soon as the SOS saw Delissi alone with his king, he got interested. The image played, but there was no sound.

"Turn it up!" the SOS said.

"It's no use, sir, all you can hear is a noise that sounds like water, sir."

The SOS was going red in impotent rage.

Then the picture fuzzed over with static.

"Get it back!"

"It resumes in a few minutes, sir, but they make no sound at all."

"Whad'ya mean? The equipment must be faulty."

"No, sir, it's picking up the clock. They are simply not making any sound."

Dumbfounded, the SOS stared at the screen.

They watched the eerie mime of Dante grabbing the Atlantean ambassador's arm and looking intently into his eyes, then Delissi bowing after not saying a word.

They watched in absolute fascination. All present came to the realization for the first time that their dubious allies were telepathic.

The SOS straightened and stared ahead of him. *These aliens were running rings around them. Something had to be done.*

Bonaci Corporation, New York Office

Jay had been working late and was just finishing up for the evening. He had loads of work to catch up on after his extended stay in Barbados with Tia and the kids. He couldn't help smiling to himself as he gathered his paperwork together. *Who'd have thought it, him a family man?* He was loving every minute of it, even Dante's little terrors. And JJ, he was besotted already. He couldn't help himself.

Still, he sighed, they couldn't stay in Barbados forever, even though it had been tempting, living in their own little bubble. Tia had been back for weeks and still hadn't officially presented Dante with his children. And there was the bond, which he knew now had to be fed at intervals, otherwise both sides could get sick. She hid it well, but the tiredness was creeping up on her; he could sense it.

As much as he hated the time she had to spend with Dante, he knew that both of them needed it for health and for the crown. That was why he'd coaxed Tia into moving partway to New York in the hope that it was a short stepping stone to Ireland. He knew his old friend well, and waiting would piss him off, like nothing else.

With another deep sigh of resignation, he switched off his laptop and put it away in his briefcase. The door clicked, and he looked up sharply.

Christian Dubonnetti, Dante's Stepfather, stood by the door. "Christian?" Rarely did things catch him off guard, but this impromptu visit knocked him sideways.

"I think congratulations are in order. I hope you don't mind, I was passing and thought I'd pop up and see you?"

Jay frowned for a minute, then smiled as he realized he was referring to his new status as father. "Er, thanks, Christian. What brings you to New York?" He carried on clearing up. The man had been a father figure most of his life, too, albeit a distant one. He felt guilty, but his loyalty was always to Dante, and this guy was definitely in opposition to him.

Conversation wasn't a strong point with Jay at the best of times, so he wanted to hurry things along and get back to his family. Plus, he knew Christian all too well and knew there was always an agenda.

Jay put his jacket on and stood, obviously ready to go, with his briefcase in his hand. "Thanks for dropping by, Christian, but I really have to be somewhere."

"Of course, no trouble at all … just wanted to catch you before you went back to Ireland."

Here we go. Jay smiled blandly – *the catch.* Breathing out noisily, Jay leaned back against the desk. "Spit it out, Christian, it's not like you to prevaricate."

Christian laughed. "Look at you … how you've turned out. A son to be proud of."

Jay started to feel uneasy and narrowed his eyes. "What do you want, Christian?"

Christian smiled at him indulgently. "Okay. I want you to come home?"

Jay's eyes went wide and he laughed slightly. "You're serious?"

"You are Dubonnetti, you were brought up as one of my sons, have you forgotten?"

Jay sighed. "So the catch has come at last." He shook his head ruefully.

"Your place in the Atlantean world is part of the Dubonnetti House."

Jay conceded a nod. "Have you forgotten I am Bonaci as well?"

"No, of course not," Christian said, grinning. "A master stroke. You unite the two houses as you were meant to."

Jay's patience started to wear thin. "Look, Christian, I am truly thankful for the home, the education and everything you did for me, but you know Dante is more than a best friend to me, I will not fuck him over … ever."

Christian laughed heartily. "Don't you see? You won't be able to help yourself. You have already taken his Siren and, praise be to the gods, given her a child … Brilliant." He shook his head as he laughed. "Don't you see you are my son?"

Jay's face was cold and adamant as he said the words, "No, Christian, I am not. Dante and I took the test a long time ago. I am not your son."

"You need to study up on your Atlantean history and prophecy, Jay."

Jay stood up straight and his face hardened. He'd had enough of this fucking around. "What are you trying to say to me, Christian?" He wanted to get the fuck out of there. The bloke was starting to give him the creeps.

"That you are my Darkly Begotten son."

Jay shook his head and blew out a breath. "I don't know what the fuck you are going on about." Deciding to play along, he put his briefcase down and perched on the edge of the desk with his arms crossed over his chest. "Come on then, enlighten me … am I some kind of fucking messiah?"

The amusement drained from Christian's face. "Much, much darker than that. Your mother was an Oracle … a seer."

Jay's eyes went up to the ceiling and back to Christian's. "You don't have to tell me what my mother was. I grew up in enough knocking shops to know."

Christian bowed slightly in agreement. "Yes, she was a prostitute, that's true, but she also practised the black arts and foretold the future using very powerful magic. Magic so powerful it is forbidden under Atlantean law. It uses the power of blood and sex, of life and of death, in the service of creating magic. She worked for me for many years.

"Through our association, she divined that this was the generation to find the Soul Breathers, she advised me through all my business dealings. She became a close confidante."

"What has any of that got to do with me?" Jay cut in. He started to feel impatient, wanting to get back to Tia and the children and normality. He certainly didn't want to dwell on any of this shit.

"Listen to me, Jay. The night you were conceived, your mother was working for me. She had ingested a large amount of my blood, as was necessary for the purpose. To double her power, she used another male Oracle. They both ingested my blood while they had intercourse to produce powerful magic. At the height of the act, the pinnacle of their power, you were conceived."

Jay's face was a mixture of utter amazement, horror and disgust.

"It was an abominable act, against the law and everything natural and good. Through that, you came into being."

"Is this supposed to make me feel good?" Jay said, but he wasn't being funny.

Christian, having said his piece, walked towards the door but paused in the doorway. "Read up on what I've told you if you doubt me, but you should come home. Rest assured, you will destroy Dante's kingdom. You will break his heart and ruin the man you love so much. What will your Siren think of you then?"

"You make it sound as if I have no mind of my own."

"If you stay, you won't be able to help yourself." He opened the door. "I'll let myself out." Then, having dropped his bomb, he left.

Jay was left stunned. *The stupid old fucker. Dante always said he was mad.*

One minute he was on top of the world. A father to three beautiful kids, a partner to a beautiful woman, and a friend to the man he loved like a brother. The next, he was told he was a freak of nature, some sort of sleeping virus or bomb about to go off any minute. *Fuck!*

He kept shaking his head and trying to shrug it off as he turned off the lights and closed up the place. However, he had the worst kind of feeling in the pit of his stomach that his life was too good to be true, and it was only a matter of time before he lost it all.

***

Read book 3, Shield Maiden, right away!
And to receive your two 21st Century Sirens Novellas, and be
the first to know anything relating to T's books, leave your
details here: https://mailchi.mp/d18c89c14f50/
tstedmannovellas
And please don't forget to leave a review. I really appreciate
the feedback.
Much love
T

GLOSSARY

Characters in family groups

Bonaci

Alfonzo Bonaci – Head of the Bonaci royal family and uncle to the Sirens
Sebastian Bonaci – Brother to Alfonzo and father to the Sirens
Luca Bonaci – Half-brother to the Sirens
Dino Bonaci – Full brother to Luca and half brother to the Sirens
Tia Storm – Siren – First wife and most compatible to Dante – queen – bonded to Jay
Lacy Rain – Siren –Mated and most compatible with Keenan Santalini and second wife to Dante
Isla Snow – Siren – Most compatible to Malleven

Royal Children

Xavier – Son of Dante and Tia

Alexia – Daughter of Dante and Tia
JJ – Son of Jay and Tia

Borge

Darl – Lord Vionne Borge – Murr and eldest son and
successor to Darl
Naomi – Wife to Sabastian Bonaci – Mother to Sirens
of Murrtaine and father to Vionne,

Dubonnetti

Dante Dubonnetti – King and most compatible mate and
married to Tia Storm and Lacy Rain

Duke Ormond Deliss – Biological father to Dante and
Ambassador for the Atlanteans in Washington, DC
Christian Dubonnetti – Stepfather to Dante and head of the
Dubonnetti royal family
Marco Dubonnetti – Half-brother to Dante and Jay Gardiner
Paulo Dubonnetti – Half-brother to Dante and Jay Gardiner
Antonio Dubonnetti – Half-brother to Dante and Jay
Gardiner – Lover to Malleven Mancini
Stephan Dubonnetti – Youngest – Half-brother to Dante and
Jay Gardiner

Florianna

Cesaré Florianna – One of the five sons of the Florianna and
cousin to Malleven Mancini

Sandro Florianna – Eldest brother to Cesaré
David, Roberto and Mario – Brothers to Cesaré

Malleven Mancini – Cousin to Cesaré – most compatible with Isla
Rodrigo Mancini – Uncle and benefactor to Malleven

Santalini

Andreas – Elder of the Florianna royal family and uncle to Keenan Santalini

Keenan Santalini – Most compatible and mated to Lacy Rain
Ruby Santalini – Sister to Keenan
Marius Santalini – Eldest brother to Keenan
Adriano, Drago and Louis – Brothers to Keenan
Reeve Santalini – Fellow guard and cousin to the brothers

The Humans

Jay Gardiner – Protector/Lover bonded to Tia Storm – Best friend to Dante

Max Brunswick – Advisor to Dante for Atlantean history and language.
Mrs Ross – Cash's housekeeper

Protectors

Vince – Keenan's best friend and member of his crew – Protector to Lacy Rain
Rick and Dan – Keenan's close friends and members of his crew – Protectors to Lacy Rain
Sean McPhearson – Protector to Tia Storm
Cash Reynolds – Protector to Tia Storm

TERMS PARTICULAR TO THE ATLANTEANS

Divining ring – worn by all princes and forged particularly for them. Can only have one wearer. Forged from the Orb itself. Determines whether a Siren is nearby and the wearer's status to her by its color
Opaque white – default resting color
Turquoise/green – a Siren is nearby
Purple – the Siren nearby is the wearer's most compatible mate

Elixir – Potion taken by princes and those humans in contact with a Siren to prevent an extreme reaction or even death in the event of breathing her essence.

First Breath – The breath passed from a Siren for the very first time. Her power passes to the recipient only on the very first exchange. Usually reserved for the king.

The Magi – an ancient order of magicians and alchemists of which Malleven belongs. Mainly Human in origin, but have worked alongside the Atlantean nation since the beginning of their colonization.

The Orb – the ancient power source of Atlanteans. Believed to rest beneath Murrtaine and came with their ancestors from Atlas.

ACKNOWLEDGMENTS

A special thank you to my loyal readers, who have stuck with me right from the beginning, particularly Diane Burke. You're all amazing.

This is a work of fiction. All characters, names, events, businesses and places in this publication, other than those clearly in the public domain are fictitious. Any resemblance to real persons, living or dead, is purely coincidental.

ALSO BY T STEDMAN

21st Century Siren Series

Soul Breather

Blood Sister

Shield Maiden

Tiger Lily

Night Goddess

Darkly Begotten

* * *

The Dark Valentines Collection

Diablo

The Watchers

Star Child

* * *

Non-Fiction

My Migraine Story

www.ingramcontent.com/pod-product-compliance
Lightning Source LLC
Chambersburg PA
CBHW030656120726
47905CB00001B/243